The Gate Keeper

Keith Morgan Chronicles #3

Brent Jeffries

Bluff Woods Publishing LLC

ISBN-13 (eBook): 979-8-9876558-6-3
ISBN-13 (Paperback): 979-8-9876558-7-0
ISBN-13 (Hardcover): 979-8-9876558-8-7

To my beautiful wife and our incredible kids.
Without you, it wouldn't have happened.
Thank you!

Prologue

The cool mountain air was invigorating, even when the herd was misbehaving like they were that day. It always took work to get the magnificent shorthorn cattle moved out of the riverbed in the spring, but they were especially excitable that year.

Moving the herd wasn't especially difficult, but it required getting the award-winning cattle out of the potential flood zone before the spring runoff intensified. The adjacent field was slightly higher, offering a secure summer spot for the cattle. They could graze on the greening vegetation without the danger of being swept away by high water.

The last thing Thornton Caldwell needed was an unexpected clamor in the forest just west of their three-hundred-head drive. Thor, as everyone calls him, heard nothing over the continuous engine noise of his ATV, but the cattle sure heard it. So did Bailey, his brother and the closest rancher to the sudden sound of tree limbs breaking nearby.

The cattle and Bailey stopped and looked off to the left. Thor was screaming commands into his headset before he realized what was happening and paused. There were advantages to using these new earbuds during their rides, like being able to hear everyone talking in a normal speaking volume.

"What's going on?" Thor yelled unnecessarily loud, even though the headset picked up his voice just fine. Everyone on the ranch was used to his yelling, both the necessary and unnecessary versions.

Thor was the leader of this group, as was always the case when he was around. His father owned the ranch, and he was the heir to the operation. On his ATV out there in the open Montana air, he looked like a natural rancher. His brown hair was long enough to be visible under his hat, but not long enough to cover his collar. He was just over six feet tall and looked strong and controlled, even while riding an ATV.

Another rider flanked the herd on the right as they navigated their way to the next pasture. All of them were on ATVs, which were becoming more common for open area moves like this. Horses could certainly navigate tight areas more easily, but the ATVs had advantages when space and terrain allowed. They had all done this before and were comfortable with the task.

"I just caught something out of the corner of my eye. I'm not sure what it was, but something crashed into the trees just to my left. It was maybe thirty yards away, and I'm sure I heard a couple of tree limbs break." Bailey was the first to respond.

"Was it a broken branch falling? This wind might be shaking loose dead limbs," Thor said.

"No, it came from above. I saw it enter the trees. Like something fell from a plane or something," Bailey responded.

"Is that why we're all stopped and looking around?"

Kurt Abernathy entered the conversation from his position far to the right. Kurt was older than the Caldwell brothers, and had been with the ranch longer than them. He hadn't heard or seen anything but he recognized the disturbance in the herd.

"Yeah, I suppose it is. We better make sure there's nothing burning out there. Bailey, go take a look and I'll keep the herd in pace," Thor said as he twisted the throttle on his ATV and bolted to his left.

"Got it," Bailey said as his ATV veered into the mixture of aspen and evergreen trees toward the noise.

"You see anything?" Thor was impatient. Their job today was simple and should be quick. This diversion was wasting precious daylight, although they had plenty of time to get it done. His impatience was more a result of his personality versus the time limits of their task.

"Not yet. I think I'm close to where the sound came from, but I don't see anything," Bailey responded.

"Ok. Don't spend all day. I'm sure it's nothing," Thor said, unable to hide his agitation.

It only took about thirty seconds for Bailey's voice to pop back into Thor's earbuds.

"You have got to be kidding me!" It was a frustrated sound, making Thor think Bailey had discovered something simple, like a fallen branch or something.

"What?" Thor and Kurt both asked at the same time.

"It's a drone. Those Krohl morons crashed one of their drones on our land!" This time, Bailey's frustration had turned to glee.

All three of them chuckled. Thor was still grinning when he replied.

"That is just awesome! We have got to get that thing back to the ranch so we can hold it over their heads. I'll come back later tonight and pick it up. Let's get this herd moved and I'll bring a trailer. How big is it?"

"Those guys have so much money they probably won't even notice it's gone. I heard some of them talking at the Golden Bear last week. They're working with some drone company to provide drones big enough to move their hay bales! I've heard of drones for video and all that, but they're way behind that!" Kurt was still chuckling while he talked.

"No, Kurt, this one isn't that big," Bailey replied. "Thor, if I had to guess, I'd say it was a large video drone. It was probably only two feet wide before it broke up with its crash landing."

"Ok, cool. I'll get back here in a hurry before they come to get it. They may have enough money to buy more, but I want everyone to see what these guys are doing. They shouldn't be flying over our property at all. This site is a good half mile from their property line. They have no business sniffing around our operation," Thor responded, his smile fading as he wondered why the massive Krohl farm next door would want to see what they were doing with their shorthorn cattle.

The Caldwell family had won two consecutive awards for their small shorthorn herd, thanks largely to Thor's genetic research. His father had sent him to get his agriculture degree at the University of Illinois, so he'd have the knowledge to take over the Lazy J ranch and keep it running for another generation. Thor, still called Thornton when his father was around, was taking it a step further. He knew owning a small-time ranch like the Lazy J wouldn't offer the long-time fulfillment he was after.

The Lazy J shorthorn herd was earning their ranch a strong reputation in the industry, and had allowed Thor to become more than just a rancher. He was a true pioneer in his shorthand breeding and the last thing he wanted was for the Krohl's to steal his secrets. He had developed a consulting business alongside his ranching, and was even delving into social media to expand the ranch's earning potential. And, of course, his personal brand.

The idea of stealing secrets also confused Thor, as there was nothing secret visible out here in this river area of their ranch. Yes, the shorthorn cattle were out here, but all the valuable information was in Thor's head or stored on his computer.

Either way, he was going to parade this fallen drone around the other ranchers to let them know about yet another evil being executed by that mammoth Krohl ranch.

"Alright, let's get this done," Thor said through gritted teeth.

* * *

"Whatcha got there, Thornton?" George Caldwell, Thor's father, yelled. He was watching from the porch as Thor pulled his ATV into the driveway with the crashed drone towed behind him in a small trailer.

George was a stereotypical old Montana cowboy, by all appearances. His canvas pants were slim and worn, his boots were aged but clean, his off-white shirt was long-sleeved and tucked into his pants behind a massive belt buckle. He even had the obligatory matching brown cowboy hat perched above his leather-skinned face. His gray hair wasn't visible below his hat, but his long mustache and trimmed beard were.

"You're gonna love this, dad," Thor said as he shut the engine off and waved for his dad to come over.

George hated the Krohl ranch even more than Thor did.

They were the largest operation in the area, and had become a nuisance to all the nearby family operations. They seemed to have endless money, cared nothing about the impact of their ranch on neighboring land, and never tried to blend into the community. Yes, they brought work to the area with their massive herds, but that was about the only positive thing George could attribute to their existence.

Even worse, the Krohl ranch had recently been home to an elitist hunting business. That's what George called it, anyway. The business model involved taking vast sums of money from billionaires around the world so they could hunt on the Krohl land. Guided, of course, by Krohl employees who would lead them right to their game of choice. For the rest of the trip, the Krohl staff wined and dined the vacationing elites.

The thought of it made George sick. That wasn't what ranching was all about. At least it shouldn't be. Those Krohl people didn't care about the ranching way of life and didn't care about the land beyond making money. While George was a businessman, too, he didn't like the way those 'guests' of the Krohl ranch treated everyone else in the community.

Thor didn't like them either, especially while they shared their hunting thrills at the Golden Bear after their 'adventures' ended. He considered them obnoxious, although he was a little less emotional about them than his father.

"Ok, I'm listening," George said as he hobbled down the stairs and headed over to Thor's ATV. He only looked slightly bowlegged when walking on flat ground, but when navigating the stairs. George couldn't help but show what years of riding could do to your hips and knees.

"One of the Krohl's drones crashed onto our land while we were moving cattle today. I'm going to make sure everyone knows what they're doing. They can't be sniffing around our land, dad," Thor said with a sense of accomplishment.

George inspected the drone, picking up the broken pieces and evaluating them closely while the corners of his mouth turned up in an unintentional smirk.

After a few minutes, his mouth fell open in surprise as he held up one of the broken pieces of the drone frame. His surprise quickly turned to laughter.

"My boy Thornton, you may have gotten more out of this little drone crash than you expected. Look at this," George said as he handed the broken drone piece to Thor.

While Thor looked at the piece, George laughed again and summarized his findings.

"This isn't one of those typical farm drones we've all been seeing. This thing is Russian! Our Krohl friends are not only spying on their neighbors. They're doing it with Russian drones! The guys at the Rancher's Alliance are going to love this!"

Chapter One

The cool, rainy day in Castle Rock, Colorado, accurately aligned with my emotional state that day. I was on the way to the funeral for Paul Frazier, my friend of over fifteen years who had passed away. Well, more accurately, he had died from a wound he had received while trying to help me on a covert assignment.

I work for a private equity firm out of Colorado called Rocky Mountain Equity. My work assignments for the firm were sometimes intertwined with covert 'missions' that can be dangerous or even deadly. Paul was the person who gave me those covert assignments. He said they originated from a group who called themselves The Association. I didn't know who the members of The Association are, as my only interface to the organization was through Paul.

The Association assignments typically involved investigations into crimes or immoral activity waged against the United States and its citizens. I've been working with them for five years, and they've paid handsome bonuses for that work. The last mission I was on was in Nashville, Tennessee, and it led to a shootout that ultimately took

Paul's life. He died in surgery before he made it back home to Colorado.

The guilt I was carrying for his death was difficult to tolerate. He had come to Nashville to help me, but after he was injured, I left him at the hospital and flew home to my family. Sure, he insisted I do it, and there was no reason to believe his life was at risk, but that didn't remove the guilt. I should have stayed.

Immediately after he died, I was asked to take over his position as The Gatekeeper for The Association. As a tribute to Paul, I felt obligated to take over that role, even though I wasn't quite sure what that meant. I knew he, as The Gatekeeper, gave me assignments. I knew he had some level of inside knowledge of The Association. And I knew he had a list of contacts that always exceeded my expectations.

But that's all I knew. Now I was taking over that position.

Jennifer Ellis, who Paul had recently recruited to be part of The Association, was with me on the assignment in Nashville. And she was sitting beside me now. Jen, as her friends called her, had hidden her tall, athletic frame in a dark pantsuit and looked stylish, yet proper. She always looked stylish and was always proper. Her straight blond hair was down over her shoulders for this event, and her brown eyes were alert but not as sparkly as usual. That wouldn't have been proper.

We were somberly driving to Paul's funeral in my Toyota 4Runner. It was drizzling and barely over fifty degrees as we pulled into the stone and iron gate of the Cedar Hill Cemetery. The property was freshly manicured and serene, with fresh flowers and closely mowed grass. It was early May, and the greenery was a stark contrast to the otherwise brown and stony landscape of Castle Rock.

I'm not sure what size of a crowd I expected, but so far I wasn't seeing anyone at all. There were very few cars parked along the road and nothing that looked like a funeral gathering. Jordan Crawford, who Paul had described as a leader of The Association, had given me the directions to come here. I had spoken to him several times over the last few days, and he said Paul was having a small graveside ceremony near the Veteran's Memorial in the center of the Cedar Hill Cemetery. So there we were.

Following the signs at the entrance, we slowly navigated the pathway toward the large, slate gray memorial near the center of the cemetery. There were a few cars parked in the small lot, but definitely not enough for a service. And there were no tents, tables or chairs to identify a gathering was imminent. Something didn't feel right.

"This is weird," Jen said as we pulled up, observing the same situation I had.

"Yeah, it is. But this is where Jordan said to meet," I replied.

"Well, let's go see what's up. Maybe there's something near the memorial," she said.

I parked the car, and we grabbed umbrellas and walked over to the memorial. The Veteran's Memorial in Cedar Hill Cemetery was located in a small designated area. It was complete with an American flag, a Colorado flag and four stone pillars covered with names of veterans who had passed. As we walked up, the feeling of reverence dominated the scene and we quietly stood on the sidewalk in front of the memorial.

We were still deep in thought when a voice from behind us cut through the sound of rain on our umbrellas.

"Paul's name will be engraved here on this memorial," Jordan Crawford said.

We both nodded as we turned around. I had recognized his voice, but Jennifer clearly didn't know who she was looking at.

"Mr. Crawford," I greeted as I shook his hand.

"Ms. Ellis, I presume? Jordan Crawford," he said to Jennifer as he also shook her hand. She nodded in response.

He was dressed in a tailored black suit, with a black fedora on his head and a black umbrella in his left hand. I noticed Italian shoes and wondered if the water would be ruining them today. He didn't seem to care. Paul had mentioned Jordan was a partner with Rocky Mountain Equity, so he wouldn't be financially affected by buying another pair of expensive Italian shoes.

"So, where's the service?" I assumed Jordan must know where we should be going.

"It's not here, as you may have recognized," he replied.

"What? Why are we here, then? Did they move it?" It seemed Jordan had no urgency to get anywhere else.

"No. I'm sorry to have misled you like this, but you two were invited here intentionally. It was one of several requirements Paul had given me. His family and close friends are at another location, but he insisted you two be led away from there. And he wanted me to give you this," Jordan said as he pulled an envelope out of the inside pocket of his suit jacket.

"Ok, this is getting weird," I said as I took the envelope.

"I understand why you'd say that. But I'm sorry to say it's about to get weirder. A few weeks ago, Paul sent me a list of instructions to execute upon his death. He didn't give an explanation, nor did he reveal any reason for the timing of these instructions. I have, or had, known Paul for over ten years and this was definitely out of character for him," Jordan said, shaking his head slowly.

"You mean, he knew he was going to die?" Jennifer was following along, equally confused.

"He didn't mention it specifically, but it seems he was acutely aware of that risk. I asked him about it, but he didn't divulge anything specific," he said.

"Besides his specific instructions, we know nothing about his concerns?" I was trying to figure out what this whole thing meant.

"No, not really. We're hoping you can find something at his condo in Denver. I'm sure you can find a way to get in, but don't tell me what it is. If someone stops you, just tell them the family has asked you to check things out. Given his role and everything he was involved in, you should be able to find some answers there. You will, knowing Paul like I did, probably have to dig around to find them." Jordan sighed at the thought.

"Ok, I'll get to the condo this weekend. That won't be a problem," I was still shaking my head as I tried to put some meaning to this strange conversation.

"And there's one more thing you should know," Jordan said, taking yet another deep breath.

"And what's that?" I asked cautiously.

"When Paul got to the hospital in Nashville, he sent me a text that said he was going to force the two of you to leave. He didn't want you near the hospital while he was there because he thought someone was following him. Again, no explanation beyond that," Jordan said.

"So, he thought someone followed him from Colorado to Nashville?" Jen asked.

"I don't know if he thought someone followed him from Colorado specifically. He didn't say," Jordan replied.

"Did he ever go on any assignments by himself before Nashville?" I asked.

"Not that I know of, no. But I rarely see assignment details," Jordan said.

"Did he say why he decided to go?" I asked.

"Sort of. He said you guys may have stumbled onto something bigger than it appeared on the surface," Jordan said.

"What does that mean?" Jen asked.

"I couldn't tell you," Jordan said, shaking his head.

"Well, you should know more about the assignment than we did since you authorized it," I said, looking for an explanation.

"What? I didn't authorize the assignment. Paul said he was sending you out there to research something. I had nothing to do with Nashville. But that's not unusual. As the leader of The Association, Paul always kept the details to himself," Jordan said.

"Wait, a minute. Paul was the leader? I thought you were?" Jordan's statement confused me. He clearly seemed to be a step removed from what Paul had been doing.

"No. I knew The Association existed, but that's about it. I just saw the bonuses during the Rocky Mountain Equity board meetings," Jordan said, looking similarly confused.

"Ok, so Paul determined which assignments we'd take and worked out the details? How did he get ideas for the assignments?" Jordan was putting the last five years of my life into a questionable state.

"Paul did get tips and ideas from me and from my network, if that's what you mean. The board members of Rocky Mountain Equity are all involved, along with a few individuals we engage for specific activities. But Paul was the ultimate decision maker for all things related to any of the consultants, including The Association. After all, he was the one funding that whole thing," Jordan said.

"He funded it? He always said it was funded by a group of people?" Again, these were new and confusing details.

"Well, that's sort of true. Since The Association projects were officially Rocky Mountain Equity projects, you could accurately say they were funded by all the partners of Rocky Mountain Equity, I suppose. But in reality, Paul added the funding to support anything to do with The Association," Jordan said casually.

"Wow. Ok, so Paul sent us on that trip on his own, and Paul was running this thing and funding it by himself?" Jordan's response was unsettling, to say the least. I didn't realize I was agreeing to this level of ownership when I accepted Jordan's request to be The Gatekeeper.

"Look, we gave Paul a long leash because we trusted him. I'm not sure what was 'bigger' than what you guys uncovered. Paul told me it was important and gave a summary story about drugs and human trafficking. Beyond that, you'll have to do some of your own research," Jordan said.

Jen and I stared at Jordan. She had been standing there listening as her chin dropped and a surprised look consumed her. Being only recently involved with The Association, this information didn't exactly align with what she was told, either.

"And we're the only three people who know anything about this?" I asked.

"As far as I know, yes."

"What about the rest of The Association?" I asked.

"I haven't shared with anyone. But honestly, I'm not sure if he told anyone else. Like I said, Paul ran all that," Jordan responded.

"Are you sure he died from surgery complications? I mean, is it possible someone killed him?" Jen asked. She was heading in the same direction my mind had gone.

"Given his preparations for the trip, I wouldn't be surprised if that's true. I'm not trying to be dramatic, just honest," Jordan said, more matter-of-factly than I expected.

We both nodded as I looked at the sealed envelope in my hand.

"Let me know if there's anything in there I can help with," Jordan said as he pointed to the envelope.

"Sure. You don't know what's in here?" I asked.

"Nope. The less I know, the safer you all are. And again, I'm sorry to have misled you about the funeral. Now you know why I did," Jordan said as he turned and walked away.

We stood there for a minute, watching Jordan walk toward a black BMW i7 I hadn't noticed before. A large man, looking like a stereotypical bodyguard, and also in a black suit, was standing next to the car. When Jordan got to the car, he opened the door and let Jordan into the back seat. He took Jordan's umbrella, shook it out, and folded it down. He put it in the trunk, got back into the car, and drove away.

A few minutes later, Jennifer and I were driving home in the 4Runner, quietly assessing what had just happened. We had an hour on the road to Jennifer's house in Colorado Springs, and we used the time to process what we had learned.

When we stopped in Jennifer's driveway, she finally addressed one of my concerns.

"Paul seems to have been directly responsible for more of The Association than he told me. Did you know that when you agreed to be The Gatekeeper?" Jen asked.

"No, this is a lot to absorb," I admitted as I shook my head.

After Jennifer got out and went into her house, I opened the envelope Paul had left with Jordan. Inside were three bullets. One bullet had six numbers, 479701. The next had eight digits, 28574901. Those two meant nothing to me on the surface, but the '01' on the end led me to believe they were PIN codes or combinations. Adding the extra two digits on the end as '01' was an old trick we used in our security consulting days to provide a quick and easy numerical disguise when needed.

The next said 'you have to try this fishing spot' and listed some GPS coordinates. That was weird.

Then there was a warning written across the bottom of the page, adding a dangerous tone to the short list.

'Trust no one, believe nothing, question everything, and be careful!'

Chapter Two

Traveling from my home in Woodland Park, Colorado, to Paul's condo in the Denver area involved one of my least favorite stretches of highway: the section of I25 between Colorado Springs and Denver. The highway itself had the curves and hills of a typical foothills terrain, but the traffic on this section of highway always seemed too aggressive for my comfort.

Even on a Sunday, today was no exception.

I'd usually take the time on a drive like this to crank my 80s hair band music and let my mind wander, but not today. The 4Runner wasn't built for this highway terrain, especially with my off-road modifications, so I had to pay close attention to the road and other drivers. This was no place for a wandering mind.

After navigating the highway north to the south side of the Denver metropolitan area, I exited west toward the mountains to get to Paul's community. He lived in the city of Littleton, just southwest of the actual city of Denver.

It had been two days since the strange funeral meeting with Jordan Crawford in Castle Rock. The details of that conversation had bothered me since we left, and were still cycling through my head in every quiet moment. I was hoping this trip to Paul's condo would reveal more about the unusual directions he had given me and the peculiar behavior Jordan had witnessed during the last weeks of Paul's life.

After turning into the Mountain Lakes subdivision, I stopped at a security gate where a guard appeared. Jordan, or someone, had paved the way for my entrance, so after showing my identification and mentioning the situation with Paul, the gate opened and I was allowed to enter. The large, well-manicured lawns behind the gate helped me realize why there was a security gate here. The brick houses lining these streets had to cost well over a million dollars.

I followed the GPS directions just under a mile to a group of condominium buildings overlooking a lake and a walking trail. The condos weren't as extravagant as the houses I had passed moments before, but were still nicer than anything we had in Woodland Park. Each condo building was accessible via a glass-enclosed lobby in the front, or via a garage attached to the back of the building.

After finding Paul's building, I parked the 4Runner in a visitor spot in the front lot and walked through the automatic glass doors leading to a new-smelling lobby. There were dark leather chairs and couches surrounding a large fireplace to the right, with a huge television above the mantle. The gas fireplace was lit, even though the temperature outside didn't require it. There was a young woman sitting behind a counter to my left who barely noticed my entrance while she talked quietly on the phone.

I waved casually in her direction as I walked toward the elevators, like I knew where I was going. Paul's condo was unit number 328, which I assumed was on the third floor.

Even if I was wrong, I didn't want to draw attention to myself by asking questions. I also didn't know how I was going to get inside, so I had my lock-picking kit just in case.

Behind the lobby was a short hallway that, thankfully, led directly to the elevators. After hitting the button to go up, I scanned around to see an exercise room and office directly to my left and a long hallway with apparently ground-level condos to my right. Everything looked new and well maintained. Paul lived in a nice complex.

When I got to the third floor, I was relieved to see doors numbered consecutively, beginning with 301, then 302, and so on. Paul's condo was the last one on the left, next to a stairwell. I noticed a camera on his doorbell, which none of the other units seemed to have, and I also realized each door had a keypad as well as a traditional lock. Before I tried to pick the lock, I remembered the numbers written on the notes Paul had left with Jordan.

Did one of those codes open the door? Trying to look comfortable in case someone was watching on one of the hallway cameras, I punched in 4797.

To my relief, the door lock clicked without delay and I was able to turn the knob to Paul's unit. I took a breath for a second before entering. The gravity of the situation set upon me as I realized I was about to go through the personal effects of a long-time friend and colleague. A friend and colleague who wouldn't be coming back to his home.

After that moment of reverence, I opened the door and entered Paul's home.

The first thing I noticed when I closed the door behind me was how bright the place was. The natural light, combined with the light shades of paint and flooring, seemed to be intentionally designed for that purpose. I turned on the light switch anyway, which seemed to make the condo only slightly brighter.

Behind the door was a short hallway with open doors on either side. The light gray walls and white tiled flooring were common throughout, as were the white doors and trim. The door on the right opened to an office area with a simple glass desk in the middle of the room. On the left of the desk was a black high-back leather chair, and on the right was a gray leather couch.

The office room looked sterile and almost unused, with only a few papers in a basket on the desk next to a large Apple computer monitor. A wireless keyboard and mouse were visible on a pullout drawer in front of the chair.

On the left side of the hallway was a laundry room that was larger than some bedrooms. There was a washer and a dryer on the left, with a cabinet beside them. Across the back wall were clothes racks with three plastic hangers aligned tightly to the right and empty. Again, the room looked sterile.

I couldn't help but think how Paul must have been a very tidy guy. I tried to remember if that resonated with how he behaved when we were in Afghanistan, but I couldn't remember anything that might have led me to this conclusion.

Making my way past the office and laundry room, the short entrance hallway opened into a surprisingly large kitchen and living area. The kitchen was first, with a large island covered with a white marble top, and stainless steel appliances along the right side, next to white cabinets. The white and gray color tones contributed to a clean, modern feel. There was a white Smeg coffeepot on the counter and a knife block full of black-handled knives.

Beyond the kitchen was a living area with a large fireplace on the right below an even larger television mounted to the wall. Straight ahead were glass sliding doors to a balcony with a wicker table and two chairs.

The living room had a fluffy white sofa along the left wall facing the television, flanked by two gray leather chairs. There were colorful plaid pillows on the couch and a red blanket over the back of each chair. Those pillows, along with flowers on the kitchen counter and fireplace mantle, represented most of the color in the first few rooms.

Looking to my left and right, I assumed this was part of a split bedroom layout with a common area separating two bedroom spaces on either side. The bedroom door on the left was open, so I started there, finding a good-sized bedroom with a blue color palate blending nicely with the light coloring on the walls and floor. The bedroom had another sliding door along the far end, which seemed to open to the same patio I had seen in the living area. This area was clean and neat, but felt lived in and less sterile than the other areas.

On the other side of the bedroom was a walk-in closet and a bathroom. The walk-in closet had a custom-looking storage unit inside full of men's clothes and shoes. One glance told me Paul organized his things very similar to my own habitual pattern. Longer sleeves and darker colors went to the right. There were no empty hangers or misaligned colors. Everything was in order. The shoes had a similar alignment on the floor, from light gray suede slippers on the left all the way to black military-style boots on the right.

This must have been Paul's main bedroom, as it showed the most obvious evidence of human existence. The bathroom had even more of Paul's things, with an electric toothbrush and soap sitting next to the double sink. There were towels folded neatly on the rack next to the shower.

I began to wonder if Paul cleaned the place this thoroughly before leaving for Nashville or if he had someone come in to clean while he was gone. I'd have to check on that later.

Crossing the living area into the other bedroom area, I opened the door and stopped. This room was a stark contrast to the rest of the condo. The shades were drawn, leaving the room dark and lit only by the light coming in from the doorway. Well, that light plus all the flashing lights of the computer servers mounted on a rack in the right corner of the bedroom next to the closet door.

There were ten different servers in the rack in the corner. There was nothing else in the room except a camera in the corner above my head and a mobile air conditioning unit in the opposite corner. I expected the camera was part of the same system as the front door camera. It also made sense that the rack may need some level of cooling if it ran all the time, which I assumed it did.

The sight of the servers seemed weird, but after I thought about it for a second, I decided maybe it shouldn't. Paul was, after all, continuously doing research for The Association and probably required all kinds of data to do his job. At least that's what I reasoned as I nodded my head, standing in the middle of his second bedroom.

The bathroom for his second condo bedroom held nothing interesting, but the closet did. It was slightly smaller than the other one, but it contained something the other closet did not. Opposite the custom shelving similar to the other closet was a knee-high, locked safe. I'm not sure if I expected to find it, but it didn't surprise me. It also caused me to remember the second set of numbers Paul had written on his note.

Without knowing the contents, I wondered if I could

simply carry it to my car. The safe was roughly the size of a small file cabinet and appeared to be very heavy. One push on the side of it verified that appearance. I wouldn't be carrying this thing out the door.

Having memorized the numbers Paul had written, I knelt next to the safe and spun the knob to clear it. Then I turned it clockwise and stopped on 28, then the other way to 57, then back again to 49.

And then I heard a sound in the other room and held my breath.

Was that the front door? Was someone coming in?

Instinctively, I pulled the SIG from the holster in the small of my back and stood. I moved toward the bedroom door to get a view of the entrance hallway and watched the door open.

Then I saw a woman casually enter Paul's condo.

Chapter Three

The woman stopped in the hallway and took a deep breath while she scanned Paul's condo. She was dressed casually in jeans, a light blue blouse and a short leather-looking black jacket. She appeared to be in her mid-thirties, trim, and approximately five foot five. Her hair was dark and straight, and was loosely tucked into a Denver Broncos cap. She would have blended in at any Yoga class or kids' soccer game.

Or at any fashion show, for that matter. Even in her casual attire and with only a split-second gaze, I assessed the woman as stunningly beautiful.

Realizing I was caught, and that the woman didn't look like a threat, I decided to reveal myself. I casually emerged from the bedroom and acted surprised.

"Whoa, I'm sorry. I wasn't expecting anyone else to be here," I said, using my best acting skills, and still keeping my SIG in my hand behind my right leg.

Did I see her squat into a fighting stance and grab at her purse when she heard me? I hadn't even noticed she had a purse until she moved, as she had it tucked under her jacket.

It was clear I surprised her, but she quickly shifted her posture. After a brief moment of shock and tension, her face shifted out of the look of fear, or intensity, or whatever it was. She shook her head and broke into an incredible smile. A somber, yet spectacular smile.

"Oh, I'm so sorry. I wasn't expecting anyone to be here, either. You really startled me," she said.

Did I detect an accent? Was it Russian? Croatian? Serbian? It was definitely something. She was trying to hide it, but there was an accent for sure.

Her sad smile put me immediately at ease in a way that felt intentional. Pretending to be smitten by her beauty, which wasn't hard to do, I immediately volunteered my name.

"I'm Keith. I worked with Paul and his family sent me over," I blurted out, stumbling across my words and smiling broadly while watching closely for her response.

"I'm Natalie. Paul, uh, gave me a key before..." Her voice trailed off and she dropped her head. If Paul gave her a key, she must have been close to him. That would mean she was aware of Paul's death and was understandably upset.

Oddly, though, I hadn't noticed any sign of a woman's presence inside the condo. That made me cautious, so I decided to keep her talking for a moment.

"I'm so sorry. How long had you known Paul?" I asked without moving toward her. If it was really Paul's girlfriend, t may have been appropriate for a hug given the tears that were now flowing down her cheeks. But the circumstances of this encounter had me hyper alert.

"We had been dating for seven months," she responded.

Seven was a specific number, not a round one like three, six or nine. That implied she wasn't lying. Or she knew what she was doing.

"I'm so sorry. I hadn't seen him casually in some time. He didn't mention he was dating someone," I said, trying to offer condolences with my voice while staying on the other side of the room and keeping the safety on my SIG off.

My response seemed to catch her off guard.

"Really? Maybe I was more serious than he was. But when he offered the key, I thought maybe he was more serious..." Again, her voice trailed off, and she dropped her head.

"Well, maybe not. To be honest, we talked a lot, but we rarely got into personal topics," I said, again trying to offer a comforting tone.

She nodded.

"So, was there something you were looking for?" I asked.

"Not really. I guess I just wanted to get one last look at what could have been. We used to sit on the patio and drink wine while staring at the mountains. We talked about moving out there someday and getting a cabin away from all the noise and smog of the city," she said.

I hadn't noticed the patio had a view of the mountains, but without looking, I realized it probably did. Paul really had a nice thing going with this condo, this view, and apparently this woman.

"I see. Feel free to have a seat if you wish," I said, offering no reason for my presence and hoping she didn't ask.

She did.

"You're here from his work?" Natalie seemed to perk up

with the question, once again causing me to stay cautious with my hand on my SIG.

"Yeah, I guess the family thought I was the best person to check in on his personal effects before they arrive," I lied.

She nodded.

"We may not have talked about personal things much, but we've been friends a long time," I added.

"I see. Well, I don't want to bother you. I shouldn't be here, anyway. I'll just go," she said as she turned for the door and quickly left. It almost seemed like she was embarrassed to be seen in the condo.

The whole scene took less than two minutes, but it also never felt comfortable. I paused for a second while I evaluated what had just happened and decided I didn't trust that woman, regardless of her beauty and her sad story. I ran to the door and opened it, cautiously looking down the hall toward the elevator.

It was empty. Natalie, or whatever her name was, was gone.

After mentally chastising myself for having my guard temporarily shaken by the beautiful Natalie, I got back to the task at hand: the safe.

Back in the closet of the server bedroom, I quickly spun the dial back and forth on the numbers Paul had given me. The handle on the safe gave way when I turned it, exposing the safe contents.

I stopped and listened before looking in, keenly aware of the sound the unlocking front door made. It wouldn't sneak up on me if it happened again.

Hearing nothing, I bent down and looked inside the safe. The safe had a small shelf on the top and a larger compartment on its floor. The shelf held two immaculate Springfield 1911 pistols in holsters, along with several boxes of .45 caliber ammunition, two full magazines and a few empty ones. That was no surprise at all, as Paul's favorite pistol was a 1911.

The bottom of the safe was more interesting. There were multiple manila envelopes and file folders, all stacked neatly in a pile. On top of them was a small USB thumb drive. Deciding I didn't want to sit there and review everything in Paul's spare bedroom, I decided to take them with me and get out of there. Natalie's appearance and immediate departure had triggered my internal alarm.

The stack of folders was less than two inches thick when I pulled it out, but it would be difficult to conceal as I exited the building. I closed the safe door and spun the dial while considering options to get the papers out.

After a few seconds, I opted for the most immediately available option to hide the documents. I loosened my belt, tucked the folders into my pants, and covered them with my shirt. The thumb drive easily fit in the generous front pocket of my tactical pants.

Looking in the mirror, I was pleased my flannel shirt was big enough that the documents didn't show up to an innocent observer, and I walked toward the door. It took a couple of steps around the kitchen to get into a casual gait, with the folders pressing against my skin. When I felt comfortable I was walking in a reasonably normal stride, I walked out Paul's condo door.

I had put my SIG back into the holster on the back of my belt, and it was pressing the folders in the back of my pants against my skin. As I walked, I realized it was pushing the folders upward and causing them to get dangerously close to falling out. Still, I tried to walk normally.

Luckily, I made it to the elevator with nobody else emerging into the hallway. After hitting the button to go down, I reached behind me and stuffed the folders deeper into my pants while trying to avoid the elevator camera. The documents were pushed so far down now that I'd have to be careful sitting down.

The elevator door opened to an empty hallway. Emerging from the elevator, I took a deep breath and hoped nobody would be there waiting as I turned the corner toward the lobby. That hallway was also empty, so I continued to practice my casual walking with the folders strapped to my midsection.

In the lobby, the woman behind the desk at the front was no longer on the phone and smiled at me as I rounded the corner. This time, I wasn't going to walk by unnoticed. I had to get a story while simultaneously walking around as casually as I could.

I decided to use the woman's attention to my advantage.

"Hi. How's it going?" I asked as I headed toward her, setting my plan in action.

"I'm great. How are you?" She responded.

"Wonderful, thank you," I replied. I decided not to mention Paul's passing, as I suspected they probably didn't yet know. It wasn't publicized and his family had known I was the first one to enter the apartment.

"I'm Rachel. Is there something I can help you with?" The woman didn't ask who I was or where I lived, so I didn't offer.

"Maybe, Rachel, maybe. I was supposed to meet one of my friends with his girlfriend, but he wasn't there. Did you see anyone go by?" I tried to be casual and prevent questions about why I walked straight through the lobby from the parking lot when I arrived.

She didn't seem to catch the anomaly.

"I mean, people have been going by since you went up. Who is your friend?"

"Paul Frazier," I said, hoping he used his real name on the lease.

The sparkle in her eye told me he did.

"Oh Paul, yes. Well, I mean, I know Paul, but no. He hasn't been by here," Rachel replied with a smile and a quick headshake.

"Hmm. Ok. I suppose something happened. He's not answering his phone, either," I added.

"They're such a sweet couple," she chimed in.

"Oh, are they? I haven't met her before. Paul and I work together, but we rarely talk about personal things. Typical men, I guess," I said, smiling as I turned away.

"Well, I hope they weren't trying to hide it because of how people react. She told me some people didn't treat them very kindly when they were out," Rachel said.

That caused me to turn back around.

"Really? Why is that?" I asked, genuinely curious.

"Well, you know. Some people are just old-fashioned and have trouble with people who are, well, just... different from them, I guess." She leaned in as if she was revealing a big secret.

I immediately remembered Natalie's accent and was surprised that people would treat them badly just because of her Russian ancestry. Or whatever ancestry it was.

"Wow. People would be mean just because of that? I guess I didn't realize people were still that shallow," I said, genuinely.

"Oh yeah. Some people are just stuck in the past, I guess," she said, sitting back in her chair. Apparently, she was proud of her revelation.

"Do you happen to have her number? I mean, if Paul's

not answering, maybe something happened. I'd like to see if they're ok," I said.

"Sure. We gather that information when we give out cards, even if they're not on the lease," Rachel said, revealing more than she knew.

She typed on her keyboard a second, then took a post-it note and scribbled a phone number. Then she handed it to me with no further questions. Security was clearly not Rachel's forte.

"Here you go. I hope they're alright," she said with a smile.

"Me too, Rachel. Me too," I said as I grabbed the number, turned around and pulled my jacket low behind me.

I needed to find out more about Paul's friend Natalie.

Chapter Four

The drive from Denver to our house in Woodland Park was slightly less than two hours. As soon as I got into the car, I missed being able to get Paul's guidance. I had gotten accustomed to his research and advice over the years, especially when my mind was wandering around with incomplete information. Paul was always there to help fill in the gaps.

Now he wasn't.

When I got to a reasonably flat area on the interstate, I called the number I had gotten from Rachel at Paul's condo. Perhaps Natalie could help fill in some of the missing pieces Paul would have filled in if he were still here.

The call went to voicemail, which still had the standard system greeting. Reluctant to leave a voicemail without any context, I ended the call and set a mental reminder to try again later.

I had only gone a few more miles when an incoming call interrupted my head banging to an old Ratt tune. The caller ID gave me a nostalgic surprise. It was Officer Keating from

Nashville. He had been in charge of the local police investigation for the last assignment I was on for Paul.

Curious, I accepted the call.

"This is Keith," I answered.

"Mr. Morgan, this is Officer Bill Keating from Nashville. I'm sorry to disturb you, but would you have a moment to talk?" Two things hit me with the greeting. First, I realized I never knew Officer Keating's first name. It seemed strange for him to identify himself that way. Second, I realized how much of a southern drawl he had when I wasn't physically there. It wasn't as noticeable when every one else sounded similar.

"Sure, I have a moment. What can I do for you, Officer Keating?" It didn't seem right to call him Bill.

"Well, first I have to warn you, this is an off-the-record conversation. The Chief wouldn't be happy if he knew I was talking about this. But given what you went through while you were out here, I think you have the right to know," Officer Keating said.

If he didn't have it before, he had my attention. Well, he had my attention as much as was possible while doing eighty down I25 between Castle Rock and Monument.

"Ok," I said cautiously.

"We are now investigating Paul Frazier's death as a homicide," he said matter-of-factly.

"Oh, really?" I asked, surprised but not shocked after the conversation with Jordan at Paul's funeral.

"Yeah. The bloodwork from his autopsy revealed some irregularities. The doctor had mentioned his concern when it happened, but it took a while for us to find anything. Are you familiar with antifibrinolytic drugs?"

"No," I answered.

"Well, they are used to make blood clot. Think of them as the opposite of blood thinners," he said.

I remembered Paul had died of a blood clot during surgery.

"Ok," I said impatiently.

"It seems someone gave Paul a dose of such a drug just before surgery, which ultimately caused abnormal clotting and death. After researching his records, we discovered none of the doctors or nurses ordered or administered such a medication." Officer Keating stopped and took a breath.

"Then who did?" I asked the obvious question.

"Well, that was a big mystery, initially. But then we reviewed all the footage from the hospital cameras and found the culprit. We found someone on a hallway video dressed as a hospital food worker who couldn't be identified as a hospital staff member. We are now under the assumption that's who administered the lethal drug."

"What did they look like?" Again, the question seemed obvious.

"All I can say is it was someone of average female stature with straight brown, shoulder-length hair. We can't verify anything else, as the person could have been wearing a disguise and avoided direct camera exposure. They knew where the cameras were," he said.

"No entry or exit footage?"

"Not yet. We're working on it. This is sort of breaking news. I'm only calling you because of the obvious relationship you and Paul shared. I don't know why someone would want to kill him, but you might. If you think of anything that could help us, please let me know. Any initial thoughts?" Officer Keating asked.

I couldn't share all the thoughts going through my mind, so I opted to deflect for the moment.

"Well, I think we pretty well cleaned up the leaders of that trafficking ring out there, so that shouldn't be it," I said, thinking out loud.

"Oh, that reminds me. I should tell you about that, too," Officer Keating interjected.

"Should tell me what?" I couldn't help but ask another obvious question during one of his lengthy pauses.

"It seems our friend Mary Perez-Valentine has friends in high places. She is out on bail awaiting trial. She is now saying we can't prove the case against her and she expects to have her name cleared," Officer Keating said, unable to hide his disgust.

"What! She admitted to everything! We got the recording." I, too, couldn't hide my disgust. During the assignment in Nashville, we had found Mary was running a drug and human trafficking ring through the border with Mexico. She and her family had set up an operation in Zapata, Texas, that we found and shut down. At least we thought we shut it down.

"She's claiming the recording is a fake, and that it was created using artificial intelligence. She's using her husband's death to tug at people's heartstrings publicly, but behind the scenes she must have someone helping her. Normally, such a situation would never merit bail," he said.

"This is nuts. So, you're telling me she could be out here trying to track me down right now?" I asked, realizing I was now screaming into the air in my 4Runner. I probably looked like a crazy man to anyone passing me on the highway.

"Well, she has a tracker on so she can't leave the area, so I doubt that'd be possible. But nonetheless, you need to be careful. I suppose I can trust you to share the same with Ms. Ellis," Officer Keating replied.

"Yeah, yeah. I'll be careful. And yes, you can trust me to share this with Ms. Ellis. Anything else?" I was too annoyed to keep talking.

"Isn't that enough?" It seemed Officer Keating was done, too.

"Thanks, Officer Keating," I said before disconnecting the call.

I drove another few miles in a daze, just shaking my head. So, Paul's premonition was on target. He was murdered. By someone. And the woman most likely to orchestrate such a murder was no longer in custody. Officer Keating was probably right: she must have friends in high places.

Realizing Jennifer needed this same information, I called her next. She was with me in Nashville and had helped with the investigation. I could also trust her to be equally frustrated by the apparent lax treatment of Mary Perez-Valentine after her arrest.

"Hey Keith," she said casually when she accepted the call.

"Hey Jen, how's it going?" I asked automatically.

"I'm ok. Still a little shocked about Paul and that odd funeral meeting, but I'm ok. How are you doing?" She asked in a more solemn tone.

"Well, after the call I just had with our good friend Officer Keating in Nashville, I can say I've been better," I replied, my frustration slipping into the tone more than I intended.

"Uh-oh. What did he have to say?" she asked.

"Well, I have to say it was not altogether pleasant. He called to inform me that Paul Frazier's death is being ruled a homicide." I paused as I heard Jen take a breath.

"So Paul was right to be concerned!" It was more of an exclamation than a question.

"It appears he was. Officer Keating says someone gave Paul a drug that was not prescribed or administered by the hospital staff. That's what caused the blood clot that killed him. They are looking at video now, but I doubt they find much. There was a person in the hallway they think may have done it, but they covered their face and knew where the cameras were," I said.

"Wow. I guess it was nice of him to call, but that's awful. I wonder if Mary is behind that from behind bars?" Jen asked.

"Interesting you should ask that question. It seems Mary made bail and is no longer incarcerated. So, to answer your question, it's entirely possible she's behind it," I said, with no further attempt to contain my annoyance.

"You've got to be kidding me," Jen replied with a deep sigh.

"Nope. Officer Keating says she must have friends in high places. Which, of course, may mean someone else is behind Paul's death, too," I added, revealing one of my initial thoughts when Officer Keating gave me the news.

"Yeah. And I guess they know we were in on it, too," she added matter-of-factly.

"I suppose that's probably why he called me. Yeah." This time, my tone was more serious.

"I'm not sure what we're dealing with here, but it sure sounds like we should be careful. Do you really think Mary had more connections than we thought? So much that she might have known that Paul was directing our effort in Nashville?" Jen asked.

"Well, that's certainly a possibility. I need to think about this a little. Maybe we can catch up tomorrow and brainstorm what might be going on. It also might be good to call Jordan. I'm not sure how much he knows about this," I added as I began to get closer to Monument and the traffic on the highway picked up.

"Sure. Ping me when you want to chat. In the meantime, I'll be careful," she said.

"Yep, good idea. Thanks Jen." I ended the call without saying "I'm sorry" again.

I was, though. I had gotten Jennifer involved in the fiasco at Willow Creek that had set her up to be recruited by Paul into The Association. Without my involvement in her life, she would have been leading a much more peaceful existence..

After our conversation, she was watching her back for an unknown killer that may or may not have been coming after her.

Chapter Five

The rest of my drive home went without issue. I arrived in time to see the kids before we all headed out for the afternoon. This was a hockey practice night for Jamie, my twelve-year-old daughter, so we had only a little time to grab something for dinner and drive into Colorado Springs, about thirty miles away.

My parents were at our house, preparing to take the kids away later in the week. It was Jamie and Kyle's last week of school, and they were eager for their annual two-week retreat in Missouri with their grandparents. They had done this same trip the last three years, so it was becoming a tradition. This year, my parents came in a few days early to help cover some of the kids' activities so I could attend Paul's funeral. Ever since my wife died in a snowy car crash five years ago, I took all the help I could get.

I tried calling Natalie again during Jamie's hockey practice, but again got voicemail. After that, I let it go for a while. It was fair to assume she needed some time to process Paul's death, so there was no need for me to pester her.

An hour and a half later, I was sitting in the lobby of my eight-year-old son Kyle's violin lesson in Woodland park watching the Rockies play the Dodgers on television. Jamie was sitting next to me, buried in her phone. My parents were sitting in the room for Kyle's lesson, which I'm sure the instructor didn't appreciate. Jamie and I were alone in the lobby.

I hadn't noticed the vibration of my phone sitting on the table next to me, but Jamie did.

"Dad, come on. Please tell me you can hear that," she said in her most critical voice.

"Oh, yeah. I was just letting it go to voicemail," I lied.

I looked at the phone to see the number was from Detroit, but wasn't one I recognized. I had been involved in an assignment in Detroit just a few months before, so I took the risk of answering. If it was a salesperson, I could always just disconnect and block the number.

"This is Keith," I answered quietly.

"Mr. Morgan. This is Bob Riley from the FBI here in Detroit. You may remember, we met at Willow Creek," the voice on the other end was familiar, and instantly took me back to the horrible shootout that ended my last Detroit assignment. That assignment was the one just before Nashville. Bob Riley was the Special Agent in Charge of the FBI field office in Detroit.

Once I heard Bob's name, I stood and waved to Jamie to let her know I was stepping out to take the call.

"Yes, SAC Riley, I remember you," I replied.

"I'm sorry to bother you on a Thursday evening, but I have some information you'll probably eat to know," he started.

"Ok," I said, cautiously.

"I don't want to alarm you, but in the spirit of collaboration, and acknowledging your work getting that case resolved, I'm going to disclose some confidential information. This is off the record," he said.

"Ok," I said, even more cautiously. It was my second unexpected off-the-record conversation of the day.

"I'll get right to it. There have been some updates in the case here in Detroit. We had everything closed out, had the judge agreeing to a life sentence for Shawn Holmes, then something went off the rails." SAC Riley took a breath.

"During a routine facility transfer yesterday, Shawn Holmes escaped. More accurately, he had a team of his associates break him out. I don't know who he knows, but it's someone with access. They knew the route and method of transfer, even though we change it all the time. There was a traffic accident and a fake emergency crew arrived. They had all the credentials and seemed legitimate, but when the real emergency crew arrived moments later, they realized what had happened. In the end, Shawn Holmes escaped. He's on the run right now, probably already out of the country. As I mentioned, this is highly confidential, but I thought you should know," SAC Riley said, ending with a deep sigh, as if he had unburdened himself from a heavy load.

I immediately thought about the confidential call I had gotten earlier from Officer Keating in Nashville. Somehow, my last two assignments were being undone. Even worse, I didn't have Paul to go to for support or resources.

"Mr. Morgan?" SAC Riley said, making me realize I had been silent for several seconds.

"I'm sorry, this is just a lot to take in," I replied.

"I know it is, and again, I'm sorry. I'm sure there's nothing to worry about, but I'd feel horrible if something was to happen to..." his voice was trailing off, and I felt the need to stop him.

"Thank you! SAC Riley, I appreciate the call. I'll make sure my family is safe," I interjected sharply.

"I've called Agent Mason already, of course, but would you feel comfortable talking to Ms. Ellis just to be safe?" It was the second time I had heard the same request that day, both times causing me to shake my head in regret. It made sense SAC Riley would talk to Agent Mason, as she was a fellow agent for the bureau. She had played a critical role in taking down Shawn Holmes, firing the shot that finally took him down. The shot also saved Jennifer's life, and probably my own, so it was good to hear was aware of this ugly secret.

"Sure, I'll let Ms. Ellis know. Thanks," I said as I ended the call.

I'm not sure how long I stood there looking down and shaking my head, but eventually I was jolted back into the moment when Jamie knocked on the window right behind me. When I looked up, she was standing there with her palms up in a 'what's going on' pose, and Kyle, my ten-year-old son, was standing next to her with my parents, all looking concerned.

I forced a smile and pushed aside my phone call. That was what I did. Over my years in the military and with The Association, I learned to compartmentalize things. On the outside, I felt I pulled off the big switch. On the inside, I was always aware of everything. Everything. All the time.

"Hey guys, ready for lunch?" I asked with my cheeriest voice as they opened the door and joined me outside.

After lunch at my favorite local cafe, Grandmother's Kitchen, we finally encountered some down time where I could call Jen again. I was dreading the call.

Jen had been a normal workplace acquaintance just a

year ago. Over the last several months, however, things had changed. We had developed a much closer relationship when my assignment in Detroit pushed us into a shared experience that went beyond professional. During that assignment, I found out about her military history and her toughness, and she found out about some of my personal background. And about my rather fortunate, and very private, financial situation.

Then our relationship changed again. Jennifer and I dated for three months. It was great, and things were going well. Then came the night in Nashville when Paul invited Jen to become part of The Association. That invitation exposed a part of my life Jen didn't know about. She realized I had been keeping that part of my life from her and things got complicated.

Now our relationship was about to get even more complicated, as the very assignments Paul and I had introduced her to were putting her in danger. Yeah, it might be overkill to suggest that to her, but since it was possible, I couldn't accept the risk of leaving her unaware. I had to tell her.

It sucked, but I made the call, anyway.

"Hey Keith, what's up?" Jen was in her usual jovial tone, which had resumed after we left Nashville.

"Well, I'm afraid I have some more bad news," I said, feeling guilty about giving her another warning.

"We need to stop talking like this," she said in a light-hearted tone.

"You're not going to believe this, but something has gone wrong with that assignment I had in Detroit..." I took a breath just long enough for Jen to interject.

"You mean someone is pulling strings on that one, too?" Her question echoed my own concern.

Was she right? Was someone undoing the work I had done for The Association?

"Well, maybe. It seems Shawn Holmes escaped custody yesterday. He's on the run. SAC Riley called me as a courtesy." I said.

"Oh, no. I've got to tell Mason," Jen said. She and Mason were longtime friends.

"They told her, already. And it's probably nothing to worry about. SAC Riley thinks he's probably out of the country, but it's worth a bit of caution," I said, trying not to be too dramatic.

"Yeah, ok. Thanks Keith. It was nice of them to let you know. I assume that probably broke some kind of protocol," she said.

"You're welcome, of course. You know I'd never want to put you in danger," I said, realizing I was getting too sentimental. So, I continued quickly. "And you're right. SAC Riley said it was confidential, so I'm sure he stuck his neck out for us by letting us know."

"I know you wouldn't put me in danger, Keith. But thanks," she said, with a hint of a chuckle.

"Sure. I'll let you know if I hear anything else," I said, and we ended the call.

The call with Jen made me uncomfortable. Even though it was probably unnecessary, I went about the rest of my weekend in a higher state of caution than normal. I knew the security system at home was effective and my trusty SIG P365 was always on my belt, but knowing there were potential threats out there raised my awareness. Every person at the bus stop, every car that went by, and every stranger on the street got an extra dose of my attention..

And I saw nothing unusual or concerning.

Later that evening, while I was standing next to the

4Runner at the Loaf n Jug, waiting for the gas tank to fill, I got a call from Denver.

It was the number Rachel, the condo manager at Paul's place, had given me for his girlfriend. All I knew was her name was Natalie, so that's how I had programmed her into my phone.

It had been over two hours since I had last tried to call her.

"This is Keith," I answered.

There was a long pause, filled with several deep breaths.

"This is, uh, Natalie. I'm returning your call," she said in cautious, quiet bursts.

The timid voice had no Russian accent, so this was clearly not the woman who I saw in Paul's condo.

"Yes, thank you, Natalie! I'm so sorry to bother you. I was just trying to track down some information about Paul," I said, revising my planned talking points on the fly.

She said nothing, so I continued.

"I talked to Rachel at his condo, and she said you had a key," I said, pausing to see if she'd speak.

"Yeah," was all she said.

"And I was trying to determine what to do with some of his things. I'll be working with the family to clear out his condo, but wondered if there was anything that was special to you?"

I paused again.

"I don't think so. No, there isn't. We weren't dating that long," she said, still quiet and cautious.

"Look, I'm sorry about this. I probably shouldn't have called you," I finally said. Once I realized she wasn't the Russian-accented beauty I had seen at the condo, I had a whole new list of concerns.

Then I heard her sniffle. She was understandably upset.

"This is really Keith Morgan?" she asked.

"Yeah, it is. Why do you ask?" The way she asked it made it sound like she didn't trust me, which was odd.

She let out a sob. Now, she was all-out crying.

"Paul told me to trust nobody and question everything. That's all. He said you were the only person I could trust," she said, now openly upset.

"Really? That's interesting. He left me a similar message," I confided.

"Out of curiosity, when did he tell you this?" I asked.

"Just before he left for Nashville," she said.

"And had he ever told you something like this before?"

"No, not really. I mean, he was always cautious about where we went and was constantly looking around to make sure nobody was following us. I thought that was weird, but I just accepted it was part of the Paul package, you know," she said.

"Yeah, it was quite a package, alright," I said with a smile. "Ok, thanks Natalie. I appreciate the help," I said, ready to leave her alone.

"And there's one more thing," she added before I could continue.

"I don't know why this was so important, but he says you have to try one of his favorite fishing spots. It seems silly now, but since I have you, I might as well tell you. He gave me the location. I'll read it to you if you're ready."

"Sure, go ahead," I said.

Then she listed out the same GPS coordinates I had gotten from Jordan.

I tried to laugh as genuinely as I could.

"That Paul, always talking about fishing," I said with a fake chuckle.

We continued the conversation for a few more minutes

with some pleasant memories of Paul while I finished pumping gas, then ended the call.

The strange thing was, Paul and I had never spoken about fishing before.

Chapter Six

After talking to Natalie, I examined the documents and thumb drive I had gotten from the safe in Paul's closet. The thumb drive was first.

I plugged it into my laptop and a box appeared on my screen with the option of running a security program. Normally, that would be an automatic warning of a potential threat, but knowing where this drive came from, I clicked 'Ok' and ran the program.

Another box appeared in a matter of seconds that asked if I wanted to use facial recognition to access the drive. Realizing I might have no shot at seeing what was on the drive since I didn't have Paul's face, I clicked 'Yes' anyway. To my surprise, my laptop camera light popped on for a second and a file folder showed up. Paul must have programmed my facial profile into the software.

As surprising as the facial recognition was, the contents were even more surprising. There was just one text file on the drive. When I opened it, I saw a URL written that I recognized as a bitcoin wallet site, along with login credentials. I also saw a long alphanumeric number I assumed was the private key to the wallet. My initial expectation was that it was probably the wallet used to pay our assignment bonuses for The Association, so I moved on.

Next, I turned my attention to the documents.

For the next hour, between entertaining my parents and making sure the kids got to bed, I dug into the folders I had found in Paul's safe. The information was well structured and told a bit of a story. It was mostly a financial story.

The story started with a list of stock purchases Paul had made nearly ten years ago. The timing aligned with our return from Afghanistan, and represented a shocking amount of wealth. I knew Paul was well off, but I didn't know he was as wealthy as the records showed.

There were three folders of stock purchases, along with some movement between stock sales and Bitcoin purchases. I read through the transactions for a few minutes, then stopped to write down a tally of all the ups and downs. Well, they were mostly ups. There were large increases being outlined, but it was easy to lose track just while reading them.

After jotting down a few numbers and looking up some stock quotes online, I sat back in my chair and looked at the totals in amazement.

Paul had somehow started with around thirty million dollars when he returned from Afghanistan. That number alone amazed me. Our work with Hart International had paid well, so I had done ok during my time there. But I only came home with a hundred thousand dollars to show for it. And I was thrilled with that. But thirty million dollars? Paul had done amazingly well!

From there, Paul had made some brilliant investments, boosting his entire portfolio to well over five hundred million dollars. The guy had a half a billion dollars and lived in a condo in Littleton, Colorado. I understood the desire to live a normal life, but that was nuts.

The bulk of the money was not in his personal name anymore. Over the last year, Paul had moved most of his assets under a limited liability corporation called, oddly enough, The Association Equities, LLC.

The next folder showed a list of real estate assets under the LLC that included properties in Colorado, Missouri, Montana, and Idaho. It seems Paul liked his real estate in the middle of the country. I didn't have time to look up property locations, but they totaled over ten thousand acres combined.

Then there was one last folder. I opened that one, not sure what to expect, as the discoveries I had uncovered over the last hour had already been far beyond anything I would have expected. The last one was a list of the various investments Rocky Mountain Equity had made. This was officially the company I worked for, so I knew most of the technology firms listed. I had consulted with several of them over the last five years.

I was about to close the folder when the title of the company on the first page caught my attention. It seems Rocky Mountain Equity wasn't just the place Paul worked. He owned it. The official name of the company was Rocky Mountain Equity, a subsidiary of The Association Equities, LLC.

Sitting back and trying to remember what Jordan Crawford had said at Paul's funeral, I felt I missed something with how he had spun Paul's involvement. He didn't exactly reveal that Paul owned the company, but may have assumed I already knew. His comments simply indicated Paul had paid for all the assignments, not that he owned the whole organization .

That last revelation made me wonder how much Paul was actually worth. I took a closer look at the various equity stakes and corporate holdings for Rocky Mountain Equity, and quickly came to a valuation of over five hundred million dollars. That amount, combined with the real estate, stock and bitcoin, meant Paul was a billionaire. I chuckled at the thought, but quickly stopped as I related that fact to the events of the last few days.

Is this why someone was targeting Paul? Did someone know he had all this money and was after it? It was certainly a lot and was probably enough that some people would kill for it. Is that what happened?

The discoveries from Paul's safe were a lot to process. They also led me to wonder why Paul hadn't revealed all this to me when he was alive. Clearly he wanted me to find it since he passed along the safe combination, but why now?

I wondered if the bitcoin wallet from the thumb drive in his safe was the one that held those millions. Reluctantly, I opened my browser and logged in to find out. I felt my mouth unintentionally fall open as I saw the total. The wallet held over three hundred million dollars in bitcoins.

I stared at the number for some time before I shook myself back into reality. My personal bitcoin wallet had given me a bit of callousness toward wealth, but Paul's wealth was many multiples beyond mine. The guy was loaded.

Looking at the clock and seeing it was now past midnight, I closed the folders and put them in the gun safe in my bedroom. Then I did the same with the thumb drive. I could now see why Paul kept them secure, and I was determined to do the same.

Knowing I had a busy Morgan crew Monday to deal with the next day, I decided to stop for the night. I was activating the alarm system on my phone when a thought struck me.

I had stepped right by the servers in Paul's apartment and didn't even think twice about them. Did they have something to do with this whole financial windfall he had gotten into over the last ten years? Were they just support systems for some of the many technology companies under the Rocky Mountain Equity umbrella? Was there something else going on with Paul - even more than I had already found out?

All the discoveries of the day had left me without considering the one last bullet item from Paul's list: the one about the fishing location. Only after seeing Paul's envelope in my safe did that last item pop into my memory. Given everything else going on, the idea of finding a great new fishing spot for a peaceful day of fly-fishing was intriguing.

Putting sleep off for another minute, I grabbed my phone and entered the GPS coordinates for the fishing location Paul had listed. The map zoomed in on a location in Montana, just west of the northern portion of Yellowstone National Park. It appeared to be in the middle of nowhere, but there were some streams visible on the map that connected to the Madison river. That could mean great trout action.

A quick scan of driving directions showed the location was a little over a twelve hour drive from my house. Looking for nearby airports, I was disappointed to find no real good options from Colorado Springs. I could fly from Denver into Bozeman to the north, then drive down from there. The drive should take around two hours.

Considering the options, I decided within seconds that I'd rather drive twelve hours than fly out of Denver and rent a car in Bozeman. The thought of driving to Denver, leaving my car, renting a care in Bozeman, driving to the fishing spot, then repeating the process to return home made my blood pressure go up. I'd drive.

The kids were scheduled to end school next week, so the timing was perfect for setting up a trip. My parents were planning to drive them to Missouri for two weeks after the school year ended. That meant they'd be gone Wednesday night after their last half day of school. I could be past Denver by dawn Thursday and on the fishing site by mid afternoon. The thought of a new fishing destination that wasn't overcrowded, like many of the ones near my home, sounded great.

Although, I was still curious why Paul had never mentioned he was a fisherman. For a moment, I had a profound sense of loss, realizing I'd never be able to ask him about it. Then, I found myself smiling as I sat on the edge of my bed thinking about Paul out in the woods with a fly rod. I had known two versions of Paul: the military version and the business version. I was sad I had never known the fishing version.

Before dropping off to sleep, I took a minute to see what sort of rental property I could find in the area. It was clear there were no hotels near the remote fishing spot, but there were a couple of small towns nearby that looked interesting.

A quick search revealed there were numerous rental properties nearby, but most were already booked. The spring runoff had slowed, and the fishing traffic was picking up. The Madison river was a renowned trout destination so the lack of available rentals wasn't really a surprise.

After a few minutes, I found a cabin in Cameron, Montana, that seemed perfect. The location was literally right next to the Madison river and was near the only restaurant I could find. It was a place called the Golden

Bear and appeared to be a bar, restaurant, convenience store and fly-fishing shop. It sounded like my kind of place.

I even got so excited about the fishing trip that I took a minute to get a Montana fishing license online. I didn't know if the location Paul suggested was private or public, but I had to consider it might be public. If that was the case, I'd want to be legal while I was fishing there.

My mind was still buzzing, so I started making a quick list of things to take care of over the next couple of days. I needed to get my trout gear ready for a remote adventure, to get an oil change in the 4Runner, and to make sure my parents were lined up to get the kids on Wednesday. Tomorrow was Monday, so I'd have plenty of time to get prepared for the trip.

It took a little while to get to sleep that night. I had gone through a roller coaster of emotions during the day, but the thought of the fishing excursion had me wide awake. I had to dig deep into my bag of tricks to force myself to sleep, using the same methods we had to use during my military and security days.

With some intense focus on darkness and nothing else, I finally drifted off.

Chapter Seven

The next morning, our Golden doodle, Winchester, greeted me with his usual morning wake-up call. After letting him out the back door, I went into the kitchen to make some coffee and began our morning routine. Over the next couple of hours, the kids were up, dressed, fed, and at the bus stop.

Next, I lifted some weights, took Winchester for a run, and spent some time at the shooting range. It was early afternoon, and I was cleaning up after a late lunch when I noticed my phone buzzing on the counter. The call was from a Denver number I didn't recognize, but given all that was going on, I answered.

"This is Keith," I said automatically, regretting I had given away my name like every other time I answered.

"Good morning, Mr. Morgan. This is Sergeant Theiss from the Littleton Police Department. I'm sorry for bothering you, but I need to ask you a few questions," the stern female voice said.

"Oh, ok. Sure. Go ahead," I said, calm and curious.

"Were you in Littleton yesterday, Mr. Morgan?" Sergeant Theiss asked.

The question threw me for a minute as I raced to consider what I had done during my time in Littleton. Did I go anywhere that might have been problematic or illegal?

"I assume you know the answer if you've taken the time to look me up and call me. I must have shown up on a camera somewhere near where a crime must have been committed or something. Could you tell me what this is about?" I asked, trying not to sound too concerned.

"Ok, fair enough. Yes, I know you were in Littleton. And yes, your vehicle showed up near a crime scene. You were at the Mountain Lakes condominiums yesterday, correct?" It was a statement phrased as a question, but Sergeant Theiss stopped, so I felt compelled to answer.

"Correct," I said, still trying to remember if I saw anything unusual. Did someone call in because they saw me entering Paul's apartment? Did Rachel report me for something after I left? Nothing else was coming to mind.

"And what were you doing there, exactly?" Sergeant Theiss asked, pointedly.

I knew I had to be a little careful. I was certain she probably knew about Paul's death, so I leaned into that thought.

"Well, it's not a pleasant reason, I'm afraid," I said, taking a deep breath and pausing.

"I see. Why is that?" she asked.

"One of my friends lives there... well, used to live there. He was killed while on a trip to Nashville. His family isn't from around here, and they asked me to have a quick look inside his condo. They wanted to make sure there was nothing dangerous, or that needed urgent care before they got there. You know, like a pet or something," I fabricated on the fly, making sure my tone was adequately somber.

"What is your friend's name?" Sergeant Theiss asked without skipping a beat.

"Paul Frazier," I said after another deep breath.

"I'm sorry for your loss, Mr. Morgan. So, you went to Mr. Frazier's condo? How did you get in?" She didn't allow any time for an emotional exchange. She was on a mission.

"I had gotten a door code from the family," I lied again. She was looking for something, so I intentionally limited my responses until I found out what this was about.

"Where did you park?" she asked.

"In front of the lobby in the visitor section," I answered.

"And can you please describe the path you took to Paul's condo, including anyone you may have seen or talked to?" Sergeant Theiss asked, clearly trying to solve a crime in or around Mountain Lakes.

"I went in the front door, saw a young woman sitting at a desk in the lobby, went to the elevator and went up to the third floor. The woman in the lobby was the only person I saw. I didn't speak to anyone," I answered.

"And then what?" This woman was relentless!

"I exited the elevator and went directly to Paul's condo door. Again, I saw nobody else," I answered.

"Which condo is his?"

"328."

"Ok. Then what?"

"I entered the code the family had given me, and went in," I said.

"What did you find?" She seemed to get a little more comfortable, as though this wasn't really her area of focus. I used that to shorten my story a bit.

"There were no pets. Everything looked to be safe and intact. There was no food out or anything that needed immediate attention," I said.

After a pause, I added a point that made me uncomfortable.

"Then I saw a woman," I said.

"What do you mean? Someone was in the condo?"

"Not when I got there. But someone came in while I was there," I said.

"They knew the code?" she asked.

"I guess so. I heard the door unlatch, and she came in. She said Paul gave her a key," I said, my mind going back to the camera that was on Paul's doorbell. I'd need to get that data, because as I said it I realized the condo didn't use keys, it used either a code or a Fob. I was annoyed with myself for not catching that the moment she said it.

"Who was it?" Sergeant Theiss was intensely engaged again.

"She said she was Paul's girlfriend, Natalie." After a brief pause, I added the point that had been bugging me. "But she wasn't."

"How do you know?" she asked.

"Because the woman in the condo had an accent. It sounded Russian, or similar. Then I spoke to Paul's real girlfriend later. She had no accent," I answered, leaving a few gaps in the story for now. I was also cautious about putting too much emphasis on the accent as Sergeant Theiss seemed to have a similar, albeit much more subtle, version of the same accent.

"So she must have spoken if you heard her accent. What did she say?" Sergeant Theiss asked.

"She did speak, yes. As best I recall, she told me her name, and that she was Paul's girlfriend. Then she said she was there for some closure," I replied, realizing how weak it sounded as I said it.

"I see. How long did she stay?" Sergeant Theiss asked.

"Maybe thirty seconds," I answered.

"Then where did she go?"

"I'm not sure. She just got kind of emotional and left," I said.

"Did you see which way she went?"

"No."

"What'd you do next?" she asked.

I avoided mentioning the contents I had gotten from the safe, as I didn't yet know what they were or if they mattered to the police. And knowing the nature of our work with The Association, it might just open me up to more questions than I was able to answer.

"I looked around a few minutes, then I left the same way I came in," I answered.

"No sign of the girlfriend on your way out?"

"No."

"Can you think of any reason a woman would come into your friend's condo pretending to be his girlfriend?" The presence of the lying woman at the condo seemed to bother Sergeant Theiss like it bothered me.

"I've been thinking about that. No, I can't come up with a reason," I answered, somewhat honestly.

"When you left, did you see or speak to anyone?" Sergeant Theiss asked.

"Yes. I stopped at the front desk and spoke to the young lady there. I believe her name was Rachel," I answered.

"What did you say to Rachel?" It appeared she was going to keep asking questions until I was all the way out the door.

"I asked her for Natalie's phone number. I felt bad for making her leave so quickly, so I wanted to apologize," I lied, more easily this time.

"Did she give it to you?"

"Yes. She said she wasn't supposed to do it, but she understood," I answered.

"How long did you two chat?"

"I suppose it was less than a minute."

"What was her emotional state when you spoke to her?"

"She seemed fine. She was happy, smiling." I was wondering if Rachel had done something after I had left.

"Then what did you do?"

"I went back to my vehicle and left," I said.

"Where did you go after leaving Mountain Lakes?"

"I drove straight home. My parents are here visiting, and I wanted to be here," I answered, getting annoyed.

"You didn't return to the condo?" That was a strange question, but implied the crime must have occurred after I left.

"No, why?" It was time for me to find out what was going on here.

"Because, Mr. Morgan, someone shot Rachel Johnson through the head at point blank range this evening while sitting in the same lobby where you say you saw her," Sergeant Theiss replied harshly.

"Oh no. That's awful!" I said, more emotional than I intended. The news was not at all what I had expected. I immediately understood why I was being questioned and why the woman in Paul's apartment was so interesting to Sergeant Theiss.

Then a thought struck me.

"I saw cameras all over that place. Surely they would have caught someone going into the lobby and shooting Rachel," I said, realizing too late I was stepping into police business.

"It's funny you should mention that, Mr. Morgan. You noticed the cameras?" She was going back on the offensive.

"Yeah, I saw them. Since I set up the cameras on my property, I notice those things," I said, which was a partial truth.

"I'm going to have to ask you to come make a signed statement here in Littleton," she said abruptly.

After hearing what had happened, I understood why they wanted to talk to me. I also noticed she avoided answering my question about the cameras.

"Ok, I understand. I have to be here when the kids get home this afternoon, but I can head up after the kids are out in the morning. Given the traffic between here and there, it may be ten before I get there," I said, frustrated I'd have to go right back to Denver again.

"That will have to work, then," she said, clearly perturbed I wouldn't be there earlier.

"So, you didn't say whether you had footage of the killer. Why are you talking to me if I'm not on camera committing the murder?" I asked.

She paused and seemed to calm down a bit before responding.

"Because, Mr. Morgan, you're the last person we see entering the lobby. The cameras upload their video footage to the cloud. It seems the perpetrator or perpetrators were not only murders, but may have been hackers as well. Someone deleted the lobby footage from the moment you left. They also deleted the third-floor hallway footage for a few brief seconds at exactly the time you said a woman entered Mr. Frazier's condo," she said, telling me more than I expected.

"And you're comfortable that I didn't do it because I was the last person on the video," I said, as more of a confirmation than a question.

"It would have been foolish for someone to hack into the

system and erase everything except their own image, yes," she replied. "But perhaps you now understand my line of questioning."

"Yes, ma'am. I do," I said. "And would they really need to hack into the camera system? Couldn't they have forced Rachel to tell them the login information?"

"Maybe. But the condo owner doesn't think Rachel had access to the system. For now, we're going with the assumption that we're looking at a perpetrator with at least some level of unique technical capability," Sergeant Theiss said.

"Understood," I replied. Her answer made my spine tingle just a bit.

"Thanks Mr. Morgan. I'll see you tomorrow," she said as she ended the call.

As I put my phone down, a thousand thoughts were going through my mind.

Who was this woman who got into Paul's condo? How did she get in? Did she kill Rachel and hack into the video storage system? If so, why? And if it was the fake Natalie, why did she let me go?

I looked at the stack of folders I had gotten from the safe and wondered if they were the reason.

Chapter Eight

Tuesday morning, I once again received my morning greeting from Winchester at dawn and skipped the run for the day. Instead, I spent my time getting ready for the trip to Denver to be interviewed about my visit to Paul's condo.

The kids were pretty much on autopilot this close to the end of the school year, so the morning went without a hitch. By 8 AM, I was fighting traffic into Colorado Springs on my way toward Denver. I could have taken the back roads through the mountains, but even those can get congested during the morning rush, so I just took my chances with the dreaded I25.

While I was driving along, I wondered if I should give Jordan a call to let him know I'd be heading out of town. I wasn't sure how much he knew about Paul's wealth, so I made the decision to play it cool when I discussed the situation with Jordan. Since Paul had tucked away all the relevant documents in a safe in his condo, it felt like he probably didn't share the details of his wealth with people.

From what I had seen, his lifestyle certainly didn't seem to reveal how much money he had.

When I reached a lower-traffic area on the highway, which wasn't really low-traffic at all, I called Jordan.

"Hey Keith. How are things?" Jordan sounded like he was up and running, even though he was a time zone earlier than me in California.

"I'm ok, Jordan, thanks. I just wanted to fill you in on a couple of things," I replied.

"Ok, great. Sounds like you're on the road," Jordan said.

"Yeah, that's one thing I wanted to tell you. There was an incident when I went to check out Paul's condo," I said, starting slowly.

"An incident? What kind of incident?"

"Nothing to do with me directly, but the Littleton police called me yesterday to say there was a shooting in the lobby after I left. The young lady who works in the lobby was murdered," I said.

"Whoa! That's an awful coincidence," Jordan replied.

"Yeah, it was. And there's more. While I was looking around in Paul's condo, a woman walked in. She said she was Paul's girlfriend. Before I could get any information from her, she said she should leave and walked out. I tried to follow her, but she was gone," I said.

"I didn't know Paul had a girlfriend, but we really didn't talk about personal things," Jordan said.

"Well, there are a couple more things that make this disturbing. First, I don't believe it was really Paul's girlfriend. I did learn he does indeed have one, but that wasn't her. I came to that conclusion because I got the real girlfriend's number from the girl in the lobby before I left. It turns out Paul's real girlfriend, Natalie, had registered for apartment access, so they had her information. The girl in the apartment had a Russian accent, but the girl who answered the phone number they gave me did not. On top of that, the police told me all the camera footage that would have caught the girl at the condo was erased. So, it appears someone didn't want that girl to be seen," I said, leaving out any discussion of the safe in Paul's condo.

Jordan didn't ask about it.

"So, they believe you may have seen the murder?"

"They didn't say that, specifically, but it sounds like that's what they're thinking. That's why they want me to come in today," I replied.

"Does that mean you're at risk because you're able to identify her?"

I had thought about that question, but it didn't seem to be the case.

"I don't think so, or she could have tried to take care of me at the condo," I replied.

"Yeah, I suppose that's true. This sounds like a pretty capable and ruthless operation. If they were in Paul's condo and then murdered someone to cover their tracks, they must be looking for something substantial," Jordan said.

I choked back my initial response of 'yeah, like a billion dollars' and instead answered more generically. Jordan may already know about the money, but I couldn't help but remember the warning Paul had written on the bottom of his note.

"Yeah, it looks like it," I said.

"Did anything in the condo look like it was worth killing for?" Jordan asked.

"I'm not sure. I may need to go back after I talk to the police. It's possible I missed something. One more thing I wanted to tell you, though," I said.

"You mean that wasn't enough?"

"It's not about the murder this time."

"Good," Jordan said, sounding genuinely relieved.

"Paul recommended a fishing spot for me to visit in Montana. I think I'm going to head up there after the kids are out of school this week. They're going to be with my parents in Missouri, so the timing is good. And frankly, I could use a break," I said.

"That sounds like an excellent idea. I didn't know Paul was a fisherman, either. I guess I should have talked to him more often," Jordan said.

"Yeah, I said the same thing," I agreed.

I considered again whether to say anything about the computer equipment or the safe and its contents. After a brief second, I decided to keep all that to myself for now. I wanted to visit the condo again anyway, to check out the computer equipment more thoroughly.

"You better be careful out there, Keith. If they know you were one of Paul's buddies, and they're after something of his, you may be a target," Jordan warned.

"Yeah, I've thought of that, too," I replied honestly. He'd really be concerned if he knew the entire story.

"But anyway, that's all I needed. I'll get through this today and then I'll head out early Thursday morning. If anything comes up, I'll let you know," I said.

"Ok, thanks for the heads up. Have a good one," Jordan said as we ended the call.

I wondered if it was a mistake to leave my findings in the condo out of our conversation, but Jordan openly admitted he wasn't involved in the details. As I drove along the highway, nearing the exit to Paul's condo in Littleton, I decided it was best to keep some information to myself unless I needed Jordan's help.

As I parked the 4Runner in the Littleton Police Department parking lot, my phone began buzzing in the seat next to me. I contemplated just silencing it and heading into the station, but when I checked the number, I realized it was Natalie, Paul's girlfriend. Knowing the difficulty she must be experiencing right now, I accepted the call.

"This is Keith," I answered, as always.

"Keith, this is Natalie. My apartment has been demolished! Stuff is everywhere! Someone has been in here! What is going on, Keith?" She sounded frantic, screaming her words between anxious breaths.

"Oh, no! I'm sorry to hear that - is everyone ok? Are you ok?" I asked.

"Yeah, yeah, I'm ok. But Keith, this is crazy. Why would someone be coming after me? I don't have anything. I don't know anything. What is going on?" Natalie was asking fair questions, but I had no answers.

"I don't know, Natalie. I honestly don't. All I can say is I'm trying to find answers, too. I'm really sorry," I said, trying to be empathetic and honest.

"Well, I'm not staying here. I'm getting out of this place. My parents are in Phoenix, and I've already called them. I'm heading out as soon as I can get my car packed," she said as she started to cry.

I felt horrible for Natalie, but she was probably doing the best thing for the moment. Until I had an idea what these people were looking for, I had nothing to offer her.

"That may be best, Natalie. I wish I had some answers for you on all this, but I don't. I hope you can get some rest with your family in Phoenix," was all I could say.

My words felt shallow and insignificant, so I stopped.

"Bye, Keith," Natalie said as she ended the call.

I sat in the 4Runner and shook my head for a moment, hoping for the best for Natalie. After gathering my thoughts and taking a deep breath, I went inside to complete my interview.

After checking in with the officer behind the window at the front desk, I took a seat in the small lobby. There were seven other chairs in the room, but they were all empty. It must have been a slow day for criminals in Littleton.

Sergeant Theiss was in the office, so she came to get me herself. She was not at all what I expected. I don't know why I thought she'd be short, but she was tall. Probably over six feet. She wasn't thin, but wasn't heavy either. Her uniform seemed to fit perfectly, with long black sleeves that would have been uncomfortably warm for the time of year. Her dark hair was cut short, in a fashion that reminded me of the figure skater from the seventies, Dorothy Hamill. She was probably fifty years old and had dark-rimmed glasses like people had been issued when I was in the Air Force years ago.

Behind her was another officer. He had a lieutenant bar on his collar and looked the part. I guessed he was probably late-thirties, about my height, but stockier. He had a pale complexion and a crisp haircut that screamed military. His thick eyebrows above narrow, fierce eyes matched his military-style mustache. He could have moonlighted as a drill sergeant in the military. Or in a Village People tribute band.

That last thought made me smile more than I should have when they walked in.

"Mr. Morgan, thanks for coming in. This is Lieutenant Carr. I've only been here a few months, and he's got more experience in the precinct, so he's going to sit in on this one," she said with a genuine smile and a nod as she held the door open for me.

"Sure," I said as I got up and followed her through the door.

We went down a long hallway to an office on the right. It was a small, simple office with a window facing the parking lot. It had a metal desk painted a tan color with a laminate top and silver legs. There was a short desk chair behind the desk, and a laptop and monitor sitting on top. There were two metal chairs in front of the desk. The only other items in the room were cameras conspicuously located in two of the four corners up near the ceiling.

"Have a seat," she said, motioning to the two chairs in front of the desk. Lieutenant Carr stood by the door with his arms crossed.

"Do you mind if we record this?" she asked, as though she knew it wasn't an issue.

"Nope," I answered.

It wasn't an issue. I knew this was how interviews worked these days.

The interview went almost exactly like the phone call the day before, as I obviously wasn't a suspect. During the interview, however, Sergeant Theiss focused more on the visitor to Paul's condo. I shared everything I could remember, but my mind was elsewhere. I wanted to get back to the condo and check out those computers.

Lieutenant Carr chimed in here and there, but clearly it was Sergeant Theiss' show.

After less than ninety minutes, I was done.

"Thanks again, Mr. Morgan. We appreciate your help," Sergeant Theiss said as she held open the door for me to reenter the lobby. Lieutenant Carr stepped out ahead of me and disappeared down a side hallway.

"No problem. I'll call if I think of anything else," I said, knowing I had already shared what I could about the beautiful, yet apparently deadly, visitor to Paul's condo.

My next stop was Paul's condo. The police presence

was already gone, and there was no sign a murder had occurred just the day before. In fact, I saw nobody watching the lobby as I entered, so I went straight to the elevator and headed up to Paul's condo.

When I got to his door, I once again paused with a reverent breath as I acknowledged Paul's passing once again. Then I typed the code and entered the apartment.

And I stopped. Then I pulled my SIG out of the holster on my belt.

Paul's apartment had been turned upside-down.

I listened for any movement, heard none, then crept quietly into the bedroom where the safe was. If anyone was in there, they could be waiting for me. But they weren't. The condo was empty.

The place was ransacked. Drawers were open, with contents strewn across the floor. Couch cushions were torn open and scattered. The mattress on Paul's bed was askew, and the bedding was now a mess.

In the spare bedroom, all the servers were still there, but someone had switched off all the power. They were sitting there with no flashing lights at all. It was almost a little eerie seeing them lifeless like that.

Then I turned and opened the closet door.

The safe that had been on the floor was gone.

Chapter Nine

Realizing I was now standing in the middle of a crime scene, I stopped in my tracks and backed carefully out of the condo. Sergeant Theiss would certainly be interested in this.

The fact that someone, and I felt I knew who, had already been back inside the condo made me wonder again why they didn't stop me. The only thing that made sense is they must not have known I had the combination to the safe. I was going to have to watch my back even closer than before.

I don't know how long I stood by the door thinking, but at some point my thinking pivoted to the servers and their role in what Paul may have been doing for The Association. If there was data or software that might bring a negative light to Paul or any of my fellow associates, as we called ourselves, I didn't want it released.

Still standing inside Paul's front door, I considered another option. What if I didn't involve the police in this little piece of the crime? After all, I already had the critical documents from the safe in my possession. They'd only find Paul's favorite 1911 and some ammunition in there now.

And at some point, the people who stole the case would suspect I was the one who had the documents. That assumed, of course, the woman who walked in on me was part of the group who stole it. Once they realized I might have been involved, they'd come for me and I'd have to make a fresh set of decisions.

I wondered if they were already after me as I stood there.

I could also just remove the servers and report them stolen, but the logistics of secretly accomplishing that task seemed unfeasible. I was already surprised the safe was taken with no witnesses or complaints. It was heavy, so the woman I saw would have needed some help. Knowing how well they had covered up the woman's getaway, a sophisticated escape scheme didn't surprise me. They could have deleted the video evidence and killed anyone in their path.

Someone knew there was valuable information in that safe.

Before making another decision, I called a technology expert who had more hardware insight than I did. She picked up after just a couple of seconds.

"Hey Keith, what's up?" Jen's voice was bright and friendly, as usual. Hearing her voice, I felt bad giving her all this information and potentially souring her mood, but I also knew she'd be able to help me sort through it.

"Hey Jen, I've got some updates from Paul's condo, and I don't know who else to call to brainstorm," I said, regretting my phrasing immediately.

"Oh boy. With that sort of greeting, I'm flattered you chose me as your last brainstorming resort," she replied with a chuckle.

"Sorry about how that came out. It's not what I meant. What I mean is, I need your help," I said as I took a breath.

"In that case, what can I brainstorm with you?" she asked.

"First, let me bring you up to speed on a few developments. Remember that envelope Jordan gave me at Paul's funeral?" I asked.

"Yeah. What was that about?"

"Well, it had just a few things on it. The first was the entry code for Paul's condo. Then it had the combination for a safe in his condo. Next, it listed GPS coordinates for a fishing spot he suggested I try. And last, it warned me to trust nobody," I said.

"Ok, that's a short list, but a lot to process. So, he has a safe in his condo that must have something important in it?" She started with the longest topic.

"Well, he HAD a safe. I'm standing in his condo now. I was here yesterday and got some documents and a USB drive out of the safe. When I returned today, I found someone had stolen the safe," I said, leaving other details out for now.

"A USB drive? You mean like a thumb drive? Why would he leave that in a safe?" It didn't surprise me she went there first, being a technology geek like she was.

"Well, it had the login information and keys to a bitcoin wallet," I answered. Leaving the value out of it for now.

"And he sent you to get it? So he wants you to have access to his bitcoins? Hmmm." She paused, but she wasn't really waiting for an answer. She was processing that bit of information and moving to the next.

"Why would he want to tell about a fishing spot after he's dead? Do you think it's really that good?" Jen asked.

"I don't know. The strange part is, we never really

talked about fishing. Maybe it was really private or something. I plan to find out Thursday after the kids head out with my parents," I replied.

"And why the cloak and dagger stuff about not trusting anyone?"

"Well, I suppose I'm finding out some of that," I said.

"Did the documents help? What were they?" Jen asked, rolling through the points in random order.

I provided her with just the summary for now.

"They basically let me know Paul was a billionaire. He lived like a normal guy, but his crypto, stock and real estate total well over a billion." I stopped to let Jen absorb that before launching into the rest of the story.

"Whoa. You've got to be kidding me. That's pretty heavy. Does his family know?" Jen asked.

"I'm not sure. I haven't been in touch with them and don't know where they might be. That's something I'll have to find out. But, I think someone else knows about all this stuff. While I was here yesterday, a woman came in and said she was Paul's girlfriend," I said, revealing the more disturbing aspect of my story.

"You mean she knew the code? And she 'said' she was his girlfriend, which means you must know different?" Jen was catching every point I was making and some I wasn't.

I told her about the fake Natalie's accent, her quick and invisible departure, and my later discussion with the real Natalie. Then I sighed and continued.

"And I'm afraid there's more. Yesterday, I got a call from the Littleton PD. It seems the woman working in the lobby of Paul's condo was murdered after I left. Then someone erased the camera footage of the murder, and any video that would show the woman from Paul's apartment. I fear this all may somehow relate to the documents in the safe, and probably to the financial stuff that was in there," I said.

"I bet they killed the girl after she let them login and clear the camera data," Jen said.

"That's possible. The police just said the system was hacked, but your idea makes more sense," I replied.

"Wow, Keith. Paul's death seems to have thrown you into a veritable hornet's nest. I wonder if he knew that would happen?" Jen asked.

"I don't know. But yeah, it's definitely a hornet's nest. And there's even more, believe it or not. I also came to know that Paul wasn't only the Gatekeeper as we knew it, but he pretty much funded and ran The Association. Jordan alluded to it at the funeral, but I'm now thinking The Association was all Paul's idea. The corporation that owns Rocky Mountain Equity was called The Association Equities, LLC. And Paul owned it," I said, pausing again.

"Ok. Wow. I'm not sure what to think about that," Jen said, thoughtfully.

"Yeah, me neither. But after all that, there's a different reason for my call," I said, unable to avoid a chuckle. I didn't even realize how much had happened in the last day until I started spilling it all to Jennifer.

"Oh no. You mean there's more?" Jen asked with fake exasperation. At least I hoped it was fake.

"This is simpler, I promise. Paul's condo had two bedrooms. The second bedroom had a rack of servers in it, but whoever stole the safe unplugged them. I don't know if they stole any data or anything, but I'm considering what to do next. I can call the police, and they'll start digging into those servers immediately. If Paul had anything on those servers related to The Association, which I suspect he did, it will fall into their hands. But it would also put the authorities on the trail of the people who stole it," I said.

"What are you concerned about being on the servers?" she asked.

"I'm not really sure. I just know there were a lot of contacts and resources Paul had at his disposal. Maybe I'm overreacting, but I'm pretty sure some of them are confidential. I guess I really just don't know what I don't know," I replied, thinking hard about what data Paul might have stored.

"Unless you know a reason not to, I think you need to call the police, Keith. You need them going after these people. I mean, this group has already shown they have resources beyond the average citizen. And if this is tied to the murder in the lobby, they're willing to kill to get to those documents. In fact, I'd say you really need to watch your back." Jen was sounding concerned, which made me uncomfortable.

"Yeah, you're probably right," I said with a sigh.

"Glad I could help," Jen said, back to her jovial self again.

"Yeah, thanks. I'll let you know if I need any more jolts of common sense," I said with a smile.

"Bye, Keith," Jen said as we ended the call.

After thinking about it for another few seconds, I finally agreed with Jennifer. I had to call the police. Hoping I wasn't about to expose some of Paul's confidential contacts, I called Sergeant Theiss.

"Sergeant Theiss," she answered immediately.

"Hi Sergeant Theiss. This is Keith Morgan. I just wanted to let you know I came to my friend Paul's condo again to do one final walkthrough, and it seems someone has stolen a safe that was in his bedroom closet," I said, stopping there.

I let her ask questions rather than volunteering more information.

"We should have them on camera, then. Our guys have been sifting through those videos, non-stop. Was that all they took?"

"I think so. I didn't memorize everything in the place, but I see nothing else missing. At least, nothing obvious. They did sort of mess things up, though. They threw around couch cushions, messed up drawers and the bed, that sort of stuff," I said.

"So, they were looking for something. Or at least they were trying to make it look like they were looking for something. We'll get a forensics team over there right now. Do you know what Paul would have had in the safe?" Sergeant Theiss asked.

I had thought about how to answer this question, but the way she phrased it gave me a way out.

"Well, like most of us, I expect he'd want to store his weapons in a safe," I replied, hesitant to disclose what I had found.

"You think that's it? Paul had guns that might be worth killing for?" Sergeant Theiss had clearly linked the murder in the lobby to Paul's condo intrusions.

"Probably not," I said.

"It feels like you're not telling me something, Mr. Morgan. It would be best for you to come clean," she said, sounding like she meant it.

I decided to fill her in.

"Paul had given me the combination to his safe. I removed some documents from the safe yesterday. As it turns out, those documents led me to understand Paul was a very wealthy man. He had hundreds of millions in financial holdings, business investments, and real estate. He even owned the corporation we worked for, Rocky Mountain Equity, through a holding company," I said, trying to stick to only the pertinent details.

"Why did you take the documents? And why didn't you mention that yesterday? This won't sit well with Lieutenant Carr," Sergeant Theiss asked, getting agitated.

"Look, I wasn't sure it mattered until today. The family asked me to look for anything important. Knowing the safe might contain something important, I looked in there. When the woman walked in, I got distracted and went to look for her instead of sitting there reading through everything. I took it home to see what it was. The contents surprised me and I didn't know if the family would want anyone to know about it. Then the safe went missing, and I realized my error in judgment. I'll be passing all this to the family," I said, trying to placate her while keeping some details to myself.

Most critically, I avoided any mention of The Association. I also avoided mentioning the servers in Paul's condo. They'd find those soon enough.

"Ok, so I suppose this wealth would have been worth killing for? How much wealth are we talking about?" she asked.

"Paul was a billionaire," I replied.

"Wow. Yeah, I guess that's enough to kill for," Sergeant Theiss said, with a rare sound of surprise.

"Yes, apparently it is."

"Stay put. We're on our way," Sergeant Theiss said. I could hear her scurrying around as she ended the call.

So I stayed put.

Chapter Ten

Thor and Bailey walked into the Golden Bear Wednesday around 6 PM, just like many other Wednesdays before. Or like many other days of the week. Except Mondays and Tuesdays. The Golden Bear was closed on Mondays and Tuesdays.

Thor was here a lot. Bailey wasn't here quite that often, but the staff still knew him and considered him a regular. They went past the door to the store and fly shop and headed straight into the action.

The Golden Bear was the biggest bar and grill in Cameron, Montana. It was also the only bar and grill in Cameron. It was also the only bed-and-breakfast, general store and fly shop. In fact, the Golden Bear was one of the few places to go within thirty miles of the Lazy J ranch to get a drink, a meal, groceries, and supplies.

The structure was built in the 1950s and had been well-maintained. The lodge-style motif mimicked the log siding outside and gave the place a stereotypical mountain feel. There were the obligatory deer, elk, trout and moose taxidermy trophies scattered over the walls and a large antler chandelier in the middle of the room. There was an upstairs area around the edge that opened to the floor below, with barstools lining the rail.

There was a bar along the back wall of the building that was long enough for at least twenty barstools. The dining area was in the middle and the far right, with the left side comprising a dozen high tables toward the front and an open dance floor and a stage to the back left side. All the tables and chairs were made of logs, which made them appear sturdy and rustic.

When live music was playing, the place was full. Hundreds of ranchers, hunters, fishermen, hikers and vacationers would pack every stool and table to take in the only entertainment for miles. Plus, the location was close enough to the Yellowstone National Park to draw in travelers from there, too.

Wednesday, however, was not a live music night. Wednesday was instead the night for all the ranchers in the area to hang out at the bar and share stories about the state of their operations. Or their herds. Or their land. Or the weather. Or politics. Or the Rancher's Alliance. Or anything else they wanted to discuss.

Tonight, Thor was hoping to stir up some conversation about the Russian drone he had discovered on their property. Most of the other family ranchers felt the same way about the Krohl ranch as he did, so it wouldn't be hard to get them fired up. If he got them really agitated, they might go with him to launch a complaint to the Rancher's Alliance. While that wouldn't do much to Krohl, since the alliance was more symbolic than legal, it would get the word out and perhaps even get an investigation at the state level. Now that would mean something to Krohl.

The other ranchers would be annoyed, as George was,

that Krohl was flying drones on other property. The bigger issue, though, was that the drone discovery made them appear to be aligned with some sort of Russian entity. George had Bailey, the technician of the family, googled the Russian letters on the drone frame. There was no other explanation for what they found. They determined there was no way to get one of those drones without a direct relationship with someone in Russia.

Thor and Bailey took stools at the bar near the middle. There were only three other stools occupied, and the Caldwell brothers knew their occupants.

After ordering their Moose Drool, their favorite Big Sky beer, the two went to work.

"Hey Guys, how's your Wednesday?" Thor said to nobody in particular, but loud enough for the other three to hear.

He received three different mumbles in return. It was too early in the evening for any of them to be in too talkative just yet. After a few sips, a few more ranchers at the bar, and a few more pleasantries, Thor introduced the topic he wanted to discuss.

"Yo, Bailey, did you get that crashed drone fixed?" Thor asked, again loud enough for the others to hear, even though this question was targeted at his brother sitting next to him.

"No, not yet. I'm not sure we'll be able to get that thing working. May have to trash it," Bailey replied, also loud enough for the other bar patrons to hear.

As Thor had hoped, enough Moose Drool had been flowing to incite the interest of the other drinkers.

"You guys dropped a drone? That's gotta hurt," Thor heard from his right.

"Oh no, it wasn't our drone. Krohl dropped one onto

our property," he replied, excited to be getting his secret out in the open.

"Whoa! No way, that's awesome!" Thor and Bailey heard, along with other equally positive responses. Clearly, they had the right audience to bash the mighty Krohl enterprise.

"Yeah, it fell right into a tree down by the creek bed. We found it when we were moving the herd up the hill. And that's not the craziest part," Thor said, building the anticipation.

Bailey was on his third beer and couldn't wait for Thor to finish.

"It turns out the thing's Russian," Bailey blurted out before Thor got to the punch line.

"What? Russian? How do you know?" Everyone asked in varying tones.

"The label was all Russian. We looked it up on the internet. It's definitely not from one of our typical suppliers," Thor said, giving Bailey the stink eye for stealing his moment in the sun.

"I heard those guys had a contract with DJI. You sure it was one of theirs?" The question came from Thor's left, so he turned in that direction with his prepared response.

"We thought so, too. But who else around here would have a drone on our farm from Russia? The property to the south of us has no ranching whatsoever, and you guys are to the north and east of Lazy J. Who else could it be?" Thor nodded at the two ranchers to his right, both of whom represented neighboring properties.

"Wow. So Krohl's in bed with the Russians," they mumbled while shaking their heads. Thor and Bailey smiled. It was the response they had hoped to get. If they could build more animosity toward the Krohl ranch, perhaps even to the point of slowing down their growth and annoying side businesses, things would be much more peaceful around Cameron and around the Lazy J.

Having accomplished their primary goal, the Caldwell brothers set in for a typical Wednesday night at the Golden Bear. It included a few more beers, a fantastic bison burger that would have been worth the trip by itself, and more rumors and gossip from the other ranchers. They were in their element.

Around 10 PM, however, a table of ranch hands from Krohl showed up and took a table in the dining section. It didn't take long for one of the now-buzzed ranchers from the bar to make their way toward the Krohl table.

"You guys just can't try to fit in, can you? First it's the rich guy retreat with way too many hunters, then you extend your boundaries even though you have more land than all of us, and now you bring in Russian drones?" he started, leaving the confused ranchers no time to respond.

"I know you guys have the state in your pocket, but we're gonna take you down. We all know what you're doing, and this Russian thing is just taking it too far!" The drunk rancher waved toward the bar, where everyone was watching.

"What are you talking about? We use DJI drones, just like you guys. We may have more of them, but we've got more land to cover. And those Krohl bosses don't let us hire enough hands to avoid using drones. We've got no choice. But we don't use 'em anywhere but our own land," the informal spokesperson at the table responded. His name was Gil, and he had been around the area since well before Krohl came to town.

"Save your lies for the state. Lazy J has proof," the drunk rancher said before returning to the bar. His last statement caused Gil to stare at Thor and Bailey questioningly.

The brothers expected there would be more to this conversation before the night was over and they were right. It only took five minutes.

"Look. I don't know what proof you guys think you have, but we aren't flying any Russian drones on your property. In fact, we're not flying drones on your property at all. It's all we can do to cover our own pastures with those things. Plus, what would we gain snooping on other ranches? Krohl's the biggest outfit out here." Gil paused after stating his position.

"Save it, Gil." Thor said. "One of your spy drones crashed on our land and we found it. I don't know what you want with our shorthorn herd, but you need to tell your boss to stay away," Thor replied.

Gil held his position, albeit with a bit of confusion.

"I don't know what you found, but it isn't ours. We know you guys have a nice herd of shorthorns, but why would we want them? It's all we can do to keep up with everything Krohl throws at us already," he said, turning to go.

"Does this look familiar?" Bailey held up a photo of the drone on his phone. Gil came over and squinted to see Bailey's phone.

"My story won't change, Bailey. I'm telling you, that's not ours. I see why you'd be suspicious, but it's not one I've seen," Gil said with unwavering conviction.

"You wanna tell me who else might use these? And who else might fly them over the west side of our property?" Bailey asked as he put his phone away.

"I have no idea who it would be. But I'm telling you, it's not us. We don't use Russian drones and we have no interest in your shorthorns. Krohl is doing fine on their own," Gil said as he turned and went back to his table, shaking his head.

Realizing they had made their point, the Caldwell boys paid their tab and headed out. They had been loud and convincing with their story and had gotten the attention they had hoped for.

In fact, they had been loud enough that everyone in the Golden Bear had heard them, including a table of visitors they hadn't noticed.

Chapter Eleven

Within ten minutes of my call to Sergeant Theiss, Paul's condo was swarming with officers. There were three Crime Scene Investigators with jackets that described their role, and the Littleton Police Department was there in full force. There were three uniformed and three plain-clothes police officers, plus Sergeant Theiss and Lieutenant Carr.

While everyone arrived and looked around, I stood at the doorway and watched. The condo looked like it had been overtaken by a swarm of police-sized army ants. It made Paul's condo feel much smaller.

Sergeant Theiss had been looking around for a few minutes before walking my way. Lieutenant Carr stood next to me and watched over everything, barking orders here and there and rarely uncrossing his arms. I was finding I didn't really like that guy.

"Did you move anything after you arrived?" Sergeant Theiss asked once she got to my spot by the door.

"No," I answered.

"Where was the safe you saw yesterday?" Sergeant Theiss asked, revisiting questions I had answered yesterday.

"You should have seen the marks on the floor in the spare bedroom closet," I said.

She didn't respond to my statement.

"And what is all that computer equipment in there?" She motioned toward the spare bedroom when she asked the question.

"I don't know," I said, happy to be completely honest for once.

"Was it unplugged when you got here?"

"Yes."

"Was it unplugged when you were here yesterday?"

"No."

"So the intruder could have thought there was something important on those servers?"

"Could have. I don't know."

"Any idea who would want to get to the safe?"

"I told you earlier, and it's still true: I have no idea who is behind this," I said, shaking my head as I observed the surrounding chaos.

"Ok. You'll let me know if you think of something?" Sergeant Theiss looked hard into my eyes and waited for an answer.

"Yes," I said, matching her stare.

"Ok. Officer Hutchinson will take your statement," she said as she motioned for one of the uniformed officers to come over.

After another hour, I was allowed to leave Paul's condo. Knowing Natalie's apartment had also been searched, I wanted to get home quickly. If these people knew I was working with Paul, they might be there already. To make sure that wasn't the case, I plugged my phone in as soon as I got to the 4Runner and called my mom.

"Hey sweetie, how are things up there?" she answered almost immediately. I was aware I would probably never grow out of being 'sweetie' to my mom. It was what she called all three of my family members. And waitresses. And almost anyone who was younger than her. Or even a little older.

"Good, thanks mom. I'm just checking in to let you know I'm on the way home. Is everything ok there?" I asked.

"Oh sure it is, dear. Your father is taking his afternoon nap, but I'm just watching the news. Are you going to be here in time to meet the kids at the bus stop, or should we go down there?" she asked.

My parents were both lifelong rural Missouri residents. I grew up on a farm just east of Branson, well away from big cities. My mom, Kate, and my father, Robert, never left my childhood home. The farm had done well, so dad could get away some now. He'd be back in the grind as soon as he got back home later in the week, so naps at my house were probably the only ones he got during the month of May. I smiled at the thought of the southern Missouri hills.

Then a silver BMW X3 honked at a cyclist right next to me, and I was jolted back to reality.

I was cutting it close on my drive back home, but I was sure I'd be there to meet the kids unless the I25 traffic bit me. Which was always a possibility.

"Right now, I'm on track to be there in time. If something stops me on the highway, I'll let you know," I answered.

"I hate that highway! People just don't know how to drive out there," my mom replied. She always believed people in rural Missouri could drive better than anywhere else, which always made me smile. 'Farm kids learn to drive on tractors long before they get their licenses,' she'd always say.

"Yeah, I know you do, mom. I don't much like it either. I'll see you in a bit," I said as I ended the call and sped up the on-ramp to the crowded highway.

Once again missing Paul's advisory services, I made it home without calling anyone else. I made it my mission to keep my eye out for anyone who might be pursuing the safe contents I had taken from Paul's condo. Then, I went about my normal business.

The rest of that day and the next day went without issue as I navigated the last two days of school for Kyle and James. I also managed to get my mom and dad out fishing for a few hours Tuesday, landing a couple of nice trout out of one of the reservoirs just outside of town. They both seemed to enjoy themselves.

Tuesday night, we all went to hockey practice for Jamie and had a nice dinner at Dave's Barbecue restaurant in Colorado Springs. Despite the constant activity and the good times, I was constantly on alert for a tail. I watched every hiker, every car and ATV, and eyed everyone suspiciously. I only saw a couple of possible tail vehicles parked in the lot as we were sitting at the lake, but it turned out to be a park ranger in a blue Toyota pickup.

I also kept the house cameras on full movement notification for those two days. If anyone was going to be out there, I was going to know about it. But nobody came. Wildlife creatures tripped the alarms multiple times Tuesday night, but I was pretty sure they didn't care about Paul's finances.

Finally, Wednesday rolled around, and the kids were more than ready to head to the farm with Grandma Kate and Grandpa Rob. We all met them at the bus stop. Jamie bounded off the school bus first, meeting me, my parents, and Winchester at a full sprint.

"Come on, guys. Let's get going. Let the vacation begin!" Jamie was already running toward home when Kyle finally got stepped off the bus. He, too, was ready to go.

"I have waited so long for this!" he said, beaming as he chased Jamie back toward the house.

That left me and Winchester to walk back home with my mom and dad.

"I hope you guys are close to ready, otherwise the kids are not going to be happy," I said.

"Oh, we are, we are. I spent the morning getting everything ready. Although, I must say they're more excited to leave this beautiful place than I thought they'd be," mom said. She loved Colorado almost as much as home. But when pressured, she'd reveal that she liked the hills of the Ozarks a little more, only because of the large trees. Even though they had large trees in Colorado. I never questioned her thought process.

When we finally arrived at the house, the kids had tempered their excitement long enough to have a snack. That, of course, only took about two minutes. Then they were once again begging to hit the road. Their bags were by the door in fifteen more minutes and they were impatiently sitting on the couch in the living room.

"Come on, Grandma Kate. You guys about ready?" Kyle yelled for what seemed like the tenth time.

"We're coming, sweetie. Make sure you go to the bathroom. We've got a long way to go," she warned.

Kyle and Jamie rolled their eyes but didn't move. I knew dad would be stopping in an hour or so to let them go. He probably knew it, too.

Another few minutes went by before mom and dad appeared with their last remaining bags, and they all shuffled out the door to dad's Yukon. He had already loaded most everything and just needed to add the kids' bags to the pile. Once everything was loaded, hugs and kisses were distributed... as much as kids that age allowed. Then they were on their way.

It made me smile to see how excited the kids were as they pulled away. I knew they'd be busy but would have a blast, just like I used to. As I thought about the farm and the constant activity there, nostalgia swept over me. I'd have to go visit there again, too, one of these days.

After watching them turn the corner out of the driveway and out of sight, I set out to get my own packing done. I had originally planned to leave early in the morning, but after thinking about everything that had happened, I decided to take off and get some hours under my belt that evening. It only took about thirty minutes to pack everything and take Winchester to Ed Sutter's place just up the hill.

Ed was a good friend and was my go-to dog watcher. He had a yellow lab that loved playing with Winnie, as the kids called Winchester, and we always watched each other's dogs when someone was out of town. Ed's classic Ford Bronco was a mainstay in the community, as were his legendary parties, but he was also a good dog boarder. Winchester had already started zooming around his vast backyard before I was out Ed's front door.

Just before locking the door on my way out, I stood and looked around. I had a decision to make about the documents and USB drive from Paul's condo. After considering the options, I opened the safe and took out the USB drive, but left the documents. It might be good to have the bitcoin wallet details with me in case I needed to do more research. The documents were too cumbersome and remained in my gun safe.

It was 3:30 PM when I pulled out of Woodland Park toward Montana. I had decided I should probably be able to make it to Laramie, Wyoming, if the Denver traffic cooperated. When I made it to Laramie at 7 PM, however, I kept going a little further. It was a slight risk that I'd be able to find a hotel, but worst case I knew I could sleep in the truck. It wouldn't have been the first time.

But when I finally stopped just after 9 PM in Rock Springs, Wyoming, the Holiday Inn Express was waiting for me. I had booked the room on my phone while driving, so I parked in the registered guest lot when I got to the hotel.

As is my custom, I also sat there silently for a few seconds and observed the traffic. Nobody seemed to follow me and nobody turned at the next exit, either. The further away I got from Denver, the safer I felt.

The room in the Holiday Inn Express was just like every other one I had ever stayed in. It was new and clean, which was nice, and had no frills. There were also no restaurants or shopping nearby to keep people moving around, so it was quiet and peaceful. I called the kids, who had stopped with Grandma and Grandpa somewhere in Kansas at a hotel. They were loving life. Then, before I knew it, it was 10 PM, and I was falling asleep. Only the excitement of the new fishing spot kept me awake that long.

By 5:15 AM I was awake, showered and back on the road. The Flying J travel center was the only nearby location with lights on, and it had exactly what I needed for that time of the morning: coffee and a breakfast sandwich.

As the sun was coming up to my right, I was forging

ahead north to Cameron, Montana, and Paul's recommended fishing spot.

The kids called me while I was near Jackson. They had gotten up and gone swimming at the hotel, and were about to finish their trip to Missouri. After telling me how great their hotel was and how much they loved traveling, they ended the call to continue their journey. I smiled once again as I thought about how easy it was for Jamie and Kyle to have a good time. Despite the pain they had endured in their lives, they were good kids. I drove along with pride in my gut for a long time after that call.

After hours of beautiful mountain scenery, it was almost 11 AM when I turned off highway 287 toward the GPS location Paul had specified. The road changed from blacktop to gravel to dirt over just a few miles, and at noon, I parked in a small gravel clearing that resembled an ad hoc parking area. I walked from there. According to my GPS, I was only about a half mile from the specified spot. I wondered if this was Paul's property, public, or someone else's. The thought made me a little uneasy, but my desire to honor Paul's request was greater.

I loaded my pack and took off on foot.

Chapter Twelve

The chatter about the Russian drone didn't stop spreading at the Golden Bear when the Caldwell brothers left. That, of course, is exactly how they wanted it. They wanted the other ranchers to get as fired up about it as they were, and it was working.

By midnight, the drone topic even incited a skirmish between the Krohl ranch hands and a group of other locals. It didn't cause any damage, but it got law enforcement, namely Deputy Sheriff Neal Marsh, called out to restore peace and escort the offenders off the property. None of them filed charges, so that was the end of it.

The story of the Russian drone, however, piqued the interest of Deputy Marsh. He didn't care much for the Krohl organization, either, as they always seemed to find ways to bypass the local authority. While this didn't smell of a felony, it also didn't feel quite right. He made a mental note to stop by the Lazy J ranch the next day.

* * *

George Caldwell was home with his wife, Margaret, when Deputy Marsh arrived at the Lazy J ranch just after 2 PM the next afternoon. The ranch was about ten miles from Deputy Marsh's place, but the cautious driving caused by hills and curves of the blacktop road meant it took twenty minutes to get there.

The property was not huge by Montana standard, but included over a thousand acres of prime mountain farmland. The house was separate from the working area of the ranch, and was visible long before arriving at the driveway, with over an acre of grass in the front that was just beginning to turn green. Stables, corrals and the ranch vehicles were visible about a half mile away toward the rear of the open land. There were cattle and horses scattered across the fields between the house and the stables.

The house was from the early 1900s and was a two-story farmhouse that could've been on virtually any farm across the Great Plains or Midwest. It was white with green shutters and was not large by today's standards. Deputy Marsh pulled into the long driveway, aware the habitants would know of his presence long before he strode up the steps to the large wrap-around porch.

Margaret, or Marge, as everyone called her, opened the screen door thirty seconds after Deputy Marsh rang the doorbell. It was a warm May day, so the temperature was high enough for Marge to keep the front door open with just the screen door between him and the inside of the house. Screen doors were common in the area, with the breeze from outside being enough to avoid air conditioners most of the year.

"Howdy, Mrs. Caldwell," Deputy Marsh began, "I wonder if I might be able to speak to George for a few minutes?"

"Why sure, Neal. Let me get you something to drink. How are your parents?" Marge was already headed into the kitchen for the drink when Deputy Marsh answered. Even though he had been a deputy for over ten years, Marge Caldwell still treated him like he was ten years old.

"They're great. Thanks for asking. And there's no need to bother yourself with the drink. I'll only be a minute." Deputy Marsh knew better than to protest, but he felt it was polite to do so.

"Oh, don't be silly. George is in the barn. I'll let him know you're here. Is everything ok?" Again, Marge was moving around while asking the questions, causing Deputy Marsh to yell through the house to answer her.

"Yes, sure. Everything is fine. I'm just here to chat," he said, not wanting to engage Marge on the topic before George arrived.

After yelling for George, getting Neal a cup of coffee, and imploring him to sit on the mid-century living room couch, Marge finally settled down. She sat on the wooden rocking chair in the corner and picked up some sort of knitting project while they waited for George. Luckily for Deputy Marsh and the awkward silence, George crashed through the back door in just a few minutes.

"What's going on?" George sounded agitated at being pulled away from whatever project he was working on outside.

"Neal Marsh is here to see you, dear," Marge replied.

"He is? What's wrong? Did something happen?" George asked as he entered the living room.

"Nothing's wrong, George. I've just got a question about a rumor I heard at the Golden Bear last night," Deputy Marsh replied.

"Oh, brother." George replied. "Hurry up, then. I don't

have time to sit and chat about gossip going on in town."

"I understand. Let me get right to it, then. There was a skirmish between some of the local ranchers and some of the Krohl employees last night. During the conversation, I came to know that the locals were accusing the Krohl team of spying on your ranch. Not only that, they said the Krohl guys were spying with a Russian drone that crashed on your property. Would you know anything about that?" Deputy Marsh asked.

"Well, I guess this one isn't a rumor. My boys must have talked about it. Yeah, we had a Russian drone crash down near the creek yesterday. The boys recovered it and found it had Russian markings on it. The only logical explanation is that it came from the Krohl place," George replied.

"You mind if I see it? I'd be interested in finding out what type of surveillance the Krohl ranch would be doing. I'm sure I don't need to tell you they have few friends at the Sheriff's office," Deputy Marsh said.

"Sure, sure. Let's head out to the barn. It just looks like it's just got cameras on it. But you're welcome to take a look," George said as he nodded and stood with a grunt, walking through the living room toward the kitchen without waiting for a response.

"Thanks, George. And thanks for the coffee, Mrs. Caldwell," Deputy Marsh said as he stood and followed George to the barn.

The barn was to the left side of the house, about thirty yards from the back door. It, too, was from the early 1900s and had been kept up and was just beginning to showing signs of wear. It was red with large white double doors at the front. They were open, so George walked in and motioned toward a bundle of broken drone parts lying on a wool blanket to the left of the door.

"Where'd you say you found this?" Deputy Marsh asked as they walked over.

"It was out near the creek, out on the west side of the creek bed, right on the edge of our property line," George replied.

While George and Deputy Marsh surveyed the drone wreckage, a late-model white Ford F150 pulled into the long driveway. The two of them were too busy discussing the drone to notice. Marge, however, was standing at the front window watching the pickup pull in. It was rare to have two unexpected guests within a few minutes.

Both the truck and the passengers looked out of place, even before the vehicle came to a stop. The truck had a Krohl ranch logo on the side, but had Colorado license plates. The driver was clean cut with sunglasses on, but didn't look like any of the ranch hands from the Lazy J and appeared too curious for Marge's comfort. There were two other passengers in the pickup, but they didn't get out immediately.

She watched the driver emerge from the vehicle, look around as though he was surveying the property, then make his way to the front porch. His outfit was fine, by Montana ranch standards, with jeans and a flannel shirt, but it looked too new and crisp to be working attire. Marge wondered if it was a government official or a politician.

He rang the doorbell, and she answered through the screen.

"Hello?" Marge said, as she walked from the window to the door.

"Good afternoon, ma'am. I'm Robert McCoy from the Krohl ranch down the road. We've had some equipment issues that may have caused one of our mobile air devices to crash near your property. I'm wondering if you may have seen it?" The guy didn't seem sincere, but at least she knew why he was here.

Marge knew Mr. McCoy had to have seen the police car sitting in the driveway. Knowing George and Deputy Marsh were already looking at the Krohl equipment in the garage, she decided to send him their way. Having the deputy present made her feel confident nothing would escalate even if there was an argument.

"You'd have to ask my husband about that, Mr. McCoy. He's in the backyard now with a deputy from the Sheriff's office," she said, motioning toward the barn.

"Thank you, ma'am," Robert said as he turned away. He took a couple of steps before he stopped.

The man who called himself Robert McCoy made a motion toward the truck and then toward the barn. The other two other passengers got out of the vehicle and stretched. One looked just like the first guy from a distance. The other was smaller and was a female. Marge looked on as they began walking around the house toward the barn.

The guy on the porch didn't leave. She was about to ask if he needed anything when he spoke.

"Just one more thing..." he said as he turned around and pointed a silenced pistol at her head and fired twice.

The sound wasn't nearly as loud as a normal pistol shot, but both George and Deputy Marsh heard it from the barn.

"That sounded like suppressed gunfire," Deputy Marsh said as he stepped to the door and looked out.

Noticing the F150 in the driveway, he reached to his hip and grabbed his Glock. He never had time to aim. He hadn't noticed the two visitors coming around the corner of the house toward the barn.

Two shots hit him in the chest before he got his arm

extended. He stumbled backward and fell into the doorway of the barn.

George saw what was happening and turned toward the back of the barn, hustling as fast as his boots could go on the dirty, straw-strewn floor. He reached the back and grabbed his trusty Ruger American ranch rifle, typically used to protect the animals from coyotes and wolves.

He pulled the rifle from the rack on the back wall and turned to fire, but not fast enough. Like Deputy Marsh, he had his weapon in his hand, but never got the chance to aim at his target. The visitors both had their arms extended and fired two shots, hitting George in the shoulder and chest.

The man who called himself Robert McCoy then casually strolled over to Deputy Marsh, still breathing but unconscious, and shot him between the eyes.

Seeing George struggle to recover the rifle he had dropped as the life faded from him, the other male visitor rushed over and kicked George's rifle aside. Rather than risk another near miss like that, the female visitor fired a fatal shot into George's head. Within a few seconds, George, Marge, and Deputy Marsh were all dead and strewn across the Lazy J ranch.

"You're lucky we heard those idiots talking about this drone at the bar. No, no more mistakes, like your inability to fly a drone," the female visitor said sternly to the other two.

"We could have gotten it back without all this," replied the one who called himself Robert McCoy.

"It had to be done. Now, let's get your toy and get out of here," the female visitor ordered.

The visitors then gathered the drone parts and put them in the bed of the F150 with the Krohl logo on its side, walked around to pick up their spent pistol cartridges, and casually drove away.

Chapter Thirteen

I had enough outdoor and war experience to know the smell of rotting flesh when I encountered it. The smell varies by species, but it's also disgustingly similar. A version of that horrible smell hit me hard as I jumped off the rocky trail I had been descending into the creek bed below.

It wasn't the smell of human flesh, thankfully. That, however, was only a slight relief given the overwhelming intensity of the odor. I thought I noticed it earlier, but I was so busy navigating the mountainous terrain and focusing on the GPS location that I didn't stop to reflect on it.

The smell hit me hard as I reached a decision point in my hike. The stream meandered between two large rocks just in front of me. They were at least ten feet high, so I could climb or I could walk in the stream. Deciding on the former, I grasped the boulder to my left to climb over. I had been hiking for about twenty minutes toward Paul's GPS coordinates.

As I pulled myself up over the rock, the death aroma hit me even harder than before. The abhorrent smell was coupled with a gruesome visual image that explained its origin.

There, six feet from my face, lying next to the crystal clear stream, were the tattered remains of an antelope. The sight of an antelope that succumbed to a mountain lion, as I guessed this one had, was not completely unusual. The specific ravine location was unusual for an antelope, but I surmised it had probably been dragged here for dinner several days ago.

It wasn't pretty.

After a few seconds assessing fishing options nearby while acknowledging my exposure to the survival of the fittest in the wild, I moved on to start my fishing excursion somewhere else on the stream.

Having looked at the map earlier, I knew this stream was a feeder to the Madison river, which was a well-known fly-fishing destination there in Montana. Or Wyoming or Idaho, as the river traversed the landscape between multiple states up here near Yellowstone.

I wasn't sure of the name of this stream, or of my exact location relative to the surfing cities and towns, but I believed I was still in Cameron. Or maybe Ennis. The lines between them were not clear to me on the GPS. But whichever city we were in, I was close to the place that Paul recommended. And as long as my handheld GPS unit hadn't led me astray, I was walking along an area with great fishing.

After trudging away from the dead antelope far enough to avoid the smell, I stopped to set up my gear for a few hours of fishing. The GPS showed a couple hundred more yards to the target location, but the creek looked too good to pass up.

I unpacked my fly rod and reel and tied on my favorite

grasshopper fly with a small nymph below it. I watched the water for a few minutes, finding a deeper pool behind some fast-moving water. The fishing was moderately difficult in the creek bed because of the trees and boulders on either side, but the challenge only made it more fun. On the third cast, I had my first fish of the day. Paul was right, it was a magnificent spot.

After three more beautiful cutthroat trout landed and a hundred yards of creek covered, I paused to review my location against the coordinates Paul had given. To my surprise, I had veered off course and was now further away from the target location. Curiously, it appeared the location Paul had noted was off to the side of the creek I had been following. I had seen no other creeks nearby, so the thought of moving away from the water made no sense.

Backtracking to a small ravine that went up the side of the tree and stone-covered creek bed, I got back on track toward Paul's recommended location. Walking further and further away from the creek I had been fishing, I wondered if the coordinates were a little off. I considered turning back toward the creek bed.

Then, as I got nearer the exact coordinates and was about to turn around, I saw the small cabin hidden away in a steep section of the mountains. I was a quarter mile from the creek, but the terrain was so dense there was no way to know it was nearby. From the cabin location, all I could see were trees and mountains. Once again, I had to wonder if Paul's directions were a bit off.

The cabin had a rustic appearance, as if it was hand-built. The roof was newer, made of green metal, and the whole place couldn't have been over thirty feet wide and equally deep. There was a small chimney on top. There was a covered porch along the front of the cabin, with one window on each side of a heavy-looking front door. The back of the cabin appeared to rest against the side of the mountain. The place looked sturdy and recently stained, but there was no evidence anybody had been around in a long time.

I looked around again for any signs of human life and saw none. This was one of the more remote places I had been and was definitely not a fishing location.

Cautiously, I walked up to the front door, continuously surveying the area for signs of human activity. I hadn't seen any such signs when I arrived at the front porch.

Given the remote location and the lack of neighbors, I was surprised to see a sophisticated security mechanism on the door. The door had a standard, modern doorknob, but also had a fingerprint pad just below it. Initially fearing I had the wrong place, I once again contemplated turning back. Before I did, I validated the GPS coordinates again. This was the spot Paul had given me. That made me especially curious.

On a hunch, I touched my finger to the pad and immediately saw a light appear at eye level beside the door. I barely had time to evaluate what it was when the door latch clicked. I turned the knob, and the door opened. Either the device wasn't as secure as it appeared to be, or it had been programmed with my biometric data.

Two seconds after stepping inside, I realized it was the latter.

I heard the door latch behind me, which caused me to pivot around with my SIG P365 drawn from its holster. I pointed it at the door, which had apparently locked on its own. Then I heard a voice on the television, which was now powered on.

"Welcome, Mr. Morgan," the voice was saying. It was

coming from an image of Paul Frazier on the large, high-definition screen. He appeared to be alive and well, which left me temporarily dumbstruck.

"Before you get too excited, this is a recording. There's no AI derivative of me that I know of." Paul smiled at himself on the recorded video.

I stared in disbelief.

"If you're seeing this, I suppose it means I've run into a problem somewhere between here and Nashville. Or Texas. Or wherever else I've been since I recorded this video. Take a seat, and I'll explain," Paul said from the television screen. It was mounted above the fireplace, and it felt oddly out-of-place out here in the middle of nowhere.

I obediently sat on the small cloth sofa across from the fireplace and stared at the screen with my mouth open. Paul didn't wait for me to get a grip on my surroundings before he continued.

"Right now, it's 1755 local time on April 23rd. I've just decided I'm going to come join you and Jennifer Ellis on your assignment in Nashville. Before I go, however, I wanted to make a recording in case something goes sideways. There's a lot about The Association I haven't told you, and some of it will surprise you. And I suppose there are also some things about me you need to know if I'm gone. I can't tell you everything, as it would take forever. In fact, even this short recording is going to take some time. So here it goes."

Paul took a deep breath on the screen and steepled his fingers in front of him. It appeared he was sitting in front of a camera with a dark room behind him. There were several computer screens visible, but they were all turned off. I didn't see that sort of background in the cabin, so he must have been somewhere else. He was dressed just like I was, in a heavy flannel shirt. I could only see his upper torso on the screen. He looked exactly like he had looked the last time I saw him in Nashville.

"You are sitting in the place where I've spent much of my time over the last five years. I'm sure you will find more information in my condo in Littleton, too, but most of my research is here. I bought a few hundred acres up here about ten years ago and slowly built the cabin since then. There's more to it than you can see, but I'll get to that in a minute. By the way, there really is great fishing in that creek you followed up here. I can't really say fly-fishing is my thing, but I wasn't lying about that."

I had to smile at the reminder of the message from Paul that had sent me here. He knew fly-fishing was one of my hobbies, and a remote Montana stream was too enticing for me to ignore. Given the trip was apparently more than a fishing excursion, I wished I had come sooner. It seemed odd Paul didn't just mention the cabin versus the misdirection of a fishing location.

"First, let me explain this location. You are in the middle of a property that sits in Montana, about thirty miles from the Wyoming border, and even closer to Idaho. The property map is on the computer in the other room, but we'll get to that soon. I built the cabin with a long-term plan in mind. I knew I'd need a secure place to be, and while I'm not really a 'prepper,' this is that sort of place. And more. There's food and water in here, but that's not the primary reason I built it."

I took that statement as a cue to look around the cabin. The inside looked modern and comfortable. It was basically one main room with a living area and kitchen, with a loft above. There was a door to the back that was open and seemed to lead to a bathroom. The entire interior was covered with knotty pine and could have been in a vacation advertisement. If this was where Paul had been spending his time, it didn't appear to be painful.

"The walls are made from logs on the outside, but are reinforced with concrete. I won't say they're bombproof, but they're definitely bulletproof. The windows are one way bulletproof glass. People on the outside can see light through them, but that's about it. The cabin wouldn't take a direct RPG hit, but it would stand up against almost anything short of that."

I looked around again, realizing how well Paul had hidden the structural strength of the cabin. He continued while I took in the cabin anew. This was getting interesting. And weird.

"The most significant part of the cabin, however, is what you can't see from the outside. You see two doors toward the back of the cabin beside the bedroom. One, as you'd expect, is the bathroom. The other one is a coat closet. But that's not all it is. In the back of the coat closet is another door, well hidden, that leads to my, well, I guess I'd call it a bunker. Don't go there yet. I have a few more things to tell you."

Paul knew my attention would be jarred by the secret door. He was right, but I pulled myself back to his video.

"That room is where I'm filming now, and where much of my research for The Association was done. I won't get into all of that research right now. It'd just take too long. There are computer files, notebooks and post-it notes in here. Before you go in, though, I need to tell you something."

Paul seemed to be bothered by what he was about to say. Almost as if he was confessing something. As it turned out, it was a sort of confession.

"I've had more to do with the assignments you've been on than I've led you to believe. Yes, some have come from other people who have asked us to undertake them, but most have come directly from me. The most recent were the Detroit and Nashville trips from the last six months. Those trips were identified because of a long-term rival of mine... and, well, ours... swirling up activity here in the US."

Paul stumbled as he tried to explain the 'rival,' but he had my full attention.

"You remember Ivan Filipov, I'm sure."

I could feel my blood pressure go up when I heard his name. He was one of the arms traders we took down way back in Afghanistan. Back then, he didn't seem unique. He was one of many murderous, vicious monsters we ran out of the area when we were there.

"Knowing you, I'm guessing you recognize it immediately. Well, here's why I mention him. It seems Ivan is quite angry with us for costing him all his arms business in Afghanistan. He also didn't stop after we shut his Afghan business down. Now, he's shifted his focus to various interests here in the United States. That includes the political stuff we uncovered with BradComm in Detroit and, well, this trafficking business you're finding in Nashville. Before you ask, yes. I knew he was behind all this when I sent you."

I felt myself fall back into the chair and realized my mouth was open. I couldn't help but wonder why Paul hadn't told me these assignments were tied to our history. And that Filipov was behind both of them. I had heard Filipov's name mentioned during a shootout in Colorado that ended our Detroit assignment, but I never realized he was behind Nashville, too.

"I guess I should have told you sooner." It seemed Paul was reading my mind.

Chapter Fourteen

Bailey Caldwell was the first to stumble onto the carnage at his parents' house. The ranchers used a separate driveway about a quarter mile down the road from the house driveway, but he could see the house clearly as he got to the road.

He was driving up from the stable around 6 PM when Bailey noticed the police cruiser in the driveway. Curious, he stopped in to see what was going on.

Seeing the barn door wide open, and knowing he and Thor had left the drone wreckage there, Bailey smiled as he assumed his father was reporting the incident to the police. Eager to share his version of the story, he bypassed the house and went straight to the barn.

He was still smiling when he noticed an officer laying just inside the entrance of the barn. Without thinking about what might have happened, he began running toward the barn as the smile on his face turned to terror.

Bailey knelt next to the body of the officer, now recognizable as Neal Marsh, a high school classmate of Thor's from years ago. It was clear he was dead, with a hole the size of a golf ball in the back of his head. Immediately concerned for his parents, Bailey jumped up and looked around, horrified to see his father sprawled out in the back of the barn.

Again, without thinking about anything else, like keeping the crime scene clean or looking to see if the murderer was still there, he ran to his father. Bailey stopped in his tracks as he got close enough to see what had happened. George Caldwell lay dead on the floor of his barn with at least three gunshot wounds, one of which was through his head. George's trusty Ruger rifle was just a few feet away on the ground.

Bailey stopped and stood still, not sure what to do next. He saw nothing out of order around the barn, but he noticed the drone was missing. Then, he had a sudden onslaught of panic and raced out of the barn toward the house. Yelling for his mom as he ran, he stormed into the back door and began searching.

He found Marge in the living room, having received the same type of head shot that his father and Deputy Marsh had taken. Bailey fell to his knees and sobbed with his head in his hands. After some amount of time had passed, Bailey gathered himself enough to grab his mobile from his pocket and call his brother.

"Mom and dad are dead!" Bailey screamed into the phone when Thor answered.

"What? Calm down, man. What's going on?" Thor asked, not comprehending what Bailey was trying to say.

"Thor, they're dead. Somebody shot mom and dad. I'm at their house. They're dead. Both of them are dead. Somebody shot our parents. Neal Marsh is here, too. They shot him. They shot Neal, and they shot mom and dad!" Bailey began sobbing again.

"Stay right there. I'm just leaving. I'll be there in a

minute," Thor said, mashing the accelerator of his truck and spraying rocks across the parking area as he sped from the stables.

In less than a minute, he stormed up the porch stairs and into the living room. He stopped with his hands on his head when he saw his mother lying on the floor. Bailey was still on his knees in the middle of the room, now quietly shaking his head.

"What happened?" Thor asked after taking in the scene in front of him.

"I don't know. I saw the sheriff's car and stopped to see what was up. I assumed dad was telling them about the drone. When I got here, I found this," Bailey said, a glazed look on his face.

"Where's dad?" Thor asked as he stepped over his dead mother, around his distraught brother, and into the kitchen.

"Out in the barn with Neal Marsh," Bailey said, still not moving from his knees.

"I can't believe they shot Neal, too. What kind of..." Thor ran out the door before he finished the rhetorical question, leaving Bailey in the house while he made his way around the house to the barn.

A few seconds later, Thor found what Bailey had been sobbing about. He discovered his old friend Neal Marsh and his father in the barn, both very dead. He was still standing in the middle of the barn in stunned silence when Bailey emerged from the house and stumbled across the yard to the barn door, the glaze of shock still visible on his face.

"Who would do this?" Bailey said as he stopped and leaned against the edge of the doorway.

"I have no idea. This is... just... I don't know. How can

this be real? Who would kill mom and dad?" Thor asked, shaking his head.

They both stood silently for a few seconds when Bailey snapped out of his haze.

"Do you think this was just because of the drone?" he asked as he looked at the scattered hay on the floor where the blanket and drone had been.

Thor walked over cautiously, his mouth slightly open in amazement.

"That can't be, can it? Krohl wouldn't be that stupid, would they? You think they'd kill just to get that drone back?" Thor was asking himself the questions out loud as the reality of the scene set in.

They both stood silently and looked at each other. Eventually Bailey responded to the questions Thor had been asking himself.

"That can't be. What could be so important about that stupid drone? We've got to call 911, man," Bailey responded.

The boys snapped into action at that point and called 911. Then they began looking around the rest of the house and around the barn for any clues who may have killed their parents. They were walking along the gravel driveway looking for tire tracks when they heard the first siren. Before that vehicle pulled in, two more arrived. Within a few minutes, flashing lights and crime scene personnel covered the landscape of the ranch.

After several interviews with ranch hands and scouring of the house, barn, and surrounding area, one of the officers stepped over to the porch where Thor and Bailey were now sitting.

"I'm sorry, gentlemen. I'm sure you understand we need to ask a few questions. You guys feel up to it?" Sheriff

Hanson asked. He was a veteran from the local sheriff's office, known to be one of the old-school, buttoned-down types and not particularly fond of anyone who wasn't.

"Yeah, sure," Thor said, taking a deep breath.

"I'm sorry, too, by the way. I can't believe they shot Neal, too," Bailey chimed in before Sheriff Hanson got started.

"Thank you, I appreciate that. He was a good deputy and a good man. It will be a big loss to the office, to the community, and to his family," Sheriff Hanson responded with a solemn nod, then began his questions.

"You guys were both back at the stables when this happened?" he asked.

"Yeah. We were working. We're not really sure when it happened, but it must have been after lunch. I stopped by the house to bring in the mail and grab some of mom's pot roast around 11:30," Thor responded.

"You didn't see Deputy Marsh here at that time, I assume?"

"No."

"Did your parents have any sort of security cameras up here?" Sheriff Hanson scanned the property with his eyes as he asked the question.

"No, unfortunately they didn't. We tried and tried to get them to add cameras up here, but they refused. There are several cameras back at the stables, but none up here," Bailey replied.

"Do you guys have any idea who might have done this?" he asked as he scribbled in his notepad.

"I bet the Krohl guys did it. They crashed a drone on our property and we found it. It was sitting in the barn this morning and now it's gone. I bet they came here to get it, probably got into an argument, and started firing away."

Bailey was getting louder as he talked, causing Sheriff Hanson to stop writing and put his palm up to slow him down.

"Whoa, whoa. Go back a second. Tell me about this drone again," Sheriff Hanson said, trying to calm Bailey down.

"We were driving the shorthorn herd up from the valley," Thor began, taking over for the flustered Bailey.

"The guys saw something fall into the trees just to the west of us, near the edge of our property. Bailey went over to investigate and found a drone that had crashed into the trees. It was in several pieces on the ground. We went and picked it up. We put all the pieces on a blanket inside the barn and now it's gone," Thor said.

Sheriff Hanson paused and looked intently at Thor.

"Why do you think it was a Krohl drone?" he asked.

"They're the only ones with that kind of equipment around here. The property nearest that side of our land isn't even a ranch, and the Krohl property is the next closest. I bet the Krohls were trying to size up our land and our herd. They've been wanting to take over dad's ranch for years, and only those shorthorns are getting him enough income to stay afloat," Thor replied.

"That's quite a herd, for sure. I know your dad was very proud of those shorthorns," Sheriff Hanson acknowledged as he resumed his note taking.

"Yeah, they were his pride and joy," Bailey acknowledged, having calmed down.

"What can you tell me about this drone? How big was it? What type of attachments, that sort of thing?" Sheriff Hanson asked.

"Well, it looked like one of those video drones. There were no visible attachments except the cameras. No sprayer, air drop, or anything like that. It was a pretty basic unit, not very big, with a central camera and four smaller ones on each arm," Bailey replied.

"Oh, and it had Russian writing on it," Thor added.

"Really? I thought they had a contract with DJI," Sheriff Hanson said with a puzzled look.

"Yeah, we did too. It looks like they had something going on outside their DJI agreement," Thor replied with a sneer.

"It's getting dark now, but I'd like you to take me out to that location tomorrow," Sheriff Hanson said, after writing a few more things on his notepad.

"Sure. Just let us know when you want to head out there," Thor said as the boys nodded.

The line of questioning then followed a more traditional path. The boys knew of nobody who would want to hurt their parents, and they didn't have any idea who else might have done this.

Finally, Sheriff Hanson had gotten through his questions and put away his pen and notepad.

"I'll be back around 9 AM. I assume we can get to the drone crash site on ATVs?" he asked.

"Yeah, we can," Bailey said.

"Ok, gentlemen. Again, I'm so sorry about this. Your folks were great people and certainly deserved better than this," Sheriff Hanson said with a nod and a tip of his hat.

The Caldwell boys eventually went home, but didn't sleep much that night.

Chapter Fifteen

I was still trying to grasp the reality of my past life interfering with my current life when Paul continued his video. So far, I hadn't even taken the time to consume the fact that he foresaw his death well enough to record this in the first place. Paul's voice started again, so I tried to focus on the screen.

"Before I get too far into the Filipov business, let me tell you a little more about the cabin. You probably noticed the cabin knew who you were. Don't be too shocked, it knows everyone who sets foot on the property. I have satellite cameras all around the perimeter of the property, far away from where we are now. The cameras and their software do more than you'd probably expect. The software is a beta version from a buddy of mine. When the cameras pick up a human, the software can run facial recognition scans to see who's trespassing. If you came in on the dirt road from Cameron, the security system should have recorded your arrival. Most people don't get the personal treatment that you got, though. I created this welcome and granted you special access, just in case. That was just for you. How'd I do that? Well, if you got the USB drive from my condo, you know I already have your facial recognition profile. And I have your retina. And I have your fingerprints. That's how I set it up. And I expect you will have visitors, by the way. Most of the people who I find on the property are riding their ATVs, riding their horses, extending their hunting territory, or trying to swipe some of the cutthroat trout that live in the stream. But I suspect there will be others."

While Paul paused, I tried to remember seeing any cameras when I was walking in, but I didn't. Of course, I was looking for a trout stream, so I wasn't paying attention to trees and other potential camera locations.

"Of course, everything is recorded in case something with a visitor goes awry. You'll find those recordings in the bunker. So far, thankfully, no harmful intruders have been identified. In your case, I had programmed your face into the door camera as well, along with this personal greeting. You are the only one, besides me, of course, programmed into the access system. Everyone else will have to knock or ring the doorbell the old-fashioned way. So, now that you know how you got in, I suppose it's time to head into the bunker. The same facial recognition program is running there, along with a retina scan. You'll see it in the closet when you twist the coat hook on the right wall."

I stood and looked at the door next to the bathroom. This was becoming surreal.

"Now, back to Filipov. You'll find the information in the computer system, but I have compiled a good amount of evidence that he has been toying with The Association, specifically those of us from our Hart International team in Afghanistan, for several years. I'll have to warn you about something else. I believe I'm being followed by someone who knows what we're doing. That's why you have the only login to the system. This will sound cliche, but you can't trust anyone right now. I'm not sure how Filipov has gotten all our team's information, but he has way more access to our team and their lives than he should. And he seems to know I'm after him. And if something has happened to me, you should be careful, too."

I could feel my mouth hanging open as I listened to Paul's warning, and I consciously forced myself to close it.

"This video will end now, I guess. I mean, you can replay it with the remote if you want. It won't self-destruct like a Mission Impossible movie," Paul smiled at his little joke before continuing.

"But, I've got to get to Nashville. Honestly, I'm hoping I return without issue and you never see this. But if I didn't, well, thanks for taking all this over for me," he said in a more solemn tone.

And with that, the screen went blank. This was all too much to handle, but I robotically moved to the coat closet and opened the door. Inside, there were two coats and two jackets, along with six empty hangers. There were two coat hooks on the back of the door, and one on each wall to the left and right. Per Paul's instructions, I grabbed the coat hook on the right and twisted it.

The next few seconds showed me just how serious Paul had been about the security of this 'bunker' room. The back panel of the closet slid to the left about three feet, revealing a hidden metal door with a camera lens right at eye level when I squatted below the coat rack. There was a latch handle on the door, but a second after I moved the coats aside, the door opened automatically. As it did, I could see it was six inches thick, and looked like I suspected a bank vault door looked. The door had eight locking bolts that went into the frame, and it only opened a few inches when it unlocked. I had to push it the rest of the way.

I was not prepared for what I experienced next.

I stepped into the bunker that was roughly twelve feet wide and fifteen feet deep, and I paused for several seconds to take it all in. I didn't close the door behind me yet, but stood holding it slightly open in case I needed to escape. To my left was a wall of computer monitors. Some were on and some were off. The ones that were on were showing several angles of what I assumed to be Paul's property.

There were two six foot long tables under the monitors with one visible keyboard and a mouse. There was a rack in the back with six of the rack slots filled with equipment and wires routing all over the place, albeit in an orderly fashion. On the right was a whiteboard that was full of colorful writing I'd get to later, and a corkboard with pictures, cards, and notes stuck to it.

The room had a low level hum that was coming from the computer equipment and another device against the back wall. I stepped closer to see it was an air filtration system. This room was getting air from the outside. It was setup like a bomb shelter.

The walls were concrete across the front, but the back seemed to be built right into the side of the mountain behind the cabin. The ceiling appeared to be half stone and half normal wood material, but the back wall itself was all stone. There was a small metal door barely visible behind the computer equipment rack straight back. If I had to guess, I'd say Paul had built an escape route into the mountain.

I shook my head as I looked around the unbelievable

place where Paul had been working. It made me instantly aware that he was hiding from something bad or was protecting something extremely important to him. Or both. He had gone through all the trouble to create this hardened safe house in the mountains, then had died on a surgery table far away in Nashville. It was sad.

As I took another scan of the corkboard on the right, one picture pinned there caught my eye. I moved closer to inspect the photo and realized it was me. It wasn't current, but was taken in the field back in Afghanistan. At first, the photo made me smile as I saw my younger face smiling at the camera in full battle attire standing next to four of my comrades.

My smile soon faded as I looked through the rest of the photos and the notes attached to them.

Next to the group photo from Afghanistan was another photo from a similar-looking locale and timeframe. Someone had drawn circles around two of the soldiers in the group. I had to squint a little to see who it was, but in a few seconds I realized I was looking at Jennifer Ellis and Simone Mason. Jen, of course, had become a close friend over the last several months. Mason, as she preferred to be called, was an FBI agent from Denver who had worked with me and Jennifer during an assignment last year.

I only had to wonder why Paul had circled them for a second. There were pins stuck in the photos with twine strung to two far more recent photos of Jen and Mason. Those photos had sticky notes on them with dates. The date on Jen's photo aligned with the day Paul recruited her to work with The Association. I remember that day well, as I was privy to the discussion, but it doesn't make me smile. That's the day my blossoming romance with Jennifer was derailed.

The date written on the sticky note for Mason's photo was from the week before. Paul hadn't mentioned he recruited Mason, but this evidence means he must have. I wondered if any of this even mattered now that Paul was gone.

For now, the other five photos on the cork board had gotten my attention. They were much more recent photos of me and my four peers from the old Afghanistan photo. I hadn't noticed my photo earlier because of the sticky note covering my face. I read the notes pinned to each photo one by one, mine being the last one on the bottom right.

The first individual photo linked to the guy on the far left of the Afghanistan photo, Mark Stephenson. The guy was a tank. He had to be six and a half feet tall, and nearly three hundred pounds of solid muscle. I remembered some of the incredible physical feats he had accomplished during some of our downtime. He thought it was funny to pick up anything that seemed heavy, often over his head, and took great pride in showing off his incredible strength.

I smiled as I remembered the time Mark had a few too many adult beverages and fell over backwards, holding a keg over his head. I was still remembering big Mark when I started going through the bullets on the sticky note stuck to his photo. Below a date, written just like Jennifer and Mason's, were a few scribbled bullets. But the bullets for Mark seemed to list out all the bad things that had happened to him, which felt odd in that context.

The notes revealed Mark had been involved in some sort of bank fraud, and had been divorced, and had lost his job with the Bank of America. There were dates and numbers next to each bullet.

The next photo, with the smile bigger than any of the rest of us, was of Keith Bartholomew. We called him Bart because the team had given me the privilege of being called Keith. But more than that, we just referred to him as 'Happy.' He was always smiling and seemed to find the bright spot on any occasion. Before I could get to memories of Bart, I went straight to the bulleted items listed on the sticky note under his chin.

Similar to Mark, Paul had listed several challenges Bart had faced. He had a bankruptcy listed, along with several business missteps.

There were similar things for Whitney "Gerry" Cheevers. I gave Gerry her nickname just because I remembered a hockey goalie from the Boston Bruins, who used to draw stitches on his goalie mask every time he got hit with the puck. It had nothing to do with Whitney, but it was the only other person I knew with the last name of Cheevers. I called her Gerry one time as a sad attempt at a joke, and it just stuck. Gerry had some hard times too, according to the list stuck to her face.

The last photo before mine, Steve Chandler, was the one guy I had kept up with more than the others. He was a crypto expert who had helped me setup all my accounts, and who had helped with a few of my assignments in the past. His bullets were similar, but all had lines through them. It was an anomaly I'd have to investigate.

The sticky note on my photo, like the others, had a date on the top. That date corresponded with the call I had received from Paul five years ago when he asked me to join The Association. Below that date were only two scribbled bullets. One said 'assignments tampered' and the other said 'wife killed.' I was acutely aware of the fact that my wife died in a car accident five years ago, but why was Paul tracking that event? And the bullet about tampering with my assignments gave me pause.

While I was thinking about that one, I took a step back and wondered why Paul had been tracking difficulties in all our personal lives. Was this what he was tracking from Filipov? Or was he somehow involved in these things?

I stood and wondered what Paul was up to out there in the wilderness.

Chapter Sixteen

Beyond the photos and lists, the magnitude of the little hideaway also weighed heavily on my curiosity. Paul was doing some serious business for The Association, sure, but the cabin and bunker seemed like overkill. Sure, the data he'd have to store was important and would certainly be considered highly confidential, but wow. Was Filipov really so close to finding him he had to go to these measures to protect himself and his research?

I sat down in the black mesh office chair as I tried to make sense of it all. Paul clearly wanted me to come here, and even set up the system to recognize me when I arrived. There had to be something in all this that would help me see what was going on.

Turning to the wall of computer screens, I moved to the keyboard and mouse sitting on the desk, centered in front of the first two monitors. When I moved the mouse, the screen nearest to where I was sitting came to life. The photo from Afghanistan appeared on the screen, taking the entire background.

Apparently Paul was enamored with, or maybe obsessed with, that photo.

While I looked at the photo, an LED light on a tiny camera I hadn't previously noticed lit up just above the screen. It was similar to the units I had at home for my Zoom meetings and seemed to be active with a green light illuminated just above the camera lens. It must have been part of the facial and retina scan Paul had mentioned.

Then, all at once, the screen changed to a typical Linux operating system desktop. Icons and folders covered the desktop, with the Afghanistan photo remaining in the background. One icon in particular caught my eye.

It was in the center of the screen and said 'For Keith Morgan.'

I clicked on that icon, hoping to discover why Paul felt the need to build this bunker.

There was no welcome video like I had seen when I arrived at the cabin, but the details in the document on the screen would start me down the path of understanding why Paul was obsessed. And why he felt he needed a bunker. And why the bunker ultimately wasn't enough to save him.

The title of the document was 'Arch Enemy,' which meant nothing in itself. There was a list below the title with dates on the lefthand side of the page. Before I started reading, I scrolled down to see how much time I needed to devote to this list. Clearly, it was important to Paul, and I'd need to focus.

The list was four pages long. It was a long time before dark, but I'd need to make my way out of here in time to clear the woods well before that. I didn't have to worry about getting home early or getting to any events with the kids, but navigating the woods in the dark wasn't a good idea. I leaned back, stretched, then focused on the screen. I'd try to get through it as efficiently as I could.

After a couple of lines, I realized what I was reading. The first page had an outline of the events in Afghanistan, specifically focusing on some of the work our team had done working for a Hart International after I was out of the Army. That's where the photo out on the cork board had come from.

The dates included two arms dealers we had taken down, and three different oil facilities we had retaken after the Taliban overcame them. Beside each date was the location, and a brief description. The description always ended with one name: Ivan Filipov. After seeing it listed so many times, I understood how many times we had affected his business. I didn't know how much money that had taken from him, but clearly we had damaged Filipov's power and his pocketbook.

The rest of the list was more detail on each team member in the photos on the corkboard. There were dates and details of my wife's death, which was the oldest item related to any of us. Then there was a question that made my heart nearly stop.

'Was this Filipov?'

The message was staring at me on the screen. I sat back in my chair, unable to read anything else after seeing that question. I stared at the ceiling of the bunker and flashed back to that day almost five years ago. My wife, Beth, had been driving down a mountain pass to our home in Woodland Park, Colorado, and had slid off the road during a fast-moving snowstorm. I couldn't see any reason how that accident could have anything to do with Filipov.

I don't know how long I sat there looking up and doing nothing, but eventually I leaned forward again to focus on the list. It was then that I realized my eyes were blurring with tears. I hadn't felt this close to the loss of my wife in years, and it was an unexpected pain. It also drove me to dig into why Paul had typed the question.

I read the question again, then scanned back through all the dates, and realized each of them was a hyperlink. There must be more details behind each of the summaries listed in this outline. Ignoring all the others, I clicked on the date next to the item summarizing my wife's death. When I did, I was presented with a whole new layer of Paul's digging. And it made me instantly uncomfortable. And angry.

The first shock came from the photos of the crash site. I had raced to the scene that fateful evening, but by the time I had gotten there, emergency vehicles and flashing lights had covered the entire scene. Paul had somehow gotten hold of images that preceded the arrival of most of those vehicles.

After studying the photos for several minutes, I also started looking at the notes Paul had typed between each one. The notes revealed footprints and tire tracks off the side of the road opposite where my wife had veered off the side. I scanned the photos and found the one he was refer-ring to. The footprints went all the way across the road and seemed to circle in the middle several times. It's almost as if the person was waiting in the middle of the road, then went to see the crash itself.

I had always assumed my wife had encountered an animal, as she would have made every attempt to avoid one, even at her own peril. It was a constant conversation for us when a squirrel or rabbit darted in front of our car. I knew it had to be a sudden swerve, because she wouldn't drive faster than the conditions permitted. She was far too cautious of a driver for that. Even to the point of often driving 'dangerously slow,' according to her husband.

The evidence Paul had somehow obtained indicated the presence of another human at the crash site before the emergency vehicles had arrived. Even worse, they may have been present at the time of the accident. The longer I considered that thought, the angrier I got. In the photo, I could see where the footprints led down to the crash site, but I wondered if that person had tried to help. It made me feel a little better to believe they had.

I also found scanned images of the police report, where Paul had circled and highlighted several items. I'd never seen the police report before and had never even considered her death may have been intentional, so this entire line of thinking was making me angry. I was curious how Paul had gotten this information, but not curious enough to stop.

The report revealed the police had noticed the footprints around the crash site when the first officer arrived. It also included eyewitness testimony from another motorist that noted someone was parked beside the road before the time of my wife's crash. The comments in the report concluded someone had stopped, but there was no reason to investigate who it was.

Again, the thought of someone leaving my wife in her car dying on that mountainside made me furious. I could feel my blood pressure rising as I sat in the mountain bunker by myself. If Paul's suggestions were true, it meant that someone may have killed Beth. I had an instant feeling of remorse that I had let my wife's killer go free for almost five years. I could feel my fists clenching involuntarily at the thought.

I went through the file again and again, each time trying to glean more information that might help me conclude what had happened. There simply wasn't enough there to tell for sure. Clearly, Paul couldn't lock down the cause of the crash, as he never completed the report.

After considering the minimal evidence and possible reasons, I developed a frustration with Paul. While he was no longer there to defend himself, I had so many questions for him. The first thing I wondered was why he had gone down this path of research without telling me. It was obvious from the amount of data he had compiled he had spent a great deal of time investigating what happened. Yet, he never mentioned a word of it to me. Maybe he was saving me from the anger I was feeling now. Or maybe he didn't want to say anything until he had proof. Neither reason sat right with me at that moment.

I lost track of time while I sat in the bunker reviewing the data about Beth over and over, and eventually I glanced at the clock to see it was now approaching 3 PM. I needed to leave in an hour or two to be sure I'd get out of the woods before dark. Since it was my first time in that area, I was certainly not familiar enough with the terrain to navigate the route back to the car in the dark.

As I once again scrolled through the pages of information on my wife's crash, I stopped at the bottom and stared at the question Paul had typed at the very bottom of the page. It was similar to the question I saw earlier and was the one Paul had obviously been trying to prove.

'Could Filipov do this?'

Chapter Seventeen

The note about Filipov's potential involvement with my wife's death had sent me into a relentless scramble to find data. After exhausting what Paul had found about Beth's car crash, I was determined to find out why Paul thought it was possible Filipov was trying to hurt me and the other associates. I needed to see the evidence. All of it.

Backing out of the Arch Enemy file, I found folders for each of my fellow team members from our team in Afghanistan. Paul had done extensive research into their lives, including each of the bullet points he had listed on the corkboard behind me. When I reviewed their folders, I got absorbed into each of their lives, their challenges, and more notes about Filipov's potential manipulation.

As I reviewed the details about the other team members and my fellow associates, I felt almost like I was spying. Or like I was intruding on their personal lives. As that feeling made me more and more uncomfortable, I considered why for a second, and suddenly realized one reason I felt that way. I wasn't looking at publicly available data. Paul had much more data on each of us than anyone would know from public records. That was first clear with the police report around Beth's car crash, but all the details on the other team members reinforced it.

Somehow, Paul was getting more data than the average person could access.

I took a break from the intimate details of each person's finances and personal situations long enough to peruse some of the other files on Paul's system. After a few clicks, I found a folder that revealed one way Paul knew so much about each of us. He was somehow accessing data from a variety of government agencies.

Before sinking into this new area of research, I had to make a decision. It was about to get dark out there in the middle of the vast Montana wilderness and I either had to go back to my truck and drive out, or I had to hunker down for the night. The cabin reservation I had made in Cameron looked fantastic, but I definitely felt like a night in Paul's fantastic cabin wouldn't be very painful. And I'd get to keep digging into his research. Before I made the final decision, I investigated more of the cabin to see if staying was even workable.

Back out in the main cabin area, I found there were plenty of military-style MREs packed into the pantry. There was more coffee than I could drink in a month, and there were even some frozen meals in the refrigerator that seemed to have potential. Clearly, I could stay for quite a while if I needed to.

I felt I didn't need to stay for a while, though. If everything was as easy to find as the first few files, I only needed the night.

Curious about how Paul would protect himself while he was at the cabin, I looked around at the places he might store a rifle. The coat closet would have been an option, but there were no other hidden panels or storage locations visible. After another minute, however, I found an extra door in the back of the bedroom closet with another finger pad and a familiar-looking lever just below it. I scanned my index finger and heard a click. When I twisted the lever and opened the door, its weight made me realize it was more than just wood. As I should have suspected, Paul had hidden a built-in gun safe.

And no longer surprisingly, Paul also had my fingerprints.

It was a large safe. There were lots of guns. And lots of ammunition.

I couldn't walk inside the safe, but it was one of the larger ones I had seen. It must have been four feet by four feet, and was full of all calibers of rifles. The fact that Paul would have weapons out here didn't surprise me, but the volume of guns and firepower seemed excessive for a remote cabin. Was Paul expecting a battle way out here?

There were two rows of six rifles racked neatly in the safe, with boxes of ammunition carefully aligned on the floor and on two shelves above the rifles. The door had eight pockets on the back of it, with a handgun securely tucked inside each pocket. I suspected there were boxes of ammunition for each of those as well. I didn't take the time to evaluate each at that moment, but the magnitude of the discovery continued to add to the curiosity and potential danger of Paul's remote paradise.

I went outside and stood on the porch for a few minutes while I evaluated my options, and took in the clean mountain air. It was still warm, but with the sun beginning to drop below the mountains to my west, it would cool off soon. The weather report I had checked on the way in revealed no rain in the forecast, but I wasn't sure if my 4Runner was safe. The parking area was at the end of a dirt road, which Paul indicated was inside the perimeter of his property. In fact, he said there would be camera footage of me. The camera coverage gave me some level of comfort, but I wanted to validate it was true.

After making my way back into the bunker, I slid the mouse around to bring the system to life. I browsed the folders on the desktop and found one that said, thankfully, 'cabin property cameras.' When I opened that folder, I saw twenty-two more folders. There was one for each camera on the property, and a single file called 'camera map.' I clicked on that file and the screen displayed a map of the property around the cabin. Following the road from Cameron on the map, I saw the line get thin where it turned to gravel, then a thinner line where it must have become dirt. If my memory was correct about the parking location, it was well within range of camera twelve.

Opening the folder for Camera 12, I saw a link to the live camera feed, then a long list of video files named by date and time. It looked like the cameras were dumping files every hour, twenty-four hours a day, seven days a week. There were a lot of files. Finding the video that covered the noon hour, I clicked on it and saw the area where I had parked. Forwarding to the time I arrived, I saw my 4Runner pull in. Then I saw my tired self get out of the vehicle and stretch, look around, and start getting my pack ready.

To find out if the 4Runner was safe, I clicked on the live link and watched as the video feed ran in vivid color. Paul's cameras were good. While the feed displayed, I noticed the cursor highlighted when I moved the mouse around. On a hunch, I moved the mouse to the license plate of the 4Runner, barely visible from the angle of the camera. When I did, a dialog menu came up asking if I wanted to search the license plate. Not knowing what I was searching, I clicked 'yes.'

The search took a couple of seconds, but the amount of data that was displayed on the screen startled me. It had my vehicle registration, my address, the history of the car, along with links to several other pieces of my personal data. I was beginning to see how Paul got all the data on all of us. Then I got another idea.

Pulling up the video of my arrival, I adjusted the video to a point that my face was visible. Then I moved the mouse to my face and stopped. As I thought might happen, a dialog opened, asking if I wanted to search on the face. Curious, I clicked 'yes' and sat in awe as data appeared on the screen. There were links for my passport, driver's license, credit report, family members, tax records, military records, real estate records, vehicle registration, news, social media, and an option to save the image of my face. The quick display of data reminded me of spy movies I had seen. Except this was real.

What in the world had Paul linked this system to?

I was more than curious at that point, and I went on a mission to find out what Paul's system was accessing. I went from link to link looking at all the data I could think of about myself. After a while, I realized I had exhausted anything I wanted to see about my life. By the end, I was reading things in my history I had totally forgotten. If Paul had access to all this stuff on everyone with just a face, which it appeared he did, then he had good reasons to have all these servers. I wondered how he had gotten internet access so fast out here in the middle of nowhere, but decided not to fret about it.

Realizing I had once again been sitting there for quite

some time, I leaned back in the bunker chair and stretched. Then I got up and headed out of the bunker, through the closet into the cabin, and stopped dead in my tracks. It was completely dark outside. I had been digging into my personal data so long I had made my decision for tonight very easy.

I'd spend tonight in a cabin in the woods. The thought of that phrase made me smile, but also made me realize I'd better let someone know where I was. I pulled out my satellite phone and noticed I had missed a call from the kids and had a text message from Jen.

Jamie had left a voicemail saying they had made it to grandma and grandpa's house in Missouri. They were heading into town for dinner and would call me tomorrow. I sent her a text message telling them to have fun and that I loved them.

Jen's message was a simple request for any updates on the Montana trip. Boy, did I have a lot of updates for her when we got the chance to talk. But I wasn't quite ready for that. Instead, I hopped back inside the bunker to continue my research. I'd dig into the computer files for a few hours, call Jen to give her an update, get some sleep, and maybe even catch a trout or two on my way out in the morning.

At least, that was the plan.

After brewing a pot of coffee and pouring myself a cup, I eased into the office chair back in the bunker. Digging back into the folders on Paul's system, I planned to go through the folders he had on the desktop in a more systematic fashion. Starting at the top left, I found a list of research folders that seemed to be categorized. There were folders for finances, for relationships, for social media, for employment, and even for travel. They were like the ones I had seen when my face was on the video image. As I looked into each folder, I found my name, along with the names of my team members from Afghanistan.

The folders beneath our names were grouped by month. Within each month was a group of files for each day. The data inside those files made my chin drop.

Paul had data that effectively assembled all our activities and interactions for the last five years. He knew where we went, what we spent our money on, who our families and friends were, and even what we viewed and posted on social media. It was more data than I had seen before. There were images, videos, and transaction files of all different types. Once again, the volume and depth of the data made me uncomfortable.

Even more worrisome, Paul had a folder in many of the individual days that was titled Filipov. That folder, as best I could tell, showed the data Filipov had inserted or modified to be used against us. It seemed Paul was trying to track where Filipov was working to hurt our team.

The more I read, the more I felt violated. Sure, Paul may have been trying to help us, but the amount of data he was collecting was disturbing. The idea that someone like Filipov could get the same data was even more disturbing.

I decided to change my tactics for a bit and searched for a photo of Filipov. When the system found a video with a reasonable image of his face, I paused the video and held the mouse over his nose. Just like my image in the video at the 4Runner, an option to search appeared.

I clicked 'yes' and waited to see what data the system could find on Ivan Filipov.

Chapter Eighteen

The search for Ivan Filipov took a little longer than the other searches I had done. It seemed the data was more obscure, or maybe the system was struggling to find data on someone who lived in Russia. That idea made sense to me.

While the search was running, I took a minute to look around the bunker again. While most of the bunker felt oddly sanitized and empty, there were a couple of places to store things. Under the desk, and next to my left leg, were a couple of drawers. I opened the top one, a small drawer only a few inches tall, and found some pens, post-it notes and unused notebooks.

Below the small drawer was a larger one, big enough to hold file folders. When I opened it, I found that's exactly what it held. There were ten separate hanging folders, side by side, in the drawer. Each one had a tab with a label.

The first folder contained a small journal with notes scribbled inside. The notes weren't really journal entries, but were more task lists that Paul had apparently been tracking. As I thumbed through it, I saw dates in the top right corner that showed how he was tracking his own research. Scanning the tasks, I could see a mixture of items related to Paul's personal life, the business of Rocky Mountain Equity, and even some notes related to The Association.

One task that caught my eye was at the bottom of Paul's list for the last several days. In the weeks before he died, it appeared he had passed the task from day to day without checking it off. He had shifted other tasks to the next day, typically when they just couldn't get done. Within a day or two, he'd check them off. This task, however, was at the bottom of the list for weeks. For some reason, Paul kept putting this task off.

He had written the task a couple of different ways, but most of the time it said, 'Let him know about Will.' I didn't know who 'him' referred to and didn't know who Will might have been, but Paul must have been expecting a tough conversation.

I was sure I could learn a lot from all the completed tasks in the notebook, so I scanned the other folders.

There were folders for a variety of Paul's contacts, including some I had worked with over my years with The Association. There were lawyers, including William Renteria, who had saved my hide in Nashville. I was shocked to see so many contacts on the various lists, and wondered how Paul had come across all these people. It also made me realize, once again, that The Association was really just Paul. When he told me he was 'checking with The Association' for resources, I now understood he was just looking into that file drawer.

The back folder in the drawer held different types of documents. Inside that folder were two clear plastic report covers with professional-looking documents inside.

The first document was the Articles of Organization for The Association Equities, LLC. That, in itself, was huge. Given my recent discovery of that corporation, I knew it held just about everything that I had devoted my life to for the last five years. Most notably, it was the parent company of my employer. And, relative to my current location, it also owned the real estate that surrounded the cabin.

Paging through the document, I saw nothing too strange. There were the standard clauses for business name, address, purpose and other business terms. Paul had created enough of a broad brush description to enable The Association Equities to do just about anything. The ownership was to only one member: Paul Frazier, founder and CEO. There were no board members.

The Articles of Organization document was signed by a registered agent named Jack Underhill, who was with a law firm called Carter and Underhill. Their firm's address was in Denver, so I took out a pen and wrote it down. I'd need to talk to Mr. Underhill.

I was wondering how Jordan Crawford, or anyone else, fit into the whole concept of The Association. If there was really no board at all, how and why was Jordan even involved?

The very last folder in the drawer contained Paul's Last Will and Testament. This one stopped me for a moment. I had been digging so hard into all this data that I had pushed aside the memory of my friend's death. He had been doing all this work out here alone, and I once again felt a profound sense of loss. If only I had a few minutes to talk to Paul again and have him explain all this to me. It must have been a tremendous burden for him to carry all this alone.

Once again, I turned and looked at the photo from the Hart International team we had in Afghanistan. I smiled at the memory, then faded back to the feeling of loss. I had lost several friends in the Army and then with Hart International, but none as close as Paul. At that moment, I made a mental note to call each of those guys in the morning to see how they were doing. Paul's notes showed they'd had some problems, so maybe a call would cheer them up. It wasn't my typical style, but I was determined to do it.

After the trip down memory lane, I went back to the last document in the folder. Scanning to the back, I saw the same signature as on the previous document, Jack Underhill. So, yeah, I'd need to call that guy.

I flipped through the pages and noticed Paul's Last Will and Testament was a surprisingly short document. Even my personal will was longer than this one, but largely due to the trusts I had set up for Jamie and Kyle. Paul had no such items.

In fact, the disposition of Paul's property only had one beneficiary listed. That beneficiary was entitled to all of Paul's property, including his business entities, his financial assets, and his real estate assets. And the name of the beneficiary, which I stared at for a long time, was Keith Morgan of Woodland Park, Colorado.

I was set to inherit Paul's entire fortune? Why me? What about his family? Was this the task he had never completed before his death? 'Let him know about Will' now had a new meaning.

Hoping to find another relative or close friend listed elsewhere, I devoured the last two documents in the file folder. I had only recently realized how wealthy Paul had been, and the breadth of his responsibilities. There was no way I wanted to take all his stuff over without his guidance.

Once again, Paul's absence consumed me.

Looking at that clock on the computer screen in front of me, I saw it was 9 PM. Normally I wouldn't bother anyone this late, much less someone I didn't know like Jack Underhill, Attorney at Law for Carter and Underhill. But tonight was an exception. I had to get some answers.

When I first started dialing his number, I realized once again that the bunker blocked all signals, even for my satellite phone. So I walked out onto the porch and stared into the darkness of the Montana wilderness while waiting for Jack to pick up. Fortunately for me, he answered in just a few seconds.

"Jack Underhill," he said, loudly. I could hear activity behind him as though he was at some sort of event.

"Hi Mr. Underhill. I'm sorry to call you so late, but this is Keith Morgan. I've just found my name on Paul Frazier's will. Would you know anything about that?" I asked, getting straight to the point.

"Oh, so Paul finally got up the nerve to talk to you, huh?" Jack said with a chuckle.

"Well, no, I'm afraid not. I'm afraid Paul is dead," I said, feeling too overwhelmed to soften the message.

Jack's voice instantly changed.

"Oh, no! Mr. Morgan, I'm so sorry. I'm at a Rockies game right now. Let me find a quiet area and I'll call you right back." I could hear him scurrying around as he said it.

"Sure," I said as the call disconnected.

He called back in less than a minute.

"Mr. Morgan, I apologize again for my lighthearted response a moment ago. I was not aware of Paul's passing. What happened to him?" Jack said the moment I answered his call.

"He died while traveling in Nashville," I said, avoiding the details for now.

"I'm so sorry. I don't even know what else to say. Please accept my most sincere condolences," he said in an appropriately somber tone. I wondered why he didn't know about Paul's death yet, but decided it wasn't worth derailing my line of questions. Since Paul had no family to tell Mr. Underhill about his death and my name was in his will, maybe this was my responsibility.

"Thank you, I appreciate that. It seems Paul had left some vague directions for me to take over some of his affairs, but I didn't know he had listed me as the primary beneficiary in his will. I'm hoping you can shed some light on that?" I asked, taking no time for idle chatter.

"Well, I suppose I can, yes. First off, Paul had no family. He never married, had no children, and his parents died several years ago. He has an uncle on his dad's side who is in and out of rehab centers in Denver, but they're not close and Paul is...or was, afraid to leave anything to him. After several months of deliberation when we set up his new LLC, he decided you should be his primary beneficiary. He said he trusted you and believed you'd be the right person to take everything over if he wasn't available. I told him he needed to get you in here to sign the paperwork, but he was dragging his feet. He said he knew it would change your relationship, and he was reluctant to do that," Jack said, then paused.

"What do you mean by 'change the relationship' and why was he reluctant to do that?" I asked, expecting I knew the answer.

"You said you found the will. Did you find any other information about Paul?" Jack asked.

I knew where he was going.

"Yes. I know Paul was a wealthy man, far beyond his lifestyle," I said.

"Yeah, well. I think that's what he meant. He didn't want people to know about that. He thought people would treat him differently, and he didn't like that idea," he said.

"Why don't you stop by the office and we can get that paperwork signed? The LLC will be in limbo if you don't sign on as a member. Officially, the transfer upon death is only valid if the transferee is a member of the LLC. We have an amendment to the LLC paperwork that Paul has already signed. Your name is there, but your signature is not. Until you sign, we can't complete the transfer," Jack said.

Without telling him where I was or why, I deflected the question for now.

"What happens if I don't sign?" I asked.

"Well, you'd still receive his estate. Eventually. That includes his personal property and the condo, but the ownership of the LLC would be a challenge. It would take a long time and could get ugly, and the businesses under that umbrella corporation would suffer," he said.

I shook my head while I thought about that for several seconds, then thought I'd see how much Jack knew about The Association.

"Do you know why he called it The Association Equities?" I finally asked.

"Not really, but he was adamant about it. I thought it was too vague, but he said he wanted flexibility to engage in a variety of business ventures ," Jack said.

"Yeah, that sounds like him," I said.

"So, should we set up a time for you to come in?" Jack asked.

"I'm out-of-town today. Let me call you when I get back into the area," I said, again deflecting.

"Fair enough. I'll get everything ready. Again, I'm really sorry," Jack said.

"Thanks," I said as we ended the call.

After all I had learned in the past few days, I wasn't sure I wanted to sign anything. I didn't feel ready to take over everything Paul had going.

Chapter Nineteen

Thornton Caldwell was asleep in bed at 6 AM when his phone started buzzing on his nightstand. He hadn't slept well at all, and answered the phone with a huff. He lived alone in a small house on the far north side of the Lazy J acreage. As the crow flies, it was only a few miles away from the site of his parents' murders. By road, it took nearly fifteen minutes to get from their house to his. The oldest Caldwell son at thirty-five, he felt obligated to stay near his parents.

"What?" Thor said after fumbling for the phone, realizing it was Bailey, and accepting the call.

"Yeah, like you were sleeping either," Bailey said.

Bailey lived in an apartment in town. His parents had offered to give him a room in their house, but he was twenty-seven now, and he wanted to live on his own. For now, that meant he had to live in an apartment. Someday he would get a house of his own, but he wasn't there quite yet.

"No, I wasn't. But what do you want this early?" Thor asked.

"I've been thinking. If someone killed mom and dad to

get that drone, why wouldn't they want to kill us? I mean, we also know about it and can describe what was on it. We've even got pictures of it on our phones," he said, with fear emerging in his voice as he talked.

"Yeah, I've thought about that, too. What do you say we take a quick tour of the area where we found that drone? I'd like to get a better idea what's around there on the Krohl property. I don't think they've put cameras out there, but I don't really care if they have. Let's find out what they were looking at," Thor said, getting angrier as he talked.

"I mean, these guys killed our parents for that stupid drone," Thor fumed.

"Yeah, that's what I mean. We need to do something," Bailey said, the fear and anguish in his timid voice turning to resolve.

"Meet me down at mom and dad's house in two hours. We can get the ATVs from there and go snoop around," Thor said.

"Alright. Bye," Bailey said as they ended the call.

Both of them ate breakfast, had some coffee, got showered and dressed, then drove to their parent's house. At 8:05 AM, they were both parking in the lot near the stables. They got out of their trucks and headed to the equipment barn beside the stable, where the ATVs were.

"Did you see they put police tape all over the front door and the barn?" Bailey asked.

"Yeah. If they don't come back anymore today, I'm going to get rid of it. We've got to get all that cleaned up in there," Thor said, shaking his head.

"I saw Pastor Martin at the store this morning. He asked me when we planned to have services for mom and dad," Bailey said as they got the ATVs out of the barn.

"Yeah, and the funeral home called me. I guess we gotta

set that stuff up when we get back," Thor said. "This stuff really sucks."

"Yeah." Bailey said before starting his ATV and waiting for Thor. Once they were both moving, Thor took off west toward the creek bed where they had found the drone. It took about fifteen minutes to get there.

"Let's stop here for a second," Thor yelled as they arrived at the very tree where the drone had crashed. "I'm going to see if this GPS location helps us figure out where it might have come from."

"We know that's the property line right over there," Bailey said, pointing just upstream from where they had stopped.

"Yeah, but how far are we from the Krohl property?" Thor asked rhetorically as he held up the map on his phone.

"I think it's about a mile or so to the north," Bailey said, not realizing it was a rhetorical question.

"I know that, Bailey!" Thor yelled. "I wanted to be a little more specific than that."

"The GPS won't help, Thor. There are no property lines on there. Let's just ride up there and see what we can see," Bailey said, again pointing up the hill.

"Ok, but that's not the Krohl place up there," he said.

"I know, but I haven't seen anybody on that property for a long time. And if we head upstream along the creek for a bit, we can navigate the ridge north toward the Krohl place. That would be the most likely place for them to snoop on our ranch. They'd have a little elevation and the best angle to see," Bailey responded.

"Ok, sure. Let's head up the side of this creek and go north when we hit the top. Hopefully, this property owner isn't up there with a shotgun," Thor said, reluctant to agree with his brother.

With Thor in the lead, they slowly navigated around the trees and rocks up the steep hill that led to the top of the ridge. It was tedious riding, but after a few grueling minutes of careful climbing, their ATVs reached the top of the ridge and they could get a better glimpse of the surrounding area.

They stopped and grabbed the binoculars from their pockets and started scanning the area to their north.

"Do you see anything?" Bailey asked.

"No, but I'm not sure we would. They could have been navigating that drone from anywhere and we don't know where they were filming. We'll probably have to ride closer to their property to see if they've been sniffing around near our land. We'll see tracks or something, I'm sure," Thor answered.

"Ok, let's head that way," Bailey said, still scanning the surrounding area with his binoculars.

"Hey, what's that? There's someone parked over there," he said, looking back south, away from the Krohl property. Thor turned and focused his binoculars in the same direction.

"Yeah, there sure is. I guess that neighbor guy is back. I don't remember him having a lifted 4Runner, though, do you?" Thor asked.

"No, but honestly, there are so many of them out here I'm not sure I would have noticed," Bailey answered.

"Yeah, true. Let's head along the ridge and see what we can find," Thor said, putting his binoculars away.

They navigated the ridge along the property line until they came to a place where they could see the Krohl herd in the distance. They'd seen nothing unusual or incriminating along their ride and were about to give up.

Then they heard the horses.

Realizing they were probably on Krohl property, they

both looked around and thought about running. But it was too late to head back east toward their own property. The ATVs had speed, but the horses had mobility, and it was a steep and difficult path back to the Lazy J property.

"You guys lost?" It was Gil, the ranch hand they had argued with at the Golden Bear. He was riding with three other ranchers from the Krohl side of the property. They had come up the ridge ahead of the Caldwell boys, taking advantage of the steady noise of the ATV motors.

"Nah, just looking for the path back down," Thor said.

"Look. I know you guys are upset about your folks and all, and I'm really sorry, but you can't be running around out here looking for things that don't exist," Gil said.

"You guys can't get away with this. Our folks were making an honest living out here. They'd been doing it for three generations. And now, just because they see one of your damn drones, you take them out? You've got to pay!" Bailey screamed.

Gil just sat there on his horse, shaking his head.

"You've got to listen to what I'm saying, Bailey. It's not us. We use drones for all sorts of reasons on our property, but not to snoop around other ranches. We don't need to do that. The Krohl ranch already has technology and resources most of you smaller outfits don't have. You may not appreciate that, but it's the truth. We should be more worried about you guys trying to take us down than the reverse," he said.

Bailey was still fuming, but Thor was deep in thought.

"What kind of drones do you guys use, anyway?" Thor finally asked.

"Like I told you before, we use DJI. We've got a contract with them. Krohl gets some sort of kickback if we just advertise it a little. They'd cancel the contract if we used anybody else's drones," Gil replied.

"Then why would there be a Russian drone out here snooping around on our property?" Thor asked.

"If I knew that, I'd tell you. Maybe someone from Russia wants to take over your shorthorn herd. That's probably the most lucrative part of the entire Lazy J operation," Gil said.

"Yeah," Thor acknowledged.

"But don't be sniffing over here anymore, Thor. You guys are welcome to come by and ask any questions you want, but don't be out here doing any vigilante stuff. That's not going to end well," Gil warned.

Thor nodded as Gil and the other three Krohl ranchers turned and navigated back the way they came. After a few seconds, Thor and Bailey did the same.

When they got back to the stables and put their ATVs and gear away, Thor yelled at Bailey before he got into his pickup.

"I'm going to go get a closer look at that 4Runner and see what it's about. If Krohl really had nothing to do with this, maybe we're looking in the wrong direction," he said.

"You really believe those guys? They'll say anything to make us look somewhere else. You know they did it, Thor. They're the guys who killed mom and dad," Bailey said angrily.

"Maybe. But what if they didn't? I'm just going to snoop around, that's all," Thor said as he considered what Bailey was saying. He didn't trust Krohl much more than Bailey, but they seemed to make some valid arguments.

"You shouldn't go there by yourself. I'll go with you," Bailey said.

"Ok, fair enough," Thor agreed as Bailey hopped into the passenger side of his truck.

In fifteen minutes, they had navigated the blacktop, then gravel, then dirt road out of Cameron and were pulling up on the spot where the 4Runner had been parked.

It was still there.

"What are you going to do?" Bailey asked as Thor took a picture of the vehicle.

"Colorado plates," Thor replied, pointing to the 4Runner.

"Yeah, so? Didn't the owner guy live in Colorado?" Bailey asked.

"Yeah, I guess he did. But still," Thor said as he turned off the truck and got out.

"Where are you going, Thor? Even if these are the guys who killed mom and dad, do you really want to go stomping in there knowing they're willing to shoot innocent people? Let's just have the sheriff look them up. You've got the license plate number," Bailey pleaded.

"Ok, ok," Thor finally said, still standing next to the truck and staring at the 4Runner.

After several seconds, he reluctantly got back in his truck and slowly navigated back into town.

"Here's the license plate. Give Sheriff Hanson a call and ask him to find out who it belongs to," Thor said, handing his phone to Bailey.

Bailey looked at the photo, then dialed the sheriff.

"Hi, Sheriff Hanson? This is Bailey Caldwell. We have a suspicious vehicle parked near our property that we'd like to have checked out. Can you help with that?"

Chapter Twenty

After consuming several cups of coffee and digging through Paul's bunker for another hour, I paused long enough to realize I was hungry. The information I had found and the phone call with Jack Underhill had knocked me for a loop, but the rest of my time had mostly involved deeper details of the same topics. I hoped I was at the end of Paul's surprises.

After snatching a spaghetti MRE from the cabinet, one of my favorites from my military days, I felt my phone buzz with a text message and looked down to see another query from Jen. I had planned to call her, but given all I had learned, I decided to put that conversation off for a day. I texted her a simple message saying I had arrived and had a great time fishing. It was true, but it was not even the beginning of the story of my day.

By the time I finished eating, I was ready for bed. It was only 10:30 PM, but I was exhausted. With the travel, the hiking, and the endless discovery about Paul's life and research, it had been a very long day.

I closed the door to the bunker, spread out the hangers

and coats to hide the secret door in the back of the closet just like Paul had done, and worked my way into the bedroom. There were sheets, blankets and pillows laying on the foot of the bed, which I assembled into a rough sleeping ensemble. It wasn't ready for a military inspection, but it would work for one night.

Normally, evening caffeine kept me from immediate sleep, but not that night. I didn't even need to get into my military field sleep mindset. I was asleep as soon as my head hit the pillow.

Jolted awake by my phone buzzing, I was shocked to realize I had slept straight through the night and it was now sunny outside. As sunny as it could be under all these trees and next to a mountain, anyway.

The buzzing was from a text message. It was Jen, simply acknowledging my message from last night. She knew I'd fill her in later and didn't press for any details. That, of course, made me almost feel obligated to call. It was already 7:30 AM, and I hadn't slept this late in a long time. It was refreshing, but also made me feel like I was already behind for the day.

I grabbed a couple of bottles of water, made some more coffee, and got familiar with the shower in the cabin. I wasn't sure where Paul was getting the cabin water from, but everything worked splendidly. I suspected it probably wasn't clean enough to drink, but it was hot and the pressure was easily strong enough for a shower.

After cleaning up and trying to make the place look like I was never there, I considered what my next course of action would be. I needed to find out more about Filipov and why Paul was so obsessed with him, so that would need to be done before I left.

What I didn't yet know was how I would deal with the

will and the ownership of Paul's LLC. On the one hand, I had no interest in the headache of owning Rocky Mountain Equity or all of Paul's assets. But on the other hand, I felt responsible and didn't want the entire enterprise to fall into the wrong hands or get lost in a probate process. That dilemma had been bouncing around in my brain since the conversation with Paul's attorney.

First things first, I headed back into the bunker and went back to my Filipov search from the night before. I had gotten distracted with the file folder and never even noticed if the search had completed.

I sat down at the keyboard and put my coffee down, ready to start digging into Ivan Filipov, when a screen on the top right came to life with a video image. It looked like one of the cameras around the property perimeter and showed two ATVs carefully navigating along the other side of the creek. It was the very creek I had been fishing in just the day before.

Standing to get a better view, I saw the footage was indeed a live stream from camera eleven. That would have been next to camera twelve, where I had watched my own arrival the night before. The ATVs were moving with purpose, with not much looking around. They had no fishing equipment, and they weren't dressed for hunting. Plus, it wasn't hunting season.

I watched for a minute, then tried out the facial recognition search I had used on myself. It only took a second to zoom into the video and isolate the front rider's face. He had a hat on, but no helmet, and because he was looking uphill, his face was clearly visible.

After I clicked the button to search the face, it only took a few seconds to return a list of data.

The first ATV rider was Thornton Caldwell, from

Cameron, Montana. His parents owned the Lazy J ranch, which I didn't recognize. He had no criminal record, no passport, and had a current Montana license.

While Thornton and his fellow ATV rider scaled the hillside on the other side of the creek, I did a quick search on the Lazy J ranch. Like every other search program Paul had set up in the bunker, the search on the Lazy J returned far more data than I expected. The ranch was owned by George and Margaret Caldwell, and had been in operation for over a hundred years. There were links for both George and Margaret, but I didn't feel the need to dig into that just now. First, I wanted to see what Thornton and his friend were doing.

So far, it didn't seem like they were doing much. After a few slow clicks up the hill, the image on the screen transferred to camera ten. The view was now a little further away, but I could still see the riders as they navigated around the rocks and trees. It was a slow ride.

When they got to the top of the ridge above the creek, they stopped. Then they pulled out binoculars. Then I got a little nervous. To my relief, they spent most of their time looking the opposite way from Paul's property.

Then Thornton's friend turned around and looked toward my 4Runner. He seemed to pause for a moment, then motioned to Thornton. They both looked toward the 4Runner for a moment and chatted. I wondered for a moment if the cameras had sound, but I didn't have time to find out.

I considered what I'd do if they started making their way toward the cabin. Clearly, Paul didn't want anyone to find it, but there's also no reason to assume a neighboring ranch would wish him or his property harm. Before I had time to make any actual decisions, Thornton Caldwell and his fellow ATV rider took off in the opposite direction, away from the cabin.

I breathed a deep sigh of relief and felt my adrenaline recede. I hadn't even realized how worked up I was getting.

As my breathing returned to normal, so did my appetite. I realized I hadn't eaten a real meal, if you call it that, since my breakfast sandwich at the Flying J in Wyoming the previous morning. Cameron had one restaurant I had seen when I researched the rental cabin, which I had totally forgotten about. My hunger told me it was time to check it out.

I packed things up at the cabin as best I could, planning to return after breakfast, and set out for the hike to my 4Runner. If I went there directly, versus stopping to catch trout along the way, I expected it should only take me twenty or thirty minutes.

Fifteen minutes later, I paused as I heard a motor running. I couldn't yet see my truck, but I knew it had to be nearby. I slowed my pace just a little and headed toward the sound of the motor. As I got near the top of the next small ridge, the sound got much louder and I knew I was close.

I squatted and peeked over the ridge to see my 4Runner about thirty yards away. Behind it was a black Ford F150 with two passengers, idling but not moving. They seemed to be looking at the 4Runner and talking.

Then, with a quick burst of movement, the driver opened his door and got out. While he stood there next to the truck, I could see him staring at the 4Runner. I could also see the passenger leaning over and yelling at him.

It was too far for me to hear what they were saying, but it was close enough for me to make out who the driver was. It was Thornton Caldwell, the same guy who was riding the ATV along the creek earlier.

My SIG was on my belt in the small of my back, as usual, and I wondered if I might need it. There was no way I was going to let Mr. Caldwell steal or vandalize my 4Runner, if that's what he was up to. And if he was up to some other nefarious activity, I didn't plan to let that happen, either.

I reached behind me and grabbed the SIG and started inching forward.

Before I moved five feet, Thornton Caldwell nodded his head at the passenger. Then he took out his phone and took a picture of my 4Runner. I quickly hunkered down, so I didn't show up in the photo. I was too far for them to see me with the naked eye unless they were specifically looking for me, but a high resolution photo with a wide angle would have caught me.

After several seconds, I raised my head again to see what was happening. I still had my SIG in my hand and didn't know if they were going to head my way or not.

It turned out they were not. Thornton hopped back into his truck and slowly navigated his way back down the dirt road toward Cameron. I didn't know what they were up to, but it was more attention than I had hoped to get during this trip.

Debating my next move after seeing all the attention Thornton Caldwell was giving my vehicle, I moved forward with my breakfast plans. Hunger won the battle over caution. Plus, if they questioned me about my truck being on Paul's property, I could explain my invitation. I was pretty sure none of them would know about his death.

Ten minutes after Thornton Caldwell drove down the dirt road from Paul's property, I did the same. Reversing my directions from the night before, I navigated the dirt, then gravel, then blacktop roads back toward Cameron and headed into town. Pulling into the Golden Bear restaurant and bar, I noticed Thornton's truck already parked in the lot.

Weighing my options, I decided it would look worse to leave. So I went inside.

Chapter Twenty-One

The Golden Bear was a very diverse business. There was a gas station to the front right with a convenience store, a small fishing shop, and a surprisingly large bar and restaurant behind them. I walked into the bar and restaurant area, not knowing what to expect.

If Thornton Caldwell and his friend had seen me pull into the parking lot, breakfast could have gone the wrong way. But it didn't. Either they didn't see me or they didn't care.

The restaurant was along the right side of the big, open area, with a bar and dance area taking up much of the middle and far left spaces. I imagined the place could probably get pretty crazy on weekends, with ranchers and summer tourists packing into the place. The far right side, where breakfast seemed to be occurring, was pretty full. There were eight booths along the windows, and six more bordering a divider next to the bar. Between the two rows of booths, there were six four-top tables. The counting thing was something my brain did without instigation.

I was adding up the capacity of the restaurant in my head when a jovial voice interrupted me.

"Hi hon. Table for one this morning?" the twenty-something tattooed waitress with short blond hair asked as I walked toward the 'please wait to be seated' sign with a big buffalo on it. She was halfway across the room when she yelled, but nobody even turned to look at me. It appeared they were used to the yelling.

"Yes, please," I answered, smiling at being called 'hon' by someone at least ten years younger than me.

I noticed Thornton Caldwell and the other ATV rider sitting in the last booth along the right side, near the windows. That would explain why they didn't see me park. I pulled into the lot from the other side of the building and parked over there. They wouldn't have seen me from their side of the Golden Bear.

Using that fact as a reason for relief, I took in the grand atmosphere of the Golden Bear. It was a stereotypical mountain lodge motif, complete with a variety of moose, elk, deer and antelope heads mixed in with some trout. There were a few snowshoes mixed in, along with some old canoe paddles and fly rods. I was still looking around when the waitress came my way and motioned for me to follow her.

"How about over here, hon," she said as she led me to a booth along the windows but at the opposite end from Thornton Caldwell. Even if they knew what I looked like and wanted to find me, they couldn't see me from here. It was a good spot to enjoy my breakfast.

"This is perfect," I replied.

"Great. I'm Molly and I'll be taking care of you. Coffee?" she asked as she plopped a menu down on the table.

"Yes, please," I answered.

"There you go, hon. I'll be back in a minute to take your order," she said as she poured my coffee into a thick white mug with the image of a bear and the Golden Bear printed on it. I wondered if 'hon' was required or if she just picked it up on her own. Either way, it gave her an identity. As did the tattoos and the streaks of pink in her hair that I noticed when she turned around.

Molly was pleasant enough and worked hard to pay attention to all her dining guests. She scurried around from table to table while I looked at the menu. Contemplating the options, I settled on the Big Bear Breakfast. I almost went for the biscuits and gravy, but I knew they'd never be as good as the ones at Grandmother's Kitchen back in Woodland Park, so I passed on that option.

The coffee and the service were both good. And true to her word, Molly returned in just a few minutes to get my order.

As I sipped my coffee and waited for my food to be prepared, my phone buzzed in my pocket. It was Sergeant Theiss from Littleton. After looking around to make sure my phone conversation wouldn't bother anyone, I accepted the call.

"This is Keith," I said automatically.

"Mr. Morgan, this is Sergeant Theiss." The voice on the other end didn't sound friendly at all, but from what I had observed so far, she wasn't prone to a friendly tone.

"What can I do for you, Sergeant Theiss?" I asked, trying to counter her harshness with an overtly friendly response.

"I'm afraid we're going to need to talk to you again. Can you please make your way to the station?" She wasn't responding to my jovial tone, and was clearly in no mood to chat.

"Well, I'm afraid I'm a little busy right now. Can you tell me what this is about?" I asked, giving up on the jovial approach.

"Why didn't you tell us you were the beneficiary in Paul Frazier's will? The ONLY beneficiary, in fact?" She was once again straight to the point, but I understood why she was annoyed.

"To be honest, I didn't know that until last night," I answered.

"You expect me to believe that? You played me, Mr. Morgan. Now, I need you to come up here and fill us in on what else we don't know or I'm going to send someone to Woodland Park to cuff you and haul you in here anyway," she said, now beginning to raise her voice.

"Ok, I'll be honest. I'm not home," I said without elaborating.

At that moment, Molly came by with an enormous plate of eggs, sausage, bacon, toast and hash browns.

"Thank you, Molly. Could I please get some more coffee, too?" I said without moving the phone so Sergeant Theiss could hear.

"Sure, hon," Molly said as she turned away.

"Mr. Morgan, this is clearly far more serious than you believe it to be," Sergeant Theiss said.

"No, Sergeant Theiss, I would disagree with that. You see, I realize exactly how serious this is. You have evidence you don't know what to do with. In fact, I bet you don't even know what to ask me about your new evidence. I'm telling you right now, this has nothing to do with Paul's death. I just found out last night that I was named in Paul's will. Up to that moment, I had no idea. If you want to confirm this, feel free to call Jack Underhill from Carter and Underhill," I said, intentionally raising my voice.

"I'll do that right now, Mr. Morgan. But that doesn't excuse your absence of full disclosure. You need to get back here and finish your interview," she said, clearly feeling defeated.

"I answered every question you asked me. And I promise I will stop by when I'm free. Tell Jack I said hi," I said as I ended the call.

I couldn't help but smirk to myself as I picked up my fork and Molly returned with my coffee.

"Something funny?" Molly asked, making me realize my smirk was probably too big.

"Oh, yeah. You know how kids are," I answered.

"I sure do. Got three of 'em myself. But yours must not be like mine, because you were smiling," she said with a lighthearted smile as she finished pouring my coffee and headed to her other tables.

The meal was delicious, and I enjoyed all of it, along with two more cups of coffee. Somewhere in the middle of my meal, Thornton Caldwell and his friend stood up and left the Golden Bear. They walked right past my table without giving me the time of day. Seeing the two of them up close, I recognized an obvious resemblance. The other guy was either Thornton's younger brother or a close relative.

After finishing my breakfast and leaving Molly a twenty-dollar bill for her and her three kids, I headed out of the restaurant and stopped by the fly shop just outside the restaurant door. That stop cost me nearly two hundred dollars in flies, but also got me some new insight into what flies might be best for the local streams and rivers.

I was pushing the unlock button on my key fob and walking around to the back of my 4Runner when I stopped in my tracks. The phone call from Sergeant Theiss was apparently not my only interaction with law enforcement for the day.

There was a Dodge Durango painted with sheriff's colors parked crossways directly behind my 4Runner. I wasn't going anywhere.

As I rounded the back of the vehicle to see what was going on, I saw a sheriff talking to Thornton Caldwell and the guy I assumed to be his brother. They stopped when I walked up.

"Everything ok?" I asked as I opened the back of my 4Runner, dropped the bag of flies and closed the door.

"Mr. Morgan, I presume?" the sheriff asked as he walked my way cautiously. The other two stayed where they were.

"You ran my plates?" I answered, deflecting the answer.

"So, that's a yes?" the sheriff wasn't taking the bait. He was still several feet away, acting way too tense for my comfort. The sheriff was older than me and had a crisp, military look about him. He was about six feet tall, maybe a couple of inches shorter than me, and had a slender build. He had a crisp, tan sheriff's uniform on with a broad, level hat pulled low onto his head. His light colored hair was shaved close around the edges and was barely visible. His mirrored aviator sunglasses and thick blonde mustache, however, were making quite a statement.

His name plate said Hanson, but I didn't feel comfortable calling him that. He looked like he meant business, so I played along.

"Ok, so I guess that's a yes from you as well. I'm Keith Morgan," I answered.

"Can I see some identification, Mr. Morgan?" He still wasn't getting close to me.

"Sure. Can I ask what this is about?" I asked while I extracted my license from my wallet.

"You can," he replied.

"Ok. What is this about?" I asked, continuing to play his game.

"Do you want to tell me what you're doing in Cameron, Mr. Morgan?" he asked, ignoring my question.

"I don't," I answered, matching his move again.

That time, I actually saw the hint of a smile, as if he was enjoying this. He looked off into the distance, then back at me. He smiled and handed me my license.

"Alright, let's end this little dance. I'm Sheriff Hanson, and this is Thor and Bailey Caldwell," he said, instantly changing his tone. After motioning to the other two, he reached out his hand.

"Sorry for the theatrics, but we're a little on edge here," he said while I shook his hand.

"Oh yeah? Why is that?" I asked, wondering if he'd really tell me.

"Well, you see, these two boys lost their parents yesterday to a murder. Then they saw your truck near their property this morning and got suspicious. I'm sure you could forgive them for that," he said.

And in that little statement, I learned they were indeed brothers. I learned they had a good reason to sniff around the perimeter of their property, and I learned that Sheriff Hanson had decided I wasn't a threat. Or at least he was going to act that way.

"Oh, wow. That's terrible. I'm really sorry to hear that," I said, receiving hesitant yet firm handshakes from the Caldwell brothers while we nodded at each other.

"So, let me start again, Mr. Morgan. Can you please share your reason for being here in our fine town?" Sheriff

Hanson was being cordial, but sarcastic. I wasn't sure I was going to like this guy.

I paused for a second before answering and wondered if they'd know that Paul had been killed. I quickly deducted he hadn't yet done that level of research and tailored my answer accordingly.

"A buddy of mine owns the property where my truck was parked. He suggested I come out here to try the fishing on that creek, so I rented a cabin here in town and planned to see what he was talking about," I said.

"I see. What's your buddy's name?" Sheriff Hanson asked, pulling the notepad and pen out of his pocket.

"Paul Frazier," I said, without adding that he was dead. I knew he'd likely find out soon enough, and then we'd have a different conversation.

Sheriff Hanson looked at his notes.

"How do you know Mr. Frazier?" he asked.

"We go way back to my military days. And more recently, we've worked together for about five years," I answered.

"I see. Thank you for your service," Sheriff Hanson said, without looking up from his notes.

I nodded without responding. I never knew how to reply to that statement, as 'you're welcome' didn't seem appropriate.

"How long do you plan to be in town?" he asked, still scribbling in his notepad.

"Until Saturday," I answered, remembering when my cabin reservation ended.

"Do you mind if I get your number in case something comes up?" Sheriff Hanson asked as he finally stopped writing and looked up from his notes.

"Sure," I answered, and gave him my number.

"Thanks, Mr. Morgan. Have a good day," Sheriff Hanson said.

He got into his SUV and moved out of my way, but the Caldwell brothers stood there and watched me suspiciously.

I quickly found the cabin rental details on my phone and hit the link to the address. From my research, I knew it was close, but I didn't realize it was only a quarter mile away. My rental cabin was within walking distance of the Golden Bear.

Sheriff Hanson and the two Caldwell brothers watched as I got onto the highway for one block, then turned toward the Madison river to go to my rental cabin.

I hadn't planned to stay at the rental cabin after finding out how nice Paul's accommodations were, but after that encounter, I wasn't going back to Paul's cabin just yet.

Chapter Twenty-Two

I was worried the owner of my rental cabin might have determined I wasn't coming since I didn't show up yesterday. My reservation started then, but that no longer mattered. Since talking to Sheriff Hanson, I was all in on that idea now. Since my reservation only started the day before, I assumed all the entry instructions would still be the same.

Looking around subtly to see if I was being watched, I tried to look as casual as possible while unlocking the key box and pulling out the key to the front door of the cabin. The front door faced away from the parking area and toward the river, so I couldn't see if anyone had followed me or was watching the 4Runner.

Having left my fishing pack at Paul's cabin when I left for breakfast, I only had my overnight duffle bag in the back of the 4Runner. I had another fly rod, larger than what I needed for the small creek by Paul's cabin, but not the rest of my gear. I brought my duffle bag into the cabin with me, not really sure if I'd be back at Paul's place during the rest of my trip. The last thing I wanted to do was to get involved with a murder investigation and unintentionally expose details about Paul's cabin.

The cabin I had rented in Cameron sat directly next to the Madison river, which was a fantastic location. While taking a few deep breaths to get past the less-than-friendly introduction to Sheriff Hanson and the Caldwell brothers, I looked around inside. The cabin only had a rear loft as a sleeping area, with the bottom area devoted to the living area, a small kitchen with a dining table, and a bathroom. It was well equipped with fruit and snacks on the counter, several k-cups for the coffeemaker, and bottled water in the refrigerator. I started for coffee, then remembered I just had four cups at the Golden Bear and opted for water instead.

While I thought about how to navigate the rest of my day, I decided to slow down for a few minutes. I needed to catch up with the kids and to call Jen. I sat on the couch in the cabin and dialed Jamie's number. As soon as she answered, it was obvious they were out enjoying some activity and I was interrupting them.

"Hey dad. We're out. Can I call you back?" Jamie said as she accepted the call with talking and other noise in the background.

"What are you guys doing?" I asked without answering her question.

"We're in Branson at the go-karts," Jamie answered. Enough said.

"Oh, nice. That's awesome! No need to call back, honey, you guys just have fun. Love you, tell Kyle," I said, knowing my call was an unwanted deviation from their fun.

"Thanks dad. Love you, too," Jamie said as she hung up. I could hear her yelling 'Kyle, dad loves you' before the call disconnected. I smiled to think of the kids having fun, riding go-karts, and thoroughly enjoying their summer break barely forty-eight hours after it started.

After the brief call with Jamie, I walked outside to call Jen. The riverside porch was covered by the cabin's roof and had four metal deck chairs with flowery cloth cushions. There was a small table between each pair of chairs, perfect for my water. As nice as Paul's cabin was, the rental cabin had its charm, too. It had neighbors, though. There were similar cabins on either side. They weren't close enough where you'd hear each other talking, but I could clearly see both porches from where I sat.

Still, it was a nice place to be. I sat down watching the three fly fishermen in the river in front of me while I dialed Jen's number.

"Hey Keith, how's Montana?" Jen asked as she answered the call.

"It's a beautiful place. No doubt about it," I said, honestly, as I surveyed the surrounding landscape.

"So, how was Paul's fishing spot? Was it worth the trip?" Jen asked, noting the original reason I drove all this way.

"To be honest, yes. It was. But, as you probably expected, there was more to the story than that," I said, getting ready to reveal the discoveries of my last twenty-four hours to Jen.

"Why am I not surprised? So, what else did you discover in beautiful Montana?" Jen asked with a chuckle.

"First off, it isn't just a fishing spot. Paul also had a cabin up here. And using the word 'cabin' doesn't really do it justice. He has a hardened cabin built into the side of a mountain with enough computer horsepower to run NORAD," I said, obviously exaggerating a little.

"What?" Jen sounded shocked and confused.

"Yeah, ok, maybe not all of NORAD. But it's a lot. He has cameras all over the place running facial recognition software. The whole thing taps into some agency or agencies, I'm not sure who, and digs up data on everyone immediately with just the image of their face. It's almost creepy," I said, realizing I was already dumping a lot on her, even though I had a long way to go.

"Wait, what? Why would he have a place like that?" Jen asked.

Realizing I was talking out loud in an open area where my voice was probably traveling farther than I expected, I stood and went back inside the cabin to continue the conversation.

"Well, I guess he didn't want anyone to know what he was doing. It seems he drove much of The Association's research from here. Plus, he did a lot of very specific research directed at our old Hart International team in Afghanistan," I said.

"Oh, really? Why would he do that?" Jen asked, leading me through my story.

I proceeded to tell her about our old team, about some of the struggles they'd had, and about Paul's apparent obsession with Ivan Filipov. I stopped short of telling her about my wife and about being the beneficiary in Paul's will. She'd have enough to consume without those additional tidbits.

"Wow, Keith. I don't even know what to say. That's just too much," she said, making me glad I stopped where I did. Her usual cheerful tone now had an air of concern.

"And on top of that, I was stopped at breakfast this morning because it seems there was a murder at the ranch next to Paul's property. The sons of the murder victims saw my 4Runner and reported me to the sheriff. That made for a lovely exchange. Although I will say the breakfast was delicious," I said, trying to lighten the tone a bit.

"Keith, you need to go back home and never leave again!" Jen said, joking cautiously.

"Yeah, it seems that way," I said, just as a knock at the door startled me.

I looked out the window and sighed.

"And speak of the devil. It seems the good sheriff has returned," I said.

"Oh no. Be careful, Keith," Jen warned as we disconnected the call.

"Sheriff Hanson, what a pleasant surprise," I said sarcastically as I opened the door.

He wasn't impressed.

"Mr. Morgan," he said as a greeting, tipping his hat. He didn't pause.

"When was the last time you talked to your close friend, Paul Frazier?" Sheriff Hanson asked. He wasn't smiling, and it wasn't a happy question. He had found out Paul was dead.

So I leaned into the idea.

"The day before he died on the surgery table in Nashville," I answered, feeling my voice and my face harden.

"Ok, so you did know he was deceased. And why didn't you offer that bit of information over at the Golden Bear? You didn't feel that might have been important?" He asked.

"You didn't ask, and no, I didn't feel it was important to your investigation," I answered.

"Look, Mr. Morgan. I don't know what type of game you're playing, or what you're involved in, but this seems to be two trips you've taken where people have ended up dead. Let's hope they're not related. But either way, maybe it's time for you to stay home for a while," he said, echoing Jen's thought from a moment before.

"Yeah, maybe," I agreed, almost telling him someone had died in Littleton, too, but thinking better of it. He and Jen had a point.

"One thing just to be cautious. Do you mind if I look in your truck? I'd like to make sure there's nothing in there related to the murder over at Lazy J. The Caldwell boys are real suspicious of you and it would probably make them feel better if they know I had looked around," he said.

The idea got me fired up again.

"I'm not really here to make the Caldwell boys happy," I started, but took a breath when I saw his face turn red, "but I suppose it's ok."

"That's kind of you, Mr. Morgan," he said sarcastically as I closed the door and headed toward the parking area.

"Out of curiosity, what's the murder weapon you're looking for?" I asked, more out of curiosity than anything else.

"Well, a murder weapon would be helpful, but I'm more interested in seeing if you have any drones or drone equipment," he said as I unlocked the 4Runner and opened the doors.

"Drone equipment? Wow, that's a new one. I've never heard of a murderous farm drone. Go ahead and look, but that's not something I'm into," I said.

"The drone wasn't the murder weapon. It's just a potential lead. Any weapons in here?" Sheriff Hanson asked, more as a matter of process than an accusation. Everyone in that area carried guns.

"Nope, just the one on my belt," I answered. As I expected, that answer didn't phase him.

After looking around the front two rows and the back,

Sheriff Hanson seemed to get a little more comfortable.

"Alright. Thanks for your cooperation. I'll let the boys know we had this little chat," he said.

"Sure. And look, Sheriff Hanson, I'm sorry I happened to show up here in the middle of your murder investigation. I probably should have been more cooperative in front of the Caldwell brothers. I completely understand their frustration. If I was in their shoes, I'd want revenge, too. But it wasn't me," I said.

"Mr. Morgan, if I thought it might be you, I would have taken you in immediately. For your own safety as much as anything else. But even though I don't particularly like you, I don't think you murdered the Caldwells. You don't have it on your face. You were military, and I was too, so maybe it's a blind spot for me. If it is, I'll adjust. But for now, I'll try to get them to leave you alone," he said.

"Thanks. You were military, too?" I asked, following up on his comment.

"Yeah. Army, 82nd Airborne out of Fort Bragg," he answered with pride.

"Wow. Airborne, huh? Then I should thank you for your service. Middle East?" I asked, a new rapport emerging between us. Sheriff Hanson didn't look like he could hang with an airborne unit anymore, but that background forced me to respect him a little more.

"Yeah. Iraq. You?"

"Yeah, pretty much everywhere," I answered.

He nodded and turned to go.

"Thanks for your time, Mr. Morgan," he said as he tipped his hat once again.

"Sure thing," I replied with a nod.

I felt my initial feelings about Sheriff Hanson changing some as he got in his SUV and pulled away.

Chapter Twenty-Three

The brief exchange with Sheriff Hanson made me a little more comfortable being in Cameron, but not yet comfortable enough to head back to Paul's cabin. He might be convinced I wasn't involved with the Lazy J murders, but he mentioned the Caldwell brothers weren't convinced. And they seemed a little on edge to me.

I had a laptop in my duffle bag, so I pulled it out and did some independent research on some of the ideas Paul had been chasing in the bunker. Specifically, I wondered if it was really possible for Ivan Filipov to tinker with all the lives of our team in Afghanistan. I hadn't spoken to some of them in years, but decided to remedy that right then. I was going to call them to check in, and see if they believed Paul's suspicion about Filipov might be feasible.

The first one I remembered was Mark Stephenson. He was the most outgoing of all our team members, and the thought of him just made me smile. We always said he should be a recruiter or a salesman. Or even a lawyer. He could always swing people to his opinion, no matter how crazy it was.

I knew he had moved to Chicago, but that's all I knew. Doing a quick search on his name, I found a list of several Mark Stephenson's in Chicago. I scanned through until an image caught my eye. The image was a little scraggly, but it was him. In fact, the image was more than just scraggly. It was a mugshot. The sight of it shocked me, as Mark was the last person I would have thought would be in jail.

Mark had a wife named Marcia, which I remembered purely because of the similarity in their names. Mark and Marcia. I looked the names up together and found an address. It only took a few more minutes to find a phone number.

I called Mark's number, but there was no answer. Wondering if he was still in jail, I went back to the internet to find news about his jail sentence. Mark was convicted of embezzlement, bribery and some lesser offenses and had spent thirty days in jail six months ago. The whole story left me shaking my head. That wasn't the Mark I knew.

Searching more on the story, I found another link that made the jail story seem trivial. Mark's name was in an obituary, along with a more recognizable photograph. The story said he had died ten days ago. And the way the story was written, it appeared he had taken his own life.

The idea made me sick to my stomach. It also made me even more determined to find out if Paul's theories about Filipov were true. I frantically typed in the phone number for Marcia Stephenson and waited. Just before the call went to voicemail, she answered.

"Hello," she said suspiciously. Realizing she wouldn't know who I was from the Colorado number, I quickly responded.

"Hey Marcia, this is Keith Morgan. I don't know if you

remember me, but I'm an old friend of Mark's from our Army days," I said, trying to make sure she didn't hang up.

"Hi, Keith. Sure, I remember you. You're the Colorado guy, right? And Beth is your wife?" Marcia said in a friendly voice, innocently triggering pain I wasn't expecting.

"Uh, yeah. That's right." I was fumbling for words.

"What can I do for you, Keith? I've gotten a couple of calls from Mark's old buddies over the last few days," she said, sounding tired.

I debated telling her Beth had died five years ago, but decided not to. I could share that later if it was ever necessary.

"I saw the news about Mark. I'm just so sorry. And shocked. Shocked and sorry," I said, shaking my head as I struggled to find the right words. They didn't come.

"Thanks Keith, I appreciate it. I really do. But just know that Mark wasn't the guy you all remembered. The last year has been awful, and he just wasn't himself. I don't know what happened, but the man that killed himself wasn't the man I married," she said, showing more strength than most people I knew.

"Yeah, I saw some of that in old news reports. I wish I would have known about all that, and maybe helped. I don't know if there was anything I could have done, but it just feels horrible. Did he ever give any reason why he committed those crimes? Was he able to talk about it?" I asked, steering her toward my personal agenda for the call.

"No, he never really did. Right up to the very end, he just said he didn't do any of it. He refused to admit it. He said he was framed and none of it was true," she answered.

"But you think it was true? You think he did it?" I asked, realizing I might be going too far.

"Look, Keith, I know you guys try to protect each other

and stuff, but the police and the judge were absolutely convinced Mark was guilty. It would have been better if he would have admitted it, but he just never owned up to it," she said with resolve.

"Understood, Marcia. So you don't think it's possible that there was someone playing games with his life, like a puppet master controlling all the evidence?" I asked, exposing Paul's suspicion with the question.

There was no answer, only a sniff. Then a light sob. Then a quivering voice.

"That's what he always said. He said he was a puppet, and someone else was pulling the strings. Why are you asking these questions, Keith?" I felt I might have taken Marcia far enough, but her response spurred me on.

"It's more of a hunch, I think, Marcia. That's it. Can you tell me when and how this all started?" I asked, cautiously.

"It was about two years ago, give or take. Before that, things were great. He was doing well, our marriage was doing well, the children were doing well. Everything was great. I mean, we weren't rich or anything, but we were fine. He got a job here in Chicago selling stuff for a bank, and he really took to it. His commissions gave us some nice vacations, and we even had enough to start saving for a house," she started, then paused.

"And what happened?"

"There was some money stolen at the bank. They said someone made some false expense reports or something, and they found the money deposited into Mark's account. There was a big investigation inside the company, and eventually the police were brought in," Marcia said, regaining her composure as she relayed the story.

"And they fired Mark?" I asked, pushing her along.

"Yeah. First they fired him, then they filed charges against him. Eventually, they had him sent to jail, but he never had to spend time there. They gave him a suspended sentence because they were out of space up here. But he never got over it," she said, getting quiet.

"And what did Mark say happened?"

"He said he never stole anything. He said the account wasn't even his. He said that until the day...," she stopped talking at that point.

"He couldn't get another job doing something similar?" I asked.

"No, that's the thing. The publicity must have gotten him blackballed in the industry. He couldn't get anything. He tried all over the country and got nothing. People would call him back, then would just back away. He would have tried in other countries if he was able to leave," she said, reengaging.

"So he just faded from there?" I knew I was getting close to the end now, and pretty much had the information I wanted.

"Yeah. After he got fired and couldn't get a new job, he started drinking and going crazy about the whole thing. He said he felt his life was being controlled by someone else, like I said. He just couldn't take it. It got to where he sounded delusional. I had to tell him to get help with, you know, a therapist or something. He flatly refused, saying he did nothing wrong, so I asked him to leave. He was destroying our family." She began to sob again.

"That does sound delusional. You're right," I admitted.

"It does, doesn't it? But he stuck to it. And he kept drinking. He called me all the time, saying he loved me and the kids. He just wasn't right. Then, there was that night a month ago. He called me drunk again. I pushed him to get help again. He said he never did anything wrong again. Then he told me to tell the kids I love them. He said he felt there was nothing else he could do, that someone else had taken everything from him. The police found his car in the parking lot outside his apartment. He had shot himself in the head," she said, now sobbing again.

I felt horrible for pushing her to this point.

"It's ok," I said, trying to be comforting.

"No, it's not. I kicked him out, Keith. I said he was wrong. I told him he needed help. I asked the judge for a divorce. And now you're telling me you have a hunch he may have been right after all? That's not ok," Marcia said between sobs.

"I don't want to draw conclusions, Marcia. Believe me, I don't. But at least one of our fellow team members from Afghanistan has run into similar circumstances. They, too, are convinced their life is being manipulated by someone else. I'm simply trying to find out if that's true," I said, realizing the truth, as Paul perceived it, would hurt Marcia.

"That better not be true, Keith. I'm telling you that better not be true! If someone did this to my husband, to me, to the kids... it just better not be true. If it is, I'm going to kill them myself. Please tell me it's not true!" Now she was screaming and crying at the same time, and I realized I had gone far enough. Maybe even too far.

"I'm sorry, I'm sorry, Marcia. No, I can't tell you anything for sure. I'm just looking into this for our team, that's all," I said, trying to calm her a bit. It worked a little, but only after one more outburst.

"You wouldn't ask if you didn't think it might be true, Keith. My God! They killed my husband!" Marcia screamed before calming just a bit.

"Honestly, I hope I'm wrong," I responded, even though I didn't believe I was.

"Keith, if there's anything I can do to help find out if someone did this to Mark, let me know. I want them to hang," she said.

"Sure. I'll do that. For now, the only thing I would ask for is to send me any information Mark may have collected that he thought was not his doing. That might help. Again, I'm just looking at ideas right now. There's no reason to suspect it's true," I said.

"Yeah, right, Keith? I know better. And yes, I'll find whatever I can find and send it to you today," she said through clenched teeth.

I gave her my contact details, and we hung up. I almost regretted making that call, because I was convinced I had created a monster in Marcia Stephenson.

Chapter Twenty-Four

Even though the call with Marcia Stephenson was horribly painful and made me feel terrible for her, it also led me to believe Paul may have been onto something. I didn't know if Filipov was the one 'pulling the strings' in Mark's life, but Paul seemed to think he was. And Marcia's version of Mark's final months didn't derail that possibility.

My next call was going to be Bart. After hearing about Mark, I was eager to find out if Bart was alive and doing ok. I knew he was in Tampa the last time I talked to him, so I started there. Like the research on Mark, I did a few searches for Bart's contact details and eventually found a mobile number under his name. I wished I had access to all the search capability in Paul's cabin for the task.

I sat back on the couch and took a deep breath, hoping the call with Bart didn't go as bad as the previous one.

"Hello?" Bart answered the phone with a cautious question, which was odd. He was always the happy, outgoing one.

"Hey Bart, it's Keith Morgan," I said, trying to set the happy tone he usually initiated.

"Oh hey, Keith, what's up? I haven't heard from you in years, brother!" His voice brightened up a little, but still sounded strained.

"Yeah, I know, man. I'm sorry about that. I always promise myself I'll do better, but life speeds on, you know," I said.

"Don't I know it," he replied, still not the happy Bart I remembered.

"Hey listen, Bart. I'm following up with everyone from the old team based on some direction from Paul Frazier," I said.

"How's ol' Paul doin'?" Bart asked, lightening up a little.

Unfortunately, I had to bring him back down with the answer.

"Well, I'm sorry to say Paul passed away about ten days ago. He was on a trip to Nashville and had to have some surgery that ended up being fatal," I said, intentionally leaving out the details that would take too long to explain.

"Oh no. I'm really sorry about that, brother. He was a good man," Bart replied, leaving the moment of cautious cheer behind.

"Yeah, he sure was. We're all sorry, for sure. But the reason I called has to do with some research he was doing before he died. He has sort of handed it to me, and I feel I should continue looking into his ideas. From your response, I guess he hasn't spoken to you?" I asked.

"No. No, he hasn't. Why?" Bart asked.

"Paul was concerned there might be an outside party trying to manipulate the lives of our team members. I'm not sure if it was possible or not, but I'm curious if you've experienced anything that might feel like that?" I set him up to tell me the story that Paul had been tracking.

"You've got to be kidding me. Paul knew about this?

YES! I have absolutely experienced this. I'm still in the middle of it," he said.

Then he mumbled some things in the background.

"I can't believe Paul knew. Wait, what am I saying? Of course, he knew. Paul knew everything," he said quietly, mostly to himself.

"Ok, so you think it's possible? If you had to take a step back, what are the things you have seen that might have been externally influenced?" I put my phone on speaker, got my pen and notebook, and got ready to write.

"Well, it started with simple identity theft stuff. I noticed a credit card I didn't recognize on my credit report. I got that fixed, then added one of those credit protection services. A couple months later, it happened again," Bart said.

"You mean the credit protection service blocked it?" I asked.

"No. That's the crazy part. Somehow, they hacked my login to the service and changed the phone numbers. Then they just approved the accounts without me knowing it. I just noticed my credit score tanked again when I logged into my bank," he answered.

"So, that was it? They just used your credit?" Bart's story sounded nowhere near as bad as Mark's.

"Oh, no. That was just the beginning. They started toying with me. They kept running up my credit cards, buying crazy stuff with them, and keeping my credit score low. I wanted to buy a house but could never get my score high enough to qualify. These guys just stayed on me. And they were good at it. They had my photo somehow, probably from my license or passport, and knew all my personal data. Every time I'd try to block it, they'd take my identify and just keep it going. They're relentless," Bart said, his voice getting louder.

I was seeing why Bart wasn't so happy these days. He continued.

"And then they got to my bank accounts. I'd be out at dinner, or at the gas station, or whatever, and my debit card would randomly decline. I never knew if my card would ever work or not. Right now, I just run to the ATM as soon as I get paid to pull out as much cash as I can. I'm literally paying my rent in cash to make sure these guys don't get it," he said, sounding utterly defeated.

"Are the police helping?" I asked, perhaps a bit optimistically.

"Well, yeah. But they're slow and their technology just isn't as good. The criminals definitely have the upper hand on the technology front. They know it, too. I was at a Rays game with my buddies a couple of weeks ago and we went to get some beer and brats. My card declined at the counter, so I tried my backup and found out they were all full. And it wasn't that they were full, it was worse. They knew I was at the game. I called the card company and had them look up the transactions. These guys were walking around the stadium buying crap right there at the venue. They were buying memorabilia and stuff that I'd never seen. All while I was watching the game. My buddies had to help me pay in cash. Do you know how embarrassing that is?" It was a rhetorical question, but I was understanding his pain.

"So, you just live on cash right now? That's how far the damage has gone?" I felt bad about trivializing Bart's trouble, but I still had Mark in the back of my mind.

"I wish. Just last week my employer ran a background check and found out I have a horrible credit score. I'm in the financial services industry, so they watch closely for things like that. They flagged me as a potential risk because my score was so low. I'm on probation, with ninety days to get it straightened out. And yet I have no idea how to do it. It's like someone else is running my life right now and I have lost control," he said, mimicking what Mark had been saying.

"Yeah. It does sound like that. And I'm not sure how far Paul had gotten with his research, but he thinks Ivan Filipov may somehow be behind this. You remember him?" I asked.

"Yeah, that Russian dude who we took down in Afghanistan? Paul thought he was behind this?" Bart didn't sound convinced.

"That was his thought, but I'm not completely sure why he thought that. I'm still learning. Thanks for the scoop, Bart. I'll stay in touch," I said.

"Let me know if you find anything, Keith. I'd love to find whoever's doing this and give them a piece of my mind," Bart said, with anger slipping into his usually jovial tone.

"Will do. Thanks Bart," I said as we ended the call.

After the first two calls, I was thinking Paul was onto something. Gerry was next, so I started searching on 'Whitney Cheevers' to see what I could find on her.

To my surprise, much like I saw with Mark, that search immediately turned up mug shots. Gerry had been arrested for drugs and, to my horror, murder.

I sat back on the couch and thought about what I had found. Was it possible that Filipov could get someone convicted of murder? Maybe Gerry's case was not really his doing. Nonetheless, I found her location and started trying to see how I might talk to her.

Gerry was an inmate at the California State Prison, Los

Angeles County. With a little digging, I found out she had access to email and could make phone calls. After leaving my number with the contact officer, I found her email address and sent her my number. I didn't know how long it would take for her to call, so I set my sights on the last name on the list: Steve Chandler.

I had his number on my phone already, so there was no internet searching required on this one. I put my notes down and took a deep breath while I waited for him to answer. This whole idea was getting more bizarre with every call.

Steve's phone went to voicemail, so I left him a message. Then I suddenly had nothing to do and sat staring out the window at the Madison river. If only I had carried my fishing pack and net out of Paul's cabin. Then I got an idea. I had another rod and reel and some waders in the 4Runner. I had the flies I had bought at the shop in front of the Golden Bear. I really just needed a net and a few small items.

Knowing I had to wait for Gerry and Steve's calls, I walked out the door and headed for the fly shop in front of the Golden Bear. It was a nice day, and the shop was nearby, so it was a pleasant trip.

The walk from my rental cabin to the shop only took five minutes. As I meandered along, I got a sense of the little mountain town of Cameron. There were several newer cabins along the river in small clusters. They looked like rental units or vacation cabins.

The highway that went through town, 287, had two lanes. The entire town, at least the part I could see, only spread one block wide on the east, and two blocks in some places on the west. Then the west side of town hit the river valley. In the center of town, there were some older buildings that looked more like permanent residences. The Golden Bear was next to that cluster.

I went in and had no trouble picking up enough supplies to spend a couple of hours on the Madison River. The entire shopping trip only took twenty minutes, and in another ten minutes I was walking along the bank of the Madison River looking for the best place to ambush prey if I was a trout.

Before I even wet my line in the river, my phone buzzed with an incoming call. It was from a number in California. I assumed it must be Gerry. The prison communication system was more efficient than I expected.

"This is Keith," I said, answering as quickly as I could and not knowing if it would be her or some sort of automated system.

"Hey Keith, it's Whitney," she said, sounding exactly the same as she did the last time I talked to her, just a little tired.

I started walking back toward the cabin as we spoke.

"Whitney, so good to hear from you. I'd ask you how you're doing, but I think I already know," I said, not knowing a good way to start the conversation.

"Yeah. Since you contacted me, I guess you know. And you didn't even call me Gerry," she said, a slight crackle in her voice.

"I can call you Gerry if you want," I said with a chuckle.

"No, no. Whitney is fine. And look, I'm not trying to be mean, but people can't see me crying here. So if I yell, I'm doing it to make it look like I'm mad. Don't be offended," she said, hissing a little as she talked.

"Sure, no problem. And you only have fifteen minutes, right?" I had seen the time limit in my internet searches.

"Yeah, so what's up?"

"This is going to sound strange, probably, but I'm just going to put it out there," I said.

Then I received another incoming call. It was Steve Chandler. Whitney heard it.

"Don't leave me hanging like that," she said, afraid I'd put her on hold.

"I won't. But this is Steve Chandler. I've got to share the same message for him, so is it ok if I join him to this call?" I asked.

"Well sure! Might as well get the old gang back together," she said. I couldn't tell if she was angry or excited.

Either way, I joined Steve to the call and told him who he was talking to.

Then I told Gerry and Steve about Paul's research on Filipov.

Chapter Twenty-Five

My initial explanation to Gerry and Steve only took a few minutes, and both of them listened quietly. I told them about Mark and Bart. Then I told them how Paul thought Ivan Filipov was behind all of it. I stopped short of telling them I was in Montana visiting Paul's cabin.

It was Gerry who spoke first. Her voice was firm and angry. Very angry.

"I've been telling everyone this whole thing was set up from the beginning! Someone has been manipulating every piece of evidence in my case. If I find out it was Filipov..." then her voice trailed off. I wondered if she was trying to avoid being heard by the other inmates.

"We can't get ahead of ourselves. I just need to know what makes you believe you were set up. I've talked to Mark's wife, I've talked to Bart, and now I've got you two. I'm getting quite a list, but I need your thoughts to help guide my research," I said.

Steve chimed in next.

"Look, I'm guessing I've got more time than Gerry, so let's let her go first," he said.

Whitney wasn't phased by the use of her old nickname. She just launched.

"As I told the police, I was set up from the beginning. I've never done drugs. I've never sold drugs. I wasn't at the meeting site where that druggie got killed, and I never shot the weapon they found in my house. Is that about enough?" She was hissing again, which seemed to be her way of avoiding sobs.

"Ok, so start from the beginning. I don't know all the evidence they used, but I can dig through it in your court documents if I need to. Where do you think they fabricated evidence?" I asked, trying to get some direction for my research.

I had also reached the cabin porch and dropped my fly rod, net and small bag of gear there. I felt better talking about all this inside the cabin, so I went inside. While I was probably far from any sort of listening device out here in mountains of Montana, there was something about talking in the open air that made me uncomfortable.

"The first one was my phone. They claim they had my phone tracked to the location of the murder, but I was never there. Obviously, they could have stolen my phone, but I think they somehow spoofed my GPS location. Then they had recorded phone calls between me and that druggie about the pickup. But I never made those calls," she said and paused for a moment, allowing Steve to jump in.

"Neither one of those is all that hard to do these days. You can definitely spoof the phone's GPS location and you can use AI to replicate someone's voice without them knowing it. I've had similar issues with the voice imperson-ation," he said.

"Ok, what next?" I asked, trying to get as much informa-tion from her in fifteen minutes as I could.

"They had a gun with my prints that they 'found' in my house. But I'd never seen the gun. It was a Glock. I don't use Glocks. And the easiest of all were the drugs. They said they found drugs at my house consistent with what that guy had been using. That is probably the easiest one for them to set up," she said.

"That's quite a list. It's a little more extreme than the others, but it certainly sounds similar," I said.

We chatted about Whitney's arrest and trial for a few minutes, but it seemed everything was built on that original evidence. Before we knew it, the fifteen minutes were about up.

"Keith, if you find who did this, I can't tell you what I'm going to do to them. They've taken my life and destroyed it. I have nothing left," she said, hissing again.

"As I've told our other team members, we can't get ahead of ourselves. As far as I can tell, Paul was operating on a hunch. It sounds like it was a solid hunch, but a hunch nonetheless. If I find more, I'll let you know," I said.

I could hear Whitney yelling at someone in the background for a few seconds, then she returned.

"My time is up. Please let me know what you find," she said as she hung up.

That left me and Steve on the phone. We both took deep breaths after absorbing what Whitney had been through.

"Did Paul have enough evidence for you, Keith? Do you believe Filipov is behind all this?" Steve asked after a few seconds.

"Before I answer, why don't you tell me about your situation," I said, remembering Paul had lined through all the items next to Steve's name on the notes I found in the bunker.

"After listening to Gerry... or... Whitney, I feel guilty even talking about the things I've seen. It's nothing like Whitney, or like Mark, or even Bart." He paused, but I stayed quiet.

"It started maybe a year and a half ago, or more. I had some typical fraud stuff on my credit report, which I watched like a hawk. I paid for a service already, so it was pretty easy to see it wasn't mine. That was the first thing I can think of, and it was the easiest," he said.

"That sounds like Mark. That's how he said his started," I said.

"Yeah, well. I wish he knew his way around the internet and all these fraud services like I did. Maybe he could have stopped all this before it got to him like it did," Steve said, his voice beginning to verge on anger. Or maybe it was regret.

"You could have never known this was happening, Steve. Nor could I," I said.

"Yeah, I know," he said, not sounding convinced.

"So you mentioned to Whitney that you had a similar experience with an AI generated voice. How did that come about?" I asked, getting back to my notepad.

"Mine was a little different. They must have known I had thwarted their other attempts. They called my bank here in Billings and tried to get a second mortgage on my property," he said.

"Wait a minute, you're in Montana? I thought you were in North Carolina? Your phone number is..." I was surprised to hear Steve was nearby, but he cut me off.

"Yeah, yeah, yeah. I know people think I need to get my number changed, but I'm used to this one. It throws people off a little, like it did you, and it's the one everybody knows," he said.

"Ok, sorry to interrupt. What about the bank?" I asked, getting back to the topic at hand.

"It's a little bank, and they know me. So when this all started, I set up an agreement with them to call or text me if they ever got any correspondence. I expected it to be used only for email or online messages or stuff like that, but they took it a step further. When someone called in saying they were me, and sounding like me, they immediately sent me a text message to verify I was on the phone with them. I wasn't, so they initiated their fraud protection and recorded the call. They kept the person talking for several minutes. The voice sounded just like me, Keith. This AI stuff is scary good for that. But after a little while, the person realized they weren't getting anywhere and hung up," Steve said.

"Ok, so that's why..." I started to mention the post it note I had seen in Paul's bunker, but stopped short.

"That's why you never got to the point of the other three," I finished.

"I guess so," he said.

"Did they ever get to your crypto?" I asked, knowing that was where Steve kept most of his wealth. He had been heavily involved with crypto since its inception.

"Not that I can tell. I watch that stuff closely, and I've seen nothing strange there. All my accounts are intact," he said. That meant Steve was still a wealthy man.

"And did you see any other things that might have fit the idea Paul was pursuing?" I asked, seeing that Steve had escaped any impact from the other attacks.

"Now that I think about it, I have seen a major increase in hacking attempts on my network at home. As you know, I have a pretty sophisticated setup for all the sleuthing I do for The Association. I get constant attacks from the typical sources, but they really started picking up about four or five months ago. I thought it was just a normal increase based on geopolitical activity, but this makes me think I should look a little closer," he said.

"Yeah, ok. If this whole thing is really Filipov, it looks like you're the only one that avoided significant impact," I said.

"On that note, you haven't mentioned anything about yourself, Keith. You've talked about the rest of us being attacked, but you haven't mentioned yourself or Paul. Is it only us, or are you leaving that part out?" Steve asked, bringing me back to the topic I had been keeping in the back of my mind.

It took me a second to figure out how to answer without hissing like Whitney.

"I'm not sure what Paul had on himself. I didn't get that far. But I found some notes about my personal situation," I said, stopping to take a breath.

"He thought Filipov may have been behind my wife's car accident. The one that killed her. Paul thought Filipov killed my wife," I said, trying but failing to hide my anger.

"Oh no. I'm sorry, Keith, I didn't mean to drag you into a memory like that," Steve said.

"It's ok. It's a fair question. But honestly, Steve, I'm not sure about all this. That one sounds a little far-fetched to me," I said, trying to calm myself down.

"And Paul? What did he think they were doing to him?" Steve asked.

"I didn't find anything he had documented about himself," I said before admitting what I had been feeling for the last few days.

"But I think Ivan Filipov had Paul killed," I said.

"What? You said he died. You didn't say he was killed,"

Steve said. It was true. I hadn't mentioned the circumstances around Paul's death on any of my other calls with the team.

"I didn't want to get everyone spun up yet. There's a lot more research to do," I said.

"How can I help with the research, Keith? You know this stuff is right in my wheelhouse," Steve said. I had considered getting him involved earlier, but now was as good a time as any.

Then I had a sudden thought that stopped me. It was the last line in Paul's note to me.

Trust no one.

Did that include our team? Did it include Steve? I decided I need help too badly to argue, so I let him in on the first piece of the puzzle.

"Maybe I can use your help. When I was in Paul's condo the other day, there was a rack of servers in his spare bedroom."

Steve started laughing.

"I knew that guy was way more technical than he let on. His questions were always way too detailed," he said between chuckles.

"Yeah, apparently. But here's the thing. I have no idea what those servers are for or what they do. The police may have them now...," I said without thinking.

"Wait, what? The police might have them? Why is that?"

I had stepped right into the story without considering that I hadn't told Steve about what happened at Paul's condo in Littleton. Now I was past the point of no return on that topic. I decided to let him in on that piece without telling him about the cabin in Montana.

The warning from Paul still kept resonating in my head. Trust no one.

"Do you have a minute, Steve? There is more to this story than I've told you so far," I said.

Chapter Twenty-Six

I shared enough detail with Steve to get him started on the research of the servers in Paul's condo. After I spoke with Sergeant Theiss, Steve was granted permission to make sure there was no critical information for Rocky Mountain Equity on those servers. At least that was the cover I used.

Steve said he'd be at the condo later that day. He had already booked a flight.

The conversations with Steve went into the early afternoon, and I still wanted to get back out to the cabin. Knowing I should, once again, get out before dark, I felt the need to get there soon. After tidying up a few things in the rental cabin, I hopped into the 4Runner and headed out.

Forty-five minutes later, I was stepping into Paul's cabin once again. Annoyingly, his welcome message started again when I went in the front door. I immediately determined I'd have to figure out how to turn that off. That time, I didn't watch the greeting. Instead, I went straight to the closet, twisted the coat hanger and went into the bunker.

I only had a couple of hours for research and I had two

big topics to cover. First, I wanted to find out why Paul had taken on all the assignments to hurt Ivan Filipov. Second, I was determined to find any evidence Paul had uncovered on Filipov's involvement with the recent struggles of our team. The discussions with them had me fired up to right those wrongs, if at all possible. I was hopeful Paul's research would start me down that path.

Back at the keyboard in the bunker, I resumed the search I had started the day before on Ivan Filipov. Once again, the search seemed to take forever compared to the other searches I had done, but that time, I wasn't going to get distracted by other activities. Instead, I just waited for Filipov's search to complete.

Once the search completed, I had a list of links with data about Ivan Filipov. The list differed from the results I had gotten for the American searches, but still there were plenty of links. They appeared to be news stories with dates, so I started my research with the oldest one. That story was from our team's work in Afghanistan.

The link to the news about Afghanistan didn't surprise me at all. It summarized our operations against arms trading outposts in the region, and Filipov was just mentioned in passing. Most of the stories immediately following described the operations our team had completed, which I knew intimately. I didn't really need to rehash those details.

One story, however, caught my eye. It mentioned a theft of gold and cash from one of Filipov's command posts. That theft, as far as I was aware, had never happened. Our team tagged and processed everything of value from all those weapons caches, including gold and cash. It was common, however, for the story to be twisted whenever we shut down operations like this. I shook my head at the thought of the media distorting the details of our operation like that.

The next thing that I noticed, however, was the value of the stash that was stolen. It was thirty million dollars. That amount was remarkably close to the amount of Paul's investments shortly after returning from Afghanistan. I noticed the similarity, then immediately moved on. It had to be just a coincidence. There was no way Paul took that money to fund this whole thing.

Was there?

Backing out and looking at the rest of the news stories, I found a story that was only about six months old. It was the most recent one in the list. That would put it just after I was in the shootout with the Russian team at Willow Creek near my home in Colorado. The story was pulled from another source that was not public, and didn't have a news agency attribution on it. I was curious where it came from, but even more curious about the story itself.

The text indicated Ivan Filipov had been relieved of his duties in Moscow. It didn't give a reason or a new position, but simply said he was relieved. I wondered if this move had to do with the work we had done with The Association to take down his political tampering in Washington, but there was no sign of that in the story. Still, the timing was ironic.

There were several other stories about Filipov over the years, but most were of little interest. They described different positions he had taken, places he had traveled, his family members, and not much more.

The work Paul had done compiling evidence about all the things happening to our team was much more complex. I started with the data about Mark and never got to anyone else. I tried to find the evidence pointing to Filipov, but the amount of data Paul had compiled was enormous. He had network traces, IP addresses, MAC addresses, a variety of names and aliases, and more online accounts listed than I could follow.

Plus, it seemed he was using another data search capability that was getting into far more detail than a typical internet search could find. This was going to take forever. Or I was going to have to get some help.

I had already sent the most technical guy I knew down to Littleton to check out Paul's condo. And I was still cautiously curious why all Steve's attacks from Filipov had been thwarted and nobody else's were. Yes, Steve was probably far more technically savvy than anyone else, but it still made me curious.

Without more deliberation, I called Jen to see if she could come help me try to solve this. It was getting late, so I headed out of the cabin just before dark. I was still concerned about staying out there at night, knowing the Caldwell boys were already suspicious of me. I didn't need to give them a reason to dig around that cabin.

As I was trudging through the woods toward the 4Runner, I called Jen to solicit her expertise.

"Hey Keith, what's up?" Jen answered in just a few seconds, once again in her traditional jovial voice. Her attitude, as usual, was infectious.

"Hey Jen. Just wanted to give you an update from Montana and, like I always seem to do, ask for your help," I said with a sigh.

"I'm sorry, the person you have reached is not available. Please leave a message." Jen joked in response.

"Too late, sorry," I chuckled in response. "But you do always have the option to decline," I said.

"Fair enough. Let me hear the options," she said.

"I mentioned everything Paul had set up in and around the cabin. I started looking into some of the research on our old Hart International team, and quite frankly, it's just too much for one person to consume quickly. And given someone has already robbed Paul's condo to find something, probably money, I'm thinking this really is urgent," I said.

"So, you need another pair of hands?"

"Yeah, I suppose that's it," I replied.

"And there are trout in the stream up there?" Jen also enjoyed fly-fishing.

"There sure are," I said with a smile.

"I'll be there as quickly as I can," she responded.

"I should have led with the trout, huh," I said.

"Yes, you should have. Yesterday. My bag would have already been packed," she joked.

"Ok, I'll see you later. I'm guessing you can't get a flight out tonight, so I'll probably see you tomorrow," I said.

"Yeah, maybe. Or I may drive. I'm not a huge fan of airports," she replied, echoing my own thoughts.

"Ok. Let me know. I'll text you the address of my rental cabin in town," I said.

We disconnected the call, and I sent her the address. I had lots of research to do, but getting out of the woods was the right decision. Plus, I was getting hungry. Since the Golden Bear was the only place around, my dinner destination was set.

Forty-five minutes later, I pulled into the parking lot at the Golden Bear, just like I did at breakfast earlier that day. Except this time, I parked on the side where the restaurant windows were. I didn't want to be surprised by the Caldwell boys again.

Molly wasn't working the evening shift. The server's name was John, and he was far more jovial than a server at the Golden Bear should be. By the time I finished my ribeye and fries, I knew more about him, his family, his friends, and his cat than I was comfortable knowing. But the food was good, and I didn't mind the conversation, even if it was a little personal.

Midway through the meal, I saw the Caldwell brothers come in again. They joined the scene in the bar area of the Golden Bear, which had been steadily picking up throughout my meal. Clearly, the Friday night patrons shifted from a restaurant crowd to a bar crowd as the night went on. I had arrived just in time to see the transition. The Caldwell boys seemed to notice me, but didn't pay much attention.

I was enjoying a glass of Moose Drool and waiting for John to return with my credit card when my phone buzzed with a local Montana number. The only local person I could think of who had my number was Sheriff Hanson. So I reluctantly answered the call.

"This is Keith," I said, since I was pretty sure the caller knew who I was, anyway.

"Mr. Morgan, you seem to have left out a few things about your friend Paul. And about your activities in Colorado. And about your being the beneficiary to Paul's will," Sheriff Hanson said, clearly not interested in taking time for chit cat.

I guessed Sheriff Hanson had been in touch with Sergeant Theiss in Littleton. He had done his homework.

"Ok. What would you like to know?" I said, looking around to make sure nobody could hear the conversation. The restaurant only had a few customers left, so nobody was close enough to hear.

"Well, I guess I'd like to know what else you're hiding," he said.

"To be clear, I wasn't hiding anything. You never asked

about any of those things," I replied, realizing my response would not sit well with him.

I heard Sheriff Hanson sigh deeply.

"Just tell me you're not out here to prep that property for sale to the Krohl's, and we'll leave it at that for now," he said, clearly frustrated.

"I am not prepping the place to sell to anyone," I replied, honestly.

"Fair enough. We'll be talking," he said as he ended the call.

During our chat, John had returned my credit card with my receipt and had waved goodbye. I signed for my meal and headed out to the 4Runner for my last night in the rented cabin by the Madison.

The Caldwell boys, clearly several beers in at that point, stumbled off their barstools and followed me out.

I looked for any of their buddies to follow, but none did. It seemed they were taking this venture on their own. I slowed to let them get close as I rounded the corner of the building toward my 4Runner. There were several cars still in the lot, so I weaved in and out of a couple, just to see what they'd do.

They followed my same path until I got to the truck. Then Bailey went around toward the front of the 4Runner and Thornton stayed behind me near the back. When I got to the door of my vehicle, Bailey held the door shut so I couldn't open it.

"Mr. Caldwell," I greeted in my most courteous voice.

"What can I do for you two gentlemen?" I asked, stepping back and letting the two of them get closer.

"We know you had something to do with the death of our parents. Now you're going to pay," Bailey said as he lunged forward for a swing at me. Apparently, he had more beer than I thought, as I easily dodged his lunge and pulled him forward. He crashed into his brother and turned around, fuming.

"I told the sheriff why I was here," I said, wondering if there was any chance of reasoning with them in their condition.

"I heard you. But it's just too much of a coincidence that you showed up on that property the day after we find the Russian drone. And I know you have that drone out there somewhere on that property. We're going to find it to prove you did it," he said, bringing his fists up to his chin like a boxer.

But I wasn't paying attention anymore. All I heard was 'Russian drone.'

"Wait a minute. The drone was Russian?" I asked.

The question confused them.

"Yeah, why?" Thor asked, stepping in front of his brother. He didn't seem quite as irritable, or drunk, as Bailey.

"Then I'm not sure the drone was looking at the Lazy J after all. I'd like to know more about what you found," I said.

The entire focus of my trip just changed. Someone was snooping on Paul's property, not the Lazy J ranch.

Chapter Twenty-Seven

The Caldwell brothers calmed down a bit when I started asking questions, but they were still amped up from the volume of alcohol they had consumed. Still, I was able to look at the photos on Bailey's phone and to get an idea of what they found. They knew very little about the drone itself, but all I needed to know was that it had cameras on it.

I couldn't share everything I knew with them, but I certainly wanted to fill in Sheriff Hanson. That was especially true after his discovery of my 'involvement' in Paul's life. He deserved to know if Filipov had sent his goons to Cameron to snoop around on Paul's property.

At the same time, my mind was churning about how they might have known about Paul's property up here. Did I leave some paperwork in the safe that might have been found? I didn't think so. Did they find out Paul owned The Association Equities and trace it that way? Possibly.

Or there was always the possibility that someone had told them. Someone who I had told about my trip. And that list was very short. As I considered the options, the warning from Paul once again began echoing in my head.

Trust no one.

Did Paul know someone close to him was working with Filipov before he died? Is that the reason for all the security out here? Did he know they were coming?

A call from Steve Chandler, one of the people who knew about my trip, interrupted me before I got to my cabin. I was now suspicious of everyone I had spoken to up to this point, so I accepted the call with no plans to disclose anything new to Steve.

It turned out he was the one with things to disclose.

"Hey Steve, What's up?" I said as the call came through the speakers of the 4Runner.

"Well, I've sorted through some of the stuff on these servers in Paul's condo," he replied, getting right to the point.

"And what did you find?" I asked as I drove the small distance to the cabin.

"Well, it seems they're just echoing signals and transferring traffic to different networks. There is some heavy encryption going on here, so I'm not sure of all the endpoints, but it appears this entire rack of stuff was just to leverage the internet connectivity available here in Littleton. Paul had three different internet service providers, and all were leveraging the highest bandwidth available. He was pumping some serious data through here," Steve said.

"Can you tell where the other networks were?" I asked, a theory forming in my mind.

"The only one I can see is routed somewhere in Montana. Oddly enough, it's not far from where I live up there. Somewhere around Cameron or Ennis. I can't nail it down much more than that," he said.

Perhaps I had found out how Filipov knew where Paul's cabin was, and why there was a Russian drone flying around up here. If they had scanned the servers like Steve did before they turned them off, they would have reached his same conclusion. But it was still possible someone told Filipov, and he never got the data from the servers. Now I had a decision to make. Did I bring Steve in or leave him outside?

I paused a little too long.

"You still there?" Steve asked.

"I may know where the Montana endpoint is," I said, sheepishly. If I couldn't trust Steve, who could I trust?

"And how is it you know this?" Steve asked, sounding annoyed.

"I've been here the last two days. Sorry, I should have told you sooner, but I got a cryptic warning from Paul that made me cautious. I'm in Cameron, Montana right now," I said.

Steve was silent for a moment.

"You were right there near my home and you sent me down here to Denver?" Steve asked, still sounding annoyed. Or hurt. Or confused.

"Yeah, I know. I felt bad when I did that. But look what we've found! So, you're saying Paul wasn't doing any of the direct processing there in the condo?" I asked, trying to change the subject.

"Yeah, that's what I'm saying. And by the way, your buddy Sergeant Theiss has been attached to my hip. I'm not sure she trusts you. Or me," Steve said.

"That could be my fault, I guess. Sorry about that," I replied.

"Yeah, she mentioned you weren't completely forth-coming with some details. Anyway, she knows what I found, if it matters. And by the way, that encryption stuff Paul was using is pretty crazy. I've never seen anything this sophisticated. It appears Paul was passing packets of data here, then distributing the packets through all these internet connections. He must have needed a faster batch of connections than he could get up there in Montana," Steve added.

"That sort of fits with what I've found here. Paul has a cabin out here near Cameron. There is some pretty serious processing power in the back of the cabin that seems to search through large amounts of data that's not publicly available," I said.

"Ok, lots of questions on that, but I'll stick to the topic. Are you thinking he has some sort of government access or something?" Steve asked.

"That's what I'm thinking, yeah. And it's attached to some slick search capability, including facial recognition. And it's fast. Very fast," I said. That got Steve out of his doldrums and more engaged with the cabin.

"Ok, so there's a cabin in Cameron. That would explain why he needed to hop to Littleton to use all the internet available here. It would definitely be better than the boon-docks of Montana," Steve said.

"Yeah, that does make sense," I replied.

"Can you send me the details of the cabin? I think I'd better sniff around and see what he was up to. I don't think I can get there until morning, though. It's getting late," he said, resuming his frustrated tone.

"That sounds great, Steve. And I apologize for the misdirection earlier. We really did need those servers inves-tigated. That was a huge help," I said, trying to repair the damage I had done to our friendship.

"It's ok, Keith. I get it. I suppose I would probably have

done the same thing. What was the warning Paul gave you, anyway?" Steve asked.

"Well, to be specific. He left me a note that said, 'Trust no one, believe nothing, question everything, and be careful.' He had given it to Jordan Crawford before leaving for Nashville," I answered. I wondered if Steve knew who Jordan was, so I waited.

"You mean the guy from the Rocky Mountain Equity board?"

"Yeah, that's the one." It seems Paul had described Jordan the same way to both me and Steve.

"He gave you a note from Paul?"

"Yeah. Why?"

"Do you think he read it?" Steve said, bringing up a point I had pondered earlier.

"That's a good question, and honestly, I'm not sure. Someone, however, knew Paul had a place up here and has been snooping around," I said.

I told Steve about the drone found near the Lazy J ranch the day before I arrived.

"Ok, that raises the stakes here, Keith. So Jordan could have read it and sent a team there before you got there. Paul always treated him as though he had connections. Maybe Filipov is one of his connections," Steve said, once again echoing one of my thoughts over the last two days.

"That's true, Steve. But if it was him, why would he give me Paul's note? He could have just tossed the note as though it never existed," I said.

"Yeah, or he could draw you in to have you wiped out. Or he could have needed you to bypass the facial recognition stuff at the cabin. Or..." Steve stopped. More accurately, I cut him off.

"Ok, ok. Yeah, it could be Jordan. Or they could have dug into the servers at Paul's condo just like you did," I said.

"Yeah, that's true," Steve said, not sounding convinced.

"You don't think so?"

"Not really. I mean, if it was me, I'd have taken them offsite to investigate that encryption. I really don't think they could have gotten any further than me, Keith."

"Ok, I get that. But remember, they had police all over that building soon after they snuck in. It would have been close to impossible to unpack those servers and somehow carry them out without being noticed. Maybe they only wanted to get to the cabin out here. I have to believe they found the connectivity to an endpoint out here just like you found," I answered.

"Yeah, ok. I guess. But I'm also just taking Paul's warning to heart. I don't trust anyone," Steve replied.

"Touche," I replied.

"Alright, I guess I need to get going. ...Back home...," Steve said.

"Barb noted," I replied as we ended the call.

There was one more call I needed to make, but I had been sitting in the parking area outside the rental cabin long enough. I headed inside to relax and talk to Sheriff Hanson.

"Mr. Morgan, how can I help you?" he said when he accepted my call.

"Hey, Sheriff Hanson. Just wanted to give you a possible lead on that drone near the Lazy J. And the Caldwell murders, I guess," I said.

"A 'possible' lead, Mr. Morgan?" he asked.

"Well, yeah. Nothing concrete, yet, but I think you have the right to know some of what's been going on between here and Colorado. And, well, other places," I started.

"I'm on pins and needles, Mr. Morgan," Sheriff Hanson said, impatiently.

"Ok, ok. Here we go," I said, and dumped the entire story about our team in Afghanistan and about the issues the team had been having. And about the cabin I had found in the woods. I left out the details about The Association. ... I could always add that later if needed.

Sheriff Hanson listened silently while I unloaded. Then stayed silent for another minute before asking his questions.

"How much money did you guys take out of Filipov's pocket back in Afghanistan," he said, starting way back at the beginning.

"I was never really sure, but the papers said it was tens of millions," I replied, leaving out the part about the missing stash of gold.

"And this has been going on for all that time?" he asked.

"Well, I guess. It seems to have picked up in the last five years, though. Even more in the last year and a half," I replied as I thought about the team's recent difficulties.

"And this drone. What do you think they were looking for?" I realized I left out the part about the internet connectivity in Littleton. When I added that part to the story, Sheriff Hanson perked up.

"Is that why all those antennas are on top of the mountain on your friend's property above his cabin?" he asked unexpectedly.

"Probably so," I said, remembering the cables that ran into the cave behind the cabin. "I've never seen them, to be honest. But something had to connect the cabin to Littleton," I said, thoughtfully.

"And why didn't you tell me you knew about the cabin?" I asked after a brief pause.

"You didn't ask me," Sheriff Hanson said with a smirk.

"Ok, I guess I deserved that," I said, smiling at his sense of humor.

"It's my job to know what's going on in the county. I saw your friend Paul hauling all kinds of construction materials into that place. It took him a couple of years, and he was careful. I doubt anyone else noticed, but I did. Then I checked it out one day after he left. I'm sure he saw me, with all the cameras he has out there," he said, surprising me yet again.

"You knew about the cameras, too?" I asked.

"Once again, it's my job. I feared it was drugs, but he didn't look like the type. I've been very curious about what was going on in there. He was always kind and courteous and never gave anyone any trouble when he was here. I had no reason to question anything nefarious was going on, so I left him alone. Honestly, I kind of miss him. He seemed like a good guy," Sheriff Hanson said, shifting to a solemn tone.

"He was a good guy, indeed," I said, reflecting on the stolen gold once again and hoping my concerns were misplaced.

Chapter Twenty-Eight

That night, I called Jamie to find out how she and Kyle were doing with their grandparents, and caught her in a chatty mood. It sounded like they were covering the entire summer in the first few days.

Jamie was still talking when I got a notification on my phone of someone on our property back home in Woodland Park. I looked at the time, and expected I'd see Ed Sutter stopping by to pick up something for Winchester.

But it wasn't Ed.

Watching the live camera streams on my phone, I saw three uninvited guests entering my property. They walked in from the woods across the street and were brazen with their tactics, not really worried that they were being caught on camera. Either that, or they knew I wasn't there and couldn't do anything about it. I considered calling Ed Sutter and warning him about the intruders so he could scare them away, but thought better of it. It might put him in danger.

After a few minutes, I was sure they knew I was gone. They had gone around the side of the garage and peered into the window, apparently looking for my vehicles. Obviously, my 4Runner was in Montana with me. Then they went to the back of the house, where there was a door to the kitchen. One of the three picked the lock to my house while the other two stood lookout. In less than thirty seconds, the door was opened and the three of them went inside.

In another thirty seconds, I had an alarm on my phone from my home alarm system. It reiterated the details I had already witnessed: the kitchen door was opened. I watched in horror as the house went back to its calm, normal state on the outside. At that moment, I wished I had set up interior cameras so I could see what they were doing. The thought of someone in my house while I was miles away was infuriating.

While the alarm blared inside the house, and my phone showed it was about to alert the Woodland Park police, the intruders stayed inside my house. I was pressing the button on my phone to call the police myself when the three intruders simply walked out the back door, looked around, and left. They were in my house less than a minute, and must have known the alarm would alert the police. They'd be long gone before any police could arrive on the scene.

As they were walking away, one intruder took off their mask just as they neared the camera at the end of the driveway. It was an intentional move. They knew I was watching. When the face became visible, I was only moderately surprised to see it was the stunning woman from Paul's condo. She stared into the camera for a minute with dead eyes, then turned and escaped into the woods with her two cohorts. The stare was haunting and targeted. She was after me.

The break-in at my house made it obvious that the fake Natalie from Paul's condo knew I had the coveted documents from Paul's safe. At least I had to assume she stole it.

There was no evidence of the theft, but adding everything together, I was certain.

If these were the same people who were so savvy with technology like they showed with the other guys on our team, I was going to have to be careful. So far, they must not have known I was in Cameron. Or they did know and went to my house, anyway. In which case, why would they be there? Just to scare me, or were they hoping to find me and find out if I had the documents?

Then another chilling thought went through my head. Did they realize I was gone and went to the house to get my kids? Would these guys be that bold? After a moment, I shook my head at the thought. Paul thought they were that bold, because he already thought Filipov had killed Beth, my wife. If they'd kill her, they'd sure kill the kids. Or at least hold them for ransom until they got what they wanted from me.

"Dad?" It was Jamie on the phone, jolting me back into the moment.

"Yeah, sorry, hon. Got sidetracked for a minute," I said. She was used to these temporary trips my brain sometimes took, but didn't need to know why I was distracted this time.

"I said I'm getting ready for bed," she said, sounding frustrated with me. I didn't have time to argue with her on this one, as I had another thought while she was talking. If I can load the video of the condo woman's face to Paul's facial recognition program in the cabin, maybe I can find out who it is.

"Bye, dad. Love you. Here's Kyle," Jamie said as I once again got quiet.

"Goodnight, Jamie. Love you," I said, then repeated a similar message to Kyle.

After the call with the kids, and before I even considered calling the police about the break-in at my house, I downloaded the video footage from my house to my phone and jumped into my 4Runner. The Caldwell guys might have been watching Paul's property, but I doubted it. They were pretty tanked at the Golden Bear, and they seemed to be assured I was not their parents' murderer.

The drive at night took a little longer, even though I was in a hurry. As I drove, I wondered what made the woman from Paul's condo come after me now. Did she just now figure out who I was? I hadn't told Rachel in the lobby what my name was, so she couldn't have told them before she died. Then I considered what I had talked to Rachel about and wondered if the woman had coaxed that information out of Rachel before she died.

That thought made me wonder about the real Natalie's safety, since that's whose number I'd gotten from Rachel. Did she give the same information to the people who killed her? I had to check on Natalie.

It was past 9 PM but I didn't care. I put a call in to Sergeant Theiss.

"Mr. Morgan, how are things in Montana?" Sergeant Theiss asked as she answered.

"They're lovely, thank you. But I have a quick favor to ask," I said, matching her desire to get to the point.

"Ok, what's going on now? I already met your friend Steve at the condo and got an update from the team, if that's what you're going to talk about," she said, sounding like she was trying to hurry me off the phone. I also heard noise in the background.

"I'm sorry, that's not it. I don't mean to bother you while you're busy, but do you have a minute?" I asked.

I heard a sigh, then she responded.

"Sure. I'm at a crime scene. Let me step away," she said. I heard the noise fade as she walked away.

"Ok, what's going on?" she said when she got to a quieter spot.

"Well, I just saw someone break into my house in Woodland Park. I have quite a few cameras around the property, and the intruders seemed to know all about them. But, for some reason, they didn't care. They picked the lock on my back door, including the deadbolt, and went in. Then, well before the police would get there, they came back out and walked away. Then, as they left, one of them lifted their mask. It was the woman from Paul's condo. She was sending me a message. I don't know how she linked me to Paul, but she did. She could have seen a photo or something, but there's also another possibility," I said.

"And what's that?" Sergeant Theiss asked.

"What if they got to Natalie, Paul's girlfriend? If they questioned Rachel in the lobby before they killed her, they may have found out about Natalie. Then, if they knew that was Paul's girlfriend, they might have gone after her for more information. I mean, she'd have been an easy target, right?" I asked rhetorically.

"Maybe. Didn't you say you warned her, though?"

"Yeah, I did. Plus, she said she was leaving town. But I'm not sure when. Can you guys stop by there?" I wondered if it was a good idea when I said it.

"You want us to stop by and scare the poor woman to death at nearly 10 PM on a Friday night? After losing her boyfriend a couple of weeks ago?" She clearly didn't agree with the idea.

"Ok, I'll just call her," I said, thinking I should have done that in the first place.

"Let me know what she says," Sergeant Theiss said as we ended the call.

I immediately dialed Natalie's number as I arrived at the parking area on Paul's property. I got no answer. Rather than call Sergeant Theiss back, I left her a text. Maybe now she'd go check on Natalie.

The walk from the parking spot to the cabin was especially tough at night, even with my strongest flashlight. I felt like I was visible for miles trying to hustle through the woods in the dark, but I didn't care. If the Caldwell boys or Sheriff Hanson showed up, I'd just invite them in.

During the walk, I searched for the cameras I knew were positioned around the perimeter. I couldn't see a single one in the dark, even with my flashlight. Then I wondered how to get all the surveillance cameras from the property visible on my phone. Given the rest of the technology at the cabin, there had to be a way.

Upon arrival at the cabin, I made coffee and headed into the bunker. It was going to be a long night.

The first task was to upload the video from my phone to the computer I had been using for research in the bunker. At least I assumed that's where it should go. I dug through the drawers and found a cable and connected my phone to one of the USB connections on the server racked right in front of the monitors.

That worked out a couple of my problems. The first thing it did was validate my identity using the camera. After tapping through a couple of validation messages, I received a message asking if I wanted to sync the available files to my device. I assumed the message was regarding the camera footage I was looking for, so I tapped yes. My phone blinked on and off twice, then installed a 'Dell secure camera and chat' service on my phone. The logo was red, which seemed odd for Dell, as the logo I was familiar with was blue. The odd colors of the logo made me briefly consider whether the app was authentic, but given the other technology in Paul's cabin, a rare software application from Dell wasn't surprising.

That installation process took less than a minute. When it was complete, I could view every camera on the permitter of Paul's property on my phone. It was a little cumbersome to view on the small screen of my phone versus the large computer screens, but it worked. I also found an alert feature that was similar to the app for my cameras at home. It allowed me to receive alerts on my phone for vehicles, animals, people or motion of any kind.

The chat feature in the software also looked similar to my cameras at home. Based on how my cameras worked, I suspected I could hit the chat button, select a camera, then talk through a tiny speaker embedded in the device. That didn't seem useful, given Paul's cameras were positioned so high in the air.

Next, I shifted my focus to the server. Within a few minutes, I had explored the files on my phone, found the video file from the cameras at my house, and uploaded it to the server. Then I played the video and found the place where the woman looked at the camera. I paused the video and zoomed in on her face as best I could.

Next was the moment of truth for my research of the mysterious woman. Would the video footage from my home camera be good enough to trigger the search tools on Paul's system? I put the mouse cursor over her face and, to my relief, a search prompt immediately popped up.

I clicked and waited. And waited. The search icon kept spinning and didn't return any results. Finally, an error popped up saying the resolution was poor, and asked if I would like to reload or sharpen the image. I selected the option to sharpen the image and waited again.

After extracting a photo, sharpening the image, and going through the same process to search on the face, the search links finally showed up. The links next to her face didn't have all the American options. They were similar to the ones that appeared in Ivan Filipov's search, which indicated she wasn't an American. Given her accent, that wasn't really a surprise.

The first link next to the photo was a news story, which I clicked first.

The first headline was all I needed to see to know who I was dealing with. And it sent the rest of my evening in a new direction. It was a news clip from 2008 that showed a graduation photo that showed a younger version of the woman I had seen in Paul's condo. Like some of the articles about Filipov, there was no news source identified. But it was an American graduation. From Harvard.

The headline read 'Natalia Filipov graduates from Harvard Business School.' She was shown shaking the hand of the school staff at the graduation ceremony.

Could I be seeing this correctly?

Was the woman from Paul's condo really the daughter of Ivan Filipov?

Chapter Twenty-Nine

I spent the next few hours digging into the life and times of one Natalia Filipov. I discovered she completed her undergraduate education at MIT, then went to Harvard for her MBA. By all accounts, she was a smart woman.

Clicking a link labeled Travel, I also found surveillance videos of her in Europe and in Moscow. It seemed Natalia traveled a lot. There were also lots of travel photos with no source and no context. It's almost as if one of the systems Paul was using had been tracking her privately.

There were few details about her, even in the news stories. After her education in the United States, she seemed to go back to Russia and to hang out in Europe. Her travel over the years covered most of Eastern and Western Europe, but she never returned to the United States.

That all changed five months ago, when she was photographed with another woman inside a small, private airport. It was a unique airport, and I recognized the interior immediately. She was in the same airport I had used to get in and out of Zapata, Texas, during my last assignment with The Association. That was the place we busted the human trafficking and drug smuggling operation along the Mexico border. It was also the assignment that got Paul killed.

So, Natalia had apparently come into the country through Zapata just a few months before we shut them down. And Paul knew Filipov ran that operation, because he mentioned it in his video. I also remembered the Zapata locals talking about VIPs coming through that trafficking process now and then. Natalia Filipov must have been one of those VIPs.

It made perfect sense that she would have then gone to the private airport to avoid prying eyes via more public routes. Someone, however, had a camera there that caught her.

I had downed several cups of coffee but was starting to fade. When I finally forced myself to look at the clock, it was 2 AM. I needed to get at least a few hours of sleep to be of any use when Jen and Steve arrived, so I shut down my research.

Remembering I had downloaded the security camera application to my phone, I pulled it up and looked through the alerting options again. I was extremely cautious after the intruders on my home property, so I selected the option to trigger for all animals, people, and vehicles. That meant, I found out a few minutes later, that every deer, fox, coyote and elk would trigger a camera alert on my phone.

After the fifth one jolted my adrenaline and sent me scrambling to find my phone, I set the system to alert only for humans or vehicles. Hopefully that would be enough to keep the place secure while I slept for a few hours.

It was.

I slept like a log until my phone alerted me to a vehicle on the property at 7:30 AM. It was Sheriff Hanson pulling up behind my 4Runner. I called him immediately rather than waiting around for him to find me. He knew I had cameras anyway, so he was probably expecting it. In fact, as I watched him on the video, he just got out of his SUV and casually looked around. He made no attempt to walk onto the property to find me. He was waiting for me to call.

"Mr. Morgan, what prompted this call at such an early hour?" Sheriff Hanson asked sarcastically as he answered my call.

"I just thought you might be bored. Maybe you wanted to chat about your childhood or something," I replied, matching his sarcasm.

"Ok, now that we got that out of the way, I wanted to share something with you. I sent word around to see if anyone knows about these Russian drones. I didn't get much on that, but people are still looking," he said.

"Ok," I replied, aware I could probably do the same thing with Paul's search system. I chastised myself for not thinking of that earlier.

"But I also asked people to keep on the lookout for a stranger with broken drone parts in their vehicle. It was a long shot, but I think I got a hit," he said.

"Oh, really? What'd you find?"

"It seems a white Ford F150 pulled into a service station near the private airstrip outside West Yellowstone two days ago, with drone parts in the back. The video is fuzzy, but I'm pretty sure it's the drone the Caldwell boys found. While they were there, they pulled the drone pieces out of the truck, extracted the cameras and kept them, then smashed the broken pieces into small chunks right there on the ground. Then they scooped the pieces up and dumped them in the trash like it was no big deal," he said.

"How many people were there? What did they look

like? Did they head toward the airstrip?" I asked, realizing too late that I needed to give him time to answer.

"Before I get to that, one more piece of data. The truck was an unmarked fleet vehicle from the Krohl ranch. It was reported stolen that same day. The thieves had changed the plates. These guys are pretty bold, walking right in there and stealing a vehicle from a neighboring ranch like that. I'm guessing they probably had another vehicle somewhere else. We'll probably find that Krohl truck dumped some-where," he said.

"Probably near the airstrip," I agreed.

"And to your other questions, there were three of them. Two of them got out to dispose of the broken drone, but one remained in the car. They had hats on, so we couldn't see faces, but the two we saw were big guys. After they disposed of the drone, they casually got back in the truck and drove toward the airstrip." Sheriff Hanson paused, apparently done with the story.

I watched him stand there for another minute, looking around.

"Are you not going to come get me so I can see your new digs? I assume you spent the night out here?" Sheriff Hanson now looked straight at the camera as if he was talking to me. I knew he was aware of the cameras from our previous conversations, but it was still weird.

The thought of bringing him to the cabin put me in a quandary. The cabin without the bunker was very nice, but nothing extraordinary. More importantly, it wouldn't need any antennas like Sheriff Hanson had seen. I suspected that was what had prompted him to stop by.

"I tell you what, you start heading in and I'll head out. You know where it is, anyway. You're not fooling me," I said.

"Ok, fair enough. I'm on my way," he said as I watched him head into the woods from the parking area.

I quickly got dressed and started another pot of coffee. I had a dilemma to resolve. Did I show Sheriff Hanson the whole property, including the bunker? Or was there another way? I looked around to see if I could quickly stack a couple of computers on a counter or something, to make it look like they might be connected to the antennas. Finding no good option, I decided I'd have to play it by ear.

I headed out of the cabin toward the parking area. It would take Sheriff Hanson at least fifteen minutes to get here, assuming he was accurate with his directions. I'd meet him in less than ten minutes. That's how long I had to decide how much of Paul's cabin to show.

Five minutes later, I saw him trudging along the creek below the ridge I was walking along. He was taking the path I had taken the first night while I was fishing. That seemed like months ago.

I yelled at him and motioned for him to climb up to where I was. The cabin was several hundred feet above the creek, two ridges to our west.

"He didn't put the cabin right on the creek?" Sheriff Hanson asked, clearly not as aware of the property as he had led me to believe.

"No, I think he wanted a view from above," I lied, planning to avoid a discussion about the bunker in the side of the mountain if at all possible.

"This is a great property. There are some nice cutthroats in that stream. Nasty antelope incident stinking it up right now, though," he said.

I was just about to respond when I was saved by my phone buzzing. It was an unrecognized Colorado phone number.

"This is Keith," I answered automatically.

"Mr. Morgan, this is Lieutenant Carr from the Littleton Police Department. Do you have a minute?"

"Hi, Lieutenant Carr. Did you find Natalie?" I asked, assuming he had been working with Sergeant Theiss, and that was why he called.

"Yeah, we did. But why did you ask that?" he asked.

His question was almost accusatory and put me in a defensive mode.

"I had asked Sergeant Theiss to look in on her last night, that's all," I replied, trying to diffuse his tone.

"You did? Hmm. Ok. Well, we're at her apartment now," he said, now sounding like he was about to deliver bad news.

I realized Sheriff Hanson was staring at me, and I knew he had already talked to Sergeant Theiss before, so I decided to include him in the conversation with Lieutenant Carr.

"I'm standing here with Sheriff Hanson. Should I bring him into this?" I asked.

"Uh, sure," he responded, sounding a little surprised.

I put the call to speaker.

"Ok, we're here," I said.

"We found Natalie in her apartment. It looked like she was packing to leave, so it must have been just after you talked to her. Someone had gotten to her before she could get away. Nobody saw or heard anything, but we're scouring the area cameras now," Lieutenant Carr said.

"So, she was killed?" I asked, forcing him to state the obvious.

"I'm sorry. I thought that was obvious. Yes, she was killed," he said with minimal emotion.

"How?" I asked. Sheriff Hanson was listening quietly.

"That's the tough part. It appears she was beaten. They may have been looking for information about you or they may have thought she knew where the money was. Or the documents. I guess we'll never know," he said, with the same emotion he would have if he were reading the news.

"That's horrible," I said.

"I'd be curious about the specifics of the perpetrators," Sheriff Hanson said, breaking his silence.

"Ok. I'll let you know what we find. Why do you ask?" Lieutenant Carr asked.

"We have a video recording of some suspects from a murder up here. I'd like to see if they match," he answered.

"Ah, ok. Yeah, I'll let you know what we find. It should be later today," Lieutenant Carr said.

"Ok, thanks," we both said.

Then I had a thought.

"Hey, Lieutenant Carr. The place where Sheriff Hanson found the video was near a local private airstrip. This may be a stretch, but maybe we should look around the Denver area at any of the private airstrip videos? I know there are some that have no video surveillance, but it might be worth a shot," I suggested.

"It's not a bad idea. Let me see what I can find," he said.

"Thank you," I said again.

"Alright. We'll get back to you later," Lieutenant Carr said as he ended the call.

We were ready to resume our trek to the cabin when Sheriff Hanson's phone started buzzing. He looked at the number and held up his hand to stop.

"Sorry, I've got to take this," he said.

He listened for a few seconds, clearly agitated by the message he was hearing.

"Alright, I'm on my way," he finally said.

He put the phone back in his pocket and turned back toward the parking area.

"Sorry. We'll have to do this another day. Looks like we've got some rustlers caught red-handed. Don't want that one to escalate," he said as he hurried away.

I stood there for a second, then turned back to the cabin. As I walked, I realized I was hungry. It felt like time for another trip to the Golden Bear, for the third time in two days. Once the cabin was locked, I would be on my way.

I had cleared out of the cabin and was just leaving the front porch when my phone buzzed again. It was Jen. I took the call as I hurried toward the 4Runner.

"Hey Jen, what's up?" I asked, assuming she would say she was heading out of Colorado. I was a little behind.

"I'm pulling into Cameron," she said.

"What? I thought you were flying in later today?" I said, shocked to hear she was already in town.

"This sounded too urgent. I got a few hours of sleep at a rest stop, but I'm good. Although I will admit coffee sounds nice. So, are you at your rental cabin?" Jen asked.

"Actually, I'm on the way to breakfast. You hungry? On second thought, forget that question. Meet me at the Golden Bear whether you're hungry or not. It's the only place in town with coffee and the breakfast is fantastic. I'll see you there in about thirty minutes," I said as I hurried along.

"Sounds great. See you there," Jen said and ended the call.

I hadn't even started the 4Runner yet when I got another call. This time, it was Steve. Surely, he wasn't in town, too?

"Hey Steve, what's up?" I said, repeating my greeting from Jen's call.

"I just landed, wanted you to know I'd be there in about an hour," he said.

I thought for a minute. There was no public airport that close, and there weren't any incoming flights from Denver this early.

"Did you get a charter flight?" I asked.

"Yeah. This sounded pretty urgent," he said. I must have been too emotional with Jen and Steve the day before. But, it turns out they were right. We needed to get going on finding out if Natalia Filipov was hunting me.

I got in the 4Runner and sped down the path toward Cameron. It felt great to get some help on this ridiculous project.

In another hour, I was having breakfast with Jen and Steve at the Golden Bear.

Chapter Thirty

Molly was hustling around the Golden Bear on Saturday morning even more than during the week. She kept our coffee full and hot, and threw in a smile and joke here and there when time allowed. Jen, Steve and I were enjoying ourselves

We caught up on light talk for a few minutes, then dug into the reason they had gone to Cameron. I shared what I had found out about Natalia Filipov, filling in the details I hadn't been able to share over the phone. Steve talked about how the servers in the condo were used and explained his plan to investigate the connectivity from the cabin.

"You guys made a lot of progress while I was driving up the Rocky Mountains," Jen finally said.

"So, you were the one who helped solve that political thing in Detroit?" Steve asked Jen during a quiet moment.

"Well, Keith did most of it. But yeah, I guess I helped," Jen said.

"Not true. Jen is a data wiz. She was at Diverse Data when Rocky Mountain Equity acquired them. She helped with that assignment in Detroit, then helped us nail that

Nashville mess, too," I said. I could have gone on and on about her military expertise and outdoor skills, too, but I stopped short of that. It didn't feel appropriate to brag on her to Steve.

Molly came by with my credit card and the receipt, and I took a second to add her tip and sign the bill.

"Nice. And an Air Force vet, too?" Steve continued while I was writing, sounding a bit smitten with Jen. I stifled a hint of jealousy that surprisingly emerged from my gut.

"Yeah. That, too," she said, not sounding quite as smitten with him. I suppressed a smile.

"So, are you guys ready to head out to the cabin?" I asked, trying to shift the mood.

"Yep" and "Sure" came out as we got up and headed out. We were ready to get started.

"Let's take the 4Runner to Paul's cabin. You guys can park your vehicles at my rental cabin. Follow me," I said as I climbed in. Jen got into her SUV and Steve got into his rental car, and they pulled in behind me as I left the Golden Bear.

In thirty minutes, we were parking on Paul's property and grabbing our gear out of the 4Runner.

"Wow! This place is amazing," Jen said as she grabbed her bag and looked around.

"Yeah, it really is. The trout fishing is great, the terrain is awesome, and wait until you see the cabin!" I said.

"And smile at the cameras as you walk in," I said, once again looking for the camera I knew was pointed toward this spot. I still couldn't see it.

"I don't see them," Steve said. "He did a good job hiding them."

"Yeah, he did. Come on, let's head in. It's about fifteen minutes to the cabin," I said as we set off toward the cabin.

In fifteen minutes, we were standing on the porch of Paul's cabin. Jen and Steve were staring out into the wilderness, taking it all in.

"Wow. I just can't quit saying it," Jen said.

"And facial recognition on the door? Nice!" Steve said.

"Yeah," I said as I stepped forward and heard the door unlock. "And you haven't seen anything yet!"

Jen and Steve followed me into the cabin, mouths agape as they looked around.

"Paul did a fantastic job with this. I saw no visible evidence of a bunker from the outside, and this interior is great! I could live here!" Jen was saying, still enjoying the normal part of Paul's property. She was reacting much like I did when I first arrived.

When we walked in, the TV once again started with Paul's welcome video. I had forgotten to turn it off. I reached for the remote to turn the television off, but noticed the way Jen and Steve were looking at Paul's face. Then I just let it run. They both sat down while they solemnly watched Paul go through the message once again. I watched the two of them, not the video. When the video ended, they both dropped their eyes to the ground.

"Yeah, I know. It's weird, isn't it?" I said.

"I know you told us about it, but it's just not right that Paul's gone," Steve said, still looking down.

"Talking about the video just isn't the same as seeing it," Jen added.

After a few more solemn seconds, they both took a deep breath, stood up, and looked around. I got a cup of coffee while they looked around. After a few minutes, they came into the kitchen and got their own coffee cups.

"This place is incredible, even without a bunker. Now, how do you get into this hidden bunker?" Jen asked after a sip.

"Watch this," I said. Then I led them to the coat closet, slide the coats aside, twisted the coat hook on the right, looked into the camera, and watched the panel slide away and the door open.

I turned around to see Jen's mouth open like she had seen an impressive magic trick. Steve, on the other hand, looked like he had just gotten his favorite birthday present.

"Awesome," Steve whispered as they walked into the bunker behind me.

Steve was digging through servers and walking around while Jen just stared.

"Once again, this is so much crazier in person," she said.

"Yeah, I know," I said, nodding.

"Is this an air filtration system? With an external vent mechanism? Cool," he said, asking rhetorical questions while he continued to snoop.

"I've been using this keyboard over here, but honestly, I haven't even gotten into the rest of this stuff," I said, showing them where I had spent my hours in the bunker.

"Ok. You can stay on that keyboard. I'm going to dig into what I had learned from the condo. There has to be some sort of external connectivity being initiated from here," Steve said. He had already found another keyboard and mouse in the corner, and was clicking away.

"Keith, can you get me an ID on the main identity management system? It looks like we will need access granted before we can do anything," he said.

"Sure, just a sec," I said as I logged in, realizing I should have done that earlier.

It only took a few seconds to add users to Paul's system.

"You guys want facial recognition included? Step over here and I'll add it. Steve, you're first," I said as Steve nodded and moved to the camera.

"Got it, thanks. You should be all set," I told Steve.

Then I went through the same process with Jen. To test the system, she clicked the mouse and moved toward the camera. The system welcomed her just like it had welcomed me. On cue, she grabbed the keyboard and started clicking away.

I stood there for a moment, staring at Jen and Steve working away on Paul's bunker computers. After a few seconds, I started looking around for another keyboard. Steve saw what I was doing.

"There's another one over here," Steve said, pointing toward the drawer in the corner.

I pulled the keyboard out of the drawer and noticed a folder at the bottom of the drawer. It had been hidden by the two extra keyboards before, so I hadn't seen it. I grabbed the folder and opened it. Inside were several old newspaper clippings and some handwritten notes. Jen and Steve saw me staring at the open folder.

"What'd you find?" Jen asked.

"I'm not sure," I said, just beginning to take in the folder's contents.

"Well, what is it?" Steve said, standing to look over my shoulder.

"That's from our raid," he said, reading the top article.

"Why would he keep a story about the theft?" Steve asked.

"What theft?" Jen asked.

I filled her in on the stolen gold and cash from our raid, and how it was never recovered. She stared for a moment, then had a look of shock in her eyes.

"You think Paul stole millions from Filipov?" she said, thinking out loud.

"I'm not sure. But he sure seemed interested in it," I said.

Steve was still reading.

"I think it was him. He also has notes here about the number of gold bars, the amount of cash, and all the exchange rates with US dollars and bitcoins," Steve said, closing the folder and standing there in shock.

Jen and I stared as well, saying nothing. I was trying to figure out what to say next. Nothing seemed appropriate.

Finally, Jen shared what we were all thinking.

"So, Paul stole from Filipov in Afghanistan. Then, when he finds out about Filipov's activities here in the US, he doubles down on him? Why would he pick on Filipov? I mean, I'm sure he's a bad guy, but there are lots of bad guys in the world. And does that mean Paul caused all this pain your friends have experienced?" Jen asked, again thinking out loud.

"I'm not sure," I said, still wondering what to think of the new bunker discovery.

"Well, I'm not sure it changes our immediate next steps," Steve said, reading my mind.

"Yeah, I guess not. We still have someone bearing down on us, apparently after me. Or, at least after the money Paul left me," I said, finally admitting the truth of the situation.

"We'll have to figure out Paul's link to the Filipov theft at some point. But for now, we need to find evidence that Filipov tampered with our friends," I said, as Jen nodded and turned back to her keyboard.

"And figure out how Paul was getting all these systems to work like this," Steve said, also turning back to his keyboard.

"Yeah, I guess that's true," I said, smiling at the sight of the two of them pounding away on their keyboards.

They ignored me while I watched them.

"Anybody need some more coffee?" I finally asked, as a joke.

Steve didn't answer.

"No, I'm good," Jen said with an uninterested smile.

"Ok, I'll just refresh my own," I said, turning to walk back into the cabin.

I got some coffee and stood on the porch of the cabin for a minute. Jen was right, it was a fantastic place. It was exactly the kind of place I'd look for when the kids grew up. Beth and I would have loved the place in retirement. I began to miss Beth and the life we had planned together.

I was still feeling a sense of loss when Jen stepped onto the porch.

"Paul had good taste," she said.

"He sure did," I said.

"Don't worry, Keith. You were right to bring us into this thing. Don't think twice about it. We need to get this mess cleaned up for good," she said in a comforting voice. I must have looked sad when she walked up. I didn't tell her the real reason for my sadness.

Instead, I decided to double down on this investigation. The thought of Beth had reinvigorated me. It didn't matter why we got into this, or why Paul started this deadly feud with Filipov. Paul thought this guy had killed my wife. And we know he caused Mark's death, Rachel's, Natalies, and the Caldwell couple at the Lazy J. We needed to stop the madness.

"Thanks Jen. And you're right, we need to clean this mess up for good!" I said, still staring into the wilderness.

We stood there a few more minutes before we heard Steve yelling from inside the cabin.

"Hey Keith! I think I found something," he screamed.

We hustled back into the bunker to see Steve hunched over the desk and shining a flashlight at the back of the servers in the racks.

"What'd you find back there?" Jen asked, as we both entered the bunker.

"This server is exactly like a server in the condo. It has a strange red Dell logo on it I've never seen before. When I saw the one like this in the condo, I thought it was weird but I thought no more about it. But this one also has a small sticker on the back. The one in the condo had all stickers, serial numbers, and other identifying marks removed. Paul left the sticker on this one," he said, still digging around.

"What does it say?" I asked, as Steve stood and turned off his flashlight.

"You're not going to believe this, but it says National Security Agency," Steve said, looking bewildered.

"Paul Frazier was working with the NSA?" Jen and I echoed in unison.

Chapter Thirty-One

We weren't sure what to make of the NSA server sitting in Paul's bunker, so we all sort of stood there looking at each other for a minute. Finally, Jen broke the silence.

"Keith, you said Paul was getting access to lots of information that wasn't public, right? Maybe this is how he was doing it," she said.

"Yeah, but how did he possibly get this? And who knows about it? And why is it here?" My mind was slinging questions faster than anyone could answer.

"He has to be working with someone over there, even if it's not in an official capacity. Someone gave him an appliance. If I had to guess, I'd say it was designed to connect securely to government systems, and someone designed it for this unique purpose, whatever that is," Steve said, still stunned by the discovery.

"It feels like we should tell them Paul's gone, unless they already know. And if they know, why haven't they reclaimed their hardware," I said, still absorbing this new information and thinking out loud.

Then I remembered the drawer with all Paul's contacts listed. But Paul wouldn't just list out an NSA contact on a piece of paper, would he?

"How would we let them know if we didn't know his contact?" Steve said, reading my mind.

"I'm not sure. Maybe we can find something in the system somewhere," I said, not really hopeful that would happen. Even if we found a name or number, I was pretty sure an NSA agent would be more difficult to contact than just dialing a phone number.

Then I had a thought.

Just the day before, I had encountered a similar red Dell logo on the software I had downloaded from Paul's servers. Did that software also have something to do with the NSA? I kept that thought to myself for the moment, not really sure if it was worth sharing.

"Does he have a list of contacts in here somewhere?" Steve asked rhetorically while he clicked away on his keyboard.

The question reminded me of the files I had found earlier in Paul's bunker. There were several random contacts listed, but I didn't scan each one specifically to see if there might have been a Dell contact. For now, I kept that to myself. Steve had gotten awfully aggressive with his research into this NSA topic, and it was making me uncomfortable.

Trust no one.

"We'll have to look around in his files. Let me know if you find a list like that. I'm going to keep digging into the research Paul was doing on the team," I said, putting the application on my phone on the back burner for the moment. If it really was NSA software, I suspected it wouldn't be good to share that knowledge with too many people.

"I'm going to see if I can find any data correlation with the hacking that seemed to go on with your Hart International team. Maybe they left a trail," Jen said, her voice trailing off as she dove into her task.

For the next hour, between coffee refreshes, we all worked on gathering data from the system for our individual, yet overlapping, purposes. Each of us was scribbling things on post-it notes we had found in stacks by the cork board. When I felt I was at a stopping point with my research, I paused and sat back. My back was aching from sitting on a stool I had found next to the table in the kitchen. Steve was stretching, too, as he also had one of the kitchen stools. Jen didn't have the same struggle, since she was using the desk chair that had been originally in the bunker.

"Maybe it's a good time for a checkpoint," I said as I stood and looked at the clock. It was past noon already.

Jen sat back and stretched. Steve didn't stop typing and kept his eyes focused on the screen.

"Just a second," he said.

"This whole bunker thing is surreal," Jen said as she stood and twisted her torso to stretch out her back. Then she calmly bent over and pressed her hands flat on the floor.

"Whoa. That's some flexibility," I said too emphatically.

She stood up quickly.

"Oh, sorry. I guess I just retained some of that childhood gymnastics agility," she said with a smile.

Steve stopped typing and linked his fingers, pushed them out in front of him, and cracked his knuckles.

"Yeah, I'll say this thing is surreal. A private NSA-linked bunker in the middle of the mountains in Montana?

Yeah, it's surreal alright," he said with his eyebrows raised and shaking his head.

"So, you think that server was Paul's link to the NSA? And that's where he was getting all that extra information on these searches?" I asked.

"Yeah, I think that's what it is. It looks like he has some sort of custom software package that links through that server into some unknown entity. I have to believe it's the NSA or something similar. The amount of data and speed that it's returned is phenomenal," Steve said, still shaking his head.

"And I think I'm seeing the trend Paul had spotted regarding the hacks the team had experienced. The credit card hacks, credit applications and online transactions that killed their credit scores were all launched from the same group of servers somewhere in the Balkans. Each would look like a typical cyber attack in isolation, but the fact that there are so many of them in a short period shows a targeted attack from a single source," Jen said.

"Can you show me the IP Addresses and MAC addresses you've found? I've found his research into apparent locations and timing of different sources myself. Maybe we're about to narrow this down enough to look for specific people," I said.

"If you guys can find addresses and times, I think I've found a way for this search system of Paul's to locate cameras near those locations. I'm not sure how deep the data goes, but just the thought makes me concerned about the level of access the government has to all this stuff," Steve said.

"Ok, there are about twelve different servers in the cluster. I don't see a printer in the bunker, so let me write down all these addresses," Jen said as she started scribbling.

"Doesn't he have a printer?" Steve asked, still staring at his screen.

"Let me see... there's a Dell printer setup here. I'll print it there. Keith, have you seen a printer?" Jen asked.

"I don't think so. I didn't even know Dell made printers. Let me look in the other room," I said as I headed out of the bunker.

I looked around in the living room, then the kitchen, but saw no printer. Then the phone in my pocket buzzed. I looked at the screen, expecting a message from the kids, but that wasn't what I saw. Instead, there was a notification from the camera security app that had installed on my phone. It was the one with the same red Dell logo that was on the server that Steve believed was from the NSA.

The notification was for a message in the security software. Remembering it had a chat function, I tapped the app. The chat function wasn't with the cameras as I had thought, but was a separate chat altogether. And someone was messaging me.

The first message was simple enough.

What are these addresses?

Someone had received the document Jen had tried to send to a printer. I was hesitant to engage the person without knowing who it was, but the idea that Paul had been communicating with them made me feel a little better. While I was still contemplating a response, another message popped up.

Is this Keith?

I stopped. They knew who I was? And they knew I was

in Paul's cabin and bunker? Did Paul tell them he was bringing me in, or did the software just read data from my phone? And who was on the other end of this chat?

"Did you find the printer, Keith?" Jen yelled from the bunker.

"No, there's not one in here. It must have been an old printer setup. I'm going to make some more coffee, though," I yelled back.

"Ok, I'll write these server addresses down, then," she said.

I was still staring at the message. After some thought, I decided to reply. If these servers were from the NSA, and if the app was not really a standard Dell app, then maybe I should find out who this was.

Who is this?

Answering their question with another question wasn't very sly, but it made me feel like I had at least some control. Their response was immediate.

A friend.

Do you know what happened to Paul?

Maybe we should talk.

I still don't know who this is.

Talking will help.

I still wasn't sure I should have Jen and Steve involved, so I decided to table the unknown chat from the security app for later.

Now is not a good time.

Ok. When? It should be soon.

This was getting uncomfortable.

When I get some privacy.

Good idea. Chat here when you are alone.

If nothing else, I had bought myself some time. I busied myself with coffee while I thought about the strange chat exchange. Was it really someone from the NSA?

"Hey Keith, you may want to see this," Steve yelled from the bunker, startling me away from my NSA thoughts.

"Yeah, Steve. What'd you find?" I asked when I got back inside the bunker.

"Some of this stuff Paul was researching is pretty old. It goes all the way back to Afghanistan. It almost looks like Paul was targeting Filipov way back then, including the raid where the gold stash was stolen. There are some photos of Filipov in that area at the time, too. Paul was obsessed with the guy," Steve said, continuing to stare at the screen.

"He set up raids specifically targeting Filipov?" I asked, trying to get my head around what Steve was saying.

"Yeah, he did. And the same goes for the work you guys did in Detroit and Nashville. Paul was looking for Filipov. Only in the past few years did technology allow him to find what Filipov was doing," Steve replied.

"But why? Why was he so intent on going after Filipov? There have to be other criminals with even more of an empire than he had," I said, trying to sort through Paul's motives.

"Well, that's why I called you in here. Look at this

message from almost six years ago. It looks like Paul and Filipov had some sort of message exchange back then," Steve said as he pulled up a photo on his screen.

It was a photo of a piece of paper, similar to an old dot matrix paper printout. There was no name on the message, and no way to tell where it came from. But the contents of the seven sentences in the message made the meaning and participants clear.

This is what happens when you steal from the wrong enemy. There was a fatal automobile crash this evening that will appear to be an accident. It wasn't an accident. You can explain to your friend why his wife is dead or you can just live with it yourself. Either way, you've got to face the consequences of your actions every day. And I'm not done. There will be more. You will learn your lesson while you watch your friends suffer. -IF

Jen and I stood silently while we contemplated the message Steve had found.

"My God, Keith. Filipov killed your wife. And he did it to get back at Paul?" Jen said in a horrified voice. That part of the message was eating away at me. Paul's research was trying to prove what he already knew.

"I guess I know why he was trying to get that evidence now. But yeah, this puts an ugly light on a lot of things," I responded, trying to control the anger that was building inside me. I wondered if it was also why I was the one he sent on these assignments.

"And we've been on missions just to help Paul avenge what was happening to your old team? I'm not sure how I feel about this. It's like the whole reason I agreed to join The Association was a lie. Like it was someone else's personal vendetta, and we were just pawns in his deadly chess game," Jen asked while she looking at me and then Steve. And then me again.

"Yeah. It sort of makes The Association itself feel dirty. I'm not sure what to think about this," Steve said quietly.

My mind was elsewhere. Filipov killed Beth. He stole our perfect life. I was beginning to wonder if Paul didn't know I'd someday find this bunker. And then I'd realize why I was the one he sent to take down Filipov's criminal enterprises. Maybe he thought it would give me a feeling of purpose beyond the assignments.

But that's not what happened.

Instead, this new revelation burned at my gut. It just made me more intent than ever to finish this. Oh sure, I was angry at Paul for stealing that stash and getting my wife killed. But Paul was gone. And he wasn't the one who had come to my hometown and set up that horrible crash.

Filipov had to pay for killing Beth.

Chapter Thirty-Two

I stormed out of the bunker and out to the porch. The pain of Beth's loss was consuming me again, but not as much as the anger. The adrenaline-spiking, blood-pressure-raising, teeth-grinding anger I hadn't felt in a long time. I just wasn't sure who to be angry at. Paul had put us in the position of risk. As our leader, he should never have done that. And for what, a few million dollars of gold?

From what I just read, Paul's greed had gotten Beth killed. And it didn't stop there. It had also led to Mark's death and the despair in our other team members.

The phone buzzing in my pocket pulled me temporarily away from my anger. I looked at it to see a message from Jamie. She was having a great time fishing with grandpa. And she loved me.

After a temporary smile at her message, the anger again swept over me for a different reason. Jamie would have her mom today if Paul hadn't done what he did.

I was still seething five minutes later when I realized I had been out on the porch by myself without explanation. Jen and Steve must have decided to leave me alone.

"I'm going for a walk," I yelled into the cabin. I was sure they'd understand.

The creek bed was only about a quarter mile below the cabin, and I made it there in record time. When I got to the water, I paused and found a rock to sit on. Even when my emotions were on fire, a stream like this had a way of helping bring brevity. The quietly babbling noise of the water falling through the canyon clashed with my emotional state.

And it helped. A little.

I took some deep breaths and contemplated what I was going to do next. That one message Steve found had changed my objective. Now I just had to find the path to fulfill that objective. The path that would bring down Ivan Filipov for good.

Sitting on the rock for a few more minutes, I eventually felt the phone in my pocket buzz again. Thinking it may be Jamie, I smiled again and looked at the screen.

Only this time, it wasn't Jamie. It was the security chat application again. Whoever was on the other end of the chat was getting impatient. The message was just one word.

Now?

Sure.

My phone rang seconds after my response.

"Are you going to tell me who this is?" I asked, as I accepted the call.

"Maybe. But first, I need to know a little about what's going on there. You seem to have downloaded some software that I monitor. Would you like to tell me where you got it?" a computer-altered voice asked.

"I've been working at a friend's house on one of his

servers. The software automatically loaded when I connected my phone," I replied.

"Paul is your friend?"

I contemplated more stonewalling, then decided it wasn't worth it. If Paul was working with these people, they probably know who I was already.

"Yes. At least, he was my friend," I said.

"And, just so I know for sure who this is, what is your name?" the voice didn't stop to offer sympathy.

"Keith Morgan," I answered with a sigh.

"Thanks for clarifying, Keith. I'm sorry to hear of your loss. Paul was a good man," the voice said.

"I used to think that, too," I said a little too quickly and harshly. The anger was still there.

"Used to? Why do you say that?" the voice asked, sounding concerned.

"Before I get into that, maybe you should tell me who you are and why your software is running on Paul's servers," I said, deciding I wanted some answers before I gave any more details.

"I can't tell you exactly who I am just yet," the voice said before I quickly interrupted.

"Then at least tell me if this is the NSA," I blurted.

The voice paused.

"Would it help if I said yes?" was the eventual response.

"I guess not." I said, still with no idea why I was talking to them.

"We were working with Paul," the voice said after a second.

"How?"

"Let's just say we were both interested in disabling a common enemy."

"Filipov?"

Another pause.

"Yes. So, you know about that?"

"Paul left me a video with a vague message about it. Then I started digging into the servers in his cabin and found out what he'd been doing. Well, at least I found some of it. But if you guys wanted someone like that, it seems you would have far more resources than a single individual like Paul," I replied.

"It wasn't quite like that. I'd say Paul was more of the aggressor on this one. We just gave him access to some data and some resources, that's all. He helped us with a few business investigations over the years, so we let him snoop around a bit. He was happy with the arrangement," the voice said.

"These business investigations, did he help with those investigations by himself?" I asked.

"You know he didn't," the voice replied, answering my unstated question. As we suspected, Paul was using The Association to do his bidding.

"So, you were giving Paul assignments that were carried out by The Association?" I asked, just to verify the rest of what I had just learned.

"Some, yes. But they didn't get dangerous until recently. Before that, we were just helping build evidence for the local authorities. Your team was a tremendous help," the voice stopped before getting into any details.

"There was an organization driving The Association, then. Just not like I thought," I murmured to myself.

"Yeah, there was. You guys were instrumental in taking down some bad people," the voice said, reassuringly.

"And in exchange, you were supporting Paul's vendetta with Ivan Filipov? And the whole thing started with Paul's theft back in Afghanistan? This doesn't make any sense," I said, intentionally letting my frustration surface while ignoring the affirmation.

"Before you get too hung up on that, you need to know that's not the complete story. ... so, it sounds like Paul didn't tell you," the voice said, pausing with a sigh.

"Tell me what?" I yelled, getting even more frustrated as I found out I was missing something once again.

"Yes, Paul stole some gold and currency in Afghanistan. We knew that. But that wasn't the beginning. Paul did that to avenge his father's death," the voice said in a solemn yet still robotic voice.

"He avenged what? His father's death? What are you talking about?" I was lost.

There was yet another pause and a sigh on the other end of the call.

"I'm about to share some classified information with you. You need to keep it to yourself. I can't give you all the details, but I can at least let you know what was going on in Paul's head," the voice said.

"Why don't you tell me first? Then I'll let you know if I will be keeping it to myself," I replied, my temper getting shorter.

"I guess I'll keep it in general terms, then. The reason Paul was going after Ivan Filipov in Afghanistan, and here in the US right up to his death in Nashville, was because of something that happened years before." The voice paused again, but I didn't speak.

"Ivan Filipov killed Paul's father. Paul's father was deep undercover for an American agency when Paul was just a teenager. We were trying to turn Filipov, and thought we had him, but he double-crossed us. And when I say us, I mean he double-crossed Paul's father. We believe he was murdered far from home, although his body was never recovered. There is no official record of it because of the nature of the mission, but years later, Paul found out about it. To make things worse, soon after his father's murder, Paul's mother committed suicide. When he discovered what had happened, Paul made it his life's mission to make Filipov pay. Since Filipov was an enemy of the US, we allowed Paul access to our systems to gather evidence against Filipov in exchange for some occasional 'off the record' assignments. Which he and, well, your team, completed with stellar results. Paul helped us complete our initiatives and also helped close down several Filipov criminal ventures here in our country. The success of all his efforts, and the impact those efforts have had on our country, have been tremendous."

The voice paused long enough for me to jump in with another question.

"That's a pretty heavy burden for him to carry, I guess. Did Filipov know Paul was avenging his parents?" I asked, although it really didn't matter.

"Paul never told me if Filipov was aware of his motives. But Paul and Filipov did exchange a couple of communications over the years, so it's possible Paul let him know," the voice replied.

"But why would Filipov kill Paul after torturing him all that time? Did something change?" I asked.

"Believe it or not, the story has evolved even more over the last couple of years. After you exposed Filipov's scheme in DC, he was fired and basically thrown out of Moscow. He lost everything. Word on the street is he drank himself to death. Or became such a disgrace the Kremlin couldn't allow him to live. Either way, our intelligence indicates Ivan Filipov is now dead. Which would make you think this would be over. But it's not. About six months ago, his youngest daughter showed up on the scene on a hell-bent mission to avenge his death and to find his stolen money. I'm not sure if vengeance or greed is her motive, but it's deadly either way. We believe she entered the country through the trafficking operation you helped shut down in Zapata, Texas," the voice said. I didn't ask how they knew I was in Zapata. Apparently, Paul was pretty open with these people.

This last bit of information lined up with details I had uncovered in the bunker and made me realize this whole situation had now come to my doorstep.

"So, the children of the two people originally involved were pursuing vengeance for their parents," I said, shaking my head.

"Yeah, I guess so. But now, only the Filipov side remains," the voice said.

"I saw some information about Filipov's daughter on Paul's computer. He must have known she was coming after him," I said.

"Yeah, he did," the voice replied.

"Do you think that's who got to him in Nashville?" I asked.

"It could be. We're looking into that," the voice answered.

"And did you know she broke into my house in Woodland Park, Colorado? I wasn't there since I'm in Montana, but I saw her on my cameras. I believe she saw me in Paul's condo, figured out who I was, and went to get the documents I had gotten from Paul's safe," I said.

Since the voice had revealed Paul's history to me, I then told the voice about the drone incident at the Lazy J ranch. Apparently, that was new information.

"So, they were there before you got there?" the voice asked.

"Yeah, apparently. I'm not sure how they knew, but I've wondered if they figured out the servers in the condo were linked to the Montana cabin," I said, trying to see how much this voice knew about the servers we suspected were from the NSA.

"Maybe. But what if someone tipped them off? You need to go back over everyone you spoke to before you got to Montana," the voice suggested.

"Yeah, I've done that," I said. "I believe they probably figured out where I was going by torturing Paul's girlfriend before they killed her."

"Natalie is dead? When did this happen?" The voice once again seemed behind on the events of the last few days.

"Two days ago. The Littleton PD said she was beaten badly," I replied.

"I'm surprised we didn't hear about that. We follow the Littleton PD scanners pretty closely. Who, specifically, told you this?" The voice needed to catch up on things, apparently.

"It was Lieutenant Carr. He sat in on my interview and oversaw Sergeant Theiss during her investigation at Paul's condo," I answered.

"Then you're probably right. If Natalie knew where you were, she probably had to tell them," the voice said.

"Yeah," I sighed.

Then I thought of another question.

"While I have you, I heard that the people we put away for the Detroit and Nashville assignments were both out of prison? One broke out and the other was out on bail?" I asked.

"Well, that's the message we left on the airwaves," the voice said.

"What do you mean by that?"

"We wanted to draw Ms. Natalia Filipov out of hiding, so we leaked those stories to the media. In reality, they're both still in good hands and won't be going anywhere. And in the end, I guess we didn't even need to do that. You pulled her into the open by yourself."

"I didn't do that on purpose."

"I know. And I'm sure I don't need to tell you to be careful. If she was at your house looking for the documents, she's probably on her way there now. Or she's already there. If they were searching Paul's property with a drone, you have no idea if they found the cabin or not. I'd assume they did," the voice added.

"Yeah, I'll behave as though they know exactly where I am," I said.

"Good. If you need anything, don't hesitate to use the chat app to get to me. You don't want to battle this woman by yourself," the voice said.

"How do I know who you are?" I asked, realizing it was probably a question the voice wouldn't answer.

"Just know I'm a friend," the voice responded.

"Well, alright, then," I said with frustration as the call ended. The voice knew way more about me than I knew about them.

But in my mind, I was absolutely ready to face the woman responsible for Paul's death. The voice had covered more ground in that phone call than I had gotten in all my hours of research in Paul's bunker.

I was now having trouble being mad at Paul anymore, but was still frustrated by his keeping all this to himself. I certainly wouldn't have left him at the hospital in Nashville if I knew Filipov's daughter was on the loose and was after him. My anger at Paul, however, was no longer on the top of my list.

The vengeful daughter of Ivan Filipov was now my primary concern.

Chapter Thirty-Three

I had just ended the call with the mysterious voice when I heard someone approaching behind me. I turned to see Jen making her way down the hill toward the creek where I was sitting. As was usually the case, the sight of her caused an involuntary smile to hit my face.

Since she had ended our romantic relationship a few weeks ago in Nashville, however, I quickly stifled the smile as she took a seat on the rock next to me.

"This is a beautiful place out here. I just can't quit saying it," she said as she sat down and looked around.

"Yeah, I know what you mean," I said, unable to deny the beauty that surrounded us since the moment I arrived.

"I'm really sorry about your wife, Keith. I can't imagine how angry you must be," Jen said unexpectedly.

"Yeah, thanks. I guess it just dredged up some old memories. Memories that are now distorted by all this new information," I said, looking down at the water.

"I'm still trying to process the fact that Paul put all of our lives at risk just for his own personal gain," Jen said. I realized at some point I'd need to tell her about the additional detail I had just gotten on the phone, but decided I didn't want to get into it at the moment. The caller was pretty clear on the confidential nature of the story about Paul's father.

Neither of us said anything for a few minutes. The silence was healing, and brought me to where I could once again engage in the situation at hand.

"I guess we're going to have to find that Filipov woman somehow, or she's probably going to find us. I'm not sure if that drone found the cabin or not, but we should assume it probably did," I said with a sigh, refocusing on who I knew to be the real enemy.

I had barely gotten the words out of my mouth when my phone buzzed in my pocket. I was a little concerned it was the unknown caller again, and I'd have to explain that whole situation to Jen, but it wasn't. It was Sheriff Hanson.

"This is Keith," I said as I accepted the call.

"Mr. Morgan, this is Sheriff Hanson. Do you have a minute?" he asked.

"Sure, what's up?" I replied.

"We took your advice and reviewed camera footage from all the private airports around Denver and Colorado Springs," he started.

"And you found something?" I asked, realizing he wouldn't call if he didn't.

"Maybe. I'm wondering if you might have time to stop by? There is some footage here on our computers that I'd like you to see," he said.

"Sure. I can be there in about a half hour," I said.

"Great. See you then," Sheriff Hanson said and cut off the call.

"What was that about?" Jen asked, watching me curiously.

"Sheriff Hanson has some camera footage he'd like to show me. I told him I suspected they'd be using private jets to get in and out of Colorado and Montana, and it seems he found something in Colorado for me to look at. I'll have to check it out," I replied, standing up and stretching.

"If you leave, can Steve and I get into the cabin without you?" Jen asked, reminding me I was the only one Paul had enabled via the facial recognition program on the cabin door.

"Let me go set that up. I'll put you on it," I said, still not confident I should add Steve.

Trust no one.

"Why just me?" Jen asked, catching my point quickly.

I paused, not sure I wanted to disclose my concerns.

"It's because he wasn't hurt by Filipov like the rest of you?" Jen asked. She always had a way of picking up on subtle things before I revealed anything.

"Yeah, I guess so," I said.

"I don't get that vibe from him. But I get your point," she said.

I nodded, and we both made our way back to the cabin. I told Steve about what was going on, but he barely seemed to notice. He kept his head buried in his research while I logged into the security system Paul had set up. Within a few seconds, I had updated the facial recognition software to allow Jen's face to unlock the cabin.

I didn't enable Steve.

A few minutes after ending the call with Sheriff Hanson and saying goodbye to Jen and Steve, I was headed away from the cabin. Knowing I had taken longer to get away than I thought, I called Sheriff Hanson to let him know I was running behind.

"Hey Mr. Morgan, you about here?" Sheriff Hanson said, as he accepted my call.

"I'm running a few minutes behind. I'll be there in about a half hour from now," I said.

I heard a pause, as if he was talking to someone.

"Ok, sounds good, Mr. Morgan. We'll see you then," he said.

"Who's we?" I asked.

"That's just a figure of speech. I'll see you when you get here," he said.

We ended the call, and I headed to the 4Runner and got in. On the way to the Sheriff's office, I called Jamie and made sure things were still going well in Missouri with my parents. Apparently they were, as they had taken a boat out on Table Rock Lake near Branson. As before, I had to cut the call short to avoid interfering with their summer vacation activities.

As I had told Sheriff Hanson, I arrived at his office in Cameron in about thirty minutes. I walked into the small stucco building and was greeted by a sight taken directly out of the movies. More accurately, it was a sight right out of a movie from forty or fifty years ago. The walls were covered with what appeared to be pine paneling. The flooring was an old commercial tile, like I remembered from my grade school days in Missouri. The ceiling was high and open to wooden rafters with hanging lights that had screen covers like a school gymnasium. The place appeared to have been transplanted from the seventies.

There was a desk situated no more than six feet from the door, with a young uniformed deputy sitting behind it. There were two wooden chairs in front of the desk, so close they were nearly touching it. Two similar wooden chairs sat next to the door on my left. There were two holding cells just behind the officer at the desk. One was empty and one contained a sleeping detainee. To the right was a small office, which I assumed to be Sheriff Hanson's.

"How can I help you?" the deputy at the front desk asked.

"I'm Keith Morgan. I'm here to see Sheriff Hanson," I answered.

"Oh. Ok. Have a seat," the young deputy said as he pointed to the chairs next to the door.

"Thanks Jason. You can take your lunch now. I'll cover the front door," Sheriff Hanson said as he appeared from the office door on the right. He must have heard me come in.

"Ok, thanks Sheriff," the deputy said as he grabbed his hat to head out.

"You can come on in here, Mr. Morgan," Sheriff Hanson said as he waved me toward his door.

I followed his direction into the office, smiling at the way a small sheriff's office in Montana worked. My wandering mind envisioned the deputy hanging an 'out to lunch' sign on the front door whenever Sheriff Hanson wasn't here to cover his absence.

"Thanks for coming in," Sheriff Hanson said, as he motioned for me to take a seat.

His office was small, maybe ten feet square, and was sparsely appointed. There was a heavy antique wooden desk that appeared out of place against the seventies building structure, and a large leather and wood chair behind it. A bookcase in the corner made of metal and some sort of plywood better matched the rest of the building interior. There were two wooden chairs in front of the desk that matched the ones near the front door.

He was motioning for me to sit in one of the two wooden chairs.

"Sure," I said as I sat in the chair nearest the wall and turned it so I could see Sheriff Hanson and the office door at the same time.

"How are things going out at the cabin?" Sheriff Hanson asked. I was surprised he was offering to engage in small talk. It wasn't his style.

"Good. I'm just getting acclimated to it, I guess. It really is a beautiful property. In fact, there's lots of beauty up here. I see why people are flooding here from other states," I said, referring to the well-publicized spike in real estate interest across the region.

"Yeah, it is. We all see why it's happening, too, but I won't say everyone appreciates it much. There's a lot of animosity from the locals about some of the newcomers," Sheriff Hanson said.

"Sorry to hear that," I replied, not sure how to respond.

"I see you had some visitors at the rental cabin. Are they friends of yours?" Sheriff Hanson asked, still not moving toward his computer as I expected. I was eager to see the video footage he had mentioned, but he seemed to be stalling.

"Yeah. I had asked a couple of friends to come up and join me on the creek. It's hard for anyone to turn down a trip to Montana in the spring, especially the way Paul had recommended it. Plus, the cabin right there on the river forces you to take a shot at the Madison, too," I replied, suspecting that's where Sheriff Hanson had seen their vehicles.

"Indeed, it is. Are they having any luck out there on the river?" he asked.

"Hadn't really gotten going yet. They're out at the cabin

right now. I left them to come here. So, what did you find in the camera footage?" I asked, trying to push the conversation along.

"Oh, yeah. Let me pull it up here," he said, moving his monitor toward him and out of my vision.

"I need to login to the site again, just a second," he said.

He seemed to be taking an awfully long time to login to whatever system he needed to get to the camera footage. So long, in fact, that the front door opened while he was still looking.

"Sorry, I have to go get that. I've got front door duty for the moment," he said, jumping up abruptly and walking out of the office.

I noticed whispers coming from the other room that made me uncomfortable. While I couldn't hear everything, I heard him mention my two friends still at the cabin. I quietly stood up and pivoted the monitor on Sheriff Hanson's desk so I could see it. The screen was not logged into any system at all. It was still showing the desktop.

At that moment, I realized he had brought me here for a different purpose and was buying time with me until someone arrived at the front door. Someone who wasn't noticed by the deputy because he was out at lunch. And now that someone had arrived. I pulled my SIG P365 out of the holster in the small of my back and gripped it tightly. Then I quietly crept to the side of the office door to listen and wait.

As I waited, I heard the unmistakable sounds of a pistol slide being racked. Then I heard someone take a deep breath. Then I heard footsteps heading toward the office door.

I waited until I heard the footsteps reach the doorway, then I crouched and sprang at the first person who came in.

It was Sheriff Hanson. He clearly expected me to still be sitting in the chair and was easily taken down as I drove my SIG into the side of his jaw. He went down, and I pivoted to take on the unknown guest.

But as I pivoted, I realized it wasn't just one guest. There were three people standing there, all crouched in defensive positions.

And all with pistols aimed at my chest.

The two on the right and left were men who appeared to be well over six feet tall and built like bouncers. In a split second, I recognized them as the individuals I had seen on the video footage from the gas station dumping the drone parts.

The person in the middle was someone I had met before.

In Paul's condo.

It was Natalia Filipov.

Chapter Thirty-Four

I stared in disbelief at the face of Natalia Filipov while Sheriff Hanson struggled to pull himself up off the floor. He mumbled a few choice words at me while shaking his head and rubbing his jaw. He flopped into his desk chair as one of the two men beside Natalia motioned for me to sit down. Feeling no other option at the moment, I did.

"Mr. Morgan, how good to see you again," Natalia said as the guy on her left grabbed the SIG from my hand. In this context, she wasn't quite as attractive as she was at Paul's condo, but even pointing a gun at me, she was still a striking woman. It was hard to put her in the category of a stone-cold killer until she spoke. There was an evil sneer in her voice that she had hidden away when we had initially met. The voice completely overshadowed her beauty.

I didn't respond. As I sat there, I wondered why she didn't just kill me at the condo when she first met me. They could have collected the safe and made away with millions of dollars. There must have been a reason for them to keep me alive. I wondered if they knew about Paul's security setup and what was behind the door of the cabin. Or maybe they thought that's where all the details of his wealth were.

It almost made me laugh to realize they were right there with all the documentation at my house in Woodland Park and they just left it behind in my safe. While I didn't know I was securing it by leaving it there, that's exactly what had happened. Even if they knew they had to use my face, and my eyeball, to get into the cabin and the bunker, it wouldn't get them what they wanted. That thought made me breathe a little easier.

Then I remembered there were two people still at the cabin. And one of them was Jen.

"Cuff him to the chair," she said to Sheriff Hanson. He obeyed, jerking my arms behind me and looping the cuffs through two spindles of the chair. I realized it wasn't a very secure way to hold me captive, but I kept that to myself.

Sheriff Hanson returned to his desk chair, and I sat quietly with my hands behind me.

"Maybe I should introduce myself," Natalia said as she leaned against the door frame of Sheriff Hanson's office. The two goons took positions against the far wall, still aiming their pistols at me.

I looked at her, then at the two goons. Then I looked at Sheriff Hanson, who caught my glance briefly, then quickly looked away. It was the look of a coward being caught in his cowardice. He had sold me out. I was still staring at him when she continued.

"Before I introduce myself, perhaps I should let you know a few things about my family. I believe you may have known my father. His name was Ivan Filipov," she said. I held my gaze to avoid letting her know I knew the name, although I noticed she referred to him in the past tense.

"I see you will not admit you recognize the name?

That's fine. I'm going to tell you about him anyway," she said, grabbing the other wooden chair and pulling it toward her.

While she did it, I once again took a glance at Sheriff Hanson, unable to contain my indignation. This time, he noticed it and didn't look away.

"Don't look at me with all that self-righteous judgment. They said they'd kill my family," he snarled abruptly before Natalia could continue.

"What was I supposed to do? I saw what they did to my deputy and to the Caldwells. I couldn't let them do that to my wife! What was I supposed to do?" Sheriff Hanson had the look of a desperate and defeated man while leaning over his desk and yelling at me.

"And from what they're saying, your friend Paul wasn't quite the saint you depicted him to be. Stealing from people as part of a government cover? Is that really why you're here? It's like an old-time scavenger hunt out here, huh? Looking for his money before anyone else can find it? Then bringing all of us into your web of death and destruction! The Caldwell's blood is on your hands!" Sheriff Hanson yelled as he continued to lean over the desk and spit out his explanation.

From his brief outburst, it was clear he was promised safety if he led me to the office. And it was also clear to me he was too naïve to recognize he was now expendable to my captors. It wouldn't surprise me if he didn't make it out the office door.

"Shut up, you idiot," Natalia finally said. Sheriff Hanson backed into his seat.

Then she turned back to me.

"Now, where was I? Oh yes, my father. You see, your friend Paul had an issue with my father. An issue that he shouldn't have taken so personally. Yes, my father killed Paul's father. But that, as I'm sure you understand, was just part of his job. My father was doing his job. I know your history well enough to know you understand what it means to have to kill to do your job. Isn't that right, Mr. Morgan?" She stopped and waited, but I wasn't planning to answer.

"Yeah, that's what I thought. But your friend Paul didn't see it that way, did he? He decided to live his life to make my father miserable. First, Paul took all his wealth from him. There was no point in that at all. And then, of course, my father had to retaliate. And I suppose that's where you come into the story. My father assumed Paul would slow down if he understood how powerful my father could be and how far he could reach. He could literally reach across the globe and snuff out a life whenever he wanted. Not only that, but he could also make it look like a complete accident. Maybe even a car accident on a snowy road in the mountains," Natalia said with a sneer. Then she stopped and stared at me.

She was admitting Beth was murdered on that mountain road, just like Paul had been researching and just like the mysterious voice on the security app had confirmed. As much as I tried, I couldn't hide my hatred for this woman.

She seemed to enjoy it as a smile crossed her face.

"Yep, that's right. But your stupid friend didn't stop there! He kept digging into my father's business. So my father started pushing more pain on Paul's friends. Their lives, as you may know, have not been all they had hoped. My father made sure of that. If Paul was going to intrude on my father's business, his friends were going to pay. But Paul didn't care, did he? He just kept going."

She adjusted in her chair as her face began to grow angry.

"He even went so far as to disrupt my father's attempts to help our country's oil production. That didn't hurt Paul at all, but he still couldn't leave it alone. You didn't even know what you were doing when he sent you to Detroit to shut down that operation. Yet, you shut it down and cost my father his job," she said, her evil smile turning to a snarl while she spoke louder.

I recognized her reference to the work we had done taking down the political tampering operation several months before. It had resulted in the shootout at Willow Creek and had ultimately led to one perpetrator slinging out Filipov's name in a vicious rant during his arrest. Back then, I thought he was just trying to get under my skin.

"And then it cost him his life. He couldn't take being considered a failure for his own country. You and Paul made him feel that way. He was a great man, but Paul took everything from him. And you helped make it happen. He took the respectful way out and ended his own life rather than go on being considered a failure," she said, now staring at me in uncontrollable anger.

"That's right. Paul and the work he assigned you to do ended up killing my father. That's why I had to finish what my father had started. Paul had to go," she said, stopping to take a deep breath and sit back in her chair.

"And now I'm here to take back what's rightfully ours. I'm here to get his money back, and to take everything Paul had gained from what he stole from my father. Which brings us to you, Mr. Morgan," she said.

I assumed I was about to find out what she knew about Paul's security system, but I was wrong. Apparently, she didn't know as much as I had expected.

"The good Sheriff Hanson here tells me Paul has a cabin out here in the woods. When I saw you had left your house and had come up here, I assumed you must not have found what you were looking for at the condo. We have the safe, so we know there was nothing there," she said, now getting into tactical mode.

Her statements were revealing just how little she knew about the situation. Still, my growing concern was the fact that Jen was still there at the cabin with Steve. If Natalia killed me here in the office, Jen would be a sitting duck out there with Steve. And even now, I wondered if Steve knew this whole thing was coming.

"So, Mr. Morgan, I'm going to lock you here in one of Sheriff Hanson's jail cells. Then I'm going to head out to that cabin. And I'm going to take back what belongs to my family. And if I find it, I'm going to come back here and I'm going to kill you, Mr. Morgan. Do you understand?" Natalia said, partially revealing her plan and not expecting an answer.

"Good. You better hope I find it, Mr. Morgan. Because, if I don't, I'm going to do whatever I have to do to you, and to those two precious children of yours, to get that money. Now, Sheriff Hanson, please see if he has a key to the cabin in his pocket," she said, motioning to Sheriff Hanson with her pistol.

Sheriff Hanson came around the desk and patted my pockets. Then he jammed his hand into each of my front pockets, pulling out the key fob for my 4Runner and my phone. He held them up for Natalia to see, then threw them on his desk next to my SIG.

"Ok, so no cabin key? Then escort our friend Mr. Morgan to his accommodations. We'll get into the cabin however we need to," she said as she stood and walked out the office door. Once again, revealing how little she knew about Paul's cabin.

Sheriff Hanson removed one handcuff so he could get them out of the chair spindles and quickly locked it back onto my wrist, keeping my hands behind my back. As he did, I looked around and evaluated my options. The two goons were still focused on me with their guns aimed at my chest. There were no windows or exits to the office, so even if I did escape Sheriff Hanson and the two goons, I'd have nowhere to go.

So I allowed myself to be led into the other room. Sheriff Hanson was trying to inflict as much pain as possible, as he pulled and tugged on my arm toward the empty jail cell at the back of the building. For that moment, I regretted hitting him in the face with my pistol.

I let Sheriff Hanson push in that direction, glancing around to evaluate possible escape routes as I went. I also remembered the deputy was out at lunch, which gave me some relief, as I knew I'd have a chance to negotiate my way out when he returned. I was still looking for escape options when Sheriff Hanson opened the door and pushed me into the cell. He left the cuffs on, which threw off my balance. I fell forward and tumbled to the floor awkwardly.

Sheriff Hanson locked the cell door and stood over me, looking disgusted.

"Is the deputy taken care of?" Natalia asked Sheriff Hanson as he continued to stand at the door of the cell and stare at me.

"Yep. I sent him on a call up north. He won't be back for a couple of hours. You guys can be gone by then," he said, locking the cell while two of my potential escape options evaporated. The cell was locked, and the deputy wasn't returning.

Behind him, Natalia had aimed her gun in his direction.

He saw me looking her direction and turned around to realize his fate.

"What are you doing? You need me to get you to the cabin," he yelled as he raised his hands.

"No, we really don't. Our drone found the cabin, you idiot. We just needed you to get Mr. Morgan here alive. And with my appreciation for that, you've served your purpose."

She pulled the trigger, and I watched as the back of Sheriff Hanson's head exploded onto the wall beside the jail cell.

Chapter Thirty-Five

"Let's take his truck in case someone is watching the drive in," Natalia said, motioning toward Sheriff Hanson's office. After getting the key fob from his desk, she turned to me as they moved toward the door.

"We will meet again, Mr. Morgan. If I find what I'm looking for, I promise you'll meet a quick yet permanent demise. If I don't... well, let's just say you better hope I find it," she said.

Then, they were all gone, and I was left alone in the cell looking at Sheriff Hanson's corpse outside my door.

During the commotion, the sleeping person in the other cell, who I had forgotten was there, had awakened and was staring at me. I was surprised to recognize the bewildered face of Bailey Caldwell. He stared in disbelief at me, then at Sheriff Hanson, then back at me with his eyes and mouth wide open. He never got up from his cot on the far side of his cell.

I nodded at him, but he still didn't say a word.

"Rough night last night?" I asked him, trying to shake him out of his shock.

He nodded.

"Any chance your brother is coming to get you?" I asked. That seemed to wake him up a little.

"Uh, yeah. Probably," he said. He continued to stare at Sheriff Hanson.

"It's probably best not to stare at him. It doesn't help. Did you hear what was going on out there before he got shot?" I asked.

Bailey nodded and looked back at me, regaining some of his composure.

"I heard some of it. So, those people are the ones who were flying the drone?" Bailey asked, focusing on the piece of the story that intersected with his life.

"Yeah," I said.

"Then they killed my parents to get it back," he said, looking back toward the door.

"Probably," I said, letting him get things sorted in his head.

"Then I started a fight last night with the Krohl guys for no reason," Bailey said, revealing how he landed in the cell in the first place.

"But your brother knows? And he's coming to get you?" I asked, hopefully.

"He should be. What time is it?" Bailey asked, looking around for a clock.

There was one on the front wall above the door. It was an old, round clock, like the ones I had seen over and over in school as a kid. That old school reminder seemed to be a theme in this place.

Bailey found it and tried to focus. The clock's short hand was just past the eleven and the long hand was on the seven. It was 11:35 AM.

"He should be here by noon. Sheriff Hanson told him to

come get me at noon," Bailey said as he finally recognized the time.

"Let's hope he's early. He's my only hope to get out there and save my friends," I said.

"I heard them talk about that. You really have friends here?" Bailey asked.

"Yeah, I do. They came to help me sort out who was behind my friends's murder. You know, the guy who owned the property next to your ranch? It turns out they found me before I found them. Now, they're on their way to my friend's property," I said.

"He had a cabin out there?" Bailey asked.

"Yeah. A very nice cabin. He spent a lot of time building it," I said.

"We wondered what he was doing. Some of us saw him out here a lot, but he didn't talk to people much. We didn't know if he was hunting or building or what. Sorry to hear he died," Bailey said.

"To be honest, I didn't know it was here either. I only found out after he died. It's kind of a shame, too, because it's an incredible place. And thanks," I said, continuously looking around for avenues of escape.

The jail cells were like cages. The bars from the front and sides matched bars that covered the top of the cells.

Bailey saw me looking around.

"I don't think there's a way out," he said, also looking around and beginning to understand my urgency.

I shook my head, sighed, then sat down on the cot with a deep sigh.

"Why were those guys looking for your friend? What did he do?" Bailey asked. Realizing we probably had some time, I gave him a high level version of the story.

When I got done, Bailey nodded, stood, and walked around his cell.

"So they are Russians, huh? We've got to get them. Let's hope Thor gets here early," he said, looking again at the clock. I was surprised to see only five minutes had passed since we started talking.

We sat quietly for another minute when we both heard a vehicle pull up in front of the building. We stood in unison and walked to the front of our cells, waiting for someone to come in the door.

After what seemed like an eternity, Thornton Caldwell came bounding in the front door.

"Sheriff, I'm here to pick up my..." He stopped talking as he saw the remnants of the back of Sheriff Hanson's head sprayed along the wall to his left.

Then he stared at me, then Bailey, then ran around the desk to see Sheriff Hanson's body lying on the floor between the desk and the cells. Only then did he speak.

"What happened?" he asked with his eyes wide open as he continued to stare at the corpse.

"It's a long story, but I can share it with you after you get us out of here. I need to get to my friend's cabin as fast as possible," I said, unable to hide my anxiety.

"Dude, I'm not letting you out of there. Did you do this?" Thornton asked, unable to take his gaze away from Sheriff Hanson.

"No, he didn't," Bailey interjected before I could respond.

"I saw everything. We need to get out of here. The people who did this are the same ones who killed mom and dad. We have to go help find them," Bailey said, shaking the door to his cell as he yelled.

"Why did they kill the sheriff?" Thornton asked, finally

looking up but keeping the look of shock and horror on his face.

"They conned him into helping get Keith here. Then they killed him," Bailey said, leaving the story incomplete and impossible to interpret.

"Why'd they kill him if he was helping them?" Thornton asked.

"They used him to get to me. Once they got me locked up, he was no longer of use to them. They shot him right here in front of us," I interjected, trying to fill in enough of the story to get him to move.

"Bailey is right, Thornton. These people are going to kill whoever gets in their way. And right now, I have a friend in a cabin on the property next to the Lazy J. These killers are on the way there, and if we don't stop them I'm afraid my friend will die," I said, realizing I had subconsciously excluded Steve and was only referring to Jen, hoping she was still alive to face the oncoming killers.

"Ok, ok. First off, call me Thor. It's a long story, but it's what everyone around here calls me. Now, let me find the keys," Thor finally said, reluctantly stepping toward Sheriff Hanson's corpse. He had fallen on his back, so it was easy for Thor to pat his pockets and find his keys. He took out the keys and walked over to Bailey's cell, letting him out first.

Bailey walked out and ran to the desk and opened a drawer. He grabbed a wallet and stuffed it in his pocket. Then he grabbed a belt and a holster, and started to strap them on. While he was getting himself together, Thor walked toward my cell cautiously.

"Are you sure this guy is ok? Once I open this, we're at his mercy," Thor said before getting close to my cell door.

"Yes! I'm sure! Just open it, we have to get going," Bailey

said, buckling his belt. I appreciated his sense of urgency and support, but I was getting more anxious with each second.

"These are the guys who flew the droid onto my friend's property, Thor. Then they came back to get it and killed your parents. It's the same people who are now going to kill my friend if we don't get going," I said, trying to calm my voice as much as possible.

After a few seconds that seemed like an eternity, Thor seemed to flip a switch in his head. He quickly unlocked my cell and ran toward the door.

"Alright, then. Let's get going. I'm not going to let mom and dad's killers go free," he said.

I ran into Sheriff Hanson's office and grabbed my phone and my SIG. When I got back to the office, the Caldwell brothers were already outside. I turned and shook my head as I looked at Sheriff Hanson's dead body, then ran toward Thor Caldwell's F150.

The passenger door was open, so I jumped in. Thor was in the driver's seat and Bailey had climbed into the back seat. As soon as I got into the passenger's seat and closed the door, Thor took off.

"Are we headed to that parking area just down Old Sage Road?" Thor asked as he took off. I didn't realize that was the name the locals had given the road, so I had to clarify.

"If that's the road where I've been parking this week, then yes," I said, knowing they had been watching me.

He didn't answer, but shot out of the parking lot in the right direction. My first task was to text Jen about her danger, which I did immediately.

"I need to make a quick call," I said while finishing my text message and opening the security application on my phone. I didn't know if a 911 call would help with Sheriff Hanson's unavailability, but I was hopeful the person from the NSA, or whoever they worked for, could get us some help.

The voice answered within seconds.

"Hey Mr. Morgan, is everything ok?" It was the same robotic voice as before.

"No, it's not. Natalia Filipov and two of her men came to Cameron. They conned the sheriff to call me into his office, and I walked right into an ambush. I lucked out and got help from two locals, but Natalia and her goons are already on their way to the cabin. We're following them now, but I'm afraid they may get there first. And Jennifer Ellis is there!" I realized my voice was getting louder as I talked. Looking next to me, I could see Bailey and Thor staring at me. I motioned for Thor to keep his eyes on the road.

"Are you with the two locals now?" The voice sounded disturbed by that idea.

"Yeah, I am," I said, offering no more information while the Caldwells were listening.

"You can't put them in danger, Mr. Morgan!"

"I don't plan to do that."

"And how do you expect to avoid danger if they're with you?"

"I'll insist they stay in the car."

Thor and Bailey were shaking their heads at me, but I ignored them.

"That doesn't sound safe, Mr. Morgan. So you said they're heading to the cabin and Ms. Ellis is there? Is she alone?" The question reminded me Steve was still near the cabin but was outside the door.

"Well, sort of," I started.

"What do you mean by that?" The voice didn't sound amused.

"There is another guy there, Steve Chandler. But I only gave Jennifer access to unlock the cabin. If Steve goes out, he can't get back in," I said, realizing how silly that would sound to someone who didn't know the situation.

"Why'd you do that?" Even through the robotic tone, it was easy to tell the voice was exasperated by my last statement.

"There were some questions about his, uh, motives in being at the cabin," I said, not really sure how to explain the whole thing to the voice while scorching down the road in Thor's F150.

"Listen to me, Mr. Morgan. You need to get Steve back in that cabin and keep him safe. He is a friend, not a foe," the voice retorted.

"How do you know that? I mean, Filipov attacked the rest of our team but Steve somehow escaped harm," I started, but the voice cut me off.

"Because we were helping him," the voice said. "Now, you get him back in that cabin now! We'll be there soon. I'm already on my way," the voice said, calming down a bit.

Only then did I realize there was a noise in the background, like a car or something.

"Ok, when will you get here?" I asked.

"We're about an hour from landing, then probably another thirty minutes to the cabin," the voice said. That meant they were flying, not driving.

"Ok, then I'm way ahead of you," I said, regretting it immediately.

"You need to hold tight, Mr. Morgan. Don't try to deal with this alone. I mean it," the voice seethed sternly.

"I won't," I said, looking at the Caldwell brothers beside me.

We ended the call, and I looked to my side, then back ahead of me.

What I should have said was, 'I won't go in alone.'

When we ended the call, I saw Jen had responded with 'ok,' indicating she got my original warning.

I began frantically texting Jen again, hoping she wasn't inside the bunker and unable to get my messages

Chapter Thirty-Six

Jen and Steve had continued to sift through data on Paul's servers while Keith was gone. They were mostly quiet, with a brief conversation about coffee, before Jen stepped into the kitchen and made a new pot.

Planning to test whether her security profile was updated, she yelled into the bunker at Steve.

"I'm going to see if my face lets me into the cabin," she said and opened the front door.

She closed the door and walked around the corner, then walked back up to the door as though she had just arrived. She stared into the small camera and waited.

She didn't have to wait long, as the door quickly unlocked and allowed her access. She smiled as she realized the system worked as designed, admiring the fact Paul had taken the time to install such an intricate system. Jen was still annoyed at the way he had played The Association for his benefit, but this cabin was impressive.

She walked back into the kitchen to grab their coffee cups.

That was when her phone started buzzing, and she received the first text message from Keith.

> Watch cameras. Filipov daughter was here and is on the way to cabin! Gun safe in bedroom closet. And be careful of Steve!

Her mouth dropped open as she saw the text, especially the part about Steve. It didn't specifically tell her to avoid him or that he was for sure working against them, just to be careful. That distinction gave her hope. And anxiety.

She responded with 'ok' to let Keith know she got the confusing message.

But knowing the Filipov woman was on her way to the cabin was enough to get Jen's adrenaline going. She was immediately in fight mode.

Keeping her emotions in check to avoid suspicion from Steve, she finished making the coffee and walked into the bunker. There were no messages on any screens alerting of intruders, so she assumed they had a little time. She handed Steve his coffee and noticed he was looking at camera footage from around the cabin. She wondered if she missed a warning while she was out and he had already seen intruders coming in.

"What's going on, Steve? Are those the cameras from around the property?" Jen asked.

"Yeah. I'm trying to find out if anyone has gotten in here over the last few months. Maybe that would give us a clue if someone is helping these guys," he answered without looking up.

"Good idea," Jen said, sitting back down in her chair. She looked at the screens with views of all the different cameras around the property and saw nothing. She took a deep breath and looked over at Steve again.

Suddenly, he sat back in his chair.

"Well, here's the drone! It looks like it flew right in from the road. Let me see if I can find a view that shows the road," he said, watching the drone fly slowly around the trees.

"Whoa! And there it went," he said as they watched the drone clip a tree branch and crumble to the ground.

"Ok, here we go. There's another alert on camera twelve, which covers the parking area. There's a white Ford F150 sitting there with someone looking at a laptop screen. That's how the drone got onto the property," Steve said after reviewing a few more videos.

"I think I need to make a call," he said abruptly and stood up.

Jen watched as he headed out of the bunker and out the front door, stopping on the porch and putting his phone to his ear. The front door closed behind him. Jen crept back into the kitchen so he couldn't see her and began frantically typing on her phone.

Before she could finish the message she was typing, she received one from Keith.

They there yet?

No. But I need to know if I can trust Steve or not.

Why?

He's on the porch right now talking on the phone

To who?

I don't know. Just said he had to make a call and went out. Do I let him back in???

...

There was a long pause while the three dots showed Keith was typing. After a few seconds, she realized he must be thinking hard about the question.

Finally, his answer appeared.

No

And with that, Jen knew what she had to do. She ran into the bedroom and opened the closet. There, she found a fingerprint pad she hoped was linked to the security Keith had set up for her earlier. She put her index finger on the pad and held her breath. Then she heard a click and let out a huge sigh.

She opened the door to the safe and found a myriad of guns and ammunition. She was still going over her weapon options when she heard Steve knock on the front door. He must have just realized he hadn't been set up in the facial recognition system like she was. And, like before, she had to admire that fact that the system was working.

She paused for a minute, then headed to the front door. Debating whether to acknowledge Steve was intentionally locked out or to ignore him, she decided to hit him with it. She walked over near the front door and yelled.

"Your friends are on the way. You're not getting back in here!" Jen yelled, realizing the front door of the cabin was probably well insulated for sound.

Her yelling was loud enough. Steve heard her.

"What? What friends? Wait! You think I'm working with Filipov? And they're here?" He was screaming at her from outside the front door.

"Why weren't you hurt like the others? Keith lost his

wife. All the rest of the team had bad things happen to them. You didn't," Jen said, thinking she would send him away with her summary of Keith's concerns.

"I told Keith about that! I just caught them before they got to me. They tried to get me. I would have been in the same shape as the others," he yelled, now looking around frantically outside.

"He doesn't believe you and I don't either!" Jen yelled.

That last statement seemed to hit Steve right in the chest. He stepped back, appearing hurt and defeated. He stood there for a second before regaining his composure.

"You said my friends are coming. Which friends were you referring to?" Steve asked.

Jen paused before she answered, wondering why Steve would ask such a question if he was in on the whole scheme. Maybe he really knew and was just trying to appear disconnected, or maybe he really had no idea who was coming onto the property as they yelled through the front door of Paul's cabin. Or maybe he had just talked to them on the phone.

After thinking about it quickly, she decided it wouldn't make anything worse to share what she knew. If he knew already, so what? If he didn't know and was really innocent, despite Keith's warning, the information might save him.

"That Filipov woman has apparently found a couple of friends. Keith says they're on their way to the property from town right now. He's chasing them, but I'm not sure if he'll get here before them or not," she yelled through the door, now questioning whether she should let him back in.

Steve seemed to be calculating his response, looking around, and thinking as he stood on the porch. This time, he looked around the property with determination on his face.

He, too, was getting into fight mode. Jen recognized the look as she watched him through the window.

"I'm going to make another call," he said and stepped away quickly.

When things got quiet again, Jen ran into the bunker and looked at the screens. Everything still looked normal, so she took a breath and sat down.

Then the screens changed. Camera twelve was showing movement. Jen looked closer and saw a view she recognized. It was the road that led them into the property from town. And Keith's 4Runner was approaching. She breathed a sigh of relief and stepped out of the bunker to text him.

Looks like you're here first. They haven't arrived yet.

She started back into the bunker when she got a response.

No!

She stopped in her tracks.

That's not me! They have my 4Runner!

Jen's heart sunk.

Then they're here. How far are you?

Ten mins

Jen ran back into the bunker and watched the screen. Three figures emerged from Keith's 4Runner and looked around. They had normal-looking outfits on but had walked around to the back of the vehicle where she couldn't see them for a moment.

While she watched, Steve began banging on the front door again. She wanted to see the approach the three invaders were taking, so she ignored Steve as best she could to focus on the screen in front of her.

The three individuals spent several seconds behind the 4Runner before emerging again. This time, they looked different. They were all dressed in camouflage and holding long rifles. At that moment, Jen realized they knew she was in the cabin and they were prepared for a battle. A battle against her.

Jen left the screen and ran into the bedroom and to the closet, where the gun safe was still open. She took a deep breath to control her adrenaline and to concentrate on the options in front of her. First, she grabbed one of the 1911 pistols out of a pocket on the back of the safe door and shoved in a magazine. She stuffed a couple of loaded magazines into her pocket.

Next, she pondered her rifle options. Thinking about the structure she was in, she realized she needed to be prepared for the potential of long-range and short-range shots. If she could get them from a distance, she would. If they got close and she had to defend at close range, she'd need an option for that situation as well.

Jen selected a shotgun and made sure it was loaded. Seeing it was a 12-gauge version, she shoved a handful of shells in her other pocket. Her stuffed pockets quickly made her realize the jeans she was wearing were not designed for this type of tactical situation. She grabbed the longest gun in the safe, which also had the largest scope. She didn't take time to inspect the brand of the empty rifle, but quickly worked the bolt action to make sure she could operate it smoothly. Then she checked the caliber, found a .308 label on the side of the barrel, and found a box of .308 cartridges in the bottom of the safe.

As Jen was trying to find the right place to store her newly acquired weapons, she heard her phone buzzing on the kitchen counter where she left it. She put her shotgun, long rifle, and ammunition down on the table and checked the phone. It was a call from Keith.

Chapter Thirty-Seven

"I've gotten into the gun safe," Jen said as she accepted the call.

"Good! I'm hoping you don't need it, but good to be ready," I replied.

"Are you about here?" Jen asked before I had a chance to continue.

"Yeah, only a couple of minutes away. But I need to let you know I received a call from someone who insists I'm wrong about Steve," I said.

"Are you sure? That decision could kill me if they're wrong? I didn't hear a good explanation from him about avoiding Filipov's terror tactics, did you?" Jen asked, getting reasonably frantic.

"Well, no, I really didn't. But the caller insisted he was working with a government agency of some kind and they helped get him out of it," I replied, realizing I had no time to explain the rest of the story about the unknown caller.

"Do you trust them? I mean, do you even know who it is?" Jen asked, fairly.

"Well, I don't know who it is, but frankly, I have to trust them at this point. They're all I have left. We've lost the local sheriff and the state police won't be able to help us quickly. I don't have time to explain how I found this person, but I'm going to have to trust them. I guess that means you should let Steve back into the cabin to help you defend your-selves," I said, finally getting to the point of my call.

Jen was quiet for a second.

"You know, now that you say that, I haven't heard him at the door since I told him I wasn't letting him back in. Let me look out there," Jen said as I could hear her moving around.

"Keith, he's gone. I'm here alone," she said after a few seconds. There was no fear in her voice, only resolve.

"What do you mean? He left the cabin?" I asked.

"Yeah, he left. I don't see him anywhere. I can look at the cameras to see if he turns up somewhere, but for now, he's not here to help me," Jen said, looking around the cabin in all the directions the windows would allow.

"Ok, then get inside and hunker down. Based on the camera positions, you can probably see your three guests coming from all directions if you watch from the bunker. When they get close, however, you'll have to rely on your own eyes. But we should catch up with them before they get there. They seemed to know where the cabin is, but I doubt they've walked the path from the parking area before," I said, trying to be optimistic.

"What do you mean, 'we' should catch up with them? Who's with you?" Jen asked, making me realize she was missing a big piece of the story from the last several minutes.

"I'm in the Caldwell brothers' F150 right now. It's a

long story, but they had to help me out of a jam at the sheriff's office," I said, trying to be brief.

"What kind of jam? And why isn't the sheriff with you? You said you lost him?" Jen asked, not letting me be as brief as I had hoped.

"Ok, I'll give you a quick summary, but then you've got to get into the bunker," I started.

"Keith, we've got at least twenty minutes, even if they come straight here. I think you've got enough time to tell me where the sheriff went and why you're racing here with the Caldwell brothers," Jen said, sounding frustrated.

"Yeah, ok," I said as the truck raced onto the dirt road leading to Paul's cabin.

"You remember I got the call from the sheriff to come into town and look at camera footage? Well, that wasn't exactly true. He called to lure me into a trap."

I paused to see if Jen had questions. She didn't, so I continued.

"We were sitting in his office when Natalia Filipov and two of her thugs came to the door. She basically confessed to killing my wife and setting up our old team, just as we thought. Then they cuffed me and put me into a cell," I said.

This time, Jen had questions.

"There were three of them? That makes sense. I just saw three people get out of your 4Runner," she said.

"Ok, that's them," I said.

"So, it was Natalia doing all this to Paul and not her father?" Jen asked. She wasn't going to let me get away with leaving out details.

"Well, it seems the assignment Paul sent us on to Detroit had caused her father some difficulty with the Russian government. So much difficulty, in fact, that he lost his job and eventually committed suicide. The increase in attacks on our team seems to have come from her. She's out for revenge and she believes getting back her father's money will scratch that vengeful itch," I said, pausing again.

"Ok, so that explains the ramp-up in online attacks we've seen lately. So, why weren't you attacked?" Jen asked. It was a question I had pondered myself, and let me to the only conclusions I could come up with.

"I think there are two reasons. First, I think they hit me pretty hard out of the gate. Killing my wife was enough to wreck my life and my kids' lives. They probably would have hit me harder if they saw how well my kids are doing," I admitted.

"Hmmm. Ok. And what's the other reason?" Jen asked, making me a little uncomfortable with her grilling. I was beginning to wonder if she was suspecting I was part of Filipov's clan.

"More than anything, I think they knew I could lead them to Paul's money, which Natalia clearly believes should be hers," I said.

"How would they know you could get them to Paul?" Jen asked, again digging deeper than was comfortable.

That question made me think for a minute, realizing I didn't have a good answer.

"I'm not really sure. I mean, Paul was directing our assignments when we shut down Filipov's US criminal enterprises. But honestly, I'm not sure why they thought I could lead them back to the money," I replied.

"Ok, so how do the Caldwell brothers come into this story?" Jen asked, finally moving past the uncomfortable questions about Filipov and our team from Afghanistan.

"Well, it seems Bailey Caldwell had overindulged last night and had landed himself in a jail cell at the sheriff's office. As luck would have it, Thornton Caldwell came in to check on his brother after Natalia and her two thugs had killed Sheriff Hanson and had taken off," I said, feeling the story was complete.

Jen still had some questions.

"They killed Sheriff Hanson? I thought you said he was involved?" she asked.

"He was, but they only used him to get to me. Once they had me, they didn't need him anymore. He thought they'd need him to get to the cabin, but apparently they already know where the cabin is. It seems their drone had uncovered the cabin location before it crashed," I replied.

That last statement seemed to jolt Jen into the reality of her current dilemma.

"Ok, so then they will probably be here in less time than I hoped. How far are you guys now?" Jen asked, shifting into gear.

"We're just pulling up to the parking area now," I replied, seeing my 4Runner already parked and Natalia Filipov nowhere in sight.

"It looks like they're already gone," I added.

"Yeah, they arrived just a short while ago. You are probably five minutes behind them. I'm pretty sure this cabin can hold them off that long," she said.

"You're probably right. Paul's message said the walls were reinforced. They'd withstand rifles but not rockets. If you see an RPG launcher in anyone's hands, hit the bunker immediately," I said, recalling Paul's video message.

"They had a tactical bag, but I didn't see what was in it. They definitely had long rifles, though," Jen said.

"Ok, good to know. We're parking now. Lock down and we'll get there as soon as we can," I said, realizing we couldn't go storming in there with guns blazing. Natalia and her thugs had the tactical advantage by arriving first. Plus, I just learned they had a substantial firepower advantage.

I ended the call with Jen as the three of us jumped out of the truck. I felt for my SIG in my belt, not confident it would do much good against Natalia's long rifles. The Caldwell boys were ranchers, so maybe they had something.

"Do you guys have any rifles I can borrow?" I asked, joining them at the back of the truck.

When I got to the back of the truck, they were already loading two rifles they had produced from the backseat.

"What are you guys doing? You don't have to come in there with me. These guys will shoot first and ask questions later. You've done enough already," I said, watching them load one round at a time into their lever action rifles.

They didn't stop. Thor had finished loading and was donning a camouflage jacket and stuffing extra ammunition into the pockets.

"We're going. These people killed our parents. There's no way you're going in there alone," Bailey said as he dug into the backseat for a jacket similar to Thor's.

After putting on the jacket, he produced another rifle from behind the seat and handed it to me. It was another lever action rifle. I wasn't an expert with this type of rifle, but I knew enough to make it work.

"Sorry, these 30-30's are all we've got. They were my dad's favorites. They're great for scaring away bears or taking out aggressive coyotes or wolves, but I'm afraid they're not so good for this type of stuff," he said with a nod toward the woods in front of us.

"This is great, Bailey. Thank you," I said, taking the rifle from him and testing the lever action.

"They'll take five rounds at a time, so you'll probably

want to load up your pockets," he said, nodding toward the boxes of ammunition Thor had pulled out of the truck.

We all loaded our rifles quickly and closed the truck. If the intruders ahead of us hadn't heard us arriving, they surely heard the doors slamming shut.

As we surveyed the tree-filled mountain terrain in front of us, a thought occurred to me.

"What are your phone numbers?" I asked when I got back to the Caldwell truck.

As they replied, I added their numbers to my phone and sent a text.

"There's mine," I said as the message went out. "Let's keep in touch," I said.

"Should we all go straight in, or spread out?" Thor asked as he snapped the lever on his rifle to load a round into the chamber.

"Let's spread out. You two take the middle and lower sections of the ridge toward the cabin, straight ahead. Keep enough distance to scan the grounds ahead of you, but close enough to communicate. I'll head around the top of the ridge to our left and circle down from the top," I said, remembering there was a tunnel behind the cabin bunker I might be able to find.

I didn't know if Natalia and her friends knew about the alternate access to the bunker, but I wanted to make sure they didn't sneak in from that direction. If they did, it would put them directly into the bunker with Jen. The thought of that spiked my adrenaline.

"You guys good? You really don't have to do this," I said as a final warning before taking off.

"All good, here," Thor said.

"Don't shoot unless you have to," I felt obliged to say.

Neither of them looked at me, nor did they respond. They were both focused on the hunt.

"Ok, let's go. Text when you find them," I said as we all headed into the woods ahead of us.

I climbed up the steep, boulder-strewn hill directly in front of the left headlight of my 4Runner while the Caldwell boys went to the right. They had a more direct route to the cabin, so I moved ahead quickly. I didn't want them arriving before I assessed the situation.

The climb up the hill burned my thighs as I jogged toward the area where I expected to see a cave and tunnel that led to the bunker. Sheriff Hanson had mentioned there were visible antennas somewhere up there, and Paul had said those should be near the entrance I was looking for.

Swinging right and left around the steepest and rockiest sections of the mountainside, I stopped in about ten minutes to scan the ridge in front of me. I could see several peaks near my estimation of the cabin's location, but nothing that looked like antenna or satellite dishes. I also saw no other humans, so I ventured ahead.

I noticed there were suspiciously few birds or other animals scurrying away as I hustled along just below the top of the ridge, making me wonder if someone hadn't scared them away before I got there. In another five minutes, I had my answer.

Ahead of me and just to my left, I saw a cluster of antennas and a small satellite dish. They were painted green and blended into the landscape surprisingly well, but they were there.

And about thirty feet to the right was a small cave entrance. It was about six feet high and was tucked away under a large rock outcropping that served as the summit to that section of the ridge.

My adrenaline surging at the sight of the cave entrance, I ran ahead to get a better look. Then, just as I rounded the last batch of trees before arriving at the mouth of the cave, I stopped in my tracks.

I saw someone's back disappear into the darkness of the tunnel.

Chapter Thirty-Eight

Knowing the person in the tunnel entrance had the tactical advantage, I paused to consider my next move. I wasn't sure if they had seen me before they disappeared into the darkness, so I'd need to be careful.

Before doing anything, I had to let Jen know her location in the bunker was about to be breeched. I raced to type and send the text message, hoping she was outside the bunker so her phone service would be working.

After sending the text, I decided my best course of action would be to find the other two members of Natalia Filipov's group and head them off at the front door. If I could get there before the person in the tunnel could descend to the cabin, Jen wouldn't have to confront them. I scampered around to my right toward the downward slope of the ridge, hunkering down as I got near the edge.

There was a near vertical drop of over a hundred feet just ahead of me that stopped my forward progress, but provided me with a good view of the slope below. My view was partially obstructed by trees, but I could still see to the creek bed. That meant the cabin was directly below me, even though I couldn't see it.

I paused and sat silently, looking for any sign of movement. I pulled the rifle out and aimed it downward, not pointing at anything in particular.

The absence of any optics or magnification meant I had to rely only on my eyesight, but after just a few seconds, I realized that was good enough. I caught movement out of the corner of my eye to the right. It was slow and subtle, but as I focused, I could make out a camouflaged shape moving along the ridge, about halfway down to the creek.

Judging by the distance from the creek at the bottom of the ridge, I determined the invader to the right was probably on a trajectory to the cabin door. If I was setting up this ambush, I would have sent someone in from the highest point of the ridge and someone from the creek bed below. That way, all elevations would have been covered.

Since I had just seen someone enter the tunnel from the high side above the cabin, and had noticed one intruder to the right, I now scanned the creek bed below the cabin to see if I could find the third person.

The creek bed provided a good amount of cover, as the sides were steep from years of erosion and had been worn into near-vertical walls well over ten feet high. A human could stay near the edge of the creek bed wall and move virtually unseen along the length of the creek. At some point, however, they'd need to leave the creek bed to ascend to the cabin from below. That was the next place I scanned for Filipov's team.

It only took a few seconds to find the last team member slithering out of the creek bed and heading straight up toward the cabin. I couldn't get a shot from my distance, so I had to find a way down. I backed away from the cliff's edge and scanned my right and left.

I hadn't seen the Caldwell boys yet, so I assumed they were still behind the invaders somewhere between the truck and the cabin. I started texting a message to the two of them to let them know what I had seen.

While I was typing the message, I received a call from a Denver number. Realizing my time was limited, and I didn't want to talk to anyone from Denver just then, I declined the call and kept texting. I sent the message and slid further away from my vantage point overlooking the hillside below.

The caller from Denver left a voicemail, so I took a quick second to view the transcript of the message. It started by saying, 'Hi Mr. Morgan. This is Lieutenant Carr from the Littleton Police Department. I'd like to talk to you urgently about Sergeant Theiss. I've found some irregularities with some of her activity in your friend's case and now she has gone missing,' but I turned the screen off before continuing. I didn't need to help give the lieutenant a review of his new sergeant just now.

When I got far enough away from the edge to stand and look around without being seen from below, I found the nearest cut away that led down from the rocky ledge was just to my left. As quickly as I could, I descended the side of the cliff toward the cabin, not really sure when I'd be visible from the invaders I had seen below. I assumed a rifle shot would probably let me know when they saw me, but to my surprise, I made it through the first crevasse unscathed.

As I reached the opening near the bottom of the cliff, I readied my rifle and slowed down. By my estimation, the two invaders I had seen from above should be very close to the cabin by now. I peeked around the corner to see where they were.

And then I saw stars as something smashed into the back of my head.

And then the lights went out.

* * *

Jen watched the cameras in the bunker for a few seconds, then ran back into the cabin to peer out the windows. She was on alert for the three intruders, but the cameras didn't provide complete coverage of the woods outside the cabin. There was plenty of coverage on the outermost portion of the property, but she had to rely on the windows to see closer to the cabin.

After watching for twenty minutes that felt like days, she finally saw signs of movement straight down toward the creek. She pulled back from the windows to avoid being detected, and watched closely. The movement was one of the two men Jen had seen get out of Keith's 4Runner. He was inching slowly up the hill, trying to stay low and hidden.

Jen resumed her search for more movement to the right, toward the parking area where the 4Runner and F150 had stopped. Judging by the distance of the intruder from the creek bed, the others should close in soon. She instinctively readied her rifle and pulled up the scope to get a better look.

She was still looking through her rifle scope to the right when she heard a beep from the bunker behind her. The door inside the closet that led to the bunker was still open, so the noise seemed to echo through the cabin. Jen ran into the bunker to see what alert had made the noise.

To her surprise, she saw another F150, this one white, arriving at the parking area. She had little time to investigate, but the only person she saw getting out was a woman.

The woman looked around for a second, then grabbed a rifle case out of the backseat of the truck and headed into the woods. She wasn't dressed in camouflage like the others, but seemed to be in a police uniform. And she handled the rifle like she was an expert.

The sight of the latest guest on Paul's property made Jen uncomfortable. Paul had a lot of acreage, but it was feeling crowded.

Jen ran back out of the bunker, closing the door behind her. She moved into the cabin to see if she could find Natalia and the other two uninvited guests. She had only seen the one person emerging from the creek bed so far, so she readied the rifle, took a breath and brought it up to her shoulder.

When she checked out the window again, she saw the person from the creek bed was now only about fifty yards from the cabin. Through the rifle scope, she scanned to the right, expecting to see at least one more person arriving from that side.

Less than a minute later, she did. Lurking behind a big spruce tree to her far right was another camouflaged intruder. She adjusted the scope to get a better view, bringing the crouching figure into focus. It was Natalia Filipov.

That was two of the tree people from the 4Runner, leaving only one more to find. She pondered the approach they may have taken to cover the cabin and decided the other must be coming from the left or directly behind her above the cabin on the mountain. She was just about to turn her focus to the left when she noticed the guy directly down the hill from the cabin stood up.

She gazed in amazement as he brushed himself off and started walking casually up the hill. Looking to her right, she saw Natalia do the same thing, both of them acting as if they were engaged in a military exercise that had just ended.

Then Jen looked out the window to her left and saw why they had relaxed their posture. To her left, coming out of the woods, was the third member of Natalia's team. He was dragging someone else, apparently unconscious. Or dead.

As they got closer, Jen cringed in horror. She held her breath as they drug the body to the front door and held his face to the camera. Then the front door unlocked. Then they opened the door.

She crouched in the kitchen with the shotgun aimed at the door, unsure what to do. If Keith was still alive, she couldn't be sure she would miss him with a shotgun blast. Yet, if she didn't fire, she was giving up her position in the cabin. She was stuck with no good option.

Natalia yelled into the house as they pushed Keith's body in the door, hiding behind him.

"We know you're both in here. Show yourselves or your friend Mr. Morgan is dead. Got it!"

Jen stayed back, inching further away past the kitchen. She considered running for the bunker, but decided she didn't have time. Instead, she inched into the bedroom and closed the door before Natalia and her goons pushed Keith inside. At least they wouldn't find the bunker. Not without a pretty significant search, anyway. Maybe that would buy her some time.

She peeked through the bedroom door to see if Keith was alive. Aside from a little blood dripping down his neck, he didn't look to be in bad shape. Then she saw Natalia raise her pistol to Keith's head.

"Ok. I'm dropping my gun! I'm dropping it! Here, it's

on the ground," Jen said as she slid the shotgun toward the front door and stepped out of the bedroom.

Natalia's head appeared around the front door as they pushed Keith forward and inspected the inside of the cabin. She looked around for several seconds and stopped.

"Where's the other person? The sheriff told me there were a 'couple of people' waiting for Keith at the cabin. So, where's the other person? You've got ten seconds, then your friend Mr. Morgan is going to die. We're in now, so we don't need this pretty face of his anymore, anyway," she yelled as they stayed behind the door, revealing her lack of knowledge about the bunker.

"I'm the only one here," Jen said, wondering what happened to Steve as she said it.

"Not good enough, I'm afraid. Time's up," Natalia said as she pulled out a pistol and held it to Keith's forehead.

"I'm telling you, I'm the only one here!" Jen yelled. "There was another guy here earlier, but he left before you guys got here." She realized she probably wasn't sounding convincing, as the story sounded fake to her, even though she knew it was the truth.

"Look around," Natalia said to the guy who didn't drag Keith into the cabin.

He peeked cautiously around the door and then inched inside. Holding his rifle in front of him, he crept around the living room and kitchen. Natalia and the other guy stayed put at the door, standing behind Keith, who was still unconscious.

As the intruder crept into the bedroom, Jen's blood pressure spiked as she wondered if she had covered the bunker door up well enough. Her breath was short while he snooped around in the bedroom, opening and closing the door to the closet and snooping under the bed.

Lastly, he went into the bathroom. Again, he clunked around in there, opening and closing cabinets and eventually returning to the front door.

"I don't see anyone," he said.

Natalia didn't seem to trust him, as they squeezed into the door while still staying behind Keith's lifeless-looking body.

"Is he alive?" Jen finally asked.

"Oh, he's fine. Just a little sleepy," the guy dragging Keith said with a smirk.

Jen wasn't sure she believed him, but she really had no choice. Then, without notice, Natalia lunged at her from behind Keith. Jen sensed the movement in time to lean to the side and grab Natalia's arm, forcing it downward.

When she did, she noticed something in her hand. It wasn't a gun, but she was lunging forward with it. So, Jen pulled that arm forward and down, then locked her legs around Natalia's waist and launched backwards. The movement pulled Natalia forward and down, with both of them crashing to the floor of the cabin.

Jen hadn't had time to think about what to do next, but was automatically reacting to the attack. She was grappling with Natalia and looking for a way to get ahold of her throat when she felt a piercing in her hip. Then she realized what must have been in Natalia's hand.

It was a needle. And Jen was fading away.

Chapter Thirty-Nine

I felt like I was awakening from a deep sleep, but with an intense headache. It wasn't a hangover. It was different. And worse.

As I opened my eyes and attempted to focus, I tried to pull my hands up to rub my temples. But my hands were stuck behind me. In fact, I couldn't move them at all. Shaking my head, I started getting a grasp of what was going on.

I was sitting in Paul's cabin, in one of his kitchen chairs. My arms were tucked between the spindles in the back of the chair and my hands were taped together, wrapped around the spindles. My legs were stuck, too, feeling like they were tied or taped to the front legs of the chair. The throbbing in my head made me realize I had been knocked out.

Someone had smacked me on the head and had moved me inside Paul's cabin, then had taped me to a chair. I didn't have to see the other side of the room to know who had done it.

"Good morning, Mr. Morgan," Natalia said before I saw

her sitting on Paul's couch. "It's nice of you to rejoin us here in this beautiful cabin."

I didn't say anything as I surveyed the room. Natalia was lounging on the couch with one of her thugs. The other member of her murderous team was sitting on the chair beside the other two. They were all casually drinking coffee as though they were on vacation. But there wasn't a fourth person.

The lack of a fourth team member confused me. If I had seen the third person go into the cave toward the tunnel down to the cabin, who had been waiting at the bottom of the rock crevasse?

Then I remembered Steve.

I heard movement and looked next to me. There, taped to the other kitchen chair, was Jen. She seemed to wake up just like I did. She had duct tape around her hands and feet, and was taped to the chair like I was. The sight of her restrained like that infuriated me, apparently in a visible way.

"Oh, I see a little life in you. Don't like to see your friend as a hostage, huh?" Natalia said with a smile. I had accidentally given her a bargaining chip, as though she needed one.

"What do you want? We're not dead, so you must want something," I said, my mouth feeling dry and thick.

"Oh, I do want something, indeed. But we'll get to that," Natalia said. "First, I want to know where your friend is."

"What friend?" I replied, wondering how she knew about Steve.

"Your good Sheriff Hanson told me you had 'a couple' of friends waiting for you out here. I only see one. So, where is the other 'friend' who was waiting? You better produce them, or the one friend I see here will pay the price," she said, aiming her pistol casually at Jen.

"I don't know! He went out earlier. Maybe he's fishing, I don't know," I replied, now hoping I knew who I saw enter the cave earlier.

My answer seemed to confuse Natalia. She motioned for one of her goons to watch the front door.

"Ok, then, let's get to business. We know your friend Paul had moved my father's money into a variety of businesses and investments. We also know he was operating some sort of sophisticated interference into some of our, uh, operations, over the last few months," she said.

"What operations?" I asked, pretty sure I wouldn't get an answer.

"The sort of operations that made your team's lives very uncomfortable," she smiled.

The thought made me wonder what Paul had been doing. We had seen his data research, but hadn't seen any specific activity trying to interfere with what Filipov had been doing to our team. But still, the thought didn't surprise me.

"And that sort of operation requires a large amount of computer horsepower. Far more, in fact, than a tiny laptop could produce," she said, pointing to a laptop on the counter. I assumed they had found it in my bag. Or Jennifer's. Or Steve's, the thought of whom made me curious once again.

"So, the question is: where is all this computer horsepower? The systems in Paul's condo were hard-wired here. We know that. But, we don't see any computing power here at all. So, where is it?" Natalia asked.

I thought about it for a second, but Jen's voice sliced through my thoughts.

"Are you ok?" Jen asked, looking groggily in my direction.

"Yeah, I'm fine. Are you alright?" I asked. She nodded. Then she looked around, trying to focus.

"You'll both be a little groggy after your medicated nap," Natalia said with another evil smile. "We needed you to be compliant while we immobilized you."

"Why didn't you just kill us?" I asked, curious how much they knew about Paul's money and, for that matter, my place in it.

"We will, but don't get ahead of yourself. Before you go, you need to help me get back everything Paul stole from my father. You see, I am pretty savvy with computers myself, thanks to your American education system. Besides making your friends' lives miserable, I also did a little research over the last several months. I know Paul had moved some of his money to cryptocurrency. I also know he owned a large venture capital firm that held significant business entities. That would make him, I believe, a billionaire and then some," Natalia said, pausing for effect as if this was some great revelation.

Jen was better at acting than I was.

"He was a billionaire? No way!" Jen yelled. It was a brilliant move that kept Natalia talking.

"Oh yes, he sure was. And not only that, I believe your friend, Mr. Morgan here, knows all about that. And I also believe he knows all about this business Paul owned. Because, you see, Mr. Morgan is listed on the LLC paperwork. In fact, if my research is correct, and I think it is, I believe Mr. Morgan here now owns the whole thing. I think Keith Morgan now owns The Association Equities, LLC," Natalia said.

Jen's acting suddenly faded as she stared at me.

"Oh, you didn't share that with your sweetie here, huh?" Natalia said, enjoying any shock she could provide.

I almost interjected that Jen wasn't my 'sweetie' but thought better of it and sat quietly.

"So, here's what we're going to do. First, you're going to send me the contents of Paul's crypto wallet. All of it. I know there's at least fifty million in there and probably more. That will get us moving. Then, you're going to sign over The Association Equities, LLC to one of my corporations. I already have the paperwork," she said, motioning to one of the goons. On cue, he produced a plastic folder out of a tactical backpack I hadn't previously noticed.

"You know I won't do that. And even if I did, you'll need legal review and authorization," I replied, trying to buy time while I thought about my next move. I had been wiggling my hands against the spindles, but was struggling to loosen the tape.

"Oh, we've got that covered. I have plenty of legal representation to help make this official," she said. I was suddenly glad I hadn't signed the paperwork to become an LLC member back in Denver. Maybe that would give me a way out of this if I was forced to sign.

"Now, how about you let me know where Paul's computer is out here? If it's not in this cabin, then where is it?" Natalia asked. The question gave me options.

I was about to make up an answer when my phone buzzed on the kitchen counter. Natalia motioned to one of her thugs, who picked up the phone and held it up to her.

"Thornton and Bailey Caldwell? Do you have them working with you? So, it's not enough for Paul to get their parents killed, but now you want to get them killed, too?" Natalia asked, with her ever-present evil smirk turning to anger.

"And they say they're in position, by the way. A little too late, but they're ready," Natalia sneered with a sinister smile.

"They also say you've got an officer approaching the front door. Go check it out, and leave the front door open," she said, motioning to the other thug.

He jumped up and walked out the front door, leaving it ajar so he could reenter later. I sat quietly, wondering what would become of the Caldwell brothers outside and which officer would be approaching alone. If only they had gotten to the cabin earlier, they would have seen me being carried inside and could have responded.

"I can show you where the computers are," I finally blurted out. I could feel Jen shudder next to me when I said it, but I didn't look her way.

The statement also seemed to take Natalia by surprise.

"Oh, is that right? Then let's hear it. Where might they be?" she asked, clearly suspicious of my sudden willingness to share.

"Let my friend go, and I'll show you," I offered hopefully, nodding toward Jen.

Natalia laughed at my suggestion.

"I don't think you're in the position to negotiate, Mr. Morgan. How about you show us where Paul's computers are and I'll let her live another minute," she replied, adopting the evil sneer once again.

I sat still for a minute, as though I was thinking about my options.

"Alright. He said he'd show us where they are, so there must be computers around here somewhere," Natalia finally said to her remaining cohort. "Find them. Tear this place apart if you have to. Do it now!"

With one thug still outside, the other began digging into

the kitchen cabinets. He pulled pots, pans, dishes, food, and everything else out and threw them on the floor. It was mass chaos for the next few minutes, while Natalia sat on the couch and smiled at us with a penetrating stare.

I had hoped the thug would find the door in the back of the coat closet, but that wasn't the first thing he found. To my dismay, he instead found the keypad in the bedroom closet that opened the gun safe.

"Hey, I found something!" he yelled from the bedroom.

Natalia casually stood and went into the bedroom, leaving me and Jen taped to our chairs alone for a brief moment. As soon as Natalia was in the bedroom, Jen stared at me in disbelief.

I nodded, trying to let her know I knew what I was doing. That was partially true. She slowly resumed her prisoner-appropriate appearance and stopped glaring at me.

"Get him in here. We need his finger," I heard Natalia telling the thug.

Obeying her orders, he ambled back into the living room area and grabbed my chair from each side, and picked me up. Since I was nearly as big as him, he struggled to haul me through the doorway and into the bedroom to the closet door, nearly dropping me multiple times.

"Get the tape off his hand and put his finger on this pad," Natalia instructed.

He did as he was told, unbinding my right hand from the chair and holding my index finger on the biometric pad for the safe. I considered telling them this was the wrong one, but decided to let it play out. The safe unlocked.

Natalia opened the safe door and looked inside. Her eyes opened wide as she took in the ample array of weapons and ammunition Paul had stored inside. But her amazement only lasted a second.

"Where are the computers, Mr. Morgan?" she said after the gun discovery wore off, emerging from the closet to stare at me again.

"This isn't the right place," I said.

"Obviously. Now, for the last time, where are the computers? I've lost my patience," she snarled.

"Inside the coat closet," I said, nodding toward the room we had been in before.

Natalia didn't seem to believe me, but nodded for the thug to carry me and my chair back out of the bedroom. He did, again bumping against walls and nearly dropping me along the way. I grabbed the chair with my now untaped right hand.

When we got to the living room, Natalia had already opened the door to the coat closet and had moved the coats and hangers aside. She could see the cuts in the back of the wall that covered the door to the bunker.

"Well, what do we have here?" she said as she looked at her discovery.

We were about to reveal Paul's bunker to Natalia Filipov. I glanced at Jen to see she had lost her poker face and was glaring at me again. I nodded again, but she didn't seem to take any comfort in it.

"Twist the coat hanger on the right wall," I said, watching as the thug followed my instructions. The wall slide away and exposed the metal door and retina scanner.

"Bring him here," Natalia said to the thug, still staring at the camera in the back of the closet.

He did as he was told, then tried to hoist me up to the camera. Since my left arm was still tied to the chair, he struggled to get me up that high. Natalia took a step back, pulled a pistol from her belt and held it up toward the door as the thug struggled to get my face in front of the camera.

After several agonizing tries, he finally got me in position.

Just like it was designed, the door unlocked and opened.

As Natalia watched with her pistol drawn, the bunker behind Paul's cabin was revealed. And I was about to learn if my plan was going to work or if I had made a fatal mistake.

Chapter Forty

The open bunker door first gave Natalia and her thug a moment of shock as they stood with their mouths hanging open. I was abruptly dropped to the ground in my chair just outside the closet as my carrier shifted his focus to the door. He needed both hands to push the heavy door open.

Natalia jumped around me toward the door, then slowed and peered around the corner and inside the bunker. Both she and her thug had forgotten I had a free hand, and now was the time to find out if my theory about the bunker was true.

As Natalia passed beside me next to the closet, she lowered her pistol slightly to peer around the door. I used my free hand to grab her pistol-wielding arm and pulled her backward, toward me in my chair. The move threw her temporarily off-balance, and she stumbled my direction.

At the same time, her thug was entering the bunker and finding that my theory was indeed correct. A shot rang out as he turned into the bunker and disappeared to the left inside the bunker entrance. Natalia, who was falling into me, tried to turn toward the bunker but couldn't move fast enough with me doing my best to hold on to her arm.

The bunker door pushed open and Steve came busting through from inside the bunker as he delivered another pistol shot into the head of Natalia's thug, now lying still on the bunker floor. Steve immediately turned to focus on Natalia, who was struggling to free her arm from my grasp, which I could barely contain in my one-handed situation.

As she freed her arm and swung her pistol around toward Steve, he left from the bunker door and met her forearm with his own pistol, knocking her weapon to the ground and fracturing her arm with an awful crunching sound. She lunged toward him awkwardly, pushing both of them into the bunker and out of my sight.

For a moment, there was silence while Natalia and Steve struggled in the bunker. The two of them struggled for several seconds, leaving me and Jen in the cabin closet area alone, still taped to our chairs. I used my good hand to loosen the tape from my other arm and from my feet. It took several seconds to get my own tape removed, then I stepped over and removed the tape from Jen's arms.

By the time I had gotten loose and ran inside the bunker, Steve was aiming his pistol at Natalia, now sitting on the floor in front of the rack of still-blinking servers. She was holding her right arm awkwardly across her body and still held onto her angry sneer.

As soon as Jen had freed herself, she also ran into the bunker. Surveying the situation, she tugged Natalia's thug away from the bunker door and drug his body into the cabin area.

When she returned to the bunker, we all took a step back and looked at each other.

"I guess that was you I saw heading into the cave up there," I said to Steve, motioning upward.

"Apparently. And you're real lucky I made it down here in time. In fact, you're lucky I didn't leave altogether," he nodded. Steve seemed miffed.

"I'm sorry I told Jen to leave you out of the cabin," I said.

"It turns out that was a good idea, but that really sucked. I can't believe you didn't trust me," Steve said. He was still watching Natalia with his Glock 19 pointed at her head, but his face revealed his disappointment.

"I misread the situation, Steve. I don't know what else to say. Let's deal with what we have here," I said, trying to change the subject.

Jen was now looking at the screens in the bunker, reminding me there was another thug to deal with outside.

"There's someone else heading in, not sure where they are," she said.

As I glanced over at the screens with Jen, Steve filled us in while keeping his Glock on Natalia.

"I reviewed the footage and saw all you guys come in, and Jen's right. There's another woman on her way in. She should be here any minute now," he said.

"Can you show me the footage?" I asked Jen.

She made a few clicks and brought up the video of the latest guest to arrive on Paul's property.

"See if you can get a good view of her face," I said.

After a few seconds, Jen found a good view of the woman's face and stopped the video.

"Now, click on the face and see if a search link appears," I said, remembering how the system had worked for me earlier.

Just as it had before, the system brought up a search link

and Jen clicked it. As the system was completing the search, we heard a commotion at the front door.

Jen lunged out the door and disappeared for a few seconds. When she returned, several items clicked into place. And not in a good way.

The woman from the surveillance video was holding Natalia's thug at gunpoint as they both came through the bunker door. It was true she was in an officer's uniform, but it wasn't a local one. The uniform was for the Littleton, Colorado police department. It was Sergeant Theiss.

Before I could register what was happening, she and the thug had taken offensive positions and were both pointing their pistols at me, Steve, and Jen. Natalia was smiling smugly and standing up, while Jen and Steve looked on with confused expressions on their faces.

"Get his weapons out and drop them. Slowly," she was yelling. Knowing they had already taken my and Jen's guns, the thug searched Steve and found two pistols in his belt, then tossed them on the floor toward the bunker door.

"Get back there away from the door," Sergeant Theiss yelled at the three of us.

"Are you ok?" she asked Natalia.

"I'm fine. They got Alex, but I'm fine. What took you so long?" Natalia asked Sergeant Theiss.

"I saw Alex over there. They'll pay for that. The walk from the car was longer than you said. I still can't run as fast as you," Sergeant Theiss replied.

"Mr. Morgan, please meet my sister, Nikita," Natalia said as she stood.

"I guess I know how you got into the country, but how'd you get a job at the police department?" I asked, ignoring the introduction. They were both more free with their accents, and now that they stood together, I could see the resemblance.

"You thought my sister Natalia was only good at ruining your friends' lives? That's not true at all. She can create a life just as well as she can ruin one," the woman I knew as Sergeant Theiss chuckled.

"Sisters, huh? How sweet. And you created the life of Sergeant Theiss from nothing?" I asked, trying not to be surprised.

"It's easier than you think. I just entered fictitious data into the right systems, then laid the groundwork for an open position at the department and made sure she got the job. Your American hiring systems are so predictable," Natalia said, still holding onto her injured arm.

Before we got any further with the explanation, we heard yelling from outside. The front door was still open, and it was clear the voice wasn't directly in front of the cabin, but was several yards away.

"Mr. Morgan, are you in there?" Bailey Caldwell was yelling.

"Go check that out," Natalia said, nodding at the thug.

He went into the cabin, and we all heard him yelling.

"Mr. Morgan is busy. You can come on in," the thug was saying in a surprisingly pleasant voice.

"We'll wait to talk to Mr. Morgan," Bailey yelled back.

"It will be a while, but I'll let him know," the thug replied.

Then we heard a gunshot outside. Then Natalia and the woman I now knew as Nikita turned around toward the front door of the cabin. When they did, I slammed into the back of Natalia, causing a pileup at the front door, with Nikita and the thug falling outside and Natalia stumbling behind them in the doorway. That gave Steve, Jen, and I a brief second to launch ourselves toward the closet and the bunker door. While shots rang out behind us, we piled into the bunker and slammed the heavy door behind us.

The whole thing took only a second or two, and during the brief skirmish, one of the two women got a shot off inside the bunker. But that was it. It was a mad scramble, then a gunshot, then the bunker door slammed and the three of us were immersed in complete silence.

A weird, eerie, uncomfortable silence.

"I wonder if there are any cameras near the cabin," I finally said.

"I don't think so, but I'll check again," Steve said, jumping into action.

The bullet that Natalia had gotten off before the door closed had taken out one of the monitors, but had done no other damage. Steve sat at his keyboard while Jen and I watched the screens. After a few agonizing minutes, it became clear there were no outside cameras near the cabin. They were setup with a thorough mesh pattern around the perimeter, but not so much for the areas nearest the cabin.

"I know there's a camera at the front door, so maybe that's all we've got," I said.

"Yeah, I see that one. Let's see what it shows," Steve said as he displayed the front door camera.

We could see the woods outside the cabin immediately in front, but the details beyond the first layer of trees were blurry. But even with that limited visibility, we could see the two Caldwell brothers squatting near trees to the front and right of the cabin. They were exchanging sporadic gunfire with the cabin. Someone must have opened the windows to shoot out, because Paul had mentioned the windows and walls were bullet proof.

It seemed they were keeping the cabin locked down for the moment.

"So the Littleton police woman was Natalia's sister?" Jen asked.

"Yeah, apparently. It didn't register until I saw her walking into the bunker, but I think I had seen her picture on the camera footage from Zapata. I also remember her lieutenant saying she had only recently started with the department. And just a few minutes ago, I had a message from that same lieutenant saying he wanted to talk about Sergeant Theiss. I didn't take time to answer it, but now I guess I know what it was about. I should have caught that sooner," I replied.

"Oh, come on. How would you have known they were that sophisticated? So, two Filipov daughters after Paul's money? Or, I guess they believe they're after their father's money," Jen said.

"Ok, so we know who it is. Now, how do we want to handle this situation? I called in some reinforcements, but they won't be here for a while yet," Steve said.

"What reinforcements?" I asked.

"When Jen left me out outside, I called Jordan. I told him the situation, and he mentioned he had help headed our direction," Steve answered.

"Good. I think I've got help on the way, too, but I'm honestly not really sure who it is," I said, not wanting to say anything to Steve about the computer-altered voice I had been talking to via Paul's security app.

"So, we know we've got three people just outside this bunker door in the cabin. Do we think that's it? Are they working with anyone else?" Jen asked.

"Well, after that latest surprise, I can't be one hundred percent sure, but as far as I know, that's everyone," I said.

"How long can those two hold up?" Steve asked, motioning toward the Caldwell brothers still hunkered down in the trees outside the cabin.

"Well, they've just got a couple of five shot rifles and their pistols, so probably not long. That's especially true if those three start cracking into Paul's safe," I replied, shaking my head.

"They got into Paul's safe?" Steve gasped.

"Yeah, I'm afraid they did," I replied.

Almost on cue, a barrage of gunfire erupted from the cabin that sent Thornton and Bailey scurrying for cover deeper into the woods. Immediately after the shots ended, we saw two people head out of the cabin after them.

"Who was that? Was that Natalia and her thug?" I asked.

"I think it was your police friend and the 'thug' running after the Caldwell brothers," Jen said, smiling as she accentuated the word 'thug.'

"Ok, if not thugs, what would you call them?" I asked in response to her smirk.

"Thug is fine. I think that applies," she said.

"Good. So, Natalia is still in the cabin, nursing her arm. Maybe one of us should stay here and watch for her to leave? If she does, we can take over the cabin. Right now, we're sadly lacking firepower," I said, looking at Steve's two pistols we had picked up off the floor.

"I can stay. But I think the most urgent need is to get outside. I think the Caldwell brothers are outgunned by a big margin," Jen said.

"Then I'd say we better make our way out of this bunker and try to help them," Steve said, already moving toward the back of the bunker.

"That's how you got in here?" Jen asked.

"Yeah. Jordan told me there was an access point where cables and an air duct were run. I followed it down from up above. It will be a steep climb out, but we can make it in probably fifteen minutes or less," he said as he squatted to enter the dark cave.

Steve and I pulled flashlights out of our pockets, glad we still carried them with us like our old military days.

"Let's hope we can get there before the Caldwell brothers run out of ammo," I said, crawling into the dark tunnel and fearing we might be too late already.

Chapter Forty-One

The tunnel behind the bunker wasn't as tight as I had feared. It was certainly dark, but our flashlights did enough to light the way. It took fifteen minutes of steep climbing that felt like hours, but soon enough Steve and I were emerging into sunlight at the top of the ridge above Paul's cabin.

Steve was the first to peek out the edge of the opening.

"I don't see anyone, but I still hear random shooting," he said.

He stepped out into the light and slid toward the edge of the cliff above the cabin. I followed him over and looked out over the boulders and trees covering the hillside below.

"The shooting seems to have slowed. I wonder if the Caldwell brothers are running out of ammo," I said as we surveyed the trees below. As before, I couldn't see the front of the cabin, but I knew it was directly under us.

As if on cue, we saw one of the Caldwell brothers jump from his hiding spot and race toward the creek. It looked like Bailey, although it was difficult to tell from my distance. We could see the other brother trying to lay cover fire from the right, but the five shot limit proved to be less than was needed for that task.

After a few shots rang out from the trees where the other brother was hiding, a barrage of gunfire erupted from just outside the front of the cabin directly below us. It appeared Nikita and Natalia's thug had taken positions in the trees near the porch. It also appeared they had acquired weapons and ammunition from Paul's safe.

While we watched, the brother running toward the creek bed was hit in the back just before he reached the safety of the drop-off at the creek. He stumbled a few more steps, then tumbled down into the creek bed and out of sight.

That left only the one Caldwell brother against the two heavily armed assailants now spreading out into the trees away from the cabin. They were on the hunt for Thornton Caldwell, and he was no longer firing back.

After a few seconds, we saw him leap from his hiding spot and retreat further away from the cabin toward the parking area. He was far enough away from his pursuers that they didn't have a good line of sight to him, but they fired anyway. When we couldn't see the three of them anymore, Steve and I backed away from the cliff's edge and began running across the ridge toward the parking area.

"It looks like they know they've got him," Steve said as we ran.

"Yeah, we've got to get to him before they do," I replied.

"I don't think they know about our escape path, so we should have the element of surprise on our side," Steve added as we navigated the boulders and trees that covered the ridge. We were running in parallel to where we saw Thornton Caldwell running, but were far enough away that he and his pursuers couldn't see us.

Or so we thought.

Just as we started descending from the ridge about a quarter mile from the parking area, a bullet blew a chunk of bark off the tree I was walking next to. The sight of the tree trunk being hit was quickly followed by the sound of a rifle shot echoing through the valley.

Nikita and Natalia's thug had found us before we realized we were visible.

Steve and I dove for cover behind two trees about twenty feet apart. Judging from the sound, we were still much further from the shooter than our pistols would cover. They had a substantial advantage over us, and we needed to move fast.

"Pssst. Hey, that wasn't from them," Steve said, nodding forward.

"What?" I didn't quite understand what he meant.

"That shot came from behind them, toward the cabin. The angle is wrong," he said, pointing to the damaged tree.

I turned and looked, and he was right. The shot couldn't have come from Nikita or the thug chasing Thornton Caldwell. The tree damage would have been behind the tree from that angle. No, someone else was firing at us from behind them.

That meant Natalia had left the cabin and had realized we were up here. I wasn't sure how she knew, but that how didn't matter just now. What did matter was that she had found a long-range rifle from Paul's safe and was firing at us. Firing at us while we hid behind trees with only a couple of pistols in our possession.

Our tactical position wasn't optimal.

My only hope was that Jen saw Natalia leave the front door and was pursuing her from behind. For now, however,

Steve and I had to figure out how to protect ourselves until Jen could intervene.

While we sat there trying to find cover in the trees and boulders, another bullet splintered a tree branch and ricocheted behind us. The angle of the ridge behind us gave us no chance to retreat up the hill. We'd be fully exposed in that direction. And if we fired toward Natalia's position back near the cabin, Nikita and the thug would see our location and could pick us off with little effort.

Steve and I spent the next few minutes focused on the wooded area below us toward the creek. We were over halfway back toward the parking area, and the creek ran parallel to the ridge all the way back to our cars. Somewhere between our location and the parking area were Thornton Caldwell and his two pursuers. Then somewhere back to our left, between our location and the cabin, was Natalia Filipov. We didn't know which way they were going or how fast they were moving.

And that lack of knowledge was horrifying.

Then I had a thought. I pulled out my mobile phone and opened the app from the security cameras. I navigated to the front door camera of the cabin and pulled up the video. There, in crystal clear view, was Jen emerging from the cabin onto the porch. She was inches from the camera when I texted her, telling her to go back inside so I could call her.

"Where are you?" Jen asked as she accepted my call.

"We're about halfway to the cars, but we're pinned down on the ridge above the creek. Natalia has some sort of long-range rifle and is taking shots at us from behind, while Nikita and the thug are somewhere between us and the cars chasing Thornton Caldwell," I replied.

"Yeah, Natalia took the rifle I had set out in the kitchen.

She can probably see all the way to the car with that scope, so you guys need to be careful," Jen said, adding more weight to our already precarious situation.

"Was she moving quickly? Did you see the direction she took from the cabin?" I asked.

"She was moving along the creek. At first I assumed she was looking for the brother that fell down there, but she wasn't. She turned and started heading your direction. You should have the elevation advantage, but I guess it's tough to use it if you don't know where the other two went," Jen said, accurately assessing our predicament.

"Yeah. That's the problem. If we could find them..." I was saying as I peeked carefully to the right. Just as I did, another shot sprayed bark over my head and I had to duck back down.

"Maybe I can see if they've made it back to the cars. Hang on, I'll go in the bunker and check. I'll leave my phone out here so it doesn't disconnect," Jen said.

In twenty seconds, she returned.

"Ok, Thornton made it to his truck. It looks like he got some more ammunition and headed off to the east," Jen said. That meant he was circling back around on the Lazy J side of the creek. I hoped he knew what he was doing.

"Jen, can you see the other two? Are they anywhere near the cars or did they stay back? If they're near the cars, then we can make a run in that direction without getting too close to them. We've got to get away from Natalia. Right now, we're sitting ducks," I said.

"Give me two minutes, Keith. I found another hunting rifle in the safe, and I think I can provide you with some cover. I'll throw some shots toward Natalia to slow her down, then you guys can get moving. Just wait until you hear me shooting," Jen said.

It made me uncomfortable to put her in the line of danger yet again, but the plan really made sense.

"You got it. Just get back into the cabin before she returns fire," I said, cautiously.

"As always, you don't need to worry about me. Just try not to get shot," Jen said, remarkably calm for the hostile environment we were sitting in.

"That's the plan," I said, ending the call.

I told Steve what was going on, and we waited. Less than two minutes later, we heard shots erupting toward the cabin and we took off, running back up the hill toward the top of the ridge. From that vantage point, we could make our way back toward the cars to help Thor and still be high enough over the cabin to help find Natalia.

First, we had to get to a point where Natalia couldn't see us over the ridge, then we needed to find Nikita and the thug.

After a few seconds of running up the side of the ridge, we were able to get a large boulder between us and Natalia's position behind us. Then we sat and looked through the trees toward the parking area. We weren't yet close enough to see it, but we saw movement below us toward the creek. Natalia and the thug had seen us running, and they were focusing in on our position. We had put cover between us and Natalia, but we weren't completely visible from the creek bed below.

We burrowed down behind the boulder and waited, hoping we were low enough to avoid taking shots from below. The angles seemed to be to our advantage for the moment. Now, we needed help from Jen. I had asked her to get back inside the cabin for protection, but I wasn't sure if she had done it. In these hostile situations, she didn't always do what I asked.

With no sound or movement for another minute, I was getting nervous. My phone still didn't show movement near the parking area, so Nikita and the thug were still in the woods. I also hadn't seen Thor or anyone else moving around the perimeter of Paul's property.

But all of that was about to change.

Steve peeked around the edge of the boulder to our right to see if he could see any movement. That turned out to be a poor decision. Shots immediately rang out and rifle rounds began pinging off the surrounding rocks. Someone had seen us take our positions and was waiting for us to move. We were trapped.

Next, my phone began buzzing as cameras on the far side of the creek began picking up movement. I didn't have time to inspect it, but there were several people creeping in from the Lazy J and Krohl side of Paul's property. I could sense the field was about to erupt.

Then it did.

It started with a couple of shots from the far side of the creek, furthest away from us. It was answered by a few shots of return fire from just below us on our side of the ridge. Then all hell broke loose.

Realizing we were still sitting ducks if someone got high enough on the opposing ridge opposite our position, I frantically texted Thor Caldwell to make sure he knew where we were. The shooting didn't stop, but somehow he got me a return message saying he knew our position. Their shots were focused on the intruders. Steve and I took that opportunity to bug out of our position and get back to the top of the ridge and out of sight.

We raced back toward the cabin, eager to see what had happened with Jen and Natalia.

Passing the overlook where we watched before, we

again found the crevasse that allowed me to descend the ridge on the far side of the cabin. Shots were still ringing out in the distance toward the parking area while we quickly navigated the steep and rocky path toward the cabin.

My phone buzzed in my pocket, but I was too busy navigating the steep terrain to stop and look at it. We continued as quickly as we could without falling, stepping over and around the boulders that formed the crevasse. Just before we came to the opening at the bottom, I turned the last corner to get a glimpse of the cabin and the porch.

I couldn't see that far. All I saw was the barrel of Natalia's rifle pointing at my chest.

Chapter Forty-Two

"I thought that might be you kicking up all that dust," Natalia said from behind the scope of her rifle. Her good hand was holding the rifle over her damaged arm, using it for balance.

"Now, throw that pistol right down on the ground in front of you or I'll be putting a hole right through your chest," she said.

I did as I was told, hoping Steve was far enough behind me that she wouldn't notice. Unfortunately, she was one step ahead of that thought.

"Where's your buddy who ambushed us in the bunker? Tell him to step out and to throw his weapon down here, too," she said, motioning behind me but keeping the rifle barrel directly on my chest from ten yards away. She was too close for us to run but too far away for me to go after the weapon.

"Come on, Steve," I said, begrudgingly. We'd have to come up with a plan without our pistols.

Steve slowly emerged from the crevasse into the open and threw his pistol on the ground next to mine.

"Now, step slowly toward the porch. You're going to let me back into the cabin before we all get shot," Natalia said. I recognized I had heard no shots recently, which was surprising at first. Then I realized Natalia had positioned herself between us and the woods. Anyone who fired at her would have me and Steve directly in their sights.

Unfortunately, or fortunately, depending on one's perspective, that was one of the primary rules of gun safety. Nobody was going to shoot at Natalia with a risk of human collateral damage. At the moment, I was glad everyone was aware of that rule.

"Come on, get over there. You go in front," Natalia said, nodding at me.

"You! Follow him to the door. Either of you try anything and I'll be putting holes in you before your friends out there start shooting. Then, we'll all go down together," she said. Her voice was icy, with an edge of unhinged desperation.

"Get in front of that camera and get that door open," Natalia said as we neared the porch. I did as I was told, wondering if Jen was still inside.

As the door opened, I considered diving behind it and slamming it shut. But that would put Steve directly in her line of fire, which wasn't an option. So, I walked into the cabin again and scanned for Jen. She was nowhere to be found. Maybe she was in the bunker.

"I noticed this cabin takes more shots than a typical cabin would. Reinforced walls and windows, huh? I suppose that's what Paul needed to hide his efforts at taking down my father," Natalia said.

I didn't reply, so she continued.

"Now, let's go find your girlfriend. I'll enjoy taking her away from you just like we did your wife," Natalia said, noticing my involuntary clenched jaw as she said it. She sneered at the sight and motioned me toward the coat closet that led to the bunker.

Realizing Natalia wouldn't walk into a trap twice, I wondered what her plan was. Why would she take us into the bunker? She could have had us walk her out of the woods with me and Steve on either side to prevent anyone from shooting. Or maybe she knew about the tunnel.

"Get inside and go straight to the back wall," Natalia said to me as the bunker door unlocked. "But you stay right in the door," she told Steve.

I nodded his way, once again wondering if Jen was inside. I took a breath, pushed the door open, and headed in. And saw nobody in the bunker. If Jen was there, she was now somewhere in the tunnel. I hoped she was already on her way to safety, leaving me and Steve to sort out a new plan.

Natalia motioned for Steve to join me in the back of the bunker, and she followed us a few steps behind. I'm sure Steve thought about slamming the bunker door, but the opportunity didn't really present itself. Natalia held the rifle at Steve's chest the whole time and stayed just out of arm's reach.

Once we were all inside, she slammed the door behind her with her foot, keeping her eyes on us and her finger on the trigger.

"We're all going to leave here together, don't worry. But before we do, you're going to transfer Paul's crypto wealth to me. All of it. I know he's made millions from the money he stole from my father. And now, I want it. All of it," she said, staring at me with glazed hatred.

I evaluated my options, but only for a second. If it would keep her talking, I'd transfer the money. I didn't have a use for it, anyway.

"It's right on this drive," I said, pulling the USB drive out of my pocket.

"Oh no, I'm not going to do it. You are," Natalia said. "Sit down and start typing," she said, motioning me toward the chair I had spent hours in over the last few days.

I followed her orders, sitting in the chair and logging into Paul's bitcoin wallet account. Within a few seconds, Natalia could see she was right about how much money Paul had made. It almost seemed like her eyes twinkled for a second before she started barking out more orders.

"Ok, here's the account information you're going to transfer it to," she said, tossing a small piece of paper on the floor from her pocket.

I picked it up and opened it, stared at her for a second while I considered my options, then started the transfer while she waved her rifle back and forth between me and Steve. She could have killed us right then, but I didn't think she would. She still needed to escape, and we were her best option for protection.

As I expected, her trigger finger stayed put. She let out a deep breath, but then moved on to the next phase of her plan.

"You got in here earlier from a different entrance," she started talking to Steve, now. "Show me where it is," she barked, motioning for me to join Steve at the back of the bunker.

We looked at each other and nodded, and Steve motioned towards the covered cave entrance in the back of the bunker next to the air filtration system and cables. As he did it, I hoped Jen was long gone, if this was how she got out of the cabin.

"Perfect," Natalia said with a smile as Steve moved toward the tunnel.

"Here's what we're going to do. If you do this well, I'll have no further need for you and you may even survive," she started, with minimal conviction.

"You two are going to head up the tunnel ahead of me. If either of you makes a wrong move, I'm going to start firing. With all the rocky angles in here, we may all die with one bullet. But I, of course, don't care about that. At this point, the money is back where it belongs. You don't have it, and that's all that matters," she said, back to her cold gaze. It almost felt like she was resolved to die, which didn't make me comfortable at all.

"How do I know you won't just shoot us as soon as we get out?" I asked. It seemed like a logical question.

"I guess you don't. But what choice do you have?" she said as she motioned for us to head into the tunnel.

"You first," she said to Steve.

Again, we looked at each other, each of us clearly evaluating our options and finding none. We both took deep breaths and nodded, and Steve headed into the tunnel. I followed.

If someone wasn't waiting on the outside of the tunnel to save us, we were climbing to our deaths.

Steve and I used our pocket flashlights to find our way up the tunnel toward the entrance at the top of the ridge. Natalia had strapped her rifle onto her back and was climbing up behind us with a pistol that also had a strong flashlight. Between the three of us, there wasn't much darkness left inside the narrow tunnel.

"Why'd your father kill my wife?" I asked as we climbed. I didn't think I'd get an answer, but for some reason, I had to ask.

"You needed to pay. You led the team when they raided

my father's team outside of Malistan," she said with no emotion. Then, she got suddenly angry.

"My fiancé was on that team. You killed him. He was just protecting my father's business. He did nothing wrong, but you killed him anyway! You had to know my pain," Natalia said, spitting the words out in anger. It was the most emotion I'd heard from her, and it made me wonder about what really happened to Beth on that slippery highway in Colorado.

"It wasn't your father, was it? You did it. You killed Beth?" Before I recognized what was happening, my anger was matching hers as I fired my questions. I already knew the answer, but she was eager to answer me, anyway.

"She didn't die in the crash, you know. I had to help her. Yeah, she would have eventually frozen. But she was still alive when I got down to the car in that ditch. It was a tough climb, but I had to be sure. We couldn't have her make some sort of miraculous recovery or something. No, she had to die. So I made sure she did. Just a little squeeze of her nose was all it took," Natalia said, getting way too much pleasure out of the story she was hissing out.

I couldn't remember hating anyone more than I hated Natalia Filipov. The more of the story I heard, the more I realized she was the one that had stolen the love of my life. She had taken my kids' mother. She had left me with all those memories and unfulfilled dreams.

And she was a holding a gun to my back as we climbed.

We said nothing the rest of the way. The climb took less than fifteen minutes and then we started seeing daylight.

"Don't get any big ideas. Step out and stand to the side. Move too quickly and I'll shoot," Natalia said.

We were about to find out if my hunch was correct about Jen. Was she outside the top of the cave waiting for us, or was Natalia about to shoot us and walk away with her millions?

To my horror, Jen came running to Steve and me as we got out of the cave, not realizing Natalia was behind us. She was just a couple of steps away from us when Natalia emerged from the cave entrance with her pistol drawn. Jen slid to a stop in a puff of dust.

Now she had all three of us lined up.

"Well, isn't this convenient?" Natalia snarled as she motioned for us to stand together. "I know I said you may survive, but you had to know that wasn't true."

Natalia reached behind her to pull her rifle around from her back and I decided I had to make a move. If not, I feared she'd be firing away in seconds and we may all be dead.

I was several steps away, but I had to lunge in front of her to protect my two friends. That would give just enough delay for them to follow and tackle her. It was the only chance I saw for the other two to come out of this alive.

But as I readied myself to lunge forward, shots rang out from behind us. Lots of them.

Then holes appeared in Natalia Filipov's chest. And everywhere else.

Chapter Forty-Three

We ducked and watched Natalia fall. I ran to her and grabbed her pistol, ready to deliver the final shot, but she was dead before she hit the ground. After watching Natalia die, I turned around to see who had fired the fatal shots. From the tree line just behind us toward the parking area, Thor Caldwell and a couple of familiar-looking ranchers appeared. They were still holding their rifles up, ready to fire again if needed.

"If you got the other two down by the creek, she's the only one left. You guys just saved our lives," I said, putting my hands up to ease their tension.

They slowly lowered their rifles as they approached us cautiously.

"How'd you know about this entrance?" I asked, not really sure how they knew to head toward the entrance to the tunnel.

"Your friends told us," Thor said, motioning behind him.

Only then did I realize there were two more people

emerging from the tree line. I recognized both of them from Paul's funeral meeting back in Colorado.

It was Jordan Crawford and his bodyguard. The sight of them puzzled me for a moment, then it came together. And when it did, I wasn't thrilled. Jordan must have been the voice I had been talking to on Paul's security app. Which could only mean he had set this whole thing up. But why?

Before I could ask questions, however, Steve yelled toward Jordan.

"It's about time, man! You guys could have gotten here a little sooner. And you could have brought some help," he yelled.

Then I remembered Steve had talked to Jordan, so maybe my thoughts were wrong about him. It appeared he was coming to Steve's aid and had nothing to do with the security app and the unknown voice.

"This isn't an easy place to get to," Jordan said. "Of course, that's why Paul loved it. Luckily, you guys had these three covering your backs."

Jordan was nodding at Thor Caldwell and the other two ranchers, who were watching us all curiously.

"So, you guys know each other?" Thor finally asked.

"Yeah, I guess we do," I replied, looking at Steve and at Jordan.

"And you guys? Where'd your friends come from?" I asked, nodding at the other two ranchers.

"When I realized Bailey was shot, I ran over to the Krohl ranch looking for help. Gil and Mike here were out tending cattle when I came over the hill. They knew about my folks, so when I told them what all this gunfire was about, they came to help. We may not always see eye to eye, but we're all still ranchers and we take care of our own," he said, nodding at the two Krohl ranchers as he mentioned their names.

"Well, I'm glad you do. Thank you," I said to Thor and his two helpers.

They both tipped their hats but said nothing. I still had more questions.

"You called him?" I asked Steve, while nodding at Jordan.

"Yeah. When Jen wouldn't let me back in the cabin, I realized she must think I was working against you guys. Which sucked, by the way. So I called Jordan and asked for some help," he answered.

"We saw him pull up and get out of the car, looking at your 4Runner. They followed us in when we went after those other two. We all saw you go inside the cabin and I wasn't sure what to do next. But then Mr. Crawford told us there was another entrance," Thor said, again nodding at Jordan.

"We got here just in time. It looked like that lady was going to take you guys out," Thor added.

"You're right, she was. Once we got her out of the cabin, she thought she was free. She didn't need us anymore. You guys saved our lives. And you also took out the person who had your parents killed," I said, making sure Thor knew the impact of what had just happened.

"Yeah, we figured that out," he replied somberly.

"Doesn't make it feel any better, though, does it?" I said. It wasn't really a question, but Thor answered anyway. I could have been asking myself the same question.

"No. It doesn't," he said, looking sadly at the ground.

"How'd you guys get around the other two?" I asked Thor, knowing he had been chased toward the parking area by Nikita and Natalia's thug.

"When we got back to the creek, they were still looking for me. Let's just say they're not looking for us anymore," Thor said.

"They're dead?" I asked, just to be clear.

"I assume so, yes. I didn't stop and check for a pulse, but it didn't appear that was necessary," Thor replied. Then he had his own question.

"That one woman had a police uniform on. Was she a cop?" Thor asked.

"Yeah, she was. Sort of. But not a good one. Her visit was a surprise to me," I said, looking toward Jordan.

He nodded, but said nothing. I wondered how much he knew about this whole situation. I decided I wouldn't find out in front of everyone.

"Do you have a minute?" I asked Jordan.

"Sure, Keith. Let's walk back toward the cars. There will be an army of officers arriving any time now," he answered.

After we got away from the rest of the group, I started in.

"You knew about the bunker and how it was setup?" I started with an obvious one.

"Yeah. Paul kept me in the loop on that," he replied.

"And you knew why he wanted a bunker in the first place?" I asked, realizing too late that I couldn't get Jordan talking with simple questions.

"Yes."

"And how much involvement did you have in this whole thing? I mean, with Paul, with The Association, the cabin and all his security, with all of it?"

No more one-word answers.

Jordan stopped, took a deep breath, and looked around for a minute.

"I'd known Paul a long time. I also knew his father. Both of them were good men. When Paul found out I had access to information about his father's death, he wouldn't let it go. He couldn't. I suppose I get that. I helped him get insight and access, and he did all the research. He got especially intense about it when Filipov started tampering with his team. He felt responsible for them, so he was utterly consumed with proving Filipov was behind all the issues in their lives," Jordan said.

"So, you gave him access to data? Including the link to the NSA?" I asked, focusing in on my hunch about the unknown voice.

Jordan looked into the distance.

"Yeah," was all he said. But it answered one set of questions while triggering a whole new set.

"And Steve knows who you are? You mentioned you knew he was ok?" I asked.

"No, no. Steve doesn't know who I work for. He only knows that I was helping Paul with this whole Association business. We assisted a little, but Steve took care of most of his own protection from Filipov. He's probably as good as our own people at that," Jordan answered.

"So, you were just letting all of us get strung along by Paul to do his bidding? Did you know Paul was sending us to take down all Filipov's dealings? The political tampering, the drugs, the human trafficking at the border? We were just being used by Paul to get back at his father's murderer? And you helped him do it?" I asked, trying not to get emotional.

"Look, Keith, it was much more than that." He was staring at me now. "Paul genuinely had the best interests of his country in mind with all this. You can't tell me you regret any of those assignments? This Filipov guy was evil. His daughter was evil. Their work was evil. Paul was doing the right thing, even if he may have had another motive," Jordan said sternly.

After staring at each other for a few more seconds, we started walking again.

"Yeah, ok. I guess that's true. But, you keep mentioning only one daughter. You didn't know about her sister?" I asked as we continued toward the parking area.

"Nikita? Yeah, we knew Natalia had a sister. Why do you ask?" Jordan responded with his own question, revealing he didn't really know she had been operating in Littleton right under their nose.

"Nikita became a sergeant in the Littleton Police Department. She's been shot in the valley between here and the cabin." I watched Jordan, taking pride in the fact that I had information he didn't. He nodded, but didn't show any emotion.

"So that's how they were doing it. We knew someone was watching Paul, but we hadn't isolated who was behind it. I wondered about his girlfriend, but when they killed her, that sort of removed that concern. Looking back, that makes perfect sense," Jordan admitted, nodding to himself as we got to the parking area where three vehicles now sat.

"You knew someone was watching, but you sent me there, anyway? You're the one who handed me the note that you said was from Paul. It wasn't from him, was it? You put me right in front of them, knowing who they were!" I was putting even more of the situation together and getting angrier about it.

"I know it looks like that, Keith. And you may never believe this, but I knew you'd somehow be ok. You always are. Paul knew that, too. The note was his. He wrote it. But yes, I knew about it," he replied.

"Which means you also knew about Paul's bitcoin

wallet and all his business holdings," I said, as more of a statement than a question.

"Yeah. I know Paul is a billionaire. And I know he handed it all to you." Jordan paused and looked at me calmly. "And I fully supported it. You need to get back to Mr. Underhill and sign the paperwork. Paul believed you were the only person who could run his organization with as much passion and expertise as he did."

That one caught me by surprise, which caused me to pause for a moment before revealing my interaction with Natalia in the bunker.

"But there's no need for The Association anymore. Paul's mission is finished. He got what he wanted, even if he's not here to witness it," I replied.

"The future of The Association is up to you. But the empire Paul built is still very much alive. He has a thriving investment portfolio of companies that need leadership. Plus, someone needs to look over his fortune," Jordan said.

"If you know me at all, you know that's not my thing. And much of the wealth is gone now. Natalia had me transfer it from Paul's wallet to hers while we were in the bunker. His bitcoin fortune is gone," I revealed.

Jordan chuckled.

"Well, not really. We had that wallet flagged in case something like this happened. We'll watch the target wallet for any access, but Paul's fortune will be back in place by tomorrow. And I suspect the only two people who would have had access to it are strewn across this property," Jordan said.

I almost fired at him again for using the bitcoin wallet as another lure to attract Natalia, just like my access to the condo, the safe, and the cabin. Instead of responding, I kept my anger to myself and just stared at the ground, shaking my head.

"You don't care how he got that money in the first place? The stash he took from Filipov in Afghanistan that started this whole thing?" I asked.

"Let's just say it's not a priority for us. As long as you continue to take my calls like Paul did," Jordan answered with a smile that made me uncomfortable.

"I don't really like the sound of that," I said.

Jordan continued to smile and turned, spreading his arms toward Paul's property.

"Come on, Keith. Just look at this place. Don't tell me this isn't a fabulous property. And there are more like this. Paul had great taste in real estate. Take it. Enjoy it. Bring the kids out and let them enjoy it, too. You don't have to wear the wealth on your sleeve, but you can certainly enjoy it," he said, sounding remarkably close to a human being again.

We stood in silence for several seconds while I contemplated what he said. It was a lot to think about.

And then, all at once, an orchestra of sirens emerged from the direction of Cameron. The cavalry was arriving. While the police cars, emergency vehicles and unmarked SUVs of all kinds appeared in the distance, Jen, Steve, Thor, Jordan's security guy and the two Krohl ranchers appeared from the woods.

Jen and Thor were chuckling about something, which felt out of character for the situation but also made me smile. I wondered if I'd ever share everything I had learned from Jordan with either Steve or Jen, but that was a decision for a different day.

Jordan and I didn't talk anymore that day. In fact, he quietly disappeared while chaos ensued on Paul's property.

Over the next several hours, as the sun set, Paul's property was covered with investigators. The FBI led the questioning, and didn't probe into anything tied to Jordan or The Association. It almost seemed like they knew the story before they got there.

I took a moment to step away and call my kids. After the chaos of that day and surviving another day of gunfire and death, I needed to get back to what was really important.

Chapter Forty-Four

The events at Paul's cabin in Montana were a month behind me. The kids were back home, and we were settling into our normal summer life. Well, mostly normal. Today, we were in Denver to go to a Rockies game.

And to pay a brief visit to Jack Underhill.

We arrived at Jack's office just before 5 PM. It was downtown and close to the stadium and was just as nice as I expected a law office to be. There was plenty of wood, leather, and polished aluminum all around, and the space was sprinkled with plants and tasteful advertisements for the firm. The office was on the twelfth floor of the building, with the lobby in the center of the floor. From the lobby, there was enough glass to see through a large conference room and out to the Denver skyline and the mountains beyond. A young, red-headed receptionist sat behind a large wooden counter with a headset on.

"Hi, welcome to Carter and Underhill. How can I help you?" the receptionist asked as we walked into the lobby. She was way too cheerful for the end of the business day, but I couldn't help but smile back at her, anyway.

"Keith Morgan to see Jack Underhill," I said as I took in the space.

"Sure, Mr. Morgan. Have a seat for just a second and I'll let him know you're here," she said as she motioned to the plush leather chairs around the edge of the lobby. As we sat down, she returned her focus to the large computer screen in front of her.

We were sitting in plush leather chairs admiring the scenery when Jack Underhill appeared in the doorway.

"Mr. Morgan?" Jack asked as he stepped into the lobby.

Jack Underhill was a tall, thin man who appeared to be in his mid-forties. He had thinning blond hair and round tortoise-shell glasses that made him look competent but not intimidating. He had a genuine smile that would put a client at ease, but I could quickly sense I wouldn't want to argue a case against the guy. I instantly understood why Paul had chosen him as his attorney.

"Keith," I replied. "And these are my kids, Jamie and Kyle."

"Ms. Morgan, Mr. Morgan," Jack said to each of them as he smiled and shook their hands like they were adults. They clearly enjoyed the formality.

"Mr. Underhill," Jamie said with a chuckle as he shook her hand.

"It's Jack," he replied with a smile.

"Should they stay here or go to your office?" I asked, not sure if he had a private place for them to sit in his office.

"Hey Sharon, why don't you get the kids something from the kitchen? We'll be back in just a second," he said toward the receptionist, answering my question.

The kids scampered off with Sharon into a door on the other side of the lobby, and Jack motioned for me to head through the door he had come in.

"Just this way, Keith. Last door on the right," he said as I walked past him and down a long hallway with glass doors on either side.

We passed two offices and two conference rooms before we arrived at Jack's office. It was an impressive corner office with glass windows all around and a stunning view of Denver. There was enough space to have four offices in there. Jack had a huge wooden desk, a matching credenza along the wall behind the desk, and a similarly designed conference table toward the corner of the windows. The table had eight wood and leather chairs around it of medium height, and there were two similar chairs in front of the desk.

"Have a seat. I'll grab the file," Jack said, pointing toward the conference table.

I took a seat at the table on the end toward the windows, not sure where Jack preferred to sit. He went around the corner of the table next to me and flopped down a file before sitting down.

"Ok, here we go. Just as we discussed, you'll need to sign onto The Association Equities LLC first. From there, the rest of the entities will transfer via the structure of trusts we've set up. There's a list of the entities here," Jack said, pushing a piece of paper toward me.

The list was broken into three categories under bold headings. There was one heading for financial assets, one for real estate, and one for business entities. The values for each were listed on the righthand side of the page, with totals at the bottom.

All the lists were longer than I expected, and the amounts were larger. The sight of them made me suddenly uncomfortable, as I wasn't planning to devote my life to managing Paul's assets.

"It's not as bad as it looks. These businesses have boards and effective management structures. Paul saw to that. Once he set them up, he spent very little time with the businesses themselves, only reviewing their performance monthly during the board meetings." Jack must have seen the concern on my face.

"Ok, I get it. It's just more than I expected," I replied, not sure whether to be angry with Paul or grateful.

"Yeah, I get it. Two billion dollars looks intimidating, no matter how well it functions. Paul had quite an eye for this stuff," Jack replied with a reassuring, yet impatient, smile.

Finally, Jack pushed the document toward me that contained my signature blocks. There were little arrows stuck to the pages where I was to sign.

"Read through it if you wish. I know this is a big decision," Jack said, again with that smile. He was good at this.

"Sure. Just give me a second," I said as I scanned the documents. After scanning the LLC paperwork and the document I was signing, I took a deep breath and signed them. Then I sat back in my chair and looked out the window. With just a few signatures, all the things Paul had worked for were transferred to me. Just like that. It gave me a strange realization of how little all this wealth really meant in the end.

"It's oddly anticlimactic, isn't it?" Jack said, once again reading my emotions well.

"Yeah, it really is," I replied.

"At a time like this, that's a typical reaction. But don't underestimate the significance, either. You really can make a difference with this. Thanks for coming in, Keith. Paul would have appreciated it. Now, go enjoy your night. It's a great night for baseball! Then, maybe you guys can head up to Montana to enjoy that cabin this weekend," he said as he gathered the paperwork and stacked it back into the folder.

He stood and shook my hand and led me back to the lobby. The whole thing took less than ten minutes.

We left Jack's office, went down the elevator to the parking garage, and got back into the 4Runner to head to the baseball game. The kids had a few questions, but not much. They were used to accompanying me to meetings for various reasons, so the whole thing wasn't all that unusual.

I didn't tell them their father's estate had just grown by two billion dollars.

While we were walking into the stadium, I got a call from Jen.

"Hey Jen, what's up?" I said, as I answered.

"Not much, just checking in to say thanks for the crazy bonus," she said.

"Sure. You and Steve earned every penny, believe me. Consider this a high-risk bonus payment," I said.

"I'm not sure if it was a seven-figure risk, but thank you. That was really generous," she said, but it sounded like she had something else on her mind.

"Don't mention it. Well deserved," I replied. We'd had this discussion before. I had made a bitcoin transfer to her and to Steve immediately after I returned home from Cameron. The same day, I upgraded the security around my home to prevent another intrusion.

Jen remained awkwardly quiet, so I felt obligated to speak again.

"We're at the game in Denver tonight. Just came from the attorney's office," I said. Jen knew some of the story about Paul's estate, so I didn't need to explain the visit.

"So, you've done it, huh? How do you feel about it?" Jen asked.

"Well, it's strangely simple. Yet huge. I can't explain it. I'm sure it will set in at some point," I replied, staying vague as I walked along next to the kids. They seemed uninterested, but I knew they heard every word.

"That's sort of why I called," she said.

"Oh yeah? What's up?" I asked again.

"Well, you remember Thornton Caldwell?" Jen asked. Of course I remembered Thor.

"Sure. Why's that?"

"He invited me up to visit. Maybe to help set up some security around the Lazy J. They saw what Paul had, and I think he's envious. Plus, his parents' prized shorthorns are his only path to survival. It seems the ranch wasn't doing well at all, and his parents had fallen into debt, trying to keep things afloat. Thor's worried about protecting the assets they do have," Jen replied.

I could sense there was more to the visit, but I didn't say it.

"Oh, good. Yeah, I felt horrible for him. How's Bailey doing?" I asked. Bailey was recovering from the gunshot he took at Paul's cabin. We all feared worse when we saw it happen, but he had survived.

"He's recovering well. He'll be fine. He'll need some more surgery, but he's mending. But I was wondering if maybe I could stay at Paul's cabin during the visit?" Jen asked, finally getting to the point of her call. She sounded uncomfortable asking, but I could understand why she would. It was a great place.

Before I could answer, she started backtracking.

"I mean, I can get an Airbnb in town if that's better. That place you rented was great," she said quickly, making me feel like I was taking too long to answer.

"Oh no, please don't do that. Of course, you're welcome

to stay there. I mean, you're the only person besides me who can walk right in there, anyway," I said, remembering the security settings were still the same as when we left after the shootout.

"That's awesome, Keith. Thanks so much! If something changes, please let me know. I can get a place in town, really," she said.

"It's no issue at all. You and Thor have a good time," I said.

"Oh, we will. He said there are some great streams up there that are only accessible via ATV and hiking boots, so we're going to check them out," she said, stopping quickly. I could hear the energy in her voice. She was into Thornton Caldwell.

"I'm sure there are. Enjoy the visit," I said, ending the call. She deserved the fun. And the relationship I couldn't give her.

"Why didn't Jen come with us?" Jamie asked, having been listening just as I expected.

"She's busy. I think she's heading to Montana," I said with a smile.

"She's going alone? Why is she going alone?" Jamie clearly picked up on the situation.

"Jen's going to visit a friend we made last month when we visited," I said, realizing she wouldn't stop until she got the details she wanted.

"So, she won't be coming around much anymore, huh?" Jamie was making a statement, not asking a question. Her insight sometimes surprised me. I was thrilled to get another phone call before I had to answer another question from Jamie.

I looked at the phone to see Jordan Crawford's number.

His real number, not the fake voice he was using over the security app at Paul's cabin.

"Hey, Jordan," I said as I accepted the call.

"Hey Keith. I hear you finally signed the paperwork. Congratulations."

I shook my head as I realized how quickly that information had traveled.

"You know, Jordan, the biggest concern I had about it was being in your debt. So, I'd like to pay that debt and return everything Paul stole in Afghanistan from Ivan Filipov, including interest," I said, knowing that wouldn't fly.

"Whoa, there, Keith. That's completely unnecessary. I don't have specific plans for you or anything like that. It was just a casual comment. It's just good to have assets in the field you can rely on when you need them, that's all. And nothing I would ever ask would be out of line. It's the same as with Paul," Jordan responded.

"See, that's the thing. I'm not your asset. I'm just a normal guy out at a baseball game with my kids." I almost mentioned the fact that Paul's actions had gotten their mother killed, but knowing they were listening, I decided against it.

"Ok, fair enough. That was a terrible choice of words. I promise I will leave you alone unless I can't. How's that?" Jordan asked, using his most sincere voice.

I didn't believe it, but I knew it was all I was going to get.

"I guess I have to take that, don't I?" I said as we were getting to the gate.

"I wish it didn't feel that way, but I guess you do," Jordan replied with a sigh.

"And I can do whatever I want with all this, then?" I

asked, keeping the question generic in front of the kids, but knowing Jordan understood.

"You can do whatever you want with anything and everything you just gained. Paul would be happy you agreed to take over. And you have my word I will not step in," Jordan said.

"That, Mr. Crawford, is why I did it. And thank you for that. Although, with the pain this situation has caused, I believe it's the least you could do," I said, this time unable to avoid the loosely veiled reference to Beth's death.

"Yes, it's probably not enough," Jordan said, sounding as if he was finished with this conversation.

"No, it's not. But it's what I have. Now, I'm going to enjoy my time with my kids. Not just tonight, but all the years I have while they still enjoy time with their dad," I said, looking down and smiling at Jamie and Kyle.

They nodded and smiled in return.

"Enjoy the game. And enjoy your time with the kids. And enjoy your life," Jordan said, symbolically and physically ending our conversation.

I smiled as I put my phone back in my pocket.

"I will indeed, Mr. Crawford. I will indeed," I smiled to no-one but myself.

Epilogue

Marcia Stephenson fumbled through her purse for the key to the mailbox at her apartment complex. She had her arms full of groceries while trying to hold on to her two-year-old daughter's hand.

"Here, Millie, can you hold Madalyn's hand please," she said to her five-year-old as she struggled.

She finally found the key, opened the mailbox, and stuffed the mail into her purse before heading upstairs. Only then, after getting the kids settled and putting away the groceries, did she look at the mail she had carried in. And only then did she notice the hand-written envelope with a Colorado return address.

Inside, she found an official-looking letter from a law firm called Carter and Underwood, and another letter hand-written on a small stationary pad. It was on one side of the page and was not very long. Marcia found herself automatically reading the hand-written note out loud, maybe because it was the first piece of mail written by hand she had seen in years.

Hi Marcia. I want to once again express my most sincere

condolences to you and the girls about Mark. I know there were difficulties, and I may never understand what you and the girls have endured and will endure. Please know my heart aches for you. I honestly don't know any more words to say.

And now to the reason for this note. You will find a letter in this envelope from my lawyer here in Colorado. He has helped me set up some financial programs for you and the kids. First off, there are trust funds for both girls they will receive when they're eighteen. It should cover college and more, assuming those costs don't keep going up like crazy!

Marcia chuckled at the smiley face Keith had drawn behind the exclamation point.

You'll also see a request for wiring instructions on some money we want you to have. Please provide the details and the money will be wired to you immediately. This is part of the settlement of Paul's estate, and he'd want you to have it. And I want you to have it. No strings attached, no expectations whatsoever. Just let me know if you need any help with taxes or investments, and I'll get you some help.

I hope you and the girls have a great life, and that this gift provides some level of support to do things you enjoy. Your friend, Keith Morgan.

Marcia stood there for a minute before looking at the more official letter. She read through it once, and her mouth fell open. Then she read it again, pausing on the amount of money they were asking to send to her bank. She wondered what would happen when the same bank that kept sending her overdraft notices realized she was getting a transfer of twenty million dollars.

* * *

Keith Bartholomew couldn't believe the words he was reading as he stood in his driveway. He'd been bitten by so many criminal scams before that he nearly threw the letter away. Then he saw the handwritten note from Keith Morgan. He stood there for several minutes before deciding what to do next.

He decided the one person from the team in Afghanistan he had kept in touch with over the years. He called the California State Prison, Los Angeles County, where Whitney Cheevers was serving her time. The officer told him to hold, which he did. He knew the process.

"Hey Bart, how's it going?" a cheery voice answered.

"Hey Gerry," Bart said, still calling her by her old nickname.

"Is everything ok?" she asked when Bart didn't respond quickly.

"Well, I think so. But I'm not really sure," Bart said as he tried to figure out how to describe what he'd just read.

"Did you get a letter too?" Gerry asked while Bart quietly collected his thoughts.

"Yeah, how'd you know I got a letter? It was from Keith Morgan, but I'm not sure it's real," Bart finally said, reading the letter again.

"I did too. And I got mine from my new attorney. The one Keith got me. The one that has already started work to get my case overturned because of evidence Paul Frazier had found. So yeah, it's real. Can you believe this?" Gerry screamed, while the reality of the letter came rushing in on Bart. He felt tears on his cheeks.

"I don't even know what to say," he finally whispered, his voice cracking.

"I can't even think about what twenty million dollars

will do to my life when I get out of here," she said, trying hard to keep her voice intact in front of the other inmates.

"This is incredible. It's just incredible," was all Bart could keep saying.

They reveled in the newfound prosperity for a few more minutes when Bart chuckled.

"What?" Gerry asked.

"I'm just looking at the bottom of the note. There's a PS that says I have to call Steve Chandler's digital protection services if I run into any more issues," Bart said while shaking his head and smiling alone in his driveway.

* * *

Jen met Thor at the Golden Bear for dinner when she arrived in Cameron. She'd been driving since early that morning, but she was excited to see Thor again. They had hit it off immediately when they met and had been on a nearly constant video chat since then.

This was the first time Jen had seen Thor since they left the aftermath of the shootout at Paul's cabin.

After they exchanged greetings outside, then went inside to wait for their table. There was another group ahead of them, which gave them a few minutes to chat.

"I saw the sign for the new police station. That's pretty cool," Jen said.

"Yeah, someone donated funds to build a new one. They're doing it in honor of Sheriff Hanson. Nobody knows where it came from, but frankly, we don't care. That old office was a dump!" Thor exclaimed.

They laughed and talked as they were escorted to their table by the host. In less than a minute, their waitress headed over.

"Hey Thor, how are things at the Lazy J?" Molly asked as she sped to their table.

"All good, Molly. How are you?" Thor replied.

"Great, thanks. Can I get you guys something to drink?" Molly asked.

"Sure. I'll have a Moose Drool. And Molly, this is Jennifer," Thor said as he nodded across the table.

"You can call me Jen. And I'll have a, uh, Moose Drool also," she said with a hint of embarrassment. That name always got her.

"Great! Nice to meet you, Jen. I'll get that right out," Molly said with a smile as she hustled toward the bar.

Jen suddenly jumped, as if she'd been shocked.

"Oh, that's Molly! That reminds me," she said, reaching into her purse.

"Reminds you of what?" Thor asked.

"Keith wanted me to give you guys these," Jen said, pulling two envelopes out of her purse.

"One for you and one for a waitress at the Golden Bear named Molly. He asked me to bring these along when I told him I was coming out to the cabin. Is she the only Molly here?" Jen asked as she handed an envelope to Thor.

"Yeah, she is," Thor replied as he took his envelope with a confused look.

Jen hustled to the bar side of the Golden Bear where Molly was giving the bartender their beer order. She saw Jen coming over and turned to greet her.

"Hey Jen, did I forget something?" Molly asked.

"No, no. Actually, I forgot something. Do you remember the guy we were here with last month, Keith Morgan?" Jen asked.

"Of course I do," Molly said, maybe a little too quickly.

"Good. Well, he asked me to give you this," Jen said, handing Molly the envelope.

"Oh, ok. Thank you. I hope," Molly said with a confused look similar to the one Jen had seen on Thor's face a moment earlier.

Jen nodded and turned to head back to her table. Before she got halfway there, Molly came bounding across the restaurant area. Jen heard her coming and turned around. When she did, Molly came crashing into her with a spectacular hug.

She had tears in her eyes that took Jen aback.

"What's wrong? What was in there?" Jen asked, not understanding why Molly was upset.

"You didn't know what was in this envelope?" Molly asked through sniffs while she released Jen from the bearhug.

"No. Keith just told me he didn't have any cash during his last visit and wanted to make sure he got it to you," Jen said, reciting Keith's message.

Molly smiled and looked at the letter. There was a typed page and a hand-written page, one in each hand.

"It's not a tip," she said, wiping her eyes. "It's a trust fund for my kids. I mean, I barely talked to him about my kids, and he's setting them up for life? And handing me a million dollars on top of it? Who does that?"

Jen didn't know what to say.

"I guess Keith does," she replied.

"There's no way I can thank him enough for this. My life, and my kids' lives, will never be the same," Molly said, shaking her head.

"I don't think he expects you to pay him back or anything," Jen said, not really sure how to respond.

"Please, please, tell him thank you. Thank you so

much," Molly said as she turned and ambled back to the bar, staring at the letter.

Jen smiled, and turned to head the rest of the way to her table when she saw Thor with his phone to his ear, staring at his letter. After hearing Molly's story, Jen wondered what could have been in Thor's letter, since he had no kids. She sat down softly while Thor ended the call and put his phone in his pocket.

"Is everything ok?" Jen asked, watching Thor sit silently with his mouth open in a daze while she slid into the booth.

"Yeah, sorry. Everything is great," Thor said.

Jen sat silently, waiting to see if Thor would tell her what was in Keith's letter.

"Is this real?" Thor finally asked, looking up at Jen with a shocked expression.

"Yeah. I got it directly from Keith, so whatever it says is real," she replied.

"So, you don't know what it says?" Thor asked.

"No," Jen answered, again waiting for an explanation.

"This says Keith paid off the debts for our ranch. It's free and clear. No debt at all. All the loans mom and dad had to take out were paid. The balances are zero. I just called the bank to confirm, but they're closed," Thor said.

"If that's what it says, then I would expect it's true," Jen said.

"But it was millions of dollars, Jen. My parents had leveraged the place to the gills. Bailey and I didn't know what we were going to do. This saves the ranch! If this is true, we can keep it in the family. I mean, it basically preserves our future," Thor said, shaking his head and clearly trying to keep his emotions in check.

"I mean, the note makes it clear. He says we saved his life. And the money from Paul was more than he expected and he believes Paul would have wanted this. But still, who writes a check for millions of dollars to save the ranch of someone they met just a month ago?" Thor asked rhetorically, still shaking his head in disbelief.

Jen smiled to herself and replied, anyway.

"Keith Morgan. That's who does stuff like this. Keith Morgan does," she said proudly.

Follow Brent Jeffries

Watch for new adventures from Brent Jeffries and follow Keith Morgan using the links below.

Web Site (www.brentjeffries.com)

Facebook (www.facebook.com/authorbrentjeffries)

Instagram (www.instagram.com/authorbrentjeffries)

TikTok (www.tiktok.com/@brentjeffriesauthor)

Twitter (twitter.com/@AuthorJeffries)